Draconian Rapture

Draconian Rapture: Book 1

By Allison Bruning

Published by Marfa House

Marfa House
Marfa, Texas

Marfa House
Marfa, Texas

Draconian Rapture
Published by Marfa House

This book is a work of fiction. With the exception of recognized historical figures, the characters in this novel are fictional. Any resemblance to actual persons, living or dead, is purely coincidental.

All Rights Reserved

Copyright 2017 by Allison Bruning
1st Edition

ISBN: 978-1-946072-46-7

Other Books By Allison Bruning:

Novels

Calico (Children of the Shawnee #1)

Bailey's Revenge (Irish Twist of Fate #1)

Elsa (The Secret Heritage #1)

Poems

Reflections: Poems and Essays

Shorts

The Legacy (Christian Fiction)

Lady of Wild Rose Pass (Paisano Paranormal Patrol #1)

Who is the Real John Wilkes Booth (Nonfiction)
Sequoyah: The Man Behind the Legend (Nonfiction)

The Jew Behind the Revolutionary Money: Haym Salomon (Nonfiction)

Daniel Boone in Love

Dedication

To an amazing author, Bianca D'Arc - Thank you for inspiring me to write this series and challenging me to expand my writing into erotica.

To Chasity Tarantino - Thank you for encouraging me to write in this genre.

To my husband, Delfin Espinosa - Thank you for always being there for me as I pursue my writing career.

Dragmoc Hold –
Kingdom of Tinu'deh

1

The powerful cliffside castle towered over the deep ravine, encasing the mighty Mipan River. A long iron bridge crossed over the gap between the rest of the kingdom and Dragmoc Hold. Iona stared out the window towards the river recalling the ancient stories about the seven kingdoms her mother used to tell her. Just to utter the names and the races who dwelled in each one was a crime in her father's kingdom. But there was something deep within her heart that yearned for her to believe that dragons, magic and creatures other than humans actually existed. The nineteen-year-old, blonde, blue-eyed princess laid her forearms on the stone windowsill and stared at the bright double moons. Her mother had once told her that the moons travelled in opposite orbits and only came together once a month to remind them that even though men and woman live different lives they needed each other. Oh, how much she wanted to believe this was true. But it was hard to believe something so wonderful when your world was only filled with darkness, repression and dread.

The clanking of metal echoed off the cliffs as the bridge lifted slowly into its place. Built entirely from the mountainside, her father's castle was impenetrable. She leaned on her arms, thinking of the secret catacombs and passageways her mother had once told her existed within the mountain. No one could recall just how old the castle was; only that it had been one of the first buildings constructed by the dwarves to honor the dragons. All the clans lived together in unity within the mountain while members of the Great Draconian Council lived with their families within Dragmoc Hold. The tallest towers had been built high above the castle with enormous space at the very top to

house the Silver and Gold dragons and their riders, the Dragon Lord and Dragon Lady.

The clank of the bridge clasping in place startled her from her dreams. She listened, patiently waiting for the sound of the metal gates and doors to fall into their place. Clank. The outer doors closed and a metal gate fell into place barring anyone from tampering with the doors. She silently counted to twenty, the amount of time the guards had to reach the outer sanctum of the castle. Clash. Another gate fell, barring anyone from reaching the doors. She should feel safe with the knowledge that she was well protected from any invaders. Safe. She wasn't safe. How could she feel safe? She was her father's prisoner; all because she had been born a girl.

Iona sighed, staring down at the dark fall that would end her life if she dared to jump from her bedroom window. She wondered just how long it would take for someone to discover her body. Would her father even care that she would rather have jumped to her death than continue to face her torments? Oh, she had tried several times to kill herself. She thought of different ways she could do it. Yet, she never had the guts to actually go through with her plans. She leaned out the window and stared up the turret to the bulging, round top. "Gods, if only I had a dragon to escape from my misery," she muttered, dreaming of the giant, flying, fire-breathing mythical creatures.

Iona sighed. There was just no use in thinking she could ever escape from this horrible place. The slender, blonde teenager sat on her bed and flipped through the empty pages of the ancient book she had found in her bedroom this morning. She didn't know where it had come from, nor would she allow anyone to know that she had it. It had appeared just that morning, seemingly out of nowhere. She had spent countless hours searching every corner of her cell, and yet she had never seen it before that day. She didn't even want to think of what her father would do if he learned she had been trying to read *The Magic of Tinu'deh*.

Born the only daughter of five children to King Nomiki and his late wife, Queen K'Lara, her destiny had been decided for her since the day she was born. Although she was of royal blood, she would never assume her father's throne. Her only duties were to marry, give her husband plenty of children, sew, raise the children and keep up with the housework. But there was something inside her that wanted more. It wasn't fair that her brothers had a tutor who taught them reading, writing, science, history, geography, philosophy, religion and languages.

When she was little, her mother would secretly teach her how to read and write. Sometimes, they would sneak into the royal library and read different kinds of books. Oh, how much she loved doing that with her mother. She never knew how her mother knew so much.

Iona had enjoyed a wonderful relationship with her mother. Every night, her mother would tell her stories full of dragons and magic. She loved listening to her mother's tales. The memories of the wonderful years she had with her mother couldn't always mask the deepest pain she felt in her heart from the hardest season of her life. Her imprisonment in the tower was nothing compared to watching her mother suffer from a deathly illness ten years ago. Her father called countless healers to cure her mother but nothing had worked. The queen's health slowly and painfully declined for a little over a year until her death nine years ago. She would never forget the funeral.

King Nomiki should have buried her within the catacombs with her ancestors, yet he had decided to lay his wife to rest among the ancient ruins in a secluded valley beyond the village. The people were outraged at the audacity of the king. His insistence on breaking from tradition incensed them. Mobs had gathered around the royal family shouting so loud she could barely hear the Righteous One priest's words. The crowd had grown more violent as the acolytes had lowered her mother's body dressed in her royal robes into a stone vault buried deep within the ground, followed by her golden crown, scepter, and dagger.

The crowds had yelled "Queen Iona. Those belong to Queen Iona! Long live Queen Iona!" Her father ordered his knights to attack the crowd. Blood spilled, cries lifted, houses burned; all while her father closed her mother's vault, chained with the thick chain and buried it deep within the dirt. He had waited a long time before he ordered the soldiers to immediately gather the survivors and bring the bodies to the small hill of dirt he had just created. The knights complied with his order. Iona would never forget the stack of fifty-five men, women and children pilled on top of her mother's grave nor what her father had done afterwards. The remaining two hundred villagers had gathered around them. Her father held a torch over his head and declared, "The time of the Dragonmoon Empire ends today with the death of K'Lara Dragonmoon! You will bow to me in the name of the one and only true god, Prince Zurggash! Anyone who defies me and the creeds I brought upon your heathen kingdom will find a fate worse than this," he declared, then lit the pile of bodies on fire. "I'll torture your bodies until you beg for mercy and then burn you alive from the inside out," he

sneered into the crowd. "Kneel before your king!"

The crowd had no choice but to comply with her father's desires and no one ever went against his commands again. He arrested Iona and threw her into the tower. Every day a servant would place food through a metal slit in the bottom of the door and then run away. It was as if even the servants were taught to be afraid of Iona. As if a small girl could be the source of such fear! As soon as Iona grabbed the tray, a thick metal plate would close over the hole and she was left alone to eat the meager slop. Her father deemed if it was suitable for a pig, it would be suitable for his daughter.

Not long after she had been locked away, he passed a decree outlawing any magic, mention of magic or magical creatures. They were only to serve the Righteous One, Prince Zurggash. In an effort to control the population, another law was passed soon afterwards. Every family was only allowed one girl until the girl came of legal age to marry. The legal age for women to marry was raised to twenty in order to prevent the overpopulation of females within their kingdom. Each year, the king would survey every household and register every member of each household. If he discovered the family had more than the one allowed girl in their home, the child was arrested. At the end of the day, he would gather all the extra girls and have them executed in the town center along with the mothers, who dared to break the law. Of course it was the mothers who were felt to be at fault. So much blood had been spilled on the town center that everyone had begun to call it Blood Square. Iona didn't know what her father had against women but his hatred towards the female persuasion only grew stronger the longer he reigned without her mother. More and more laws passed to control the female population and eventually the female villagers were reduced to nothing but slaves. Every year, when the moons gathered together Prince Zurggash would deliver more female slaves to her father. She had never met nor seen the prince before but she knew he existed.

At first she didn't know how much time had passed from her imprisonment. But then it had occurred to her she could keep time by the screams she heard rising from Blood Square when the moons merged together. She had forgotten her birthday but she knew she was ten years old when her mother had been buried. Iona accepted the unification day as her own birthday. Each passing year, she hated hearing the cries of the condemned women and children but she knew there was nothing she could do about it.

Strange things started to happen to her around her twelfth

birthday. Her body tingled every now and then with bursts of energy. At night, her dreams were so vivid it was as if her soul had been transported to a magical place that yearned for her constant companionship. The dream world was so peaceful and beautiful she only wished she could stay there forever. Oh, if only she could remain there in sleep, never having to wake!

She would often wake up exhausted and her body would be in all kind of different places within her small, confined chamber. One night, she awoke to find her body falling from the air to her bed! The more time passed, the more she realized the dreams of her body levitating over her bed weren't a dream but a reality! Once she realized that, she became so scared to go to sleep that she tried to deny herself sleep. But that only made matters worse. She would fall into a deep sleep and wake up, what she assumed could only be days later, even more exhausted then before.

As time passed, her symptoms became worse. During the day she experienced fevers, nausea, headaches and lower stomach cramps. Yet there was no one to help her through it all. At night, her exhausted body would return to the dream world. Over and over again, her body constantly battled against her mind. Her symptoms eventually subsided only to be replaced with such severe stomachaches that she couldn't stand the taste of food. She should have died but somehow the food she ate in the dream world sustained her. She was constantly in a foul mood and wanted nothing more than to sleep all day. Every month, once a week, her body endured its agony until soon after her fifteenth birthday she awoke to find blood in her bed and between her thighs. Her lower stomach ached and she couldn't stop the blood. The blood flow only grew stronger the longer it flowed and it wouldn't stop! She feared she would bleed to death until on the eighth day her body had returned to perfect health except a few days later she had the overwhelming sensation between her legs that it was missing something. She couldn't quite figure out what the problem was. She just ignored it and eventually it would go away.

~~~~~~

"Iona." Iona smiled, biting her lower lip at the sound of Prince Kilean Dragonsun's voice in her mind. Her handsome, muscular lover had appeared in her dreams a month ago. She had never encountered anyone before when she travelled into the mysterious land. Kilean and Iona had been so shocked to see another person that they never spoke on that first encounter, only silently studied each other. Iona had awoken from her trip into the Plains of the Great Dreams never expecting to see the handsome, dark haired warrior ever again. The following night, she reappeared in the same area and before her stood Kilean. The couple introduced themselves and spent the entire night talking. Night after night, she visited upon the seasoned warrior.

Her world started to make sense the more she listened to her new friend's words. Kilean had told her the Plains of the Great Dreams was a place of sanctuary that could only be accessed by the Dragon Lord and Dragon Lady. The power of the dragons was passed down from one generation to another through the unification of the Dragon Lord and Dragon Lady. Thirty - five years ago, that union had never occurred between his father and the woman chosen to be the next Dragon Lady, the consequences of which had been traumatic for the entire world. The magical energies holding the world together were falling apart throughout the seven kingdoms. The Council of Dragons had done everything in their power to prolong the destruction of the magical world but their efforts were in vain. If the next Dragon Lord and Dragon Lady don't merge, then magic and all magical creatures would disappear forever.

Iona had left the Plains of the Great Dreams not entirely believing Kilean's story. Dragons? Magic? Weren't those just in fairytales?

"Thank you for the book," Iona smiled, turning another page.

"What book?"

"You're such a tease. How did you get into my room?"

"Iona, I don't know what you are talking about. I can't cross over the Plains of the Great Dreams into your kingdom."

"Then how did it get there?"

"Are you certain you didn't just misplace a book and then find it?"

"Females are forbidden from an education. I haven't seen a book in over ten years."

"Are you certain it's not one of your mother's books?"

Iona sighed, "My father destroyed everything my mother owned when I became a woman."

"When did you first notice the book?"

"I woke up to find it on my bed. Kilean, if you didn't give it to me and it doesn't belong to my mother then how did it get here? Father has strictly forbidden anyone from coming near me, especially men."

"Perhaps, it came to you?"

Iona laughed, "Came to me? Books are alive?"

"You believe dragons exist..."

"...I never said I believe in dragons. Magic, maybe. But dragons and books that are alive? I'm doing well to believe that you actually exist."

"How can you enter the Plains of the Great Dreams and not believe that magic exists? Let alone, me? That kiss we shared last night was amazing!"

Iona grinned, recalling the slow, passionate kiss she shared with Kilean last night underneath the forest canopy. He had held her tight to his firm body, pinning her between his strength and the ground. Their arms and legs embraced. The heat of their bodies tempting them to go farther than just one, amazing kiss. "Iona." She cleared her throat and pushed her thoughts aside.

"Say, that I believe all your claims about magic, dragons and who I am, what use would I have with this weird book?"

"Weird? How so?"

"The pages are empty. There's two dragons intertwined on the front and back covers. They come together in the middle to form one body but their heads are apart."

"*The Magic of Tinu'deh*," the young man muttered.

"How do you know the title?"

"Because mine says *The Magic of Huitgan*."

"Yours?"

"It appeared on my bed this morning sometime between when I woke up and returned from my training. I didn't think anything about it but when I showed it to my father he said I should contact you to see if you had received yours."

"How much have you told your father about me?"

"Everything, Iona. He's known about you since the first time I saw you in the Plains of the Great Dreams. You don't understand just how important you are to me." Iona closed the book and held it tight against her chest. Important. The only person who had ever told her how important she was had been her mother. "Come to the Plains of the Great Dreams and bring that book with you," Kilean suggested and disappeared from her mind. Iona lay on her back, holding the book tighter to her chest. Kilean may have told her plenty of stories but he's never hurt her. Deep in her heart, she wanted to believe all of his tall tales. A handsome man who loved her unconditionally. That was far better than any man her father could find to be her husband.

K'nza Caverns – Valley of Li-tli

2

The soft purple silk sheet lightly covered General Roan Tharg's well-defined warrior physique. He lay on his back staring up at the early evening sky through the open ceiling of Asa's large, bedroom chamber. The twin moons were almost perfectly aligned. It would be only a few more days until the portal opened for his soldiers, Kilean and Vashti to enter into the mating grounds. The mating season. He just couldn't believe it had already been almost ten months since the last time the portal had opened. Time had flown by so fast. Gods, how much he hated the mating season.

Every ten months it only became harder to watch Asa fuck Kilean. He never thought he would fall in love with a dragon twin. Hell, he remembered the day her mother had laid the egg she and Sina had hatched from a hundred fifty-years ago. The birthing had been routine for him. In his five hundred years of life he had seen female dragon twins come and go. He knew the Draconian Laws by heart. Dragon Twins existed only to fuck, conceive, and heal the Dragon Lord and the male dragon. The green scaled, blue eyed, purple haired beauty had captured his attention the first time he had laid eyes upon her. He knew the rules and for a hundred years maintained his distance from her every time he escorted the Dragon Lord into the lair to mate with the twins. He tried everything to keep his feelings hidden, even participating in orgies with several of the more experienced priestesses and his officers. But even after he left the Valley of Li-tli he couldn't keep his mind off of her. He thought he could sooth his need to be with her by taking a dracnoid as his lifemate. The Dragon Twins were dracnoid, weren't they?

Even though the dracnoids accepted Draco and Razil as the supreme deities they each had their own household gods – D'stanian, D'varla, T'linda, and T'nal – the firstborn dracnoids of Draco and Razil. The four minor deities had their own personalities and gifts to bring those who faithfully served them.

D'stanian and T'linda had mated together to create the dracnoids, humanoids with the scales of dragon as skin, human colored eyes with a variety of bold hair colors. A perfect blend of dragon and human traits, the dracnoids were more aggressive than the humans. When D'varla and T'nal had mated together, T'nal gave birth to two eggs. When the eggs hatched, a human male and a dracnoid male emerged from one egg while the other egg had a human female and dracnoid female. The dragons were confused. How could they give birth to humans? The humans had been created by a different god. The first Dragon Twins had inhabited the earth for a few days when they couldn't satisfy their insatiable hunger to mate. The four children went to a field and had an orgy with the first draconiods. From the union between the six of them, the human female gave birth to the first Dragon Lord and the first dracnoid Dragon Twin gave birth to the first dragon. The gods were happy until the Dragon Twins died in the birthing process. They resurrected the twins and told them to mate again. This time only with the male Dragon Twins. They did so. The draconiod Dragon Twin gave birth to a female dragon and her sister gave birth to the first Dragon Lady but once again the process of laying the eggs had killed the mothers. D'varla and T'nal mated again and T'nal gave birth to a new set of female Dragon Twins. She and her mate, created separate lands for them to dwell in and restricted each set of twins to only mate with the Dragon Lord, Dragon Lady or their dragons. The dracnoids never forgot the first pair of dracnoids, the Dragon Lord, the Dragon Lady and the Dragon Twins stories. They worshipped idols representing one of the first beings created and held festivals to honor each one.

Roan's marriage to his lifemate might have lasted longer if the idol of the first dracnoid didn't look so much like Asa. He tried hard to be the good husband to Ti're, especially during the early stages of their marriage when during the second year of her gestational period she lost the egg she had been carrying. She was heartbroken. But he reminded his beloved wife that she was only a hundred and eighty years old. Draconoids could live ten to fifteen thousand of years. They waited a few months and tried again. Ti're successfully delivered their first egg three years later. He visited Ti're everyday in the nursery while she coddled the egg. Eighteen months later, it hatched and they had a handsome baby boy. Ti're was so happy. And for a time, so was he. But once again, his thoughts had turned to Asa. He eventually began to image Ti're was her whenever they had mated. She gave him three more children within a ten-year time span then she was no long in heat. He tried. Oh, he tried so hard to keep his life balanced between his duties as Dragon Master, husband, and father but fifty years ago, he couldn't fight his feelings any longer. He had snuck into Asa's bedchamber while the Dragon Lord was sleeping with Sina and declared his true feelings to her. She had told him she had always felt the same. They made love but he made certain never to spill his seed inside her.

Roan's thick right arm wrapped around Asa's slender body. She purred in her sleep, stroking her hand on his chest with her head over his heart. Gods she was so perfect! He mindlessly played with her nipple, periodically pulling on the tit ring attached to the metal chain that hung between her breasts.

"Hmm," she moaned and moved her hand down to his crotch as she rubbed the side of her cheek on his firm chest. She moved her long leg over his own and snuggled closer to him.

Roan gasped at the touch of her fingers upon his penis. "Asa," he muttered between his teeth, glaring at her with a warning look.

"You're the one getting me excited," she said, opening her eyes and motioning towards his finger.

"Sorry," he apologized, removing his hand and pushed himself into an upright position. He leaned upon the ornate headboard. Roan fixed his eyes upon the overly spacious bedchamber large enough to fit two dragons. He couldn't escape the feeling of what would happen to them should Sina catch her sister and him together.

Asa pushed back her long raven hair and softly stroked his penis. "What's wrong," she asked then licked the top of his penis nearly making him cum.

"Shit, Asa," he gasped.

"Too much," she asked.

"If you want me to get off then at least let me enjoy it."

"I was trying to but you're thoughts are elsewhere," she whined, playing with the hair on his chest. "Are you tired of me and want to fuck your wife," she asked.

"You know I love you and not Ti're. I am your true mate."

"Have you fucked her," she sung playing with his nipples.

"Asa," he warned her.

10

"She's a dracnoid. If you're not going to fuck her then at least buy her a sex slave to release her frustrations. Dracnoids can go without their lifemates for twenty years but then their bodies will eventually crave to mate with their lifemate."

"I visited her and the children ten years ago. She was molting."

"Molting only lasts for five years. You're an idiot if you think she doesn't need you after she molts. Her sexual urges are increased for three years after she gains her new scales. And if she doesn't mate for at least a year she'll lose her mind," she explained walking her fingers across his strong chest."

"And do you need me, Asa," he asked, peering at her hard nipples.

"Of course I do."

"Then why are you pressuring me to mate with Ti're," he asked placing his hand on top of her fingers, halting her seductive trace.

Asa sighed, "I don't want her to suspect there is anything between us."

"You don't have to worry about my wife. I bought a sex slave as soon as I knew she was going through her first molting experience and told her my duties prevented me from being with her. She agreed to use him."

"She actually cast the spell that made him look and act like you when she needs a fuck?"

"Yup."

"Which of the seven races did you procure?"

"A human. She like being dominant in bed and humans are the only race that are weak enough for her to conquer," Roan explained, pushing her underneath him. He suckled her breasts causing her to almost lose her train of thought.

"You made certain the human wouldn't be too scared of her teeth, fire breathing and roar when she reaches the final orgasm," she pushed through the intensity of his kisses down her body.

"I did. And he has enough stamina to endure her during mating. Dracnoids never conceive an egg while they have sex after a molt so I'm not too concerned about the repercussions. The only stipulation she had was that I return to her when she's in heat," He explained, kissing her clit then rising over her.

"Shit," she swore, fighting the urge to mate as he chuckled.

"How long do you have until that happens," Asa asked, taking her hand to his penis and thoroughly licking his penis. She gave him a blowjob as he spoke.

"Ugh, about a month after the mating season. She's in heat about every ten years. I went back to her the last time but found she had entered into her first molt. I don't know how often she'll molt."

"She's what? Two hundred?"

"Close to that. Her mother molts every two hundred thirty five years and her father every two hundred. I'm thinking since she had her first molt around two hundred it will be that often. So I'll have to return to her and fuck her regularly for at least five years next month. I'm more concerned with Sina than Ti're. Sina's not an idiot."

"Sina, smina," she huffed, rising over him with a stern look. "What is it with you and this preoccupation with my sister. I'm beginning to think you like her more than me. Is it because she's human?"

Roan stared at her with a blank look on his face. "Asa," he whispered.

"I'm sorry. I forgot your first wife was human."

"I can't...please just don't bring it up. Zarsi is dead."

"Roan, it's been five hundred years and you still love her?"

"I don't want to talk about her!"

"Do you love me?"

Roan grabbed her tit chain, lean closer and kissed her passionately. He moved his lips down her neck. She arched her head back, purring a soft, sensual sound of perfection. He knew every hidden spot on her body that heightened her desires.

"You're avoiding the question," she murmured.

"I could always stop," he whispered in her ear then nibbled on her earlobe and slid hand down her stomach to her clit.

"As much as I, hmm, love the attention. Shit," she arched her head back as he nibbled on her tit, inserting his fingers inside her. Roan grinned, lifting his eyes to her. "What are you not tell me?"

"This is highly illegal. We could...."

"We've been together for fifty years and now you're questioning the relationship? We already eliminated the loose ends. We killed the priests that found us having sex in the forest...."

"...hmm, and the guards that found us together in the barracks...."

"....don't forget the priestesses that joined us that orgy. Eight people are dead because of us. What else do you want," she pushed through as he played with the highly sexual creature's clit.

Roan pushed her onto her back and kissed down her long body. He suckled between her tits, gently massaging one as he suckled the other then vice versa. Asa rocked her body. Her soft purrs and moans enticed him to continue even more. "We've killed for each other, committed treason and yet I can't help but think this wonderful relationship of ours is about to get us in even more trouble than we've had before."

"You're paranoid," Asa sung thoroughly enjoying his sensual touch.

"What if when we interfered with the Bonding of Dragons we didn't completely eliminate the bonds that unite the Dragon Lord and Dragon Lady," he questioned, staring between her breasts.

"Roan? There hasn't been a Dragon Lady since Queen K'Lara and she's dead."

"I just feel as if we didn't exactly complete our mission but made matters worse. Prince Zurggash is protecting us but for how long?"

"Why are you questioning that," she pushed him off her body. "We promised to extinguish the bond between the Dragon Lord and Dragon Lady. We did that perfectly. And every person we have killed has mysteriously disappeared before either Sina or King Tavir learned of our deeds."

"Vashti's been acting strange."

"Strange, how so?"

"Loss of appetite, irritable, exhaustion and loss of interest in her training."

"She's in heat?"

"Isn't she too young to begin? The last dragon was already 900 years old when I became her Dragon Master and I don't recall my trainer ever informing me of the transitional period for a dragon to become an adult. How old are dragons when they make the transition?"

"A hundred, just like dracnoids."

"It doesn't make sense. Vashti's egg hatched fifty years ago."

"Vashti completed her entire first ten years of life in her egg?"

"Why wouldn't you know the answer to that question? Weren't you and Sina conceived at the same time as Vashti?"

"It's different when the Dragon Twin gives birth to the twins."

"How?"

"As soon as the twins conceive they are separated and secluded within the High Priestess' temple."

"Why is that?"

"The twins don't share the same gestational period."

"Nine months for the human and three years for the dracnoid," Roan asked.

"Yes, humans can't survive the birthing of a dragon egg. That's why it's forbidden for human females to mate with dracnoid male but perfectly alright for a human male to mate with a dracnoid female. I've heard horrible stories about the human dragon twin being torn apart by the egg during the birthing process and the surviving dracnoid twin falling into a deep depression after her sister's death."

"Do you believe them?"

"I don't know. I've never been that close to Sina. Seems to me she cares more about me than I do about her."

"Who provides your services during that time? Wouldn't the world be unbalanced if the female Dragon Twins are missing from the time?"

"No, the male Dragon Twins join the females."

"Why?"

"The babies need the mothers to transfer sexual energies to them while they develop. The only way to do that is have sex with another creature like us. The human mates with the human and the dracnoid mates with the dracnoid until after the human's death. Then the human joins his brother and the three of them have constant sex with the dracnoid mother or something will go wrong with the baby."

"Who provides for the services the Dragon Twins offer when that happens?"

"The Dragon Lord and the Lady mate with each other while the High Priest and Priestess mate. Sometimes they have an orgy."

"And afterwards the dracnoid twin returns her duties?" Roan asked.

"No, the birthing process kills the mother just as it did with her human sister. It takes up to ten years for a dragon to hatch but not so for Dragon Twins. We mature faster so we can assume our mothers' duties. There have only been a few dragons that have entered puberty early and those who weren't guided through the ceremonies properly became insane."

"Vashti can't become insane. How do I help her?"

"She'll need to mate...," Asa pushed him underneath her and kissed his entire body until she reached his penis. She played with his balls. Roan breathed deeply, "We broke the cycle when we helped King Nomiki interfere with the Bonding of Dragons. Wouldn't that mean she wouldn't enter this period of her life?"

"No, a dragon is still a dragon no matter if the Dragon Lord and Dragon Lady are unified or not."

"What good does that do anyone if she doesn't have her mate," he pushed her underneath him, kissed her passionately as he fingered her.

"I'm starting to understand her predicament quite well, lover." She stared down at Roan's still fingers inside her vagina and his thumb resting comfortably on her clit. He followed her gaze downward.

"The nodes inside my vagina and on my clit are super sensitive to any touch. I was created for sex, Roan, you can't do that to me. Either continue what you were doing or let me masturbate."

"That's such a waste of your body."

"Then fuck me already!"

Roan pulled her legs around his waist and sat her on his lap. Asa gasped as he thrust his large, erect penis deep within her vagina. She rocked up and down, holding firm to his back. Oh, she was so fucking wet! "Hmm, feel better," he said, grabbing the back of her head, he kissed her passionately, making certain his tongue missed her sharp, razor like canines.

"Oh yeah, much better," she whispered with a grin. She slowed her rhythm, fully enjoying the deep, slow thrust of his cock. Roan inhaled a deep breath. The highly sensitive bumps in her vagina clung around his penis delivering extra stimulation. He pulled her closer to his body. The slower she rocked the more stimulation she provided. Asa caressed his muscular chest then pinched on his tits. He grabbed her firm ass and pulled her closer to his waist, thrusting deeper. He stared down at her breasts. Silver juice poured from her tits. The sacred Milk of the Dragons poured abundantly from the Dracon Twins' breasts to nourish, strengthen and heal either the Dragon Lord or the dragon she was mating with. He had always avoided her milk but this time he couldn't help but be drawn to the thick juice. He tugged on her tit chain, making the milk pour down even more and Asa groan. "Fuck it," he swore and drank from her. The power soared through his body. He had never felt such strength! He took her breast into his mouth and suckled harder.

"Ugh," she groaned as he rolled her underneath him and ravished her breasts while pushing his penis hard into her. She clawed his back with low roars in the back of her throat he had never heard from her before. Roan swallowed a large amount then licked his tongue up to her neck, her mouth and kissed her as the juice poured even faster, lubricating their lower stomachs.

"Fuck you, bitch," he snarled, grabbed her left breast and suckled, pushing even deeper within her. Oh, such power! He sat upright and pulled her to his chest. She was more aggressive with him than he had ever seen of her! He moved his hand down to the silver girdle around her waist. Asa grinned, fully understanding what he was about to do to her. He traced the silver cords to the back of her ass where they met at a silver disk on her lower back then came out of the disk as one larger braided cord ran between her legs. The powerful cord's job was simple enough. Dragon Twins were technically dracnoids and as such had a higher sexual drive than most humans. She constantly needed to be sexually stimulated, especially here. The Valley of Li-tli wasn't just her home. It was the sacred mating lands of the male Dragon Rider, his army and his dragon.

D'varla and T'nal had created two sanctuaries, one for the female dragon rider and her female army and the other for the male dragon rider and his male army after they secluded the Dragon Twins and wrote strict laws within the Draconian Codex about them. Mortal priestesses who were chosen by the High Dragon Priestess were trained by the Dragon Twins and given the duties to sexually serve the soldiers in any ways that pleased the men. Yet not every man could be served by just any priestesses nor could they explore the entire lands. There was an order that had to be followed. The most experienced and sexually satisfying priestesses were reserved for the officers while trainees and new ordained priestesses were given the task of pleasing the enlisted men. The best part of Roan's duties was that he had been given permission to be with any of the priestesses, no matter what rank they were, except for the Dragon Twins.

Roan traced the silver cord at the back of her ass. The cord made certain her sexual needs were always provided for should she not be able to mate with either the Dragon Lady's dragon, the Dragon Lord or her twin sister. During sexual encounters, it could be used to stimulate and sustain her body's higher sexual possibilities. Roan pushed the cord close to her asshole. The magical rope pushed into her asshole and became a large anal plug. Asa growled loudly, arching her head back. Her screams became more intense with every push of his penis deeper within her vagina.

Roan pushed her onto the bed. She grinned rolling onto her back, opening her legs wider, moving the rope back and forth against her very, wet pussy. He grabbed her thighs, pulled her legs wider and drank from her pussy. "Shit," she exclaimed arching her back as his tongue entered into her vagina.

Oh, gods. Oh fucking gods, she was so intoxicating! He had to have more from her. So much more! Up and down, he moved suckling between her breasts and between her legs. The more he took from her the hotter and more aggressive in bed she became. Power, glorious power surged in his veins! He wanted more. He had to have more! His blood ran hot in his veins.

He grabbed her legs and pulled her to the edge of the bed, and pounded his enormous erect penis hard inside her. She called his name several times, begging for more. Her wet pussy tightened against his enormous penis. It never ceased to amaze him just how much she could please him. Her body always knew what he liked. He placed her legs on his shoulders, knelt over her and thrust even deeper continually sucking her breasts. She growled louder, her sweaty body uncontrollably fidgeting as the cord between her legs vibrated against her clit and the ass plug became a large vibrating dildo, matching the depth and rhythm of his assault.

Roan breathed heavy, matching her sensual moans and groans.

"That's it...oh, baby...yeah, like that...hmm, I like that. Fuck me! Oh, gods, fuck me harder," she pleaded.

His body tensed with pleasurable tension. He held her body down and leaned closer, sandwiching her fidgeting sweating body between him and her firm bed. Who was he to deny her the pleasures this sexual creature wanted? She called his name in between her sensual moans. Her uncontrollable body fidgeted with even more intensity in between her screams. He placed his hand over her mouth. "Asa, shh. We can't be discovered. Sina's going to hear your roars."

Asa grabbed his wrist and sucked on his fingers. The pressure was almost too much to contain. He could feel his large penis grow to its full thickness. The walls of her womb wrapped tighter around his penis. He breathed deeply between his deep thrust until he couldn't handle it anymore. He pushed one last time, reaching an orgasm with her.

"Oh," he heaved, lowering his head to her breast with a grin.

"Roan."

He grinned with a slight chuckle. "I don't think I have ever had sex with a woman that intense before. I feel as if...."

"Roan."

"...huh, gods, I could fuck you all over again." He spread her legs but she wouldn't budge. "What's wrong, baby," he asked looking up at her. A sharp wave of intense, nauseating pain as if knives were stabbing every nerve, muscle and bone in his body overwhelmed him. He screamed, grabbing his stomach and fell off the bed. Every move, every breath he made only made matters worse. Roan leaned over his knees with his hands over his head, in complete agony. He vomited profusely in between his cries by her bed. Asa crawled to the edge of the bed, leaned over and rubbed his back.

"Don't touch me. Oh gods, don't touch me," he protested.

"I'm sorry," she apologized lifting her hand. "I could see the scales on your body and I knew I had poisoned you."

"Poison me? I've seen Dragon Twins milk their rider and dragons plenty of times before. They never poison them."

"Actually, we do. It's a safety precaution D'varla and T'nal placed within the Milk of the Dragons and the Seed of the Dragons to prevent anyone other than the Dragon Lord and the Dragon Lady from mating with the Dragon Twins and stealing the power we bring upon the riders. Kilean was poisoned by us the first time he drank from our breasts."

"Was? There's an antidote?"

"No."

"Then what!"

"He is the antidote. Every Dragon Lord is immune to our poison. The same is true for the Dragon Lady when she drinks the Seed of the Dragons. They don't get sick just exhausted after the first time the venom is delivered into their system. Their bodies recognize the poison and immediately deliver the antidote which causes their body to change."

"Change?"

"The venom actually never leaves the body but merges with the antidote to create a lining inside their organs, blood, muscles and bones to strengthen their bodies so they are as strong as a dragon whenever they mate with us."

"But you said until the bonding occurs Kilean has to drink from you."

"We are adding more venom so the process can continue. It takes years to make him strong enough to endure what a dragon can. The same is true for Dragon Lady. That's why they have to mate with us twice a year before they fully assume their roles. If you were mortal I'd tell you that the poison was going to kill you but I don't know what happens to immortals."

"You could have warned me!"

"I never thought you would have crossed that line! We have another problem."

"More than this," he yelled, then vomited.

"I'm with child."

Roan tightened his jaw and looked up at her. The seasoned warrior lifted his brown eyes to meet her blue ones. He swallowed hard, realizing he had spilled inside her womb instead of her mouth.

"You're...what?"

"You pushed so deep your sperm made the connection. I felt the outer shell burst."

"Oh, gods," he mumbled. He couldn't believe he hadn't allowed her to suckle on his penis at the end of their sensual experience.

"The poison should have killed you so you couldn't continue but you grew in power just like Kilean does when he drinks from either Sina or I."

"I felt as if I could conquer the world."

"That's how Kilean feels when he does that. Are you certain you felt that?"

"How else did you expect me to fuck you with poison in my veins," he bellowed.

"I'm sorry. I really am. It just doesn't make sense."

"Maybe I didn't break the egg's shield?"

"I know what I felt. It burst. Your sperm made contact."

"How do we know if my sperm even works? I'm immortal."

"Are you fucking insane! Ti're laid four healthy eggs from you!"

"She miscarried our first egg before she had those four. Maybe you'll do the same?"

"There has never been a Dragon Twin who's miscarried an egg!"

"And you just said there has never been a man who was poisoned by your milk that was able to finish fucking a Dragon Twin! You could be the first to lose an egg!"

"Roan, you're an idiot. My egg sack can only be penetrated once. I'm with child whether you like it or not."

"Oh, gods, what have I done?" Roan groaned.

"You're overreacting."

"Overreacting," he bellowed at her. "Nine hundred years ago, a Dragon Twin gave birth to a mortal man with immense supernatural powers. Those powers drove the man insane! Do you know what became of that man?"

Asa sighed, "His name is Prince Zurggash. His mother raised him until he was ten years old. The power within him was too much for him to bear. He became violent and couldn't control the magic within him. He killed his father and subjected his mother to the most horrible of things. So horrible, that many do not speak of his deeds. He killed his mother then committed atrocities throughout the world for twenty years. During that time he gathered an army. He sought to control all magic and believed by murdering the council he could control all magical creatures. The world was at war with The Righteous One for forty-five years. It only ended when the Dragon Lord and Dragon Lady were able to capture him. They tried to help him but when they couldn't they had no choice but to kill him but he resurrected."

"Prince Zurggash only wants to destroy magic, Asa."

"Isn't that what we want, Roan? It's magic and the Draconian Codex that keeps us apart when in our hearts all we want is to be together. Why should all the seven races be allowed to mate with whomever they want when we can't!"

"The seven races have restrictions placed upon them as well, Asa."

"Not like ours!"

"Prince Zurggash is a threat to our world and it is our world that created him! He's going to declare war on the seven races. It's just a matter of time."

"Then so be it. I hope this time he actually defeats the Draconian Council. Eleven times he's tried and eleven times he's lost."

Roan groaned, pulling his hands down his face. "Prince Zurggash is powerful. Perhaps powerful enough to cure me and take the child from you but he'll demand more upon us than he has ever done so before."

"I told you, I only have one egg sack and that's been compromised with your sperm. If we ask Prince Zurggash to remove the child then I will never conceive. We don't know what my poison will do to you and I don't want you to die," Asa protested, rising from the bed.

"And you want to die having my child?"

"Maybe their just stories to scare my sister and I into complacency."

"Oh, sure. That knowledge would just make me want to fuck and conceive right away if I were you," he sneered.

She hissed at him. Her silver cord returned to its normal state, inserting a softly vibrating dildo into her vagina. The cord lowered a see-through, white fabric in the front of her legs. White silk wrapped seductively around the top and bottom of her breast and tied together in the center of her back. Her tit rings and chain showed through the slit of the fabrics.

Roan stared at his beauty, mesmerized by her appearance then vomited. "Roan?" she asked, stepping towards him.

"Ugh, I can't return to King Tavir and Prince Kilean like this. They'll seek help from the council. If the council learns of what we have done then we'll be arrested."

"There has to be a solution. Surely they wouldn't let a Dragon

Master die?"

Roan rolled onto his back, shivering uncontrollably. His pale face white as a ghost. "Shit," she swore, kneeling by his side. He lifted his wide eyes to her, barely breathing with the look of death upon his face.

"Contact him," he pushed out of his mouth then swallowed hard.

"But I don't ...." Roan closed his eyes and fell limp.

"Roan," she said, tapping his cheek but felt nothing. She placed her fingers on the side of his neck and felt for a pulse. Nothing. How could he not have a pulse? His heart was supposed to beat eternally. "Roan," she roared, shaking his body but he never responded. She didn't know what to do. She had never killed nor heard of anyone other than the council killing a Dragon Master before.

Asa paced the floor trying to think of what to do. Where would his soul go? How soon would the council know of his death? There was only one solution. The love of her life was dead. There was no use in complying with whatever the Draconian Council wanted from her. She wanted his child to know how great a man its father was and how she never meant to kill him.

Asa lifted the purple drapes separating her bedchamber from the rest of the cavern. Sina was nowhere around. She peered at Roan's body then walked into the largest chamber. Bookcases lined the walls. Long tables with a multitude of paraphilia scattered the floor. She walked between a row of stone tables that used to be used by the priests and priestesses during the mating moons.

"Oh, good you're here. I'm so fucking horny for some reason," Sina said, walking into the room and stared down at a table. Sina rubbed the vibrating chain between her legs.

"How big is it," Asa asked, glancing between her sister's legs.

"Not large enough," Sina roared, grabbing the edge of the table. She lowered her head and roared. "It doesn't matter how large the dildo gets it can't satisfy me."

"Weren't you bleeding this week?"

Sina lifted her eyes to her. "Do you know how much I hate that dracnoid body of yours? You've never have a menstrual cycle in your life nor gone into heat a few days after it."

Asa faked a smile towards her white skinned, raven haired, green-eyed twin sister. "Give me fifty more years and then I'll experience that."

Sina rolled her eyes, "Ugh, my bleeding stopped this morning but I'm horny as fuck and my dildo won't satisfy it. It's usually more intense if I'm ovulating while we're fucking Kilean."

"Must be close to the time when Roan brings Kilean to us" she lied, walking to her sister.

"Hmm, perhaps. Oh, what I wouldn't give to just lie on this table and let you fuck me hard, sister." Asa peered over her shoulder to her bedroom.

"Asa, is something wrong," Sina asked between moans

"No," Asa replied, turning back to her sister. "How big do you need it?"

"I want a Dragon dildo. I'm so wet I need something larger than a human penis inside me." Sina grabbed her sister's hand and started towards her bedchamber. "You're room is closer to mine. Let's mate in there."

Asa pulled her sister back. "Wait!"

"What's wrong, sister," Sina asked, pivoting to her.

"I..ugh...well...I want to have sex outside. It's such a beautiful day and it would do well for the priestesses to prepare themselves for the soldiers' return. Do the priestesses have their fake penises?"

"Yes, the more experienced have been instructing the new priestesses how to give a blowjob. I think they will be ready for the enlisted men."

"Then let's get all of them so wet and horny with the energy we give off outside that they'll want to practice fucking each other."

"That's an excellent idea. Come, sister," Sina enthusiastically said, pulling Sina towards the entrance of the cave.

Asa grabbed the largest, fullest fake dragon penis from a table, attached to the front of her hip chain and the chain between her legs then exited from the cavern exchanging a grin with her sister.

Draconia Temple of the Gods - Plains of Great Dreams

3

Lush, ancient forest surrounded Iona. She stared up at the tall canopy wondering where she was and what was happening to her body. She had become use to the fevers, illness and fatigue that her body often endured without the help of a nurse or servant. Most days she thought her conversations with Kilean were just a figment of her mind trying to escape from her high fevers. The only sanctuary she found came from her time inside the Plains of the Great Dreams. There was no pain, no illness only peaceful bliss. She had quite enjoyed her solitude within its alluring charms. The strangest parts of her experiences were when she awoke from the deep sleep. She would find a wet cloth on her forehead, a basin of water with other clothes inside it and drinking water on her nightstand with a tray full of her favorite foods. Any mess she had made from her vomiting had disappeared. Iona always found fresh clothes and towels by the window along with a bath filled with water laced with luxurious perfumes and bubbles. Yet no one was in her chamber nor had her door been unlocked. Every time she emerged from her bath it would magically disappear. She had searched many times to learn the identity of her nurse but only came up with more questions than answers. Eventually, Iona settled into the fact that perhaps her nurse feared that if her identity were made known King Nomiki would execute her using magic and helping his daughter, let alone pamper her.

Iona lowered her attention to the marble path before her. She pushed her hands down the skirt of her beautiful white dress. Two large strips of white fabric ran up from her golden belt barely covering her large breasts and tying at the back of her neck to form a V pattern that left most of her torso exposed. Golden bracelets dangled from her tiny wrists. Her long blonde hair clung at the back of her head masterfully designed into an overflowing bun tied back with ribbons. A golden tattoo of a large serpentine dragon ran from the back of her neck to her lower back, wrapping its back claws around her breasts. Its front claws clung inside her thighs. She had never felt so beautiful in her entire life.

Iona slowly walked down the long path wondering what other wonders she would find. With every step she took it was almost as if nature itself was declaring how beautiful and powerful she was. Too bad this was only a dream in her feverish state. She could get use to this. She pushed aside a group of large leaves barring her way and gasped. Kilean stood on the steps of an ancient temple dressed only in tight white pants declaring his well-endowed manhood. The same golden dragon wrapped around his chest with its neck disappearing through the lips of his pants. A long red cape flowed down his back, clasped together with two silver dragons at the base of his neck. She swallowed hard, never taking her eyes off of the bulge in his pants. His eyes stared at the fullness of her large breasts.

"By the gods, you're absolutely gorgeous," he muttered, taking a step towards her.

Iona lifted her eyes to his. She swallowed hard, lowering the leaves behind her. "I...where are we?" she asked stepping towards him. She looked around the area, taking in the immensity of the ancient temple before her. A large stone altar stood on a raised platform within an open courtyard with decorative pillars surrounding the courtyard. Rose petals littered the marble floor. Flowers of all shapes and sizes dotted the courtyard. Pestles with assortments of food and wine scattered throughout the room.

"Draconia Temple of the Gods in the heart of the Plains of the Great Dreams," Kilean answered. Kilean gently took her right hand and drew her closer.

She smiled nervously, glancing down at her dress. "It's not something I would normally wear. I'm sorry if it...."

"I like it on you. You're magnificent," Kilean declared.

Iona smiled, biting her lower lip. He lightly traced his fingers down the side of her left cheek. "I love you," he whispered, leaning his mouth close to hers.

Iona slowly opened her mouth, letting him kiss her slow and deep. They nibbled on each other's lips periodically between their kisses. The dragon tattoo on her chest and back glowed a light hue matching

Kilean's glowing torso. She closed her eyes and embraced his strong body. His hands wrapped around her back, pulling her closer to him. His strength. His warmth. The power! Oh, she felt such power between her legs! Iona pulled away from him, trying to catch her breath. The tattoos returned to their normal tone. She huffed with a slight smile. "Hi," she greeted lightly.

"I believe we already said that," he reminded, as he swallowed hard.

"Right," she said tapping his firm chest. "What are these?"

Kilean placed his hand on the knot at the back of her neck. "May I," he asked. She swallowed hard, heaving with anticipating. He released his hands. "We don't have to but it might answer some our questions."

"Untie it," she ordered, placing his hands on the knot.

Kilean smiled at her as he fumbled with the large knot. "You're nervous. So am I," he whispered in her ear.

Iona smiled back at him then cast her eyes on the chain that hung between her breasts. "What is that," she nodded.

He lowered his eyes to the golden chain. "Breast chain. I've seen them before on the priestesses and the Dragon Twins. It's used to heighten the stimulus when having sex." He untied the knot. The two pieces of fabric gently fell to her hips exposing her full, large breasts. Kilean stared at the emerald studded barbells perfectly pierced through her tits. The tattooed dragon's claws pinched the nipple. "They match," he said, nodding to his own nipple barbells and dragon tattoo.

"What do they...?" Kilean pulled her closer to him, lowered his mouth to her left breast and stroked the nipple with his tongue. She inhaled a deep breath, separating her legs as a wave of ecstasy came over her.

"That," he said, rising to full stature.

Iona held onto his shoulders, stabilizing herself, taking deep breaths. "Holy...."

He chuckled. "Like it, did you?"

She nodded as he pulled her close to his chest. He lightly stroked her slender back. "Where's the book," he whispered into her ear.

"I'm lying on my bed with the dragons over my heart but when I came here it wasn't with me."

"Hmm, why did you place it over your heart?"

"I don't know. I just felt like I needed to do that. Why?" she asked, lifting her eyes to his own.

"I didn't think you would know to do that. I was afraid this wouldn't work."

"What do you mean?"

Kilean shrugged his narrow shoulders. "When I showed the book to my father he said it only appeared when the time comes for the Rite of Dragon Souls."

"The Rite of Dragon Souls?"

"Our souls have sex. He said in order for us to obtain our Dragon Souls we have to go through the ceremony. After I left you I told my father you had the book. He took me to his nest...."

"Nest?"

"It's a secret place in the castle where the Dragon Lord can go to recuperate and prepare for missions. You should have one to."

"I've never heard of anything like that and I'm certain if father knew of it he would have destroyed it in the Great Cleansing. What happened to you after your father took you to his secret place?"

"He and his guardian ceremoniously prepared me for this. I drank the blood potion, fell asleep and here I am."

"Guardian, blood potion, ceremony?" she asked nervously.

"It's alright, Iona. Sometimes I forget that you haven't been prepared for any of this. Did you feel the power we both had when we were kissing?"

Iona grinned, "My lower stomach ached for you."

She peered down at his crotch.

He followed her eyes then chuckled. "You want it, don't you?"

"What. No," she protested, shaking her head and backed away. Yet honestly, she liked the strange feeling she had felt. Kilean's face fell. "I mean. Wait, do you want that from me?"

Kilean grinned. He silently walked into the outer courtyard. Tiny pockets of grass sprouted between where the ancient cobblestone floor had given way to the ground. Tall marble walls prevented any outsiders from viewing whatever happened in the courtyard. He motioned for her to follow him. Iona gazed up on the elaborate images of dragons and humans in acts of passion on the walls. "What you see on the walls are not what you think," Kilean whispered in her ear. Iona turned to face him. "Dragons and humans have co-existed for so long no one can remember a land before our kind encountered them. They came to mankind in our darkest hours. We were about to destroy ourselves through war, pestilence and violence. No one knows where they came from only that they brought magic into our world."

"Magic...again," Iona huffed, crossing her arms over her chest.

He glared at her with a disappointing look, "Just listen and stop trying to doubt everything I am telling you."

"Father...."

"...your father neglects you and yet you still defend him?"

Iona's cast her head downward. He lifted her chin up with two of his fingers. "Don't."

"Don't what?" she asked.

"Iona, you're a very beautiful, intelligent woman. Don't let your father convince you otherwise. You were born to lead not just underneath whomever your father deems fit to be your husband and bear him children. You are not a sex slave."

"Sex slave," she gulped. "Is that what I ...."

"It is and all seven races have them, especially the Dracnoids."

"Seven races? Dracnoids?"

"Iona, there's more to this world than what your father told you. Elves, Humans, Dracnoids, Dwarves, Fae, Nymphs, and Mermaids inhabit our world. Each of our races has their own deities. The oldest of race are the Elves."

"The youngest?"

"Humans. Our existence is just a blink in the eye compared to how long the other races have inhabited Draconia. Even though each race has their own deities that they worship we all believe in the two great supreme deities who created the lessor gods that created us, Draco and Razil."

"But father said...."

"You're father's well-known as the Destroyer. He's tortured and killed magical beings throughout the world all in order to appease his master, Prince Zurggash. No one will ever forget that day he came to your kingdom. He's the reason your mother never assumed her rightful place as Dragon Lady!"

"He's my father, Kilean."

Kilean exhaled a deep breath, "Iona, you told me that your mother use to tell you stories about dragons and magic."

"She did, Kilean. But those are only stories."

He cleared his throat and recalled in a monotone state "Long ago the world was falling apart. Humans could no longer control their destructive natures. Crestos, the crowned prince of Shotar grieved for his people. He searched for an answer throughout the la...."

Iona tapped him hard on the shoulder. Kilean lowered his eyes to her. "How do you know that story in the same words my mother used?"

she asked.

Kilean grinned, "It's a tale that the Dragon Lord and Lady pass down to the next generation word for word."

"Kilean, if I believe what you are telling me to be true then I lose everything."

"Lose? I don't understand. You gain everything, Iona. Once you accept the truth within your heart then your powers will come upon you."

"This place and you. Every encounter brings me joy that helps me endure the miserable life I have at home. If I accept that I am the Dragon Lady then I must also accept that I will never be able to rule as I should as long as my father reigns."

Kilean placed his hands on her upper arms. "Iona, I will help you defeat your father and reclaim your kingdom. You have my word. I will never forsake you nor allow you to live in misery. You are more than a lifemate to me. You're my soulmate."

Iona gently placed her hand on the side of his face, leaned in and kissed him. "I do love you," she whispered in her ear then pulled away. "You called this place Draconia Temple of the Gods."

"Yes, there are many gods. King Draco and Queen Raziel ruled over all the other deities. This is there temple. It only appears when our souls are ready to become one."

She stared at the two pedestals on either side of the steps. Each opened to the center pages without any writing upon them. "Are these our books?"

"Yes. When our souls merge and we absorb the Dragon Soul our Spirit Dragons will write special messages for us in the book. The Dragon Lord's spirit dragon is silver and the Dragon Lady's is gold. They always personalize the book to meet the personality of the rider it belongs to."

"Sounds interesting."

Kilean beamed. "No one other than the rider can open the book. When I was around six my father had left the book beside his throne while he was talking to Roan."

"Roan," she asked as he stepped closer.

"His Dragon Master. He's been preparing me to assume father's position as Dragon Lord."

"Oh, what happened when your father left the book by the throne?"

"Well, I snuck up to his throne while they were talking but as soon as I placed my hands on it the Spirit Dragon flew out of the book and attacked me."

"What?" she asked astonished.

Kilean nodded. "Father had to call the dragon off before it sliced me in two."

"Didn't it recognize you as your father's heir?"

"No, that's thing about the Dragon Spirit. They only recognize whomever has their soul inside their body and they become very territorial about their host and his or her magical possessions." He placed his hands on her upper arms and changed the subject. "Iona, whose caring for you?"

"I don't know. I never found out their identity. Maybe it's for the best that they remain hidden?"

"Perhaps not. Everything is unbalanced. We are both ill with high fevers, headaches and nausea. That will temporally go away once our souls merge and we accept our Dragon Souls. I'm just worried that if this doesn't go well you won't be able to survive the fever without help. My father said our bodies become deadly weak while we are in here."

"Why would the gods allow our bodies to reach the brink of death if we are to become so strong?"

"The dragons honor strength. They want to ensure the new Dragon Lord and Lady are strong enough to endure any circumstance they encounter."

"What happens if they are not?"

Kilean shrugged. "I don't know. I do know if we don't merge our souls our illness will consume us and we will become insane."

"And when you say merge our souls?"

"Have sex, Iona!"

"Is that the only reason you want to have sex with me?"

Kilean huffed, crossing his arms and stared at her breasts. "Really, Iona! Kiss me like we did, wear a dress like that, let me lick your tit and ask me that question?"

Iona stared down at her body then met his eyes. "Well, those pants don't make it any easier," she motioned to his tight crotch. "Your handsome and well, uhm, damn Kilean, just how large are you?"

"Care to find out," he said, grabbed her wrist and placed her hand down his pants. "Stroke it like that," he said, perfectly positioning her hand around his large cock. He moaned with pleasure, closing his eyes and arching his head back. "Ah, yes, just like that." Iona placed her arm around the back of his neck and kissed him passionately. "You feel it," he whispered in her ear. "And I don't mean my cock. You feel the passion we have for each other. The need to be together, don't you?" Iona released her hand from his pants and backed away. "It's not a bad thing, Iona. It's quite natural, especially for us."

"I'm not even supposed to be with a man or even dress like this. I don't know what's wrong with me. I'm sorry. How...?"

"...stop and give into your true self, Iona. I know you love and want me."

Iona paced the floor. Her thoughts couldn't escape from the knowledge that he was right and she needed him now more so that she had felt how large his penis was. She stared at the stone bed behind him upon the platform. Twin sets of straps hung down from the top and bottom parts of the bed. Her mind wandered to the various positions they could try on that bed. The more she thought about it the more she wanted to let go and have her way with him. But what about the good little girl she was supposed to be for her father? Just how badly would he punish her for having sex outside of marriage? But then again, was having sex in her dreams truly ever having sex? It wasn't her body experiencing the encounter.

Her blood ran hot the more she contemplated the situation. She loved Kilean as much as anyone could ever love a dream lover. If she was going to live her wildest dreams in her sleep then let them satisfy her no matter how hard it was going to be. She was tired of living her father's expectations.

Iona walked past Kilean to the altar. She ran her hand along the table and messed with the black leather straps hanging from the bed. Sexual toys of all shapes and sizes sat on tables on both sides, clearly for both their amusements. Her heart skipped a beat as Kilean walked to the altar. She nervously drops a vibrator on the table. The switch turned on and the large dragon penis bounced all over the table. "Oh," she exclaimed, captured the vibrator and turned it off.

Kilean chuckled, "Do you even know what that is for."

"No." She gently laid it back in its place then stared at her lover.

"Do you want me to teach you?" Iona bit her lower lip. "We'll take it slow and if we want to use them we can," Kilean offered as he sat on the edge of the altar.

"Ok. Cause I want to have sex with you and if we do this... you know my....well I..." Kilean placed his finger on her lips.

"Stop talking. You're safe here. Remove your clothes," he suggested.

Iona stood facing Kilean, removed her dress and handed it to him.

He threw it to the side as she stood upright. She fidgeted with her slender hip chain. Two smaller chains descended between her legs. The dragon tattoo's mouth lay open lining the opening between her legs. "Turn around," he ordered.

Iona complied. The dragon tattoo's wings folded over her back pointing to their tips on her firm ass to crevice between them as the chains emerged upwards and connected to her hip chain.

"Do the chains hurt," he asked.

"No. I like them," she replied, tugging on the hip chain. "They're loose enough not to bother me. What are they for?"

"The chains will tighten and spread the folds of your outer and inner lips so I have more access to your sensual zones."

"Sounds painful."

"Not unless you want it to be." He placed hands on her hips and gently guided her backwards. "Sit backwards on me, Iona."

He pulled the back of her ass to his crotch as she sat on him. "Now what?" she asked nervously.

Kilean whispered in her ear with his arms around her. "Lean back, close your eyes and relax your body," he coaxed, gently massaging her breasts and lower stomach. She complied. His right hand slid down her firm stomach while he kissed her neck. She suddenly closed her legs at the touch of his finger upon her clit. "Kilean," she gasped, opening her eyes.

"Felt something," he teased, removing his hand.

"I...uhm...."

"You liked that but don't want to admit it?"

"It's just...."

"Are you going to allow this to happen or listen to your father?"

Iona slid off his legs and turned to him with her hands covering her tits. "I really want this. I do."

"I know you do but what I can't understand is why you are allowing him to influence your thinking."

"I...I...I don't know, Kilean. This is all so new for me. I'm not even supposed to talk about sex let alone like it."

He huffed getting off the table and removed his pants. Kilean kicked his pants to the side. "Look at it. Touch it," he said, taking her hand and placing it on his erect penis. "This is my penis and those," he said moving her hand down to his balls. "Are my balls. I give them to you, Iona. Freely. Because I love you."

"That goes inside me," she asked.

"Yes and you will like it. No, you'll love it. You'll love it so much that you'll be begging me for more. But I'll never force it inside you. If you don't want it then I'll understand."

Iona lowered her hand with a serious look on her face. "Will it hurt?"

He grinned, "Iona, you'll feel sensations that you've never felt before and I promise you it will be an experience that you will want again. Just trust me." Iona nodded biting her lower lip. "Good," he said sitting back on the table. "Sit on me," he instructed. She humbly complied. "Spread your legs apart and lean on me" he coaxed, rubbing the inside of her thighs. Iona nervously leaned against his chest. "Close your eyes," his whispered in her ear. She complied, wondering what her strong lover was going to do to her. Iona gasped feeling a strong sensation from where he swirled his finger over her clit.

"Oh, hmm," she fidgeted, as he held her back, periodically playing with her nipple. His fingers slid down to the opening of her vagina. "Mhmm," she moaned, leaning forward. He pulled her back to his chest, held her tighter and nibbled on her ear.

"You like that, baby," he whispered.

"Oh, very much."

"Sex isn't something to be scared of. It's pleasurable Iona. Very pleasurable and once you experience it you'll want more."

Kilean grabbed the large Dragon penis vibrator from the table and slipped it into her womb. He held it tightly into place and turned it. Tentacles emerged from the top of the vibrator and lightly touched her clit, bringing a heightened stimulation. "Oh," she moaned loudly, opening her legs wider, as he pushed the large vibrator harder. The chains between her legs tightened, opening her sacred area even more. She rocked her ass with her eyes closed thoroughly enjoying the waves of pleasure he brought her.

"That's what a vibrator does."

She could feel his balls against the back of her ass. His erect penis pushed against her asshole.

"Get off me," he whispered, removing the vibrator.

Iona gasped for breath, stumbling to her feet. She leaned over her legs, not certain just how long she was going to be able to stand after that experience. "Shit," she exclaimed.

"Oh, that's nothing compared to what we could do with these other toys," Kilean informed her. "We have heightened sensuality in the temple but we have to be careful because, well, women have more orgasms then men and I want to cum inside you."

"Cum," she asked with curiosity, rising to full figure.

Kilean shook his head. "If you had access to your high priest you would have been better prepared for this," he sighed. "Spill my seed inside you?"

Iona shook her head. "Do you know what semen is?"

"No."

"Damn your father," Kilean swore under his breath. He wiped his hands down his face.

"I'm sorry if I'm upsetting you."

"Iona, you're not upsetting me. Your father is. You were supposed to be trained for this but you weren't and I can tell you're not as confident as I am with this ritual. I should not have to train you. It's not my obligation to do so. I should be able to make love to you without having to worry if you're going to reject my advances because you fear what you don't know."

"I'm sorry."

"Stop apologizing and come to me." Iona approached him as Kilean spread his legs apart. She stared at his large erection. The face of the dragon tattoo opened his jaw around his penis and balls. "Touch it," he guided, placing her hands around his cock. Iona nervously complied.

"It's stiff," she said.

"You did that to me," he said leaning back on his arms.

She looked at him then back to his penis. "How," she asked.

"When you sat on me and acted like that with the vibrator inside you, you excited me, especially when your ass was against my balls. That's why I wanted you to get off."

"Oh."

"If you want to excite me even more open your mouth and suck on my penis."

"What," she asked. "That sounds disgusting."

"It's not. I promise. Just do it but lick your lips first and then move your tongue all around it. I played with you and you can play with me."

Iona held his penis, licked her lips and descended her mouth over his penis. She swirled her tongue all around, bobbing up and down with his hand on top of her head. "Oh, shit, Iona," he groaned, leaning back. He inhaled deeply through his teeth. "Ah, baby. Yeah, just like that." Up and down she bobbed taking him fully into her mouth. It wasn't that bad and truth be told she thoroughly enjoyed making him react the way he was. It was making her want him inside her even more.

"I need you," she mumbled between bobs.

"Ugh, me too. Get up."

Kilean slid off the altar, stood before her, groping and kissing her breasts as they fondled each other. The couple pressed their foreheads together with a longing of desire. They kissed, embracing each other. Iona stroked Kilean's penis while he rubbed her clit. "Oh, I need you," Kilean whispered in between kisses.

"Hmm, me too," she replied, their hands running down each other's backs.

Oh, he was making her so hot! Suddenly the sound of something clanking into place startled them. Kilean and Iona pulled away from each other and stared at the walls. Blue tinted glass arose from the edges of the platform and encased the room as if they were inside a giant aquarium.

"Kilean," Iona panicked. He protectively pushed her behind him and examined their situation. "I don't like being trapped."

"You're trapped in a tower and don't like being trapped?"

"I'm scared. What...what if... what if we've been caught by my father and we're going to be executed for being together."

"I don't think your father has control over anything that happens in the Plains of the Great Dreams let alone in this temple."

Iona wrapped her arms around his chest and sat her head at the back of his neck. "Kilean." He turned around and held her close to his chest. "Shh, I'm not going to let anything bad happen to you. I promise. You're safe. The walls could have gone up to contain the sexual energy of the dragon souls."

"But you don't know for certain, do you?"

"No, but I have been preparing for this experience since I was consecrated by the Dragon Twins."

Iona silently looked up at him. "Consecrated by the Dragon Twins? How do you prepare for this day?"

"He's had an orgy twice a year with them since puberty," a female voice echoed off the walls. The couple looked around for the source but couldn't find it.

"Who are you?" Kilean demanded, pushing Iona behind him.

"I am the one who is protecting Iona." Iona placed her hands around him and looked at him with a strange look upon her face. She shook her head. "Oh, dear child, don't believe all the lies your father has instilled upon you. You are not whom he claims you are to become. You were destined for even greater things. Things that your father fears the most."

"Fear? My father fears nothing," Iona protested.

A metallic orange dragon elegantly appeared before them. "My name is Tayla and I am the High Priestess and Priest of the Plains of the Great Dreams."

"Priest and Priestess?" Iona questioned.

"Humans do not understand the duality of the sexes. I am both in order to provide the necessities that either Dragon Lord or Lady may require to prepare them for the Bonding of the Dragons," the dragon answered. "Perhaps, little one, this image would suit you better?" the dragon said then transformed into an orange naked dracnoid.

"How did you do that," Iona asked, pushing her body forward.

The seductive woman chuckled, "There are far more things possible in the impossible than possible with those whose minds are not open to believe. Iona, I have been with you since the time your mother died. Yet never have made my presence known to you until now. You love this man."

Iona looked at Kilean and nodded. "He's wonderful."

"Kilean loves you."

"Always," Kilean answered stroking the side of Iona's face. "Tayla," he called to the woman. "How will the transfer occur without her mother?"

"That's complicated and the request I have of you will be unusual. It has never happened before. When the council told me of it I was shocked they would have even requested it from me. But it is my duty to guard the dragon souls and ensure that the transition is smooth no matter how unconventional that experience may require of me."

Kilean looked at Iona then back to the dragon. "What does the council desire of us?"

"When Queen K'Lara died the dragon soul she possessed returned to the dragons. It dwells inside my body just as it did thousands of years ago before the Dragon Lord and Lady ever existed. The soul is wounded. It feels the humans no longer want it."

"That's not true," Kilean objected.

"It must be enticed to return to the next Dragon Lady."

"How," Iona asked.

Tayla turned to Kilean. "You will conduct yourself as you have done with the Dragon Twins."

"An orgy? But I thought our bonds were sacred and no one was to interfere," he protested.

"Normally, but Kilean these are not normal times and we must adapt if magic and dragons are to survive."

"What's an orgy," Iona asked.

Kilean faced his beloved. "The three of us will have sex together."

"No," Iona protested, pushing him. She paced the floor, glaring periodically at him. "I...I...I... can't do that."

"Iona, I've done it plenty of times. It's fun."

She snarled at him. "You've done it plenty of times. I thought you were a virgin like me!"

"You can't tell me that you haven't felt the urge to have sex since you're puberty, can you?"

"Well of course I have but I don't hire prostitutes to fulfill that need!"

Kilean groaned, "I fuck the Dragon Twins. They are sacred creatures not prostitutes. They ease the need within me to mate so I can focus on more important matters without causing harm. If our sexual urges aren't met we will cause someone harm in order to appease them, especially more so after we procure the dragon souls."

Iona huffed, crossing her arms over her chest. "Kilean, it's not right."

"And this is! You said you wanted a world away from the restrictions your father has placed upon you. I'm offering that world to you, right now! This isn't a dream, Iona. This is real! What I'm asking from you is what you were born to be. You are the next Dragon Lady."

Iona glanced between Kilean and the Tayla. A part of her wanted to explore the sensuality of a threesome. Yet the devoted daughter of King Nomiki told her that everything she was experiencing was wrong. She should reserve her body for her husband not these people. Oh, what was she going to do? If Kilean thought the orgy was fun and alright then it must be, shouldn't it. Kilean had never lied to her before.

"There must be any other way for me to obtain the dragon soul," she questioned Tayla.

"I'm afraid not. Humans use magic to transfer energy from themselves to another human. Dragons are magical creatures. They hide their souls deep within their own hearts or the hearts of one of their hosts. A bodiless dragon soul within another dragon can only occur when the dragon and creature are physically connected. Even then it may not happen. If the dragon soul finds that the creature's mind is corrupt it will remain in his host's body. The only way for me to transfer the soul is to mate with you while Kilean does so. I will join in your pleasures but only if you both agree to do so."

"I will allow it," Kilean said then looked at Iona. Iona stared into nothing, completely shocked that another woman wanted to have sex with her! Sex with Kilean was one thing but another woman? "Iona," Kilean nudged her.

Iona swallowed hard, never taking her eyes off the beautiful woman. "You once told me you wanted to experience new things. This is definitely new."

"Oh, what the hell? I've come this far, why not?"

4

Sweat poured down Iona's naked body. She pulled on the chain binding her wrists to the table with a long sensual moan, thoroughly enjoying the pounding Kilean was delivering to her. At first, the thought of someone watching them having sex had hindered the process. Iona just couldn't perform while Tayla was standing by. Despite their best efforts, Kilean and Iona had a rough start. She couldn't keep her attention on him. It was only when Tayla offered to disappear that Iona was able to focus more on her lover than the strange dragon woman wanting to seduce her. They played with all the sex toys, fully exploring each other's bodies in different positions. Iona especially liked it when Kilean strapped the wireless butterfly vibrator over her clit and had slipped his penis inside her behind completely bring her to a heightened level of sensual pleasure she never thought possible. She was glad sometime after that he had placed her ankles and wrists in the straps. The immense pleasure had almost been too much for her to bear. Kilean was an amazing lover and his penis was huge!

Kilean arched his back, closing his eyes with a deep moan. Sweat poured down his well-formed athletic body. He pressed the remote beside her to high. The clit vibrator massaged her clit even faster. She tensed her thighs as he pushed even harder and faster. Her warm body tinged with red. Her tits grew harder. The familiar strange, overwhelming feeling deep within her lower stomach returned but even stronger this time. She screamed with pleasure, calling his name several times. Her body fidgeted uncontrollably. The more he played with her tits the more her body reacted with burst of excitement. "Harder! Faster," Kilean complied, thrusting deeper and harder. She gasped with delight. "Oh, baby. Yes, yes," she screamed then felt a burst inside her. Kilean grinned as she gasped with her mouth open, "Oh, hmm, off. Turn it off," she moaned.

"Damn. I kind of like it and I'm, ugh, yes" he cringed, arching his back. "Oh, shit, yes," he swore, pushing with one last hard thrust, ejaculating just as she reached another orgasm. He exhaled a deep breath and turned the clit vibrator off. Iona cringed, uncomfortably.

"What's wrong," he asked, leaning over her.

"I feel something sticky inside me. It wasn't there whenever I ...uhm..."

"Orgasm."

"Yeah."

"That's my cum."

"Oh, and the wetness I felt inside me?"

"That's all you. It's your cum. Your body excretes it every time you have an orgasm. It's natural."

Iona nodded. "Did you learn how to be an excellent lover with the Dragon Twins?"

"You're not jealous of them, are you?"

"I was. I thought we were only supposed to be together."

"We are but the experiences we have with our twins doesn't matter because they are training us. I have yet to learn more from them."

"Damn," she swore with a grin. "Because that was... mindblowing."

Kilean chuckled, "Glad you liked it."

"It's time," Tayla said reappearing beside them.

Kilean unlocked Iona's restraints. The couple looked at the dracnoid then looked back at each other. "How does this work," Kilean asked.

"You do everything I tell you and you do not deviate from anything I say or the soul may reject Iona," Tayla instructed, climbing onto the bed. She touched Kilean's penis. "It takes human men longer to have another erection once they have experienced one unless they are in the Valley of Li-tli. I will give you a temporary dragon's ability to mate so you can receive the dragon soul from your father. Once the transfer of dragons is complete you will be able to mate with Iona as often as you like and vice versa. But remember, when you mate with her it must be mutual desire to do so or the dragons will not honor it."

"I understand."

Tayla lowered Kilean onto his back and placed her mouth around his penis. She gently stroked the sides with her mouth then licked the top of his penis. "Ugh," Kilean groaned, arching his back. Up and down, Tayla perfectly moved her head, stroking every side of his penis with her tongue. Kilean breathed deeply through his teeth, pushing her head closer to his waist. Just the sound of his sensual moans and groans was enough to excite Iona all over again. She looked at Tayla. Tayla nodded in her direction.

Iona straddled Kilean's face with her bottom and faced Tayla. She gasped, arching her head back at the sensation of Kilean's tongue inside her, his fingers playing with her clit in between strokes of his tongue upon it while he held her down. She closed her eyes, relaxing to the rolling pleasures he was granting her.

Tayla abandoned Kilean, grabbed the side of Iona's face and kissed her deeply as she repositioned herself over Kilean's erect penis. Iona opened her eyes, grabbed her by face and kissed her in between her sensual moans. Tayla joined, rocking faster on Kilean's hips. "Ugh, you feel so good, dragon rider," Tayla declared between kisses.

Iona cringed, wanting more from her lover than his tongue and Tayla's kisses. It wasn't fair that Tayla was being fucked by Kilean when it was supposed to be her! "Kilean," she yelled his name while Tayla suckled Iona's tits in union with her rocking and tickling Kilean's balls.

Tayla rose from Kilean. Iona grabbed Kilean's penis and suckled while she moved her ass back and forth over Kilean's mouth. "Hmm, yeah, baby," Kilean moaned.

Tayla pushed Iona off of Kilean. The two women looked at each other over Kilean's erect penis then kissed. Kilean leaned upright with a large grin. "He likes this, Iona," Tayla whispered between kisses. Iona glanced at Kilean. He looked at them with a stronger desire. The women moved their mouths to Kilean's penis, each giving him a blowjob, passing his penis between them. "Oh, shit," he exclaimed arching his head back. Iona straddled Kilean's waist backwards, supporting her entire weight in a crouched position. She lowered her body over his penis and moaned as it entered. Up and down, she rocked. Tayla rubbed Iona's clit with in perfect rhythm with her tongue and finger. Kilean held his beloved's ass, kissing her gently on the neck. Tayla's hand stroked Kilean's balls. He groaned louder, arching his back. Tayla removed his penis from Iona, rubbed it along the folds of Iona's labia, teased her asshole with it, then reinserted it.

"Yes," Iona yelled, jumping harder and faster. Tayla and Kilean worked in perfect unison to bring her to heightened sensuality. Sweat lubricated their bodies. Loud, sensual moans and groans echoed off the glass walls. "Oh, gods! Oh, gods, yes," Iona screamed.

"My turn," Tayla grinned. Iona dismounted and kissed Kilean as Tayla mounted him, facing them. She rocked back and forth, fully taking in Kilean's penis. Her deep moans echoed off the walls while she rocked harder. Kliean snarled, wrapping his hands around Tayla's firm ass. She slowed her rocking, pushing his penis deeper within her. They stared deep into each other's eyes, smiling from the deep sensation within them. Iona watched them react to each other as if they had completely forgotten she even existed. Tayla leaned over and passionately kissed Kilean while rocking her hips. Their sensual moans growing even louder.

"Kilean," she called to him. But he never paid her any attention. This was her man! He was supposed to be making her feel like that. Not Tayla.

"Get off him, bitch," she snarled, pushing Tayla to the ground.

"Iona, what are you doing?" Kilean asked, leaning up on his arms as Tayla rose to her feet.

"She's jealous," Tayla chimed.

"And why shouldn't I be? You're the fuck. I'm the one he loves," she declared loudly.

Tayla roared loudly in her direction with a look of fury.

"Don't be angry with her, Tayla. She doesn't understand. She wasn't trained," Kilean protested.

Tayla tightened her jaw glaring deeply at Iona with a stern look. Iona swallowed hard, hiding behind Kilean. "If you were any other woman interrupting my mating you would have been dead!"

Iona hid even further behind Kilean. She clung her hands to his chest and hid her face between his shoulders. "Did she upset the soul," Kilean asked.

"No, it wants more," Tayla sneered. "But you must cum inside me first then in her if this transfer is to work."

"Understood, but there must be a way for her enjoy the experience?"

"Get up and have Iona lie down," Tayla ordered.

Kilean exchanged glances with Iona. He rose from the altar. Iona laid down. Tayla crawled on top of the bed and straddled over Iona. "Does it help if he doesn't see my face?" she asked Iona.

Iona snarled, "As long as he doesn't enjoy it as much as you want him then yes."

Kilean crawled on the bed, sat on his knees and inserted his penis into Tayla. He thrust hard, deep and fast. Her moans lifted higher the faster he thrust. Iona wanted to hate the sensual woman on top of her but the more she reacted to her lover the more she wanted Kilean to satisfy her needs as well. She never thought it possible for Tayla to excite her the way she did. Kilean slowed his assault, rubbing Tayla's back. Tayla grinned, periodically kissing Iona. Kilean moved his hand down to Tayla's clit and rubbed it, slowly pushing. "Ah, shit," Tayla hummed, closing her eyes.

"We're going to make her come hard," Kilean smiled at Iona. "But not as hard as I want to make you."

Iona lifted her eyes to her lover. Kilean and Iona kissed Tayla all over her body, fondling her everywhere. He pushed Tayla over Iona and thrust the hardest he ever had. "Oh, yes," Tayla screamed several times. Kilean arched his head back, heaving.

"Ugh," he groaned then spilled his seed insider her. Tayla collapsed onto Iona while Kilean stood over the women with a satisfied look. "Now what," he asked looking at Iona.

Just when she thought she had experienced everything. Kilean's limp penis grew erect again. Tayla ordered them off the altar. Iona and Kilean complied with a confused look on their face. Tayla lay sideways on the bed with her legs open and her head lowered towards them. "Fuck her from behind, Kilean while she eats from me. Use the ass plug, if you want and a vibrator on me."

Kilean and Iona looked at each other for a few moments then got into position. "Iona," he asked playing with the plug.

"Yes," she agreed, spreading her legs wider and leaning over. Kilean spread her ass wide, licked his finger then lubricated the asshole. He placed the plug deep within. She screamed, arching her back then exclaimed even more when he assaulted her with his penis. He pushed her to the edge of the bed and lowered her so her face was between Tayla's legs, handing her a large vibrator. Tayla licked his balls as he thrust hard into Iona.

"Fuck. Oh yeah. I like this," he exclaimed, massaging Iona's clit as he pounded hard into her vagina. Tayla took the vibrator from Iona's grasp and placed it deep within herself. She moaned arching her back, nipping at Kilean's balls while Iona rubbed Tayla's clit and played with the vibrator.

"Oh, oh," Iona exclaimed in between thrusts.

"You're so fucking wet," Kilean yelled.

"Fuck me harder, lover. Oh, oh!"

A light glow illuminated between the three of them with a soft humming sound just barely noticeable between their sensual moans. The light grew brighter until the only light in the room came from them. Their bodies automatically pushed their sensual pleasure even higher. Iona and Kilean's souls lifted out of their spirits into the air. Their souls stared at their physical mating happening below them

"Damn, we're good," Kilean muttered.

Iona chuckled. "You were right."

"Oh?"

"I like this and I want more."

Their bodies drew closer to each other. They embraced, wrapping their arms and legs around each other. Their mouths locked in a long, slow deep kiss. Something felt odd inside her but Iona didn't care. She was safe, wasn't she? A warm, tingling sensation came over her. She closed her eyes, fully taking in every strange sensation. It was almost as if she wasn't herself anymore. Power and lust filled her entire being. Two became one. Kilean and Iona's souls merged into a large dragon. The dragon roared mighty flying all around the steamy, lustful temple. Iona could hear every one of Kilean's thoughts and vice versa. They were each their own unique person yet inside one body! Such power and wisdom consumed them. Joy, bliss, all the knowledge of the dragons unified inside them. They were the same but yet different. Their dragon suddenly burst apart and they rejoined their spirits. Kilean collapsed onto the bed and lay next to her with a large grin.

"Did you...," he started to ask.

"...What was that?" she interrupted

They laughed, holding each other then realized they were completely alone.

"Where is she," Kilean asked leaning up on his arm.

Iona searched the room but Tayla was gone. She grinned, turned to Kilean. "She said after we received the dragon's souls we would be able to mate again. Care to try?"

"Gladly," Kilean said and pushed her underneath him. "Shall we play with the toys or just make love?"

Iona squirmed and repositioned the ass plug. "Whatever you want to do but I want to cum harder than I have yet."

"Harder, hmm? Is that even possible?"

"I don't know but I like being with you. Do your worst Prince Kilean Dragonsun."

He looked over at the toys and grinned. "Oh, I can think of many things I'd like to do with you." They exchanged a knowing grin.

Drag'tharg Keep - Kingdom of Huitgan

5

The fresh scent of salt from the Talarn Sea filled the air matching the sounds of the water breaking upon the shore. Seagulls cried outside the marble balcony. Normally he would have enjoyed the view of the ocean from the highest tower of the castle. But this wasn't a normal day and his precious son was still deadly ill despite the passing of the Silver Dragon Soul. King Tavir Dragonsun peered down at the fresh charcoal black burn marks on his chest from where the silver dragon had tattooed itself upon him twenty years ago. His mark upon his chest and back had once glistened upon whomever saw it but now was just a dull grey. He was no longer a Dragon Lord but had transformed into a Dragon Elder. But how could he be an elder if the marks were no longer upon his son's chest and back. Oh, they had the matching nipple barbells that every Dragon Lord is given when they go through the Rite of Dragon Souls but not the tattoo. It was so baffling.

After he had fallen into a deep sleep he found himself under Draco's wings. The almighty dragon had cocooned him while they watched his physical body's torso burn where the tattoo used to be as the dragon left his body and Kilean's body seized as the soul took a new host. Tavir had never felt any pain until Draco released his spirit back into his physical body. Gods, the pain was so unbearable! Pain like that would have normally killed a man but Draco had sustained him. He awoke screaming, clutching the restraints binding his wrists to the bed, unable to move or breath without piercing pain in his chest and back. Thankfully, his guardian, Solon had been by his side with a potion to ease the pain. He had emptied the cup then fell back into a deep sleep.

His spirit had travelled to a mysterious golden kingdom nestled deep within a mountainous valley. Men, women and children of the seven races shouted with joy. Musicians sang songs about him. He had thoroughly enjoyed the experience especially when he was reunited with his father. The older king had escorted him into a grand council hall where he had met all the Dragon Lords and Ladies of the past, their Guardians and Dragon Masters. He didn't know how long he had been there or what they had talked about. He awoke later with a silver cape draped majestically on his back strapped around his shoulders with dark leather studded with rubies and emeralds. The image of Draco consumed the entire cape.

"Tavir," he heard Solon's elegant music like voice call his name. Tavir turned to the left to see the eight-foot elf with a silver goblet in his hands.

"What is it?" Tavir asked, taking the goblet.

"Nightsong."

Tavir suspiciously looked at his faithful friend. "Trying to kill me?"

"If I wanted to kill you I wouldn't use that to do so. You must drink the sacred elixirs of the seven races to complete your transformation."

"Wouldn't consuming any of them kill a mortal?"

"You're not entirely mortal anymore. You'll die a mortal's death but your soul will not travel into the Lair of the Undead but proceed directly to Draco's court. Drink it. I wanted to start you with an Elven one."

"Nostalgia?"

"More like it's easier to make."

"Why Solon Meleran, I never thought you'd chose something easier over something challenging."

"Eh, I blame my dwarvian side."

"Dwarves aren't lazy. They're the hardest working miners and engineers on the planet."

"Just drink the potion, Tavir," Solon said then returned to his books.

Tavir grinned to himself thinking about his old friend, confident and mentor. He had first met Solon when he was six years old. The High Priest had charged the elf with tutoring him in the Draconian Ways. Tavir had rarely interacted with the oldest race on the planet and had a healthy fear for the elves. Quiet and reserved, the elves carried a wealth of knowledge and magical abilities. Yet, they could also be very deadly if they needed to be. At first, Tavir had admired Solon simply because he was an elf but over the years his admiration had been replaced with a close friendship. Tavir couldn't get enough of Solon's interesting lessons and the constant companionship the elf had brought to him.

So many questions arose in his head over the years about Solon's life. Most of the time Solon would appease his curiosity. A few days after he became a man, his father had told him that Draco had relieved Solon of his obligations and had charged General Roan Tharg to train him. Tavir's heart had been crushed. Solon was his best friend! His father had then told him that Solon was a priest and had obligations that needed to be fulfilled within the Temple of the Moon. He asked his father if he could visit upon his old friend. His father said no, claiming that only females were allowed within the Temple of the Moon but he would ask the Dragon Lady if she would be willing to carry messages back and forth between him and Solon. Solon and Tavir had communicated through letters for years. Each brought joy to the other until that dreadful day in his eighteenth year when the Dragon Lady had visited upon her father's court with a small wooden trunk in her hands. She had given the trunk to him with her apologies. She really didn't need to say more. He knew by the tone of her voice what she had come to tell him. The only words he could formulate were "How?" She told him Solon had fallen ill with the Dwarvian Flu. His father, the High Priest, had done everything he could to save his beloved son but the flu is deadly to elves and Solon's dwarvian half wasn't strong enough to save him. Before he died he had asked his father to give Tavir a chest. Tavir had opened it to find the wooden horse he had made for his friend many years ago and handwritten note encouraging him to be the strongest, most noble, kindest man he knew Tavir could be. He went on to tell Tavir that of all the humans he had ever met he was the only one he could ever consider his elven brother.

"Oh, gods, that tastes awful," Tavir complained, placing the goblet on a pedestal beside the canopy bed. He held his hand over his stomach and lowered his head on the balcony rail.

"You drank all of it," Solon asked with his nose in a book.

"Yes, Solon," he sighed, stumbling.

Solon placed the book on a desk and quickly walked to his charge's side. "Dizzy and nauseous," he asked.

"Weak too," Tavir said.

"Don't fight it, Tavir. Let it consume you."

"I'll die."

"Have I ever done anything to hurt you?"

47

"While you were alive or after you were resurrected by your father to serve as my guardian?"

"Either," Solon challenged.

"Eh," Tavir replied. "Solon," he stumbled to his friend.

Solon picked Tavir up in his arms, carried him to the bed and laid him down next to Kilean. Tavir fidgeted, arching his back up and down, "Ugh, why does it hurt so much to breath?"

"It's bonding to the marks."

"But I don't carry the soul any longer."

"No, but you do carry the marks of having done so. Now you must be accepted by all the gods in order to assume your place as Kilean's ambassador. Once you're an ambassador you'll be able to speak on behalf of the Dragon Lord to all the deities. The pain will not last long. What do you remember from your time in Draco's Court?"

Tavir closed his eyes and focus his mind on his new memories. He pushed through his muddled thoughts but couldn't think of anything. He opened his eyes realizing the pain, dizziness and nausea had subsided. "Nothing," he answered, bewildered. Tavir pushed his hands down his firm chest with a confused look upon his face. He sat upright and looked to his mentor for answers.

"Your body will fight each of the seven sacred drinks unless your mind controls the body. When you think of the wonderful things you experienced when you travelled to Draco's Court, the body will release its urge to fight the poison," Solon counseled.

"Why didn't you tell me this before?"

"I taught you mind over body years ago. Why didn't you do that when you first felt the pain?"

Kilean painfully moaned, fidgeting and turning his head. "Kilean," Tavir called to his son, leaning over his body.

"Ugh," the crowned prince of Huitgan groaned, turning his head to his father.

Kilean coughed uncontrollably, rolling onto his stomach and leaning over the bed away from his father. Solon went to his side. "Slow deep breath, Prince Kilean." Kilean stared at the eight-foot tall elf's large shoes. It had never occurred to him just how odd the stubby feet matched the tall, slender, elegant elf's figure. "Prince Kilean," the elf called once again.

"Hmm, I feel worse than I did before I went in there. Why is it so cold?" he shivered, reaching for blankets.

Solon placed his hand on the side of the young man's check.

"You're fever's risen. Did you bond your soul to Iona Dragonmoon?"

Kilean nodded.

"Solon," Tavir said, pulling the blanket off his son. Kilean protested. "Stop, let us look." Kilean dropped the blanket onto the bed and leaned over his legs. "The tattoo's gone," Tavir whispered to his mentor.

Solon peered at the young man's strong, bare back. "This doesn't make sense. I witnessed the transfer. Your chest and back burned just as your father's did when he passed the soul to you and you are marked with the charcoal burn pattern of the serpent that will remain with you until the day you die."

"If my son dies without that mark he won't be accepted into Draco's Court."

"Hmm," Kilean moaned with a shiver. "Father," he muttered between the chattering of his teeth.

Tavir looked at Solon. Solon nodded then returned to his book as Tavir moved closer to his son and pulled him into his lap. He wrapped his arms around Kilean, pressing his son's head close to his heart.

"S...so....hmmm...cold," Kilean pushed through his teeth.

"Solon, tell me you have something that can help my son!"

Solon lifted his finger in the air with his nose in the book. Clean, cold water filled the basin beside the table with fresh cloths. A pitcher with ice water sat beside it with a tall, slender glass filled with water. "Water," Tavir asked, taking the water.

"Don't be so ungrateful, Tavir. It's unbecoming. The water's laced the petals of Atlantium."

"He's not a Merman."

"Did you know that Mermaids and Mermen must lower their body's core temperatures in order to live within the depth of the ocean? They consume Atlantium because it not only nourishes them but gradually lowers the body's temperature to a sustainable level so they are able to live within the bowels of the ocean fully able to live the lives they desire within the walls of Atlantis. Of course, they use it in other oceanic areas where their natural body temperatures wouldn't allow them to dwell. That's why there are Atlantians throughout all the oceans and seas."

"And how did you get your hands on Atlantium?"

Solon pointed to the balcony. "Princess Talaran."

"King Tritan's daughter just freely gave you a portion of her food?"

"Don't concern yourself with how I got it, only with what it does."

"Solon?"

Solon lifted his eyes to the king. "I'm the son of the High Priest and your Guardian. How do you think I got it?"

"By the gods, Solon. How does an elf have sex with a mermaid?"

Solon deflected, "Don't give him too much. It may seem cool to the touch but is ice cold once it enters the body to offset the body's increased temperature."

"What about the Dragon Twins? The Milk of the Dragons will cure any ailment a rider has," Tavir asked.

"I need him conscious enough to tell me what happened at the temple before we even attempt to find a cure. He can only travel to the Dragon Twins when the portal opens within our Dragon Hold. That will not occur for three more days. We might not have that long if his fever continues to rise as fast as it is now and you need time to consume the other six elixirs. I can only give you one elixir per day."

"Why not all at once?"

"Because after your body adjusts your mind needs to prepare itself to communicate with the gods. You'll hear their thoughts and they will hear yours. It can be quite overwhelming for a human to endure, especially so when you start with the Elven gods. I told you, I chose the Elven elixir first because it was simpler to make but, what I didn't tell you is that it is harder for your mind to merge with theirs. It could take hours, days, weeks, months, even years for the unification between their minds and yours to occur and I can't give your mind and body to the next gods until the first set has been appeased."

"So...this could take the entirety of my life to complete?"

"Perhaps but perhaps not. The Elven gods take the longest to complete. Once they have accepted you then the rest of the pantheon will be easier to complete. Give him the water."

Tavir picked up the glass of water and placed it close to his son's lips. "Kilean," Tavir coaxed. Kilean slowly opened his weary eyes and mouth. Tavir gently poured small portions of the crystal clear liquid into his son's mouth.

"Uhm, no more," Kilean protested swallowing the water and pushing the glass away from him with his head lowered.

Solon interrupted, "What's it taste like, Prince Kilean?"

"Bitter. I want to vomit it back up. It hurts my throat and stomach."

"Give him another sip, Tavir."

Kilean shook his head. "One more, Kilean," Tavir ordered with a fatherly tone, placing the cup next to his son's lips.

"Hmm," Kilean cringed at his father. Tavir eyed his son with a stern, fatherly look. Kilean humbly opened his mouth and allowed his father to pour more of the water. He closed his mouth and swallowed with the relaxing look on his face.

"Son," Tavir asked.

"It tastes like rosewater."

"That's enough," Solon ordered, motioning with his eyes for the king to lower the water. "The next sip will kill him."

Tavir placed the glass of water on the table and cradled his son close to his chest. "Relax Kilean and let the water help you." Tavir silently watched his mentor pace the room, periodically exchanging books and flipping through them. The king's thoughts turned his son's fate. The day Kilean was born had been a day of mixed feelings. He was grateful to the gods that they had given him an heir to his kingdom but he also knew Kilean would become the next Dragon Lord. He never quite knew how Kilean would be able to fully serve all of Draconia without a Dragon Lady by his side but he kept with tradition and had his son trained to assume his rightful place in the world. He had just about given up hope for his son when Kilean informed him he had not only visited the Plains of Great Dreams but met K'Lara's daughter within it. He had been so excited by the prospect that perhaps his son wouldn't have to face the prospect of living with the emptiness and sorrow of not having his soulmate within his life that he had immediately informed Solon of the incident. Their hope and joy had increased even more when Kilean had told him that he was able to communicate telepathically with Iona.

Kilean clutched his father's bare shoulder and inhaled a deep breath. "Kilean," Tavir called, releasing his tight grip. Kilean lifted his eyes to his father with nod.

Kilean stared at his father's chest then his own. His eyes bulged. "Where is it," he panicked, stroking his chest. "I had the nipple barbells and the tattoos just like you, dad. But now I only have the barbells. Where's my tattoo?"

Tavir grabbed his son's strong forearms. "We don't know. We thought you might have an explanation."

"Prince Kilean," Solon called, placing a book onto a pedestal.

Kilean opened his mouth to speak then closed it. "Take your time, son. We need to know everything that happened in there," Tavir instructed.

"Iona and I made love so many times and in so many wonderful ways," he grinned, starry eyed.

51

"I'm glad you enjoyed your experience."

"I didn't quite enjoy it at first," he admitted.

"Why not?" Solon asked.

Kilean moved off his father and sat on the bed with his back against the headboard. "She knows nothing about human breeding nor the seven races and the Laws of Bonding within the Draconian Codex. She told me her father taught her not to dress provocatively nor to enjoy sex."

"Sounds like King Nomiki fears his daughter will desire to become like her mother," Tavir said.

"He would have justification to fear that from her. You are certain she is the firstborn daughter?" Solon asked Tavir.

"She's the only daughter," Kilean yawned. He shook his head, "Oh, sorry."

"Don't be. Your body is weak without the blessing of the Dragon Soul upon you. How did you get Iona to complete the ceremony?" Solon asked.

Kilean wiped his hands down his face. "I'm very good at persuasion," he grinned. The men sternly looked at him. "What?"

"Kilean, this isn't funny. I just held you in my arms fearing you would cross the divide into the underworld and you're joking about the matter," Tavir yelled.

"Sorry," Kilean whispered. He exchanged glances between the older men. They never took their piercing eyes off of him. "Iona's naïve as I was when father took me to the Temple of the Sun for training. She found a dildo in the shape of a dragon's penis, complete with the sensual nodes and everything. She didn't know what it was so I...uhm...well...educated her."

"Well, if that was the first sex toy I had my choice of for using with a virgin, I would have chosen it as well," Tavir said.

"She liked it so much that she almost made me cum in my pants. I then taught her how to give a blowjob."

"Those are all excellent ways of introducing a woman to sex but did you have sex with her or did you spill your seed in her mouth?" Solon asked.

"We had sex after we met Tayla."

Solon's face fell. "Tayla," he urged.

"Yes, the priest and priestess of the temple?"

"There's no priest or priestess at the temple," Tavir claimed.

"What else did she tell you?" Solon asked with urgency.

"Whose Tayla?" Tavir asked.

Solon waved his hand in his direction and looked sternly at the prince.

Kilean turned his attention between the two men.

"Kilean, what did she tell you?" Solon asked with more urgency. "Did you fuck her?"

"Wha...well, yeah, she said I had to in order to pass the dragon soul from her to Iona. She said when Queen K'Lara died the gold dragon returned its dragon soul to the dragons and that it resided within her. She had to transfer it to Iona."

"Who did you give your seed to first?" Solon asked leaning over Kilean bracing his weight on his arms on both sides of Kilean's body.

"Solon," Kilean whimpered, fidgeting backwards.

"Who?"

"Solon, what's this about?" Tavir asked, stepping towards the bed.

Solon ignored the king. "Who, Prince Kilean? Which woman did you fuck first?!"

"Iona, alright. She had nine orgasms before I ejaculated inside her."

"And the tenth time you two came together?"

"Yes."

Solon looked over to the king. "It passed to him."

"How do you know?"

"Tell your son how many orgasms K'Lara had with you before you ejaculated into her?"

Kilean earnestly turned his eyes to his father. Tavir huffed and held up nine fingers. "Really," Kilean beamed. "And you released on the tenth with her?"

"Yes...."

"...just as his father did with K'Lara's mother and so on," Solon answered.

"Damn, and I thought it was just because we played with all the toys. The hotter she became, the more it affected me. It was amazing!"

"Yes, well, you won't get anymore of that if we can't unite you and Iona together at the Bonding of Dragons." Tavir informed. Tavir turned to Solon. "Where's the soul and why doesn't he have the markings?" Tavir asked.

"I don't know but when they are within the temple, they have the sexual drive of the spirit dragons. Female dragons must have nine orgasms to prove to the male dragon that she has the strength and stamina to breed his eggs. He'll only ejaculate if she can reach the tenth with him."

"Gods, it was amazing," Kilean grinned, recalling the experience in his mind. The men looked back at the young man. "Those orgasms grew in strength. I could feel them on my penis. She grew more aggressive and accepting of what we were doing...."

"Kilean," Solon called.

The young man pushed the memories out of his mind then looked at the long haired elf. "The male transfer occurs first then the female. Did you feel the soul within you?"

"You wouldn't have felt it right away. Your body would rest for a few moments while the soul nests inside you. It takes a few minutes for it to settle, then you would feel its strength within you. It would crave to mate with the female. I know it did for me," Tavir explained.

"Tayla joined right afterwards. She gave me a blowjob saying that she was going to give me the strength of a dragon to mate again. Then we had a threesome and I ejaculated inside of her while Iona helped me to seduce her."

"Shit," Solon swore, running back to his books.

"I've never heard you swear before?" Tavir asked, crossing his arms over his chest.

Solon grabbed several books and quickly flipped through them. "Did you fuck Iona afterwards?" he asked anxiously.

"Well, yeah. Tayla insisted we do that. It was weird though."

"Weird how?"

"Well we lifted in the air and became a golden dragon. We could see our bodies have sex. We reached orgasm then returned to our bodies, exhausted, but Iona wanted to mate. So we did, several glorious times."

"Solon?" Tavir asked with a confused look on his face.

"Damn it," the elf snarled then swore something in Dwarvian with a large book open in his hands. He rolled his eyes with a long drawn out breath.

"Solon," Tavir called again with more urgency.

"I knew I recognized what she did. But I never thought it would actually happen."

"Solon!"

The elf looked at the human father and son. "Who is Tayla and what happened to my son? I know you recognized the name."

Solon nodded. "You remember Prince Zurggash?"

Tavir clutched his jaw and fists. "The man who captured Roan and Asa then forced them to disguise his top general, Nomiki, into my image and present him to her. She never became my lifemate because of what they did but we are still soulmates."

"Are you more upset at Roan and Asa than Prince Zurggash? We talked about this, Tavir."

"Finish your story, old man," he sneered.

"Eh, well I'm not exactly old as being I'm only three hundred, but suit yourself. The Dragon Lord and Lady arrested Prince Zurrgash and his Dragon Twin aunt, Tayla long before I was born. She was so unbalanced by the death of her human twin that she became her nephew's lifemate and empowered him with her Milk of the Dragons."

"Isn't that deadly to any man who's not a Dragon Lord?" Kilean asked, sitting upright.

"Yes, but for some reason it doesn't affect Zurggash as it does other men. We didn't know it until after the execution but the Milk of the Dragons bonded with his Dracnoid DNA and gave him supernatural abilities that wouldn't have been activated. The day of his execution came. The Dragon Lord and Lady along with their Dragon Masters carried out the execution ceremony."

Tavir and Kilean grimaced. "I'm grateful I never had to carry out that ceremony. I don't think I could stand it," Tavir said.

"Me either."

Solon taught, "That's why the Dragon Masters stand with their riders when it is carried out."

"I can understand drawing the magical properties out of one that has it and destroying it. But for the dragons to ensure the victim remains alive during the entire ceremony so we can open up their insides, destroy all their organs except the heart and lungs then let them suffer as we break all their bones and sever the body until nothing remains but their head and torso. And only then we stop so our dragons can slowly roast our victim to death. Isn't that a bit much?" Tavir asked.

"It must be done and in public so all know never to commit treason against the gods. An execution ceremony has rarely been conducted. The Dragon Lord and Lady are the enforcers of the Draconian Codex. That is why it is so important that they know every law by heart and the legal ramifications they must deliver to those who break them. When balanced, they travel the world ensuring all are compliant to the law."

Kilean asked, "If Prince Zurggash went through all of that that, then how is he still alive?"

"We thought he had died. The following morning, when it was time for Tayla's execution, her cell was empty, but the doors were still locked. The High Priest and Priestess examined the ashes of Prince Zurrgash only to find they transformed into Brulite."

"Brulite?"

"Magical dust that remains behind when a powerful spell is cast to transform someone's identity into another. We suspected they used a slave to stand in Prince Zurrgash's place. The United Draconian Army searched throughout the world for Prince Zurggash and Tayla but never found them. Over the centuries they have amassed large groups of followers known as The Righteous Ones. We don't know how they gather them or where their headquarters are. They only make their appearances known when they are about to cause another war. Normally, they use one of their followers to cause problems for the Draconian Council. They want nothing more than to replace Draco and Razil so they can control all magic."

"But that would never happen. There are too many believers and wouldn't the Dragon Lord and Lady prevent that from happening?" Tavir protested.

"Normally yes, but when they were able to stop your union with Queen K'Lara, Prince Zurggash and Tayla gained a stronger hold upon the world. We never thought Kilean and Iona would be able to attain their positions so Draco and Razil created a way for the dragon souls to be protected should Iona be unable to assume her rightful place while they were conducting the Rite of Dragon Souls. The soul would temporarily transfer to the High Priestess until the council could determine which of Iona's ancestors were suited to return from the dead and start a new kingdom ruling as the Dragon Lady."

"Just Iona," Kilean asked.

"That was their intention. But everything in the world must be balanced between male and female energies. So the council created the same system for you."

"The ceremony," Tavir asked, exchanging glances between his son and Solon.

"Yes, I don't know how Tayla knew of it. It's a secret well guarded by the High Priest and Priestess. There's a reason the High Priest and Priestess are elves. Of all the races, we are the most capable to keep any secret."

"Who else knows of the ceremony?"

"Not many. The book I have is written in Coptic Elven and the only people other than I and the Dragon Lady's guardian who can read are my father and the High Priestess. My mother doesn't even know it existed."

"Father?" Kilean asked.

Tavir explained, "His father is the High Priest. His mother was a priestess that conceived from her induction ceremony."

"I thought we induct the priestesses?"

"There are two inductions known as The Shifting. The Chosen, that's when the inductees are presented to the High Priest. He examines them and chooses who will be trained and presented to the Dragon Lord. They're trained by the Dragon Twins for a year then presented to the Dragon Lord in The Forbidden. He chooses the ones who will precede further and which ones will become sex slaves. The Shifting also occurs on the female side."

"And your mother?" he asked Solon.

"She passed The Chosen but not The Forbidden. I was only a few months old when she didn't please the Dragon Lord. I never knew her and I don't know where she is. She was sold soon along with the other less fortunate ones after the High Priest wiped her memories of anything she had done in the temple. She doesn't even know that she gave birth to me."

"But what about the children?"

"We're raised in the temple by the High Priest if we're male and by the High Priestess if female. When we are old enough we can go through the training to become a priest or priestess if we want to or we can join the rest of the world and forget everything we know about what happens in the temples. Most of the low class peasants in Elven society are actually children of the High Priest or High Priestess. My people shun them not because they aren't pure elven but because it's common knowledge among my race where they came from. We allow them to mate with each other but not with anyone outside their caste. I went through The Shifting and passed."

"You're a priest?"

"I was until I died from a horrible illness soon after your father turned eighteen."

Kilean leaned upright in shock with his mouth open. "You're dead!"

Tavir explained, "All the guardians are dead. That way they have no ties to the outside world and can focus on our needs. But the guardian is someone that we trust the most with our lives. Solon was my tutor when I was a boy. The High Priest always sends one of his priests to tutor the next Dragon Lord when he is a child."

Kilean eyed Solon with renewed interest. "So, you've...uhm...you fucked a Dragon Lady."

"Kilean," Tavir disciplined.

Solon chuckled, "It's alright. It's not as bad as the response I got from you when you first learned of who I was and what I am." He turned to Kilean. "Yes, I have fucked, as you put it, a Dragon Lady but she's not the only one. There are different levels of priests. When you first become a monk you are only allowed to fuck the enlisted women. Once you prove that you can handle more intense training and have years of experience you are promoted to fucking the officers. And if you're fortunate enough, you can glean the attention of the Dragon Master and hopefully, but rarely, the Dragon Lady herself. But she usually secludes herself with her Dragon Twins. If you can get the Dragon Lady's attention, then you have more of a chance to become the tutor to the next Dragon Lord and that, young prince, is how I lived my mortal life, except that my father favored me over all his other sons so he taught me things other priests would never know. That in turn prepared me for my role as the guardian. Now, let's return our focus back to what happened between you, Iona and Tayla. The threesome you had with Tayla was the ceremony used to temporarily transfer a dragon soul."

"Why didn't she just take Iona's? Wouldn't it have been easier to do so?" Kilean asked.

"No, because when the Dragon Lady or Lord die they take the soul with them if they are the ones who possess it. Queen K'Lara made the transfer from Razil's Council. It's much harder to steal from the dead than it is from the living."

"How do we get it back and what use is it to her if the soul knows it belongs to Kilean?" Tavir asked.

A sudden gush of wind almost blew Solon across the room. The men covered their face as Vashti flapped her enormous wings close to the balcony.

"Vashti!" Tavir yelled over his son's body.

"I'm sorry, Tavir. But it is urgent that I speak to you."

"You could have communicated with me telepathically," he bellowed.

"You don't know. How could you not know?"

"Know what?" he asked.

Solon answered, "It is the soul that allows you to communicate with her telepathically. She can no longer hear your thoughts, feel your emotions or your pain."

"Do you have to fly so close to the room?" Tavir bellowed.

Vashti descended into the large room, lowered her wings and landed with a hard thump. "Better?" she asked with a powerfully, echoing voice.

Tavir nodded to Vashti. "You look paler than normal, Tavir," Vashti said.

Solon tapped her on the side of her body. She moved her eye to focus on him. "He is recovering from the ceremony and the first Elixir of the Gods. What brings you to The Nest, young one?"

"K'Lilith found Roan in the boat when she transported souls into the underworld."

"How can Roan be dead?" Kilean asked.

Vashti curled her body into a big ball, draping her wings behind her back. She moved her gaze to the bed. "I don't know. The discovery took the Draconian Council, The High Priest and The High Priestess by surprise."

Tavir asked, "Why wasn't his soul transported to Draco's Council?"

"It's tainted."

"How?" Solon asked, walking to Kilean's side.

"K'Lilith said he's so overcome with depression that he won't speak. He just sits in the boat not aware of where he is, who he is or in what condition he is in."

"That doesn't make sense unless his soul was poisoned," Solon said.

"Who has the power to corrupt the soul of an immortal?" Kilean asked.

"Not many. It's a punishment given by Draco to the immortal when he has committed an unspeakable sin."

Tavir huffed to Solon, "Roan is as anal about the laws as you are about your books. He wouldn't go against them."

"There's more," Vashti insisted. The men gave her their complete attention.

"Go on," Kilean said.

"The Silver Dragon Soul appeared in the hands of the High Priest for only a moment then disappeared. He doesn't know where it went nor how it came to him to be transferred. He approached the council only to find K'Lilith was there with Roan and King Tritan, who is accusing Solon of misrepresentation and theft. King Tritan said he felt some of the Atlantium missing and some of its power inside Kilean. He demanded an explanation from the council but they didn't have one to give him."

Solon asked, "Do they believe all three events are related?"

"Yes, especially since Roan has committed treason before."

Tavir protested, "Prince Zurggash placed him and Asa under a spell that they couldn't break from until they present King Nomiki as me. How can the council even think Roan would agree to betray them?"

"Because it has happened before."

"Oh come on! This is jus...." Tavir gasped, trying to breathe at the sensation of a multitude of thoughts entered his mind. So many thoughts. So many voices. Information rolled through his mind as if a giant lid off an ancient coffer of magic and knowledge had been released. His fingers tingled. Power and strength surged through his veins. A gentle female's disembodied voice spoke louder than the rest, telling him not to be afraid. He rolled to the side of the bed, holding onto the pedestal as he placed his feet on the marble floor.

"Dad?" Kilean asked. Tavir leaned over his lap with his hands on his forehead. "Dad!" Kilean yelled.

Solon pulled the prince back. "Leave him, Kilean. Give him some space. There are forty-seven elven gods and he's hearing all their thoughts at once. He needs to learn to sift between them after he greets each one."

"That didn't take long," Vashti said to Solon.

"Shorter than I expected." He turned back to Vashti's eye. "Vashti, the charges against me?"

"Under investigation. I've been ordered to take you, King Tavir and Prince Kilean to the Temple of the Moon for interrogation."

"They certainly can't believe we have something to do with any of that. I'll accept my crimes but Tavir and Kilean are innocent."

"That's not my decision to make, Solon. The council was quite clear. I am to bring the three of you to your father. I would suggest you do so willingly. I like all of you and I don't want the Unified Draconian Army to be called forth to forcibly remove you from the premises. Draco and Razil have been gracious enough to offer a peaceful transition to the temple, even supplying me with a new saddle that will hold three passengers instead of one, before they strike against the House of Dragonsun for insubordination."

Solon ordered, "Kilean, mount up. I'll help your father." Solon picked Tavir up as Kilean mounted the front set of the leather saddle. The prince yawned, extending his hand to Solon. "No. Rest your head on Vashti's neck and return to your slumber. I can mount him between us."

Kilean nodded. "They are allowed to rest," he asked Vashti.

"Yes, of course. It's a long flight," she answered.

Solon nodded, helping Tavir into his seat then mounted into the backseat. "Alright, I'll protect them. Take us to my father."

Vashti gallantly rose to her feet and took off quickly into the air.

Dragmoc Hold –
Kingdom of Tinu'deh

6

Joy. Absolute joy. Iona stood naked in front of the oval shaped full-length mirror she found in her bedroom. She had awakened from her sleep this morning to find her bed wet with her cum, her fever gone and the golden dragon tattoo on her torso. A pair of golden nipple bars clung through her nipples with emerald studs on each side. A long golden chain hung between them. She tugged lightly on the chain and moaned as her body reacted with a heighten sense of sexuality. She bit her lower lip, smiling as her hand traced down the dragon. It tickled her body with each move of her hand. She came upon a small, golden hip chain highlighting the curves of her hips. Her long finger reached between her legs and found a small clit hood piercing. She rubbed it, inhaling deeply with each stroke, opened her legs wider and moved her fingers downward. She giggled enjoying her new body. She felt strong and fearless. Iona wondered if Kilean was feeling the same thing.

"*Kilean,*" she called out to him in her mind.

Iona bit her lower lip impatiently waiting for her love. She called his name several times but he never replied. She felt odd. As if he had never existed. But surely the handsome warrior had existed. Her body was evidence enough that everything he had said was true. Kilean had promised never to forsake her but then why wouldn't he answer her call? Maybe that method of communication no longer worked. Perhaps she had to entice him to communicate with her.

Iona walked quickly to her bed, lay down and opened her legs wider. She rubbed her clit, gently playing with the opening of her vagina with her slender fingers. The dragon tattoo glowed brightly. She inhaled a deep breath through her teeth, moaning under her breath. *Oh, Kilean,* you fucking amazing man. Can't you feel this? Don't you want some of this? She questioned with her mind. Yet still he never replied. "Shit, if only I had a vibrator."

Suddenly the large, thick dragon penis vibrator from her dreams appeared beside her. "Huh," she huffed, grabbed it and thrust it deep with her. "Oh, yes," she grinned, turning the large contraption on. It immediately went to work without the need for her support. Iona leaned back on the bed, fully taking in every sensation as it pounded against her; its tentacles massaging her clit. She was fucking wet! Her nipple bars pinched and nipped at her tits. "Oh, gods," she muttered, clinging to the side of the bed, arching her back. The vibrator pushed another pair of tentacles deep within her asshole. Iona opened her mouth to scream but held back, hoping the guards wouldn't have already become suspicious of the noises in her room. She placed her hand on the end of the vibrator, rolled off her bed and crawled onto the floor on all fours. It adjusted it position and assaulted her doggy style, double stuffing her by turning the tentacles in her ass into a dildo. "Shit," she exclaimed head down. Her skin grew warm and red the harder and faster it pushed. "Yes, yes, yes!" she exclaimed pushing even harder against it until she felt the intense wave of pleasure erupt from inside. Iona exhaled a deep breath and collapsed onto the floor. The vibrator and its tentacles immediately disappeared. "Damn," she muttered with a grin feeling her own cum on her thighs. Iona rolled onto her back and stared up at her bedroom ceiling. This certainly wasn't a dream. She was the Dragon Lady.

Dragon Lady. How was she supposed to be that woman when she was locked up in her tower? "Iona," a woman's soft voice called to her. Iona sat upright and stared at her bedroom window. Morning sunlight poured gently into her prison. "Iona," the voice called to her once more. But this time it sounded much closer. As if it was outside her window. But how could that be? Her residency was in the highest tower of the castle. No human would ever be able to scale it. She thought she had heard something loud as if a gush of air was escaping from the sky.

Iona quickly walked to the window. She gasped at the sight of a large golden dragon hovering outside her window. Its large sapphire eyes declared the wisdom of ages. She was so beautiful! It grinned at her naked body and bowed its head gently to her. "Your majesty," the dragon humbly greeted her aloud.

"Wha..," she tried to speak but could only look upon the ant sized guards at the bottom of her father's castle. "Can they see you?" she asked looking at the dragon.

"No, your highness, I am not really here."

"But I can see you."

"You see me because you possess my soul," the beautiful dragon informed her. The beast stared down at the front of Iona's torso. "That is my mark on you. It matches the one on your back."

Iona looked down at her body, walked to the mirror and turned around. A long, serpentine dragon tattoo slithered with it's tail at the base of her neck and it's mouth open on her buttocks. Its claws clung to the sides of her hips "I never noticed that before."

"Our thoughts are connected. But I do have to apologize to you if my cravings are too much for you to handle. I know you are untrained."

Iona walked back to the window, grinning as she spoke, "I feel so strong. As if I could conquer the world myself and last night was SO amazing!"

The dragon chuckled. "That is my power within you but you must be careful. There are good and bad things that can happen when you possess a dragon soul."

"Good and bad things? Like what?"

"You must be trained, Iona."

Iona sighed, with a nod of her head. "Will you be my trainer, then?"

"No. My name is Kalesh. I will always be with you as long you serve as Dragon Lady but there are others who will train you."

"It's a pleasure to meet you, Kalesh."

Kalesh grinned, "Iona, you are magnificent. Never forget that. The times have changed much since I last spoke to a Dragon Lady. There is so much you need to learn, Iona, lessons that should have been taught to you years ago."

"I can still learn, Kalesh. I want to know everything."

"I'm certain that you do but now is not the time for me to tell you everything. There are more pressing matters that must be discussed. I have come to present you to your guardian."

"My guardian?"

"Yes, milady. The Dragon Lady doesn't stand-alone when she makes decisions. She has a Dragon Master who trains her to become a superior warrior who defends the seven races and an enforcer of all Draconian laws. The Guardian lives within her nest and is her source of all information from the beginning of time itself to present. The Dragon Ambassador was the former Dragon Lady and speaks to the multitude of gods on her behalf. These three important women will be...."

"Former Dragon Lady. You mean my mother," Iona asked, still focusing on the dragons words about the Ambassador.

"That I do."

"My mother's alive!"

"She has been resurrected."

"Take me to her! Oh, please, I have so much I want to tell her."

"No child. You must find her yourself. Your book, *The Magic of Tinu'deh,* lies in your nightstand drawer. Get dressed into your normal clothes. Leave your bedchamber with the book and follow the instructions on the first page. The book will disappear if anyone comes near you."

"What about these?" she asked pointing to the nipple bars and chains.

"Your clothes will not expose them. You must hurry your highness. You are untrained and are most unable to soothe my soul for very long within you. Run little one, before I desire more sexual encounters from you."

"I like the sound of that."

"No! You do not understand the power it brings upon those who cannot control it. You cannot allow those urges to master you. You must master it! Go," the dragon instructed then disappeared.

Iona grabbed her tattered clothes from the back of her tall dressing screen and placed them on. The bulky, grey colored clothes did little to flatter her curvy figure. She stared at the clean bed. Not a stain nor wet spot. "Thank you," she whispered to her invisible helper. But no one ever said, "You're welcome." She opened her nightstand drawer and removed her book. The once unified dragons stood facing each other without meeting eye contact. "Huh," she huffed, opening the book. She flipped through the pages noting the strange language consisting of curvy lines and circles. She couldn't read a single line. How was she supposed to follow the book's directions if she wasn't able to read the language? Iona gulped feeling something tingle between her legs. A strong urge to mate came upon her. She quickly flipped to the first page, recalling what the golden dragon had told her. "What the...?" she exclaimed, peering at the empty page. She flipped through the pages of the book and this time there was nothing in it. Iona rolled her eyes. A bright golden hue illuminated from the first page. She peered down and read in her own language:

"*Exit and turn right. Walk until you come to a hallway intersecting with your own. Go left.*"

"That's it?"

The book wrote:

"*More instructions will follow. Go, now, Princess Iona Celeste Dragonmoon.*"

"Huh." She opened her bedroom door and peeked outside. No sound. No one was coming. Good. Iona closed the door and followed the book's instructions. Every time she came to a stopping point, it guided her further. She didn't know how long she had meandered her way through the tower's confusing passages. She had so many questions to ask the book but it would just ignore her, only bringing her further into the depths of the castle. Finally, it stopped writing. She peered up to find she was no longer in the tower but in the oldest part of the castle deep underground. She found herself within the ancient great hall where the bravest and noblest of rulers had once held their court. The square cobblestone room still contained long tables and chairs from the Feast of the Moontide held within its confines thousands of years ago. She vaguely remembered a story her mother had once told her about how the feast had been interrupted by a war between two dragons. Humans had never known the existence of any other race other than their own until they had met the dragons. Cobwebs clung to the wooden furniture. Pitchers still filled with wine sat on the tables in between plates with what she could only assume use to be filled with food.

"Welcome, my lady," a voice called to her. Iona turned around to face the king's table only to find the ancient room had been transformed into a gallant banquet hall filled with all kinds of food and wine. Lords and ladies heartily ate, joking around with each other. Music filled the air. The festive crowd never noticed her. She peered down at her clothes. Her sackcloth dress had been transformed into the dress she had worn at the temple except the thick white fabric pieces were thinner. They crossed over each other at the top of her lower stomach and ran up her chest, small enough to only cover the nipples of her large, bare breasts and tied at the back of her neck. Her nipple chain hung delicately in full view.

She swallowed hard, pushing down the fabric of her white mini skirt. She didn't know who this woman was but this wasn't the way she should appear in public. Iona instinctively covered her breasts.

"Now, now, there's no need for that. I know who you are and truth be told I've seen more revealing royal dresses on your ancestors than that one," the woman said gazing up and down Iona's body. "You're more conservative."

"More conservative?" Iona asked, dropping her arms and looking at her body.

"The Dragon Lady's royal dress changes with the sexual acceptance of its master. It is quite rare for her majesty's dress to even have this much fabric on the tunic," the slightly overweight woman said, nodding to Iona's chest.

"Where am I?" Iona asked the slightly heavy-set, grey haired lady standing in front of the king's table.

"I think you know the answer to that question." Iona stared at the woman wanting to believe what she knew to be true but how could it? "You don't recognize them? King Asher and Queen Meleena?" the woman asked taking a step towards her.

"They were my ancestors that were here when the dragons first came to our world," Iona whispered.

"Ah, I'm so grateful you paid attention to your mother's tales." Iona stared at her ancestors almost in disbelief. "I am sorry for any misunderstanding the book may have caused you. It likes to keep secrets sometimes from the new Dragon Lady. It should have confided in you that you were to walk down through the crypt into this chamber instead of leading you on some sort of quest," the woman said, glancing at the book.

"What?" Iona asked, shaking her head, clutching the book tight against her chest.

"The book. It brought you to me so you could meet with the guardian," the woman explained.

Iona glanced at the book then to the lady. "Who are you?"

"Ah, it never fails. Your ancestors have always asked that question of me before I truly am able to explain what happens next. I am her," she said pointing to Queen Meleena.

"But you look nothing like her."

"Well I wasn't given this duty until I was much older. When Asher and I died, the Dragon Council appointed us to serve at the pleasure of the guardian."

"Serve, so you're not the guardian?"

"Oh, I once was but no longer. But perhaps it is best that the guardian explains it to you?"

"Are we in the past?" Iona asked following the queen past the tables and into a mall arched corridor on the right hand side.

"Yes. The hall was a sacred place for generations even after our family expanded the castle. But everything changed when your father corrupted your mother into believing he was the Dragon Lord. She should have known better. The image you see of the Dragon Lord within the Plains of the Great Dreams is what he looks like in real life. But somehow General Roan Tharg and Asa were able to convince her otherwise."

"Who are they?"

"General Roan Tharg is Prince Kilean's Dragon Master. Asa is a Dragon Twin. Her sister is Sina."

"I've heard of Dragon Twins. Kilean said he had orgies with them."

"Yes, it is true. It is part of his training as it would have been of yours would you have had access to the female mating grounds."

They turned another sharp right and came upon a large wooden door. "Your guardian is within this room. Most riders are shocked when they see whom their guardians are."

"Why?"

"You will see. Iona, not everyone has the same guardian. They are chosen by the council because that person was found to possess the highest of noble qualities and be of someone the Dragon Lady would trust with her very life."

"Who is it for me?"

"I do not know. The guardian changed this morning. When that happens, I am not privy to the identity of the guardian until she has met in private with the new Dragon Lady."

"Then how do you know the guardian changed?"

"Because the door is locked. The only person who can turn the knob is the Dragon Lady."

"Will I see you again?"

"Of course, my dear sweet child. I serve your guardian. When the time comes for your guardian to meet me, she will send for me. But for now, this sacred time belongs to you and your guardian. She will be able to answer more questions than I ever could. Good luck, Iona, and don't be afraid to accept who you truly were created to become."

Queen Meleena disappeared. Iona clung the book tighter to her chest and stared at the large wooden door. Her heart pounded with anticipation. Her guardian was someone she would trust with her very life? There was only one person she could think of that met those qualifications - Kilean. But he couldn't be her guardian. He was supposed to be the Dragon Lord. Her lover. The dragon had said her mother had been resurrected from the dead to serve as her ambassador so surely the guardian couldn't be her. Hopefully the Dragon Council knew what they were doing when they sent whoever was behind that door. Iona placed her hand on the iron doorknob and slowly turned it.

The large wooden door creaked as she slowly opened it. She couldn't believe her eyes. The room should have been smaller but it wasn't. The grand room was larger than she could ever have imaged. It glowed with a light golden hue. A long, king size bed lay on a marble balcony overlooking an ocean. Tall pillars in the sculptured shapes alternating naked forms of men and women in various sexual positions lined the balcony. She closed the door, never taking her eyes off the scene before her. In the center of the chamber's marble floor lay a large mosaic with a circle with golden dragons intertwined just like the image she had seen on her book before her visit to the temple.

"Iona," the familiar sound of her mother's voice entered her ears. She turned to her left to see her mother next to a row of large bookcases along a wall. "Mother," Iona cried, opening her arms wide and running to her. Mother and daughter fully embraced, clinging to each other tightly. "I missed you. I missed you. Tell me you're real, mom. Tell me you're actually here and I'm not dreaming this!"

Queen K'Lara placed her hands on the sides of Iona's face and pulled away from her teary eyed daughter. The raven-haired beauty smiled. "Oh, my sweet girl. When the council told me you had accepted the Dragon Soul, I couldn't have been any prouder of you."

"But how? You died."

"Death isn't the end of life, Iona. When a Dragon Lady or Lord die, they are honored by the dragon gods for their service. I lived with our ancestors in Razil's Court."

"Razil?"

"The goddess of all goddesses. She's a dragon just like her husband, Draco. Let me have a look at you," Queen K'Lara cast her eyes up and down her daughter's body. Iona instinctively placed her hands over her chest. "Stop it," she ordered, pushing her daughter's arms to the side.

"I'm offensive."

The queen grabbed her daughter's arms and sternly looked at her. "You are not offensive. You can't allow the thoughts your father placed inside your head to dictate how you should act. You're my daughter! This gown of yours is the most modest I have ever seen and it absolutely won't do for what is required from you."

K'Lara sighed. She lifted the fabric over her daughter's breasts and examined the nipple bars. "Is your clit hood pierced and did you masturbate to release the energies you had when you returned from the temple?"

"Mother," Iona gasped.

"Just answer the question, daughter and don't be so shocked when I ask you intimate details."

Iona sighed, "Yes."

"Good. At least that happened. You're absolutely gorgeous!"

"Father doesn't think so. He locked me away in the North Tower."

"Your father's not whom he seems to be. I didn't know that when I married him. I believed everything Roan and Asa told me. I was a fool," she sighed, lowering her hands and walking to the table on the other side of the room. K'Lara leaned over the table, examining several parchments.

"The dragon told me the former Dragon Lady serves as my ambassador. I was supposed to meet my guardian in here."

"That is true but I am not her."

"I don't understand. The dragon said I would have an ambassador, guardian and a master. Where are the other two?"

"I don't know. I'm trying to figure that out. I can't assume my position as the ambassador because I do not have a physical body in which to consume the sacred elixirs."

"But I see you in the royal dress and the crown you had when you were alive and the dragon said you had been resurrected."

"You see what you want to see, Iona."

"I don't understand, mother."

"You want me to be the person I was to you before I died but I'm not her, daughter. There are rules that must be followed. I broke those rules when I believed the lies your father, General Roan and Asa told me the night before my bonding ceremony. I was punished by Draco and Razil for my actions."

"But that wasn't your fault, mother."

"It was, Iona. I knew better. I should have consulted with my guardian before I accepted your father's request. The Gold Dragon Soul inside me tried to warn me but I never listened. I didn't know what to do. My father had been killed in battle against Prince Zurggash's army a few days before and I was still grieving his loss. The last thing I had wanted was to assume my mother's position. I wanted a man to rule over my kingdom and fill the hole that had been left in my heart from my father's death. I was angry and confused. Everything changed for the worse after I united with your father. My guardian and Dragon Master disappeared along with my dragon. I was reunited with my mother after my death. She helped me to heal from my broken heart and mind but told me I would have to offer penance for my actions against Razil. I was resurrected and placed within your nest to guide you so you never make the mistakes I made while I was alive."

"And this place?" Iona asked studying the various bookcases.

"This is your sanctuary. It's a place of rest and rejuvenation."

"I don't understand," she shook her head, stepping towards her.

K'Lara lowered the parchment to the desk with a drawn out sigh. "By the gods, he really messed with your mind." She placed her hands on the table and leaned over, lowering her head.

"Mother?" Iona asked with concern. K'Lara shook her head, tears flowing down her cheeks. "Mother, why are you crying?" Iona asked, stepping closer to the table.

"Push it aside, Iona."

"Push what aside?"

K'Lara lifted her face to her. "Free your mind from everything Nomiki taught you and you will see the real me."

"The real you?"

"The woman you see is the woman whom your father created, not the real me. What I have planned for you is never going to work because you're not ready to accept the reality of your situation. You need training."

"I keep hearing that, but if I need it so badly then why isn't anyone helping me to get that training?"

"You should have gone through an initiation ceremony after the first sign of your transition from child to woman. The blood of your first cycle would have been collected by your Dragon Twins and ceremoniously drank by them to bond them to you."

"Eww."

"I thought the same thing when I learned of it from my mother. After they drink the blood they have sex with you."

"While you're on your cycle?"

"It is most...," K'Lara smiled. "Well it was amazing. After the ceremony, you live with them until your eighteenth birthday. You return to your castle and prepare for the Bonding of Dragons while bonding with your dragon. Then upon your twentieth birthday, you return to the Draconia Temple of the Gods where you and the Dragon Lord conduct the Bonding of Dragons." She sighed, lowering her head. "A few days before that happens, the Dragon Lord is brought to your castle to spend time with you and then you visit his castle. I should have known something was wrong when I had sex with your father during the visit. It's forbidden for the Dragon Lord and Lady to physically join until after the bonding ceremony."

"How could you have known? Your mother had died when she gave birth to you. There was no one to guide you."

"My father knew what was required of me."

"He must have been a wonderful man."

"He was chosen by mother's Dragon Lord to be the father of her children."

"Chosen?"

"The High Priest chooses three priests as tribute to the Dragon Lord before the Bonding of Dragons ceremony and the High Priestess choses three of her priestesses for the Dragon Lady. The priests gather before the Dragon Lord where they exhibit their sensual strengths upon the three priestesses chosen by the High Priestess. The Dragon Lord choses the strongest lover for the Dragon Lady. The monk chosen by the Dragon Lord lives with him. The Dragon Lord and priest then sacrifice the remaining priests and priestesses to Draco and Razil. The High Priest and High Priestess then chose three more priests and priestesses and the process is repeated by the Dragon Lady where she chooses the Dragon Lord's wife."

"But why would a priest or priestess willfully comply with that if they know they will die in the end?"

"It's considered a great honor to be sacrificed by the Dragon Lord or Lady and their Holy Mate. The priests and priestess want to be chosen for the great honor, Iona. The humans compete for it. They know Razil and Draco will bless their souls for their humility. My father mourned that he wasn't able to give his life but was pleased to be chosen to share my mother's bed. He knew she was not his lifemate. His only duty was to appease her sexual desires when she was unable to visit upon the Dragon Lord or the Dragon Twins and to give her children. When my mother died and he assumed her leadership as my regent. He was a strong ruler but he knew his place. I was the true leader of our kingdom not him. He allowed the High Priestess' tutor and my mother's

Dragon Master to train me. I did everything that was required of me except for that one moment in my life." She grabbed Iona by the shoulders. "I am so proud of you. Many, including I, in Draconia never thought you would assume your rightful place as my successor. You should not have been able to hear Kilean let alone be with him in the Plains of the Great Dreams without going through your training. You have been blessed, daughter."

"My life wasn't so much of a blessing after you died."

"I know and for that, I'm truly sorry."

K'Lara paced the floor periodically picking up and reading a parchment, scroll or book. Iona watched her mother search through items throughout the chamber. She gasped as her mother's dress and crown disappeared only to be replaced by a golden leather wet looking catsuit, highlighting the curves of her body. "Holy shit!" Iona exclaimed.

"What?" K'Lara asked turning around. Her long raven hair beautifully bordered her plump breasts.

Iona couldn't take her eyes of her guardian. A small diadem clung to K'Lara's forehead with a sapphire in the middle. "You're...." she gulped.

"You see me, don't you," K'Lara asked, stepping closer to her in her high heeled boots.

"My mother wasn't so...hmm...like that," Iona exclaimed, motioning to the dominating figure.

K'Lara grinned. "You see me for what I truly am. I am your Dragon Master. I am your guide as you assume your role as Dragon Lady. I'm sensual if you need help arousing your priests but I also protect you. I'm a warrior and a teacher but it is not my obligation to teach you everything. It's good that you see me for what I have become. That means your mind is opening."

"But you're my mother," Iona gasped.

"Don't look at me like that or you won't see the real me. Yes, I gave birth to you and your brothers. Yes, I am the one who told you all the stories. But, no, I am not just her. I am more."

"Are you the one who took care of me when I was ill?"

"Took care of you?" K'Lara's face fell. "Tell me more, Iona."

Iona couldn't keep her eyes off her as she spilled every detail concerning the mysterious servant who always provided for her without question. The more she spoke of her encounters the more K'Lara seemed to know who the person might be. "Meleena," K'Lara muttered.

"I met her outside. She said she is the servant of the guardian."

"She is that but also serves as the protector of the future Dragon Lady. She was my constant companion when I went through my preparations for ascension."

"Ascension?"

"It is the moment when you claim your true existence and duties that come with being a Dragon Lady. You said this was the first time you had ever met her?"

"Yes. Why?"

"I don't know. It's just odd."

"She told me that you would meet her when the time was ready to do so."

"Well, daughter, I think that time has come. But first," K'Lara said walking to the round wooden table. She pulled out a padded, golden chair. A large, dragon dildo sat upright from the center of the seat. Its high back had two golden braces with elaborate decals of dragons with slits in the middle.

"What is that," Iona asked, stepping towards it.

"Every chair you will encounter will look like this. It won't activate unless it senses the sexual energies that need to be displaced. When you were with Prince Kilean did you ever sit on his lap?"

"Yes."

"Good, sit on the chair like you did with him," K'Lara said, pulling the braces away from the chair.

Iona slowly approached the chair, spread her legs and descended upon the dildo. "Mhmm," she moaned, closing her eyes as warmth filled her lower stomach. She opened her eyes, feeling something cold against her bare breasts. Her mother positioned a tit ring through one of the slits, locked her breast in place and repeated the process again.

"The Dragon Lady is responsible for all female sexual energies within all of Draconia. Everytime she releases those energies they spread to all the races. Your body will want to continually mate but sometimes it is impossible for you to do so. These chairs allow for you and your priestesses to expel those energies when there isn't a man to soothe you."

"And do I always have one?"

"Yes. The chair will respond to your sexual needs, Iona. Don't be afraid of it. You will be required to boldly sit on many different chairs like these throughout your life. It's best that you get used to it before you are in public. Sit up straight and lean back. You must be able to allow your body to soothe while maintaining a regal presence. The people need to know that you are in control of all your urges."

Iona complied. She swallowed hard at the sensation of a tentacle from the dragon dildo teasing her clit. Silver tentacles ascended up her torso and played with her nipples. She arched her back, closing her eyes at the strong sensations.

"Look at me," K'Lara ordered.

Iona opened her eyes and stared at her mother. She swallowed at the sensation of a tentacle pushing its way into her ass. It grew to match the dildo. "Oh," she moaned, trying to push forward. "Sit up straight and let it do what it needs to do to process that urge inside you. You must be able to enjoy the experience without letting your mind be distracted from your people. There are times for you to completely enjoy a sexual encounter in front of whomever you desire, but there are other times when you must keep your pleasures to yourself. I want you to practice maintaining your dignity while that chair gives you whatever pleasures you like."

"What about father?" she pushed through her slight moans.

"Don't worry about him. You're safe in this room. No one ever knows where the Dragon Lady truly is. Assuming everything is right on track as it should be, the High Priestess should have placed one of the priestesses in your place. She will look and act like your human self in every manner until you are ready to assume the throne."

"And if that isn't happening?"

"He can't find you in here, Iona. You are safe. Enjoy the chair, Iona. I will return," she instructed then walked out of the room.

Iona spread her legs wider and rocked in unison to the large dildo's thrusts. The more she rocked the harder the dildos pounded into her. She grabbed the edges of the chair, fidgeting. She clutched the chair, trying desperately to muffle her sensual moans. Sweat poured down her body, lubricating the tentacles. "Oh, gods," she mumbled, closing her eyes. She heaved, fully taking in the overpowering sensual experience this amazing contraption was giving her. Her legs quivered. Waves of intense pleasure rolled through her stomach. She opened her eyes and pushed hard on the side of the chair, rocking faster. Iona arched her neck and stared up at the ceiling. Her mother said she needed to maintain her dignity. Alright, she had to think of something important. Not something. Someone. She bit her lower lip thinking of Kilean. Her tits were hard. Her body flushed. She didn't think she could control herself. "Kilean," she shouted as she reached an orgasm. She felt the release of the dildo from her ass but the other tentacles never moved.

She stared down at her body. Little white lights travelled through the golden tentacles from her nipples, down her chest and between her legs. She felt the dildo inside cling the sides of vagina. She peered over the arms around her breasts to between her legs. The legs of the chair glowed.

Help...Help me...Iona...help me....please..., Kilean's frightened voice pleaded in her mind.

She leaned back. *Kilean,* she closed her eyes and tried to connect with him but all she heard was sobbing.

Help, please, Kilean sobbed.

His screams vibrated loudly in her head. She clutched the side of the chair. Excruciating pain vibrated through her entire body. She couldn't tell if she was screaming or not. Her body tensed. *Kilean! Oh gods, Kilean. Where are you? What's wrong?* She pushed her mind deeper into the darkness chasing his voice. The more she chased after him the more pain she felt. She wasn't certain just how long she had endured the torment.

It's wrong. It's all wrong, his voice echoed in the back of the darkness.

What is? Speak to me, Kilean! He screamed loudly then grew silent. *Kilean?*

"Iona," her mother's voice echoed in her head. Iona gasped opening her eyes. Blood spilled between her legs, from her nipples and down her nose. The once active chair no longer held her captive. "What happened," Iona asked, crying.

"We don't know. We heard your screams and came only to find the chair attacking you. Meleena was able to deactivate the chair. Can you move?"

"I don't feel well."

K'Lara placed her hand around her daughter's waist. "Together," she asked Iona, staring into her daughter's eyes.

Iona nodded. Mother and daughter counted to three. With the help of her mother, Iona lifted her bottom off the chair. She grimaced at the sensation of the dildo painfully rubbing its poisonous nodes against her tender vagina until she was finally free from the contraption. Blood profusely spilled between her thighs. "It hurts. Oh gods, it hurts worse than when I'm on my cycle," Iona cried on her mother's shoulder, clutching onto her mother's catsuit.

Meleena placed a blanket around Iona. "It's not supposed to do that to the Dragon Lady," K'Lara whispered to Meleena. "Why is it attacking her as if she's a mere mortal?"

"I don't know," Meleena said. The older woman handed K'Lara a cloth for Iona's nose then examined the chair. K'Lara placed the cloth next to her daughter's nose, periodically glancing between Iona and Meleena. "It gathered her cum and milk. I can see it in the reserve. The gauges show there was a transfer of sensual energy into the reservoirs."

"Which race?"

"I can't tell whose it is for. This doesn't make sense," Meleena said peering at a cylinder gauge.

"What?"

"Looks like it attacked her while it was gathering. It if was going to recognize a mortal and attack the woman for sitting upon it so after the first few thrusts. But for some reason it looks like the chair recognized her authority to sit upon it but didn't recognize her after she reached her first orgasm."

"If I remember correctly, the chair delivers seven orgasms, one for each race in order to gather the energies, cum and milk so the dragons can deliver it to the mages of the seven kingdoms. They create a potion from it and the kings of the seven kingdoms drink it once a month. The queens partake from a potion derived from the Dragon Lord's semen and blood at the same time as their husbands."

"Yes. But the gathering can only occur after the Rite of Dragon Souls. Prince Kilean should have been in his chair by now."

"I have to help him," Iona said. Why was the world around her so blurry?

"Help who?" K'Lara asked her daughter.

"Kilean. He's in pain."

K'Lara looked at Meleena. "Hurt, how?" K'Lara asked, stroking the hair away from her daughter's mouth.

"I don't know. He called for me to help him. I heard him sobbing and yelling. He said it's wrong. It's all wrong. Ugh, I feel sick," she muttered.

"We need to get her to her Dragon Twins so they can heal her," K'Lara told Meleena. "You sent me to them when I was becoming a woman. Why didn't you send her?"

"I couldn't. Her father placed a protection spell around her chambers. I was shocked when she was able to access the Plains of the Great Dreams on her own. That wasn't my doing, K'Lara. Your guardian had tried everything she could think of to help prepare your daughter for her calling but nothing worked. We assumed our efforts were in vain because the guardian wasn't attached to Iona," Meleena explained.

K'Lara glanced at her daughter then back to the older woman. "My guardian wasn't here when I arrived."

"No but hers was," Meleena nodded to Iona then back to K'Lara with a knowing glance.

K'Lara opened her mouth to speak but couldn't formulate the words. She glanced between her daughter and Meleena several times. "But the guardian is chosen by the High Priestess to serve the Dragon Lady and is someone the Dragon Lady trusts with her life. She doesn't know you."

"In times of great distress the Guardian's Protector can serve as the Guardian until a suitable replacement has been appointed by the High Priestess. I was given orders by the High Priestess to reveal my temporary position after you were reunited with your daughter."

"Why you?"

"K'Lara, your mission is to right the wrongs of your past by guiding Iona towards her true identity. The council felt it was in your best interest to have me by your side rather than allow your Guardian and Dragon Master by your side."

"Why?"

"They failed their mission when you forsook them."

K'Lara grabbed the front of Meleena's tunic. "What will they do to my sister and my Dragon Master? It wasn't their fault I didn't listen to them. It was mine!"

"The council interrogated them and understands that it was not under their guidance that you chose the wrong path. But they couldn't allow them to return as your advisors because it is obvious that you hold no regard for their advice."

"My sister was born before me. She was supposed to be the Dragon Lady, not I. She died from a terrible illness when she was eleven. I loved her."

"But you didn't respect her or you would have sought her counsel when Nomiki, Asa and General Roan came before you with their claims."

K'Lara released her grip exhaling a deep breath. She swallowed hard then lifted her eyes to Meleena. "What will happen to her and my Dragon Master?"

"Your sister is a servant in the Court of Guardians and your Dragon Master serves as a concubine to Karliz."

"My sister's a low caste servant within the Razil's Court and my

Dragon Master a concubine to the God of the Dead? Those positions are only reserved for the lowest of sex slaves after they die."

"The punishment is less severe than it could have been."

K'Lara nodded with understanding. "And what of your duties here?"

"My duties are to protect the Dragon Lady and ensure you do not cause your daughter to walk away from the path she was created for. Should you fail in your atonement, there will be repercussions."

K'Lara lowered her head in submission. "I understand."

"Good. I'm deeply concerned by the events that have transpired between the chair and your daughter. I think it would be in the best interest of all if we transport her to her sacred lands." She looked deep into Iona's eyes. "How do you feel?"

Iona shook her head and buried her face in her mother's chest.

"Iona," K'Lara asked, lifting her daughter's chin with her finger. Iona gazed her weary eyes to her mother's. "What happened on the chair?" she asked.

Iona recalled every detail of her experience to them, periodically taking breaks to vomit into a ceramic bowl. Her body uncontrollably shivered. Her pale skin became deathly white. The more she spoke the harder it became to breathe. Her head pounded with fire and all she wanted to do was sleep. K'Lara pressed her daughter's head to her shoulder. She looked up at Meleena with a concerned look. "Fever."

Meleena sighed. "She won't last for long, K'Lara. The venom works quicker on humans than any other race."

"Maybe she wasn't on there long enough to receive a lethal dose? She did say that it only attacked her after she spoke to Kilean."

"But we don't know how long they were talking before we arrived. What exactly did you tell her about the chair?"

"Not much. Only that there are different sex chairs she will have to sit upon throughout her life. I wanted her to practice her regal skills so I told her there would be times she would sit upon a chair while she was ruling and other times she would use it for enjoyment. I thought if she knew she was being gleaned she would too scared to sit in it."

"Wise decision. The Dragon Lord and Dragon Lady can communicate with each other in order to heighten the experience. The chair only allows them to communicate with each other no one else is allowed to speak to her during the gleaning. The only way it would have reacted as it did, was if it didn't recognize Prince Kilean's authority."

"But how can that be, Meleena? Why wouldn't the chair recognize him if he carried her spirit dragon's mate?" K'Lara asked. "She obviously went through the ceremony."

"She did but perhaps he didn't."

Iona grinned, "He was there and he was magnificent." She cringed with her hand over her stomach. Iona breathed through a surge of nauseating pain.

"We need answers and she needs healing. Is there an antidote," K'Lara asked.

"Yes, but it can only be delivered by the Dragon Twins and she has to be strong enough to accept it. The longer we wait the weaker she will become. Pick her up and placed her on her bed. Then lay next to her. Place your forehead on hers and say the transportation spell you learned when you were trained as Dragon Lady. The same spell works with every Dragon Lady. The mists will recognize the both of you and transport you to their lands."

K'Lara picked her daughter up in her arms. "But I'm not a Dragon Lady."

"Once a Dragon Lady always a Dragon Lady, K'Lara. You wear the marks of your rank upon your chest and back. The mists will recognize them."

Iona moaned, closing her eyes. Her beautiful mother adjusted her grip.

"Thank you," she said to Meleena.

"You're welcome."

K'Lara walked quickly to the bed, gently laid Iona upon it then laid beside her daughter. She pressed her forehead against Iona's and chanted the magical words.

Drokap Castle – Kingdom of Saloron

7

The impressive, ancient Drokap castle towered high upon the peak of Zurggash Peak overlooking the sprawling lights of the Raylor Village. Pinnacles rose from all sides of the massive ziggurat. Prince Zurggash patiently stood by his tall bedroom window staring down at the village illuminated by the moonlight. Faint echoes of music, cheering and yelling lifted in the air from the boisterous inhabitants of the village below. Tonight was just any night for his people. Twice a month, he ordained the Cleansing throughout all his lands. He had specifically chosen the dates of the Cleansing to match the ceremonious Power of the Gods Rituals the Allied Seven Draconian Races participated in each month. The Power of the Gods was a special time of the month when the Dragon Lord and Dragon Lady shared their reproductive energies with the rulers of the seven kingdoms in order to ensure each of the seven kings line of succession.

Zurggash smiled at the terrorizing screams from the village below. Twenty-five villages filled with people of all races, not just the Allied Seven Draconian Races, spread across vast distances participated in the great celebration. The strict decrees he had placed upon his villages hundreds of years ago were abandoned. Men, women and children from all castes were free to explore their fantasies without consequences. The one night period of lawlessness allowed the strongest to survive while eliminating the weak. Sex, drugs, murder, rape, infidelity, and any other horrors his people could think of were highly encouraged from sunset to sunrise. Once the sun rose, his soldiers immediately killed anyone still conducting their fantasies.

Normally, he would have joined in the revelry but he just couldn't think about that while Tayla was missing. A complete day. His beloved aunt had been gone for a complete day! Where the hell was she? What was taking her so long? Was she dead? He had so many unanswered questions. He hated feeling useless, especially during the Cleansing. The Cleansing was her favorite time of the month. They had thoroughly enjoyed spreading and encouraging evil deeds throughout their kingdom.

The sound of his bedroom door opening startled him. "Where have you been," he bellowed at the sight of Tayla.

Tayla grinned closing the door behind her. "Miss me?"

He charged to her, grabbed the side of her face and kissed her passionately, pressing her back against the door. Tayla wrapped her arms around his strong back and her legs around his waist. "Oh, fuck," she swore in between kisses, dropping a leather satchel to the floor. Zurggash pulled his erect penis out of his black leather pants and thrust hard inside her. He grabbed her legs as she wrapped her arms around his neck and moaned with each of his thrusts. She was so fucking wet! Silvery milk spilled from her tits, soaking her chest. He licked the milk off her stomach, under her breasts and suckled as he pounded harder. Oh, she was so delightful. She was just what he needed and more. Her sensual moans enticed him. Her milk lavishly poured from her tits. Deeper, harder, he thrust until finally, oh gods, finally he came inside her.

Zurrgash swallowed, slowly returning Tayla to her feet. She stumbled a bit and held onto his shoulder. "Damn," she swore with a grin.

The tall prince laughed, placing his penis back into his pants. "Did you get them?" he demanded.

Tayla sighed with disappointment. "Only one."

"One? How is that possible? There should have been two!" he snarled, pushing back his long, black cape. "You told me the ceremony would work."

"It did but I didn't have a chance to retrieve the other one. The Golden Dragon fought me."

"Why didn't you just transform into your dragon self and fight back?"

"I can't fight a spiritual being with my corporal form," she claimed throwing the square, leather case on their bed.

"We have to have both!"

"I know that, Zurggash. And we will have both."

"How?"

"I don't know. Prince Kilean's a good fuck but not as good as you," she sung. "And once Iona accepted that she could enjoy it too, she was as powerful as he was in bed."

"Is that why you are late? You enjoyed yourself with them so much that it detained you from me?"

"Aww, are you jealous, my love?"

"No, but if you wanted to be fucked hard, we are in the middle of the Cleansing. I've never known you to not be enticed by the thought of blood, violence and sex."

"I wasn't late because I wanted to have sex with them. I told you, the Golden Dragon fought me."

"I saved you from your death because you told me you could help me. Was that all a lie?"

"No, my prince," she answered with a shaky voice. "Only a Dragon Twin can touch the soul of a dragon. I stole Kilean's dragon soul in my womb and birthed it in my bedroom before I arrived. I'm sorry it took so long to get back to you. The soul wanted to nest and I had to fight hard to convince it to remove itself from inside me."

"Are you ok?" he asked tenderly stroking the side of her cheek with his long finger.

"Yes but a couple of your servants are dead. I killed them and used their blood to convince the soul to leave my womb."

"Eh, it's the Cleansing. Who cares? What about the soul?"

"It's depressed but healthy enough for you to take as a new host."

"Good."

"When I find Iona's, I will steal that one as well."

"So King Nomiki's daughter ate from you?"

"Yes," she grinned. "I think she quite enjoyed it, too."

Prince Zurggash tightened his jaw and glared deep within her eyes. "You better not be lying to me Tayla," he yelled, pushing her backwards.

Tayla flew across the room. Her back thumped against the wall and she landed on her bottom. "You're quite irritable tonight, even after we had sex. What's wrong?"

Zurggash shook his head. "I have looked forward to the time when we use the Dragon Souls for our advantage yet only to be disappointed. We need the souls to assume lordship over the seven kingdoms!"

"We'll have them, Zurggash."

"When Tayla?"

"I don't know. Iona had accepted the Golden Dragon Soul and I believe the Golden Dragon is protecting Prince Kilean. We need to find a way for the Silver Dragon Soul to convince its mate that Iona isn't the true Dragon Lady. Once the soul is bonded with a new host it will crave to mate with her. I just don't know if the Golden Dragon will accept the new host as its mate after what I saw."

Prince Zurggash hissed a stern warning at the beautiful woman. She rose to her feet and stayed away from him. He stared at the black leather straps that ran along her torso, highlighting her breasts and lower stomach. A tit chain ran between her breasts locked into place by two silver nipple bars that ran through her tits. He smiled at the sound of her vibrator ascending from the strap between her legs into her vagina. She stared downward then up at him. "I would much prefer your presence than this thing."

"I'm sure you would but that isn't happening right now. Open it."

Tayla sighed with disappointment. She walked to the edge of the bed, opened the satchel and pulled out a large orb wrapped in a light blue cloth. "I had to remove it from my womb sooner than I had hoped."

"Will that damage it?"

"No. But it calls to nest inside me and the longer it's outside the stronger that call becomes."

"Will it willingly come inside me if it calls to be with you?"

"It should. Everything our prisoner told us has been truthful so far. Why would she have lied to us about the reunification ceremony?"

"Because she's Queen K'Lara's guardian."

Tayla stared at him with a curious look, "It's the Cleansing and usually we release our prisoners to peasants to be tortured. What did you do to K'Lara's sister?"

"She's somewhere very special with men who have always wanted to fuck a Dragon Lady."

"Your soldiers will kill her. There's no restrictions tonight on how much damage can be done."

"I chose only the soldiers who don't have the heart to kill her. But by tomorrow, Larsa will wish she was dead. She'll freely give us the information we seek concerning the unification ceremony."

"You do realize she had died before she even bonded first menstrual blood with the Dragon Twins."

"We know that but no one else needs to know she's not fertile with the Dragon Seed."

Tayla chuckled, placing her hand on his firm chest. "I do love the way you think, my prince."

"Will your spell work if we have both of them?"

"Yes." She placed the globe back into the box. "Are you certain you want this? There is no going back once we complete the spell."

"I am. Do you not...?" he paused hearing a slight humming noise coming from a tall mirror. "Put it away," he ordered then walked quickly across his room. The raven haired, olive skinned prince looked over his shoulder. Tayla rose from beside the bed and quickly joined his side. She placed her hand around his waist and waved her hand over the tall, freestanding mirror. The frightened image of Asa came into view. She paced around the room periodically looking over her shoulder.

"What do you want," Prince Zurggash bellowed.

Asa turned towards the mirror, her face whiter than normal. "Asa, what's wrong?" Tayla asked.

The human Dragon Twin shook her head with tears strolling down her face. "I...we...oh...gods...I...we...need your help," she pleaded, holding tight to the mirror with both hands blocking their view of her room.

"With what?" the prince asked.

Asa wiped the tears from her eyes and silently stepped to the side. The image of Roan's dead body on top of her bed came into view. "What the hell?" Tayla gasped, stepping closer to the mirror. She pointed to Roan's body.

"Is he dead?" the prince asked, joining her.

Asa sniffed her nose with a nod. "We...were having sex. It was great but then he drank from my breasts. He didn't die right away but it empowered him. He kept making love to me, harder then he had ever done. When we were done he grew ill. We spoke for a few moments then he died. I don't know what to do! But that's not the worse of it all."

"How can that not be the worse?" Prince Zurggash asked.

"He broke my egg sack."

"Shit," Tayla swore, glancing to her beloved. "You can't even do that."

Zurggash snarled at her then walked closer to the mirror, pushing her aside. "Are you certain you're with child?"

Asa nodded, "I became ill while having sex with Sina. I've tried to hide it the best that I can but my symptoms are growing and I'm certain it's affecting Sina. The council will come for me, Prince Zurggash. I don't want to die nor do I want my sister to be punished for my crimes."

"What were you thinking, Asa?" Tayla questioned sharply. "You know the power our species have over humans. The priestesses have only half the magic we do and they still can drive any soldier insane with lust. That's why the Dragon Masters are the only ones who can have relations with the more experienced priestesses."

"It was an accident, Tayla. He wasn't thinking. We were laying together in bed and he was mindlessly stroking my tits," Asa explained.

"Well, that can make you cum hard even without penetration," Prince Zurggash grinned at Tayla.

"Eh," she sneered at her nephew. Tayla looked back at the mirror. "We told you two to be more careful!"

"Please, you have to help us. We'll do anything! Roan and I wanted to contact you before his death once we realized he had broken the egg sack."

Tayla and Prince Zurggash exchanged glances. "What do you want from us?" he asked sternly.

"Take my child and resurrect Roan from the dead. I'll faithfully serve you if you will protect them within your court. If the council learns I am with child they will deem me as corrupted. They'll arrest Sina and I, then we will be executed for treason. I don't want that."

"Let us speak to one another about this and we'll talk to you again," the prince offered.

"Prince Zurggash, how long will that be?"

"Not long. Stay there."

Zurggash exchanged a glance with Tayla then turned back to the mirror. "Keep Sina out of your room. Don't let anyone know Roan was with there and stay by the mirror. Tayla and I need to discuss the matter and we will return to you."

"But," Asa protested.

"It won't be long, Asa. We promise," Tayla encouraged then waved her hand to the mirror breaking the connection. Zurggash sighed, looking at his aunt then to the mirror. His bronze toned beautiful aunt placed her hand on his chest. The dark leather tunic highlighted every muscle in his torso. "Your thoughts," she asked.

"I don't like the situation she is in, but why should I even care? It's not like she's anyone important."

Tayla growled loudly, slapping him on the cheek. "The death that awaits her isn't so simple! They have to extract the magic from her very being. If she survives that process then she will be so weak she won't be able to protest as they sliced her body apart into fifty pieces. That was the death I would have faced had you not kidnapped me from my hold and that, my love, isn't the worst part. Roan's immortal. Have you given any thought to what they have to do to an immortal?"

"Since when have we been in the business of helping magical creatures? I I want to eliminate magic from the gods and have complete control over it. Every magical creature that serves the gods is my enemy."

"They don't have to be. There are some, like Asa, who trust us more than the gods."

"More of them trust Draco and Razil, Tayla. It's better that we completely eliminate every race that doesn't bow down to me and start with a new creation. Isn't that why we are stealing the spirit dragon souls to begin with? Once they dwell within us we will be the new Dragon Lord and Dragon Lady. We'll have complete control of all the temples and sacred breeding lands as well as the priests, priestesses, High Priestess and High Priest. We don't need Asa and Roan."

"This isn't right. Asa and Roan are faithful to our cause."

"Esh," he huffed and walked away from the slender woman. "It was your idea to help them in the first place."

"They believe in the same things we do. They willingly helped us with what they knew they were supposed to stop. What makes you think Roan and Asa won't help us again? Besides, think of the power we'd have if we controlled the child of a Dragon Master and a Dragon Twin."

Zurggash pivoted quickly to face her. "I have an army out there to help me," he pointed to the village.

"Mere mortals and why wouldn't the magical creatures try to help you eliminate them? You're never going to convince them that they should exist. At least you'd have another Dragon Twin, a Dragon Master and their child who are so willing to seek your aid and help you in any way imaginable. Hear them out to...huh," she grinned grabbing the pillar of their canopy bed and lowered her head.

"Double stuffed?" he asked, grinning.

She nodded. "I hate it when we argue and you can't satisfy me. As much as I like the way it makes my body feel this constant need for sex gets in the way. I can't have a normal argument without the aggression making me extremely horny." She pushed the mattress forward and straddled the thick wooden bar connecting the pillars of the bed. Tayla leaned back and played with her tit rings as she rocked back and forth. Zurggash watched with interest while she masturbated. Her sensual moans beckoned him to join her. "Ugh, some days I truly hate the mortal side of you that can control your dragon urges," she complained leaning forward and grabbing the bar.

Zurggash chuckled. "What value do you believe they have for me?"

"Ugh, are you absolutely that stupid not to see what you have coming to ask for your help?"

"Tayla, I have a Dragon Twin, you. And might I say you do quite nicely," he grinned.

She growled in his direction. "Get you ass over here and fuck me hard if you think that."

"Oh, I like the show I'm getting right now."

"Your crotch is tight. Did you cum too hard and too fast to soothe those dragon urges inside you? My milk must already be working on you. Can't you feel its power surging through your veins. You want more, nephew. You desperately want to fuck me, don't you?" she grinned.

"I'd rather fuck you when you can't stand the cravings any longer."

"Ugh, you're horrible you know that," she said then screamed louder. "Oh, oh, oh," she proclaimed, arching her head back. She rocked even harder.

"Come on baby. Scream."

She yelled so loud she roared with flames bellowing out her mouth. "Shit, that hard huh," he muttered as she fell to the ground.

Tayla gasped on all fours with her head lowered. "You could have had some of that."

Zurggash placed his hand on her arm and helped her to her feet. "Perhaps, later."

"It will want more," she whispered, exhausted as he held her close to his chest.

"And I will be there to satisfy it. I may only have a 1/3 of dragon within me but it will need to be satisfied soon after seeing that."

Tayla chuckled with a slight huff. "Asa and Roan."

Zurggash peered over her shoulder towards the mirror. "It won't be so easy to raise Roan from the dead. His soul would have travelled into the underworld as punishment for fucking a Dragon Twin. If his soul has been discovered K'Lilith would have transported him to appear before the gods. There's powerful magic in those halls that would make it next to impossible for me to penetrate without them knowing I am near them."

"But there is a way to extract him?"

"Yes, but I will need his body."

"I can take care of that."

"Tayla, I'm not so convinced that I should help them. Asa's not Iona's Dragon Twin. She belongs to Kilean. There is no access to the Sacred Female Dragon Temple without...." He looked at her with a grin. "You're going to hand her over to the High Priestess but then what? There's a warrant for your arrest. If you're caught you will be executed for corruption."

"I don't have to get caught. Asa doesn't even have to know until it's too late. All I have to do is kill the High Priestess then assume her place. When Iona is presented to me I can steal the soul from her and use Asa to carry it until I am ready. The extraction ceremony will approach the council as the High Priestess and leave Asa in their hands."

"And would you be so willing to betray her to the council like that?"

"All I have to do is convince them that Asa and Roan betrayed them. Kilean's devout to the council. He'll approach the council with their predicament and have no choice but to arrest Roan for corruption and treason."

"Aren't you the one who didn't want Asa to die?"

Tayla stroked her hands on his chest, "Her child is more important to me than she is. Think of it, Zurggash. Our very own child whom we can secure your lineage with."

"Hmm," he moaned, tipping her face upward. He gently kissed her then pulled away. "I do like the way you think, my love." He waved his hand towards the mirror never taking his eyes off of her.

"Prince Zurggash, Tayla," Asa greeted them with earnest. The prince lowered his arm and kissed the bronze toned humanoid beauty long and slow, ignoring Asa. Silence filled the room. Their arms embraced as they kissed deeper. He lifted his head briefly. "We will grant you what you desire on some conditions," he said, staring deeply into his beloved's eyes while lightly stroking her cheek with his finger.

"Those being?" Asa asked.

"Roan serves as one of my generals."

"Accepted."

Tayla continued, "Asa, you give birth to the child." She kissed Zurggash, pulling him closer to her.

"But won't I die?" Asa asked.

"Gods, I thought you were an idiot," Tayla whispered into Zurggash's chest. Zurggash chuckled then turned his face to the mirror. "The birthing process doesn't kill the Dragon Twin if she gives birth to a human. It is when she gives birth to a dragon that destroys her. The only reason the Dragon Twin who births the next set of Dragon Twins is destroyed is because the dragon within the twins tears the mother's stomach apart with the teeth and claws. The Dragon Twins don't have to die. The council is afraid to tell the twins the truth. That's why they are condemned from having relations from anyone other than the rider or the dragon."

"And what truth is that?" Asa asked.

"That our race was created to serve the dragons. We are slaves to a system, Asa. We have no free will as long as our twin is alive. Once our twin dies, our bonds are broken and our minds are clearer. We see the world for what it truly is. That scares the council because they believe if the Dragon Twins were allowed to be free then we would destroy the world in order to gain our freedom."

"But you are obviously still bonded to the dragon within you," Asa said, noting the bronze juice running down Tayla's thighs as Zurrgash suckled Tayla's breast.

Tayla peered down then back up. She shrugged her shoulders, "I'm working on trying to eliminate that part of me."

"And what of my child? Won't it become insane like him?" she asked motioning towards Zurggash.

Tayla laughed, "My nephew isn't insane."

"Some days I might be," Zurggash chimed.

Tayla slapped him on the chest. "Shut up," she jeered then returned to Asa. "The stories told of him are exaggerations spread by the council because they don't want to accept the reality that the world is changing. People are waking up and realizing that magic has no place in our world."

"But he murdered his parents."

Zurggash countered, "I only murdered my father because he beat my mother. But the council never tells you that side do they? As for my mother, her mind was corrupted by my father and the years of abuse she endured under his control. After I killed him she only grew worse. One day, she decided she was going to tell the council that I was a mistake. She told her rider that I was abusing and murdering the priestesses. He should have known that to be untrue. We had shared many of the priestesses in orgies. I didn't know about my mother's betrayal until his Dragon Master confronted me with all the lies she told them. We argued and fought. My mother interfered and I accidently killed her instead of the Dragon Master. I knew I had made a mistake but it was too late. He had sent the Dragon Rider to confront the council with the lies while he confronted me with them. Tayla and I were arrested shortly afterwards. I endured a two-week long trial before the council. It didn't matter what I said they had already made up their minds about me so I kidnapped one of the priests and changed his identity to my own. He and Tayla were arrested and sentenced to death. They placed the monk's execution chamber for Draco to consume. While everyone was distracted I freed Tayla."

Tayla addressed Asa, "Asa, your child would be welcome in our kingdom."

"But you want to eliminate all magical creatures."

"Not eliminate. We want to offer them mortality. We weren't created by Draco. We're products of the council. They wanted slaves so they created the Dragon Twins and Dragon Masters. Don't you want a life with Roan?"

"Of course! I love him."

"Then you must prove your loyalty to us," Prince Zurggash said.

"How?"

"You will help us steal the Golden Dragon Soul."

Asa stood silent, contemplating his request.

"I don't have all day, Asa. What is your answer?" Prince Zurggash impatiently said, fondling his aunt as she leaned her back against his chest. She rubbed her back against his chest, moaning with her arm around his neck. "My dragon self isn't going to wait. So unless you intend to watch, which I wouldn't mind very much if you were to join in, then you better give us an answer."

"Hmm, I thought you said a few hours," Tayla whispered in Zurggash's ear.

"I miscalculated."

Obviously," she grinned, enjoying his touch.

"I agree," Asa proclaimed.

"Good. Now if you don't mind. I have to take care of my wife." The prince waved his hand. The image of Asa disappeared. "I'm going to fuck you hard, bitch," he sneered, forcing her to bend over.

"You've been holding out on me," she grinned.

"You have no idea," he declared, pulling his erect penis out and thrusting it hard inside her.

8

Valley of Tli

Giant ferns scattered the lakeside shore. Soft rays of sunlight danced off the surface of the large light blue lake. Iona lay on the shore, not completely certain if this was just a dream or reality. Her weakened body shivered as she listened to the conversation.

"This is highly unusual, K'Lara," a man said loudly.

"But damn, she turned out better than when she was training as a Dragon Lady. Can you fight as well as you look?" another man jeered.

"Care to find out, Thalos?" K'Lara returned the tease. The three of them grew serious.

"How long since it poisoned her?" Thalos asked, moving a strand of hair away from Iona's mouth.

"By what little she told us, Meleena and I don't think it was very long between when it first attacked her and when we interfered. She said you have a cure?"

"We do but she needs to be receptive of it. The weaker she becomes the harder it will be for her to accept what must happen. How much blood has she lost?"

"The blood between her legs is heavier than her nose and breasts. We were able to stop those but she's bleeding as if she's menstruating and she's been complaining of cramps."

"She is. The Dragon Soul inside her is trying eliminate the venom by cleansing her womb."

"If it is trying to cleanse her then why do you have the antidote?" K'Lara asked.

"See these marks," he said pointing to sets of deep bite marks on the top and bottom of her nipples. "The dragon can only cleanse the womb not what's in her bloodstream. This is what's making her so ill, not the womb."

Iona moaned, rolling on her stomach. She clung to the mud, turning her head to the left. "She's awake," Lethos told his brother and crouched beside Iona. "Your highness," he patiently called to her.

"Ugh, where am I?" Iona asked, never taking her eyes off her mother's boots. "Mom," she called, reaching her hand out.

K'Lara knelt beside her daughter and took her hand. "Turn over and look upon them. But don't be scared of them. They are the only ones who can cure you."

Iona slowly rolled on her back. She screamed at the sight of a naked deep blue toned man, sat up and backed away. "They always do that to you," Lethos said, tapping his twin brother on the arm. "Don't be afraid of us, Iona. He won't hurt you," the white man with short raven colored hair offered, extending his arm to her.

"Not unless she wants me to," Thalos grinned.

Iona reluctantly took the twin's hand. He helped her rise to her feet. She stumbled a few steps, cringing her face. "Hmm, my head hurts."

"We'll heal you," he said lifting her into his strong arms. She wrapped her arms around his neck and laid her head on his shoulder. Her dress disappeared to reveal only her chains and tit bars. "Oh, fuck, she's more sensual than you were, K'Lara," he yelled behind his shoulders and then disappeared into the woods.

"Thanks for the compliment. Just heal so we can talk further," K'Lara huffed.

Thalos tapped her on the shoulder, "She's safe with us."

"I know she is. Thalos, this doesn't make sense. None of it does."

"Lethos and I have been talking about it ever since the High Priest told us of the investigation."

"What investigation?"

"General Roan Tharg was found by K'Lilith on the boat to the underworld. Draco has punished his soul but nobody knows why. Solon seduced King Tritan's daughter and stole Atlantium from her then gave it to Prince Kilean."

"Why?"

"The Silver Dragon Soul transferred to his body but then left it."

"Then he'll become insane?"

"No, he has Soul Sickness."

"Soul Sickness?"

"It occurs in a Dragon Lord or Lady when the soul is removed from their body before it has completed its nesting. When the Dragon Soul is removed by force it excretes a deadly poison within the host's body. The only remedy of which is for the Dragon Soul to be returned to the body but that has to be done within six days from the time it was extracted or the host will die."

"Why haven't I ever heard of it?"

"Because it wasn't something that had ever occurred before. The council feared if Iona ever learned of her true identity she wouldn't be of sound enough mind to assume her position as Dragon Lady. So after you died, they met with Draco, Razil and the Spirit Dragons to create a way for the Spirit Dragons to be protected."

"A way to kill my daughter?"

"K'Lara, she's not the one who was poisoned."

K'Lara crossed her arms over her chest with a huff. She glared at the blue toned man with a stern look of disapproval. "It could have been. What if she went through the ceremony and they found her unfit to assume my former position?"

"You're thinking too much about this."

"Am I?"

"Stop being so overprotective of her. Her mind is open to the possibility of the reality of the world we live in. What happened between her and Kilean is blessed by the gods."

"Then where's the Silver Dragon Soul?"

"It briefly appeared in the hands of the High Priest then disappeared. No one knows where it has gone. When the High Priest approached the council concerning the matter K'Lilith was already there with Roan as were King Tritan who was accusing Solon of theft. The council suspects Roan, King Tavir and Solon have conspired against Draco and Razil. They've been summoned before the High Priest for interrogation."

"And what of my daughter?"

"The council demands she continue her path towards becoming a Dragon Lady. There is one more thing K'Lara, that you should be aware of."

"Oh?"

Thalos exhaled a deep breath. "Your sister was kidnapped."

K'Lara heaved several deep breaths. "Why....how long....oh, gods!" she exclaimed falling to her knees.

"The council has been searching for her but felt it was in your best interest not to know that she had been kidnapped."

"And now?"

"We were told to tell you about it because the council believes her disappearance is related to the current events that have transpired. We believe Prince Zurggash may have her. We don't know how long she has been missing. It was a great ploy if he is the one who has taken her. The only reason we know of the deception is because your mother went to visit upon her after you departed to serve Iona and was concerned with some of your sister's irregular behaviors. Your mother apprehended her and brought her forth to the High Priestess where it was discovered under her investigation that the servant was an imposture."

"No," she cried, pulling her hair and bending over her knees. Thalos knelt before her and placed his hand on her back.

"K'Lara, we will find her."

"She's not involved in this. She would never help Prince Zurggash," she argued, pushing the Dragon Twin's chest.

"We don't know that for certain. Your sister has been displeased by her position for quite sometime."

"It was my fault, not hers! If anyone wanted to do something to right the wrong, it would have been me! Let them arrest me instead of accusing my family of treason!"

"Are you guilty?"

K'Lara huffed, rising to her feet. "Of all the....huh." She crossed her arms, turned her back on him and stared across the lake. Thalos silently rose to his feet. "How many times have we fucked and you have the audacity to ask me that question!"

"I know you're innocent, K'Lara. But you have to think with a clear mind. Your daughter's life and soul are at risk."

K'Lara exhaled a deep breath, lifting her head back, trying to break her tears. "Thalos, if anyone is to blame for this mess, it's me. I'm the one who believed the lies Roan, Asa and Nomiki told. If I had just listened to the soul inside me I would have never allowed any of this to happen to me."

"You can right the wrong with your daughter's help, K'Lara. You still trust my brother and I?"

K'Lara turned to face him with a nod. He gently placed his hand on her arm. "The best thing you can do right now is find a couple of priests. There's some here that are excited that you have become a Dragon Master. They've always wanted to fuck you." K'Lara chuckled. "There's that grin I love."

She bit her lower lip as he pulled the hidden zipper down from her neck to lower stomach then helped her arms out of the sleeves. The top of her catsuit hung down her bottom. He stared at the familiar, dark, dragon tattoo on her torso and back and the emerald nipple bars matching her daughter's markings. He pulled on the chain hung between her nipple bars. K'Lara gasped. "The men will like to see those marks," he said removing his hand from the chain.

"I'm sure they would," she whispered, removing her heels and the suit from the rest of the body.

"My brother and I personally established your hut with everything we know you like. There's new weapons in the chest."

She placed her clothes next to a tree, placed her boots back on then returned to him. "Good. What of Iona's army?"

"We don't know. We haven't been able to connect with the High Priestess nor with Asa and Sina. Follow me," he said taking her by the arm. K'Lara pushed her long, raven hair behind her shoulders and followed the man through the thick forest. Lower level priests gawked at her, muttering amongst themselves. She smiled at them then turned her attention back to trail. Every step they took brought them deeper into the heart of the woods. Men of all ages and levels stared at her with lustful desire. A network of connected treehouses with swinging bridges loomed over her. She stared at the center large hut. She didn't need to see behind the door to know what was in there. For a few years of her life that was her sacred place among the priests. The place where she had lived and enjoyed a passionate relationship with the Dragon Twins.

"K'Lara," Thalos called to her. She turned her attention to her escort. He lowered his extended hand. "She'll be alright in our care. You know this. We have faithfully served your ancestors for hundreds of years." K'Lara slightly grinned then nodded. She lifted her eyes to a row of six naked humans, dracnoids and elven priests. "When the High Priest told us who Iona's Dragon Master was we already had in mind whom we would ask to serve you based on what we know you liked."

"And they can handle how rough I like it?" she grinned, swiping her hand down a human's strong torso to his thick penis.

"Of course. Let them ease your mind, K'Lara. I'll send for you when your daughter is well." Thalos said then walked into his hut.

K'Lara walked up and down the row of two humans, two elves and two dracnoids thoroughly examining each with her hands and mouth. She kissed a turquoise toned dracnoid priest. He wrapped his arms

around her, playing with her firm ass. She stepped away from him with a grin; staring at all the men's erect penises. "I want all of you," she said walking into her hut. She was taken away by the sheer beauty of her new home among the priests. Candles lined the walls. Rose petals laid beautifully on the bed and floor. Elaborate dishes of sensual foods and stimulating toxins lay on the table by the wall. She sat on the king size bed with a grin. Handcuffs hung off the headboard. Sexual toys were all over the place. Her heart skipped a beat at the sound of the door closing behind the last of the priests who entered their room. They silently lit the candles, poured perfume all over their bodies and prepared several stimulating toys for her pleasure. A human grabbed a bottle of oil, knelt before her with his head down and asked, "May I prepare your body, Dragon Master?"

"Of course," she beamed. He slowly removed her boots, kissing the inside of her thighs. She inhaled deeply as his lips found her clit. K'Lara spread her legs wider, falling onto her back. His slender fingers rubbed the oil all over the lips then worked their way to her clit and vagina. Its warmth excited her senses. He thrust a few fingers in her vagina. She moaned, grabbing the edge of the bed, arching her back. The men surrounded her. A tall elf knelt his over her face and positioned his slender penis over her mouth. She opened her mouth, taking it fully in. The elf moaned in unison as the human touched her insides with his oiled fingers. The dracnoids descended upon her chest, each suckling on a breast as she played with their balls. The human monk lifted her knees and thrust his large penis inside her. She almost chocked from gasping with the penis in her mouth. "Oh great gods," she moaned, rolling her eyes as the other human and elven priests rubbed oil on her lower stomach and ass, periodically playing with her clit and asshole. Her warm body fidgeted. Her tits grew hard. The more she reacted the harder the human thrust inside her. If this was just the start of their time together she couldn't wait to see what else these priests had in mind for the rest of their encounters.

9

Iona sat with her legs wide open on the silk blanket on her bed. She stared up at the dome of the leathered skinned wigwam. Was this all a dream? She couldn't remember much about how she got here only that her mother had brought her. Her mother. Her mother was alive! Iona grinned from the warm sensation between her legs and the knowledge that her mother was alive. "Hmm," she moaned as Lethos held on to her thighs and licked her clit. Despite feeling so weak with fever, her body was quite enjoying the human Dragon Twins' sensual touch.

Iona closed her eyes and fell limp. "Iona," Lethos called to her, tapping the side of her warm cheek. She moaned, turning her head to face him and opened her eyes. "Stay with me." She swallowed hard, staring deep into his light green eyes. "Thirsty," she whispered. He grabbed a glass of water from the wooden nightstand and helped her to sip it. The clear liquid didn't exactly taste like water but who cared? It soothed her dry throat and eased her pain. "Don't drink too much at one time. The nectar will overpower you in this state," he informed.

Iona swallowed then turned her head away. He placed the half empty glass on the table then turned her face to his own. "We can stop until my brother comes."

Iona shook her head. "I like it."

Lethos smiled, "Ok, but if you feel you are too weak to continue you let me know. I am only appeasing your urges so you can rest without the dragon within you demanding from you more than you can handle. But in order to heal your body my brother and I have to have sex with you at the same time. I don't want your body so weak that we can't do that."

Iona shifted her body and opened her legs wider. She closed her eyes, relaxed and motioned for him to continue his work. Lethos kissed her on the lips. He slid his tongue into her mouth while fondling between her legs. His tongue slid out of her mouth and down her torso, stopping just long enough to tickle her nipples as he suckled upon both breasts.

"Oh, that's not fair," Thalos protested, entering into the large hut and closing the door behind him. Lethos pulled his fingers out and licked them in front of Iona.

"What took you so long? I was going to wait but the Dragon Soul needed to be appeased."

"Thank you," she smiled, taking his fingers and licking them herself.

"Damn," Thalos sighed, staring at the woman.

Iona turned to the strange looking man. "Who are you two and why does my body desire more of what he gave me?"

"We are your Dragon Twins. My name is Lethos and this is my brother, Thalos. Our only duty is to bring you and the female dragon pleasure when you need to mate. We also heal you but that can only come while you are mating with us. You have been poisoned by the Gleaning Chair."

"Gleaning Chair?" she asked with a curious look.

"You know what a menstrual cycle is, right?"

Iona nodded. "I spill blood between my legs once a month."

"Well the Dragon Lady and Dragon Lord spill excess sexual energy twice a month. It has to be gathered through the Gleaning Chair. It lasts for three to five days, depending upon the severity of the energy that has been stored within the body."

"Why would my body store sexual energy if I have sex?"

Thalos answered, "There are many times within your life where the dragon within you cannot allow your body to experience the intense sexual encounters it demands upon you because for a majority of your life you will mate with a priest that has been chosen as your lifemate by the Dragon Lord. The priest can handle a certain amount of intense sexual relations but not as much as either we nor the Dragon Lord can."

"Then why would I marry a priest and not Kilean?"

"You and Kilean are sacred authorities, Princess Iona. You have to be able to balance your human obligations to rule your kingdom and your mystical duties as enforcer of the Draconian Codex. The sexual powers that you possess must be controlled or they will consume your human mind. It is very tempting for you to spend the rest of your life in bed with either Prince Kilean or us but if you did that then there would be chaos in our world. So in order to eliminate that temptation from either you or Prince Kilean, your kingdoms are separated. Only the Dragon Lord and Lady can use a Gleaning Chair because they carry the soul of the spirit dragons. It is the spirit dragons who need to be gleaned of the excess energies but it can only be done through their hosts."

"Why did it attack me?"

"Were you in communication with Prince Kilean?"

"Yes, he contacted me after I was thinking about him."

"He doesn't carry the Silver Dragon Soul so when you two were in communication the chair didn't recognize him and must have deemed you an imposture as well."

"But...that doesn't...hmm," she moaned, leaning back on the thick pillows as a strange wave of energy flowed through her body.

Lethos explained, kneeling beside her. "May I?" he asked, nodding at her breasts.

"Hmm," Iona nodded. "It feels good when you touch me."

Lethos fondled with her breasts, licking her tits and pulling on her chain, always keeping his eyes upon hers. She arched her head, swallowing hard.

"Thalos and I can bring you pleasure together, if you so desire it."

"Is that an orgy?" she asked.

"Yes, you have heard of that," Lethos asked playing with her vagina.

"Huh, yeah, I had one with Kilean and Tayla."

"Tayla," the brothers repeated with shock.

"When? How?" Lethos asked.

Thalos placed his hand on his brother's chest. "Healing first, questions later, brother."

"Of course," Lethos sneered.

"Sit up, Iona."

Iona complied as Lethos backed away. The human sat on the low headboard with his legs extended behind her and stroked his penis. "Have you ever sucked on a cock before," he asked.

"Yes," she answered, crawling on all fours. She grabbed his penis and suckled with her ass in the air.

"Oh, yes," Lethos moaned. "Whoever taught you this did it the right way."

"Kilean," she mumbled in between head bobs.

Iona moaned feeling Thalos' large penis thrust inside her. "Hmm, she feels so good," Thalos said.

"She was already wet before I played with her."

Thalos thrust slow and deep. Every rhythm repeated by her on Letho's cock. Thalos grabbed her hip chain, guiding her into the perfect rhythm. Iona moaned with her lovers. She licked Lethos' balls, taking them fully into her mouth. "Oh, yeah, ugh," he moaned, arching his head.

Thalos pushed Iona to the side and slide onto the bed. "Sit on me," he ordered, grabbing her hip chain as his brother stroked his own cock. Iona faced Thalos and straddled his hips as Lethos climbed onto the bed. She inserted Thalos penis inside her and moaned with pleasure rocking back and forth. He was larger than Kilean!

"You feel like the dragon dildo I played with," she grinned, pressing her hands on his firm blue chest. Tentacles rose from his penis, stimulating her clit and ass. "Oh," she moaned, leaning backward, fully taking in the pleasure of the sensual nodes on his penis and the tentacles. A strange warm, overpowering sensation came from within her. She gasped as her lower stomach ached with each move.

"I'm a dracnoid. My twin brother is human. Most humans can't take the intense sexual stimulation we give our mates." She inhaled deeply, pushing back her hair as she paused over him. He grabbed her chain and rubbed her hips. Her lower stomach ached for more.

"Breath Iona," he coached, grabbing the side of her face. "The nodes excrete a lubricant deep within your vagina that stimulate your G spot. You're more delicate now because you're on your cycle. If you tense up too many of the sensations will be stronger. Just relax and enjoy them. You're safe. I promise."

Iona swallowed hard with a nod. He lowered his hand back to her hips then stared into the dracnoid's golden snake like eyes. Slowly she moved her ass up, inhaling deeply from the touch of the tip of his penis on her G-spot. She rocked back down hard, moaning loudly.

"Like that," he grinned.

"Yeah," she smiled back. She rocked a few times, periodically kissing Thalos as he rubbed her ass. The tentacles moved away from her asshole as his fingers drew closer.

"Ugh, yes. Oh baby, yes," she groaned. She gasped feeling something wet in her asshole. "Put it in," she demanded, grinding even harder. She screamed with delight at the sensation of Lethos' penis inside her. He pushed her against his brother's body, pinning her between them as she thrust in unison with him. "Hmm, ugh," Iona moaned loudly, clawing Thalos' sides. The sheer force of their thrusts and the sensations deep within her nearly took all of her strength. "Ugh," she cringed, leaning her head against Letho's shoulder. He pushed her head back down and thrust harder. Iona clamped her teeth onto one of Thalos' nipple rings and pulled, moving her ass harder. Faster and harder she rocked, groaning loudly with each intense wave of pleasure as Thalos played with her nipples, periodically pulling and sucking on them. Sweat filled her body. Her tits were hard. Her body, flushed. She was about to cum hard.

"You close," Lethos asked his brother.

Thalos nodded with a long groan. "You," he asked.

"Looks like you're closer than I am. I can feed her this time."

"Oh gods," Thalos declared, arching his back as Lethos removed his penis from Iona's ass and stood beside the bed. Lethos whipped his hand on his penis, purifying it as Thalos pushed Iona underneath him.

"Hard," she pleaded, lifting her legs to his shoulders and he pounded into her. She grasped the edge of the bed, arching her back. "Our semen will heal you but it only works while your dragon soul cannot control your cravings. You were about to cum hard. We stopped that from happening so you could feed. Thalos will control the dragon's sexual urges while you feed from me," Lethos said, climbing onto the bed. "Suckle," he instructed, straddling her face and placing his penis in her mouth.

Iona licked her tongue all round, moving the penis in and out of her mouth. She had never tasted anything so sweet before. She closed her eyes, moaning as the penis warmed her mouth. "Slower, Thalos, she's not ready," Lethos instructed. Iona moaned, feeling Thalos slow his deep ascents. Lethos' already large penis grew even larger. She wanted to gag as it pushed against the back of her throat. "Don't," he warned her. "I know your body wants to reject it. Don't let it," he instructed her.

She arched her back and suckled faster. "I can't stop it, Thalos. The dragon is stronger than the human. She's coming harder than she was before," Thalos shouted, pushing harder and faster.

Iona clawed her teeth down the sides of Lethos' penis. He roared and rocked hard, holding her by her forehead. Stronger, warmer the penis grew inside her until it finally erupted its delicious tasting liquid inside her mouth at the same time as she and Thalos reached orgasm together.

"Swallow it," Lethos ordered, pulling his penis out of her mouth and sitting her upright.

Iona complied. The golden liquid tingled and warmed her insides, making her very sleepy. "Hmm," she moaned, rolling on her stomach and closing her eyes.

"Sleep and when you wake up you won't be so weak. We'll have to see if one dose was enough to eliminate the poison in your system. If not then we'll do this again and again until the poison has been removed from your body," Thalos said, lifting a silk blanket over her body.

"Why does it feel different?" she asked as he sat next to her.

"What do you mean?" Lethos asked.

"Your cum and penis tasted sweet and delicious while your brother's penis didn't and when he came inside me it wasn't warm like yours was in my mouth."

"Oh, it is because mine was medicine and his was just a penis. Either one of us can give you medicine but in order for us to do so we must deny ourselves pleasure while the other is having sex with the Dragon Lady. He was closer to orgasm than I was so we chose to purify my penis to feed you rather than his."

"You can do that?" Iona asked with a shocked look.

"Yes, but the Dragon Lady and the Dragon Twin must maintain the physical connection for it to work. The sexual energies soothes the beast within you so we can tend to your human body."

Iona nodded her head and fell fast asleep never noticing the men's thin breechcloth returning to their hips. Lethos kissed Iona on the top of the head then walked out of the room with his brother. They silently walked out of the hut and paused at the sounds of loud sensual moans and yells coming from the Dragon Master's hut.

"I miss those days with her," Lethos grinned. Thalos tapped his hand on Lethos' chest and nodded towards the path. They walked towards the path leading to the river.

"We have to tell the High Priest that Iona confirmed that Tayla is involved," Thalos said.

Lethos walked backwards and stepped in front of his brother. "You know what they'll do. They'll order she be apprehended."

"They won't hurt her unless they find she willingly cooperated with Tayla and Prince Zurrgash."

"Perhaps not her but what of her mother? K'Lara wasn't with her when she went through the Rite of Dragon Souls. She couldn't guide her towards the truth until that occurred. She's in enough trouble as is, brother."

"It is not our place to cast judgment. We serve the Dragon Lady at the discretion of the council. The council needs answers. Kilean contacted Iona and then the chair attacked her. They'll take that into consideration. Besides, he's suffering from Soul Sickness. If the council deems him innocent and worthy of assuming his position as Dragon Lord then there is a way of him regaining control of the Silver Dragon with Iona's help."

10   Temple of the Sun

The large double moons hung close to the horizon baring their light pink rays upon the ancient temple grounds. Tall ornate columns rose high connecting the marble floors and open ceiling of the circular landing platform. Solon gently pulled the unconscious Kilean from the saddle and laid him upon the floor. Sweat poured down the prince's face as he shivered. "Kilean," Solon called to him, gently stroking his cheek. Yet the prince never responded.

"Solon?" Tavir asked dismounting.

"The Atlantium wore off hours ago. I was hoping he was just sleeping but I had my doubts. He's entered into the Deep Sleep," Solon answered then lifted his eyes to Vashti. "How long do we have before we approach my father?"

"The guards we already on their way as soon as we crossed over the Valley of Tli," she said, curling her tail around them.

Solon nodded then turned to Tavir. "Your head?"

"I'm fine. I've meet and been accepted by most of your gods."

Kilean arched his back with long gasp then seized. "Kilean," Tavir yelled, running to his son's side. Solon pulled Tavir away and held him back.

"No, let his body fight the poison within him. This is good, Tavir."

"He's seizing! How can that be good?"

"He's body is doing something instead of accepting death as a remedy for what ails him. That means his body is strong."

Tavir stared down at his son fighting the urge to help him as Solon's thin yet inhumanly strong arms held him back. He clutched his jaw with anguish. It seemed like an eternity had passed as his son's body violently shook but he knew it was only a few minutes. Kilean's body eased, exhaling a deep breath then he returned to his unconscious state weaker than before. Solon released his grip and turned to Vashti while Tavir ran to his son.

"You will bear witness?" Solon asked Vashti.

"Yes," she answered as the large, double wooden doors opened to reveal six guards and their commanding officer dressed in silver armor with the image of the Silver Dragon wrapped in a circular pattern along their torso. "Solon," Captain Drayson Trajeon greeted, extending his hand to his men. The elven captain slowly approached Solon. He silently lifted to fingers to his heart then his forehead in unison with Solon. The two elves touched each others fingers, lowered them and gazed deeply into each other's eyes.

"I'm sorry, old friend," Drayson said telepathically to his half-brother.

"How upset is he?"

"Remember the time when we were kids and we hid his staff in the rubbish?"

"That upset?"

"Worse."

"Dear gods. Couldn't you do something? You are the heir to his throne. Your mother is the High Priestess."

"My parents only bond during the Bonding of the Dragons and that hasn't happened in thirty-six years. They are quite unbalanced."

"And your sister? Have you heard from her?"

"There's been no contact with the Temple of the Sun. Solon, father cherishes you more than I. I thought for many years, until the day you died, he would choose you over me to replace him upon his 1,000 year birthday."

"I'm the son of a sex slave not the High Priestess."

"He doesn't have to claim me as his heir. The Draconian Codex is explicit. The High Priest and Priestess has to be of Elven descent from the former High Priest or High Priestess. They have one pair of twin children within their 1,000-year reign, a male and female. Only one can assume their parent's position. The other must be from a sex slave in order to assure the genetic markers do not become diluted. My twin wants to replace our mother and we had expected she would, then you died and we had to accept the reality that it could, neither of us ever wanted. Ever since you died, father has renewed his interest in my affairs. My sister had made every effort she could to persuade our mother to accept

her as her replacement. Our parents have been at odds with each other over the matter and when the veil was placed between them after King Tavir and Queen K'Lara did not join in their initial Bonding of Dragons matters only became worse. Father's temper is shorter than it use to be and the longer he is separated from mother the more irate he has become. Just be careful in how you conduct yourself when you appear before him."

"I will. I promise. Thank you for the warning." Solon nodded then broke the connection between them.

The elegant, elven commander apologized pushing back his purple cape and removing a rolled up parchment from a slender leather case on his right hip. He opened it up and read the scroll, "By order of Draco and Razil, Solon Trajeon, son of High Priest Aejeon Trajeon and the sex slave, Nesla, you are hereby arrested for the crime of theft, rape and treason." Drayson nodded to two of his soldiers.

Solon slowly raised his hands as the men approached him. One of the guards stood in front of him and aimed a gun at Solon's head. The guard's partner lowered Solon's hands, pulled them behind his back and placed silver, glowing cuffs on his wrists. He tightened the thick metal bar between Solon's hands. "You can't use magic with those on. I'm sorry, brother, I truly am," Drayson said, handing the order to one of the soldiers guarding Solon. "Take him to the chamber."

"Yes sir," the guards answered in unison then lead Solon away.

King Tavir watched them lead Solon down a long, dark corridor while he tended to his son. He glanced up at the eight-foot elven commander. Drayson pulled another scroll from inside his leather coat. "King Tavir Dragonsun," he commanded, motioning for two more soldiers to approach. Tavir's heart sunk. Now what? The commander turned to his guards. "Take Prince Kilean Dragonsun to our healers."

"Yes sir," the guards replied then quickly descended upon Kilean. Tavir rose to his feet. He watched the elves say a spell. Kilean's body rose in the air and followed them out of the hall.

"You can't cure what ails him without the soul," Tavir objected.

"No, but with Sina and Asa's help we might be able to delay his death until we have retrieved the Silver Dragon Soul."

"Assuming you know where it is," Vashti interrupted. Elf and human glanced at her. "Kilean claims Tayla took the soul. Problem is, no one has ever been able to locate where Tayla and Prince Zurrgash reside. How do you plan to locate someone whom even the council cannot?"

"The council believes General Roan must know more information than he claims."

Tavir huffed, "It wouldn't surprise me."

The blonde elven commander turned to the Dragon Lord. "We cannot make assumptions based upon our emotions. The council needs facts not feelings. Roan is human. He will give us the information we seek." He tapped the other scroll on his other hand.

"That's for me, isn't it?" Tavir asked with a concerned look.

"It is quite unusual for me to arrest a Dragon Lord let alone a former one."

"Charges?"

"Technically you're not under arrest, just suspect."

"I see."

"The council wants to detain anyone they suspect are involved with General Roan Tharg."

"And why would I ever want to help him? Tayla's theft of the Silver Dragon Soul threatens to kill my son. Roan and Asa ruined my life when he prevented Queen K'Lara from bonding with me. I have never forgiven him and he knows it. We kept whatever relations we had based upon pure duty. Now you are implying that Roan and Tayla worked together to bring about a horrible death for my son? Never, Drayson, I would NEVER place my son's life in jeopardy."

Drayson peered over his shoulder at the group of fifteen soldiers under his command. "Leave us," he ordered then turned back to the king. The taller man stepped closer to the human king. "I believe you, King Tavir, but it isn't my decision to make," the elf acknowledged in a hush tone with his hand around Tavir's upper arm. Tavir stared down at the firm grip on his arm. The elf wasn't even holding his arm with his full strength but he could feel the immense power within the grasp. He slowly lifted his eyes upward to the lean face. "Come with me," the elf ordered, urging Tavir forward.

They walked a few paces before Vashti's booming voice bellowed. "I serve witness."

Drayson paused. He released Tavir and pivoted towards the dragon. "Vashti, the charges are serious."

"I understand the seriousness of the charges."

"But why would you stand with...them?"

"Drayson, I only stand with your brother, Kilean and his father. I care not for Roan. Grant me passage into the chamber."

"Draco and Razil don't...."

"...They are expecting me. I sent word to the creators of my intentions. Drayson, I was chosen to serve the Dragon Lord. Let me do so. Open the portal." A thick silence fell between dragon and elf. Despite the elf's calm appearance, Tavir could tell the young man was struggling with the request. It wasn't everyday that a dragon decided to stand in the place as a criminal's guardian, let alone one suspected of treason. If the criminal was released before his or her trial but escaped from the guardian's custody then found guilty then the guardian would take upon them the punishment the criminal deserved. It didn't happen very often but he had known in some cases where the criminal had killed their guardian using the law.

"Dragons are not allowed with in the chamber for a reason, Vashti," Drayson countered.

"One would think you would be more appreciative of my support for your brother," Vashti chimed.

"I am but this is most irregular."

"Open the portal, Drayson. Draco will allow it."

Drayson nodded, turned and muttered a spell while he moved his hand in intricate circles. A large blue portal with swirling energy opened directly before them. Vashti nodded her head, walked into the portal and disappeared with the portal.

The men turned to each other in reflective silence. Never could they recall a dragon ever risking their own life to defend a criminal. "They'll listen to her testimony?" Tavir asked.

"I don't know but I pray to the gods that they do. Come," Drayson muttered, taking Tavir by the elbow and led him down the long, ivory walled maze of hallways leading to the circular round chamber. Neither man muttered a sound.

11

Tavir's heart beat fast with anxiety as he stood in the center of the massive chamber. Soldiers under Drayson's command surrounded him along the wall, ready to kill if they had to. He peered at the circular wall excluding them from the outside chambers of the temple. No doors, no windows. The only way in and out was through magic. Magic he didn't posses. He worried about his son. If Solon was right, Kilean only had five more days to live. Hopefully, Sina and Asa could prolong Kilean's life.

"She disappeared," Sina's voice brought Tavir's attention back to reality. He turned his face to the left to see the olive skinned human dragon twin speaking beside him. Roan's spirit stood silent on the far end.

"Sina, tell us the truth," High Priest Aejeon Trajeon ordered.

"I am telling the truth, sir. Asa and I had sex outside then we parted. When I returned to our cavern I couldn't find her. I didn't even feel her presence. It's as if she had never existed."

Tavir peered up to the high area where the council sat above them. The elven high priest sat in the middle of a long row of councilmen. Each of the seven races: draconid, elf, human, dwarf, mermen, fairies and halflings rulers had appointed two councilmen to dwell within the temple and help regulate laws for the entirety of their lifespan. One from each race sat on either end of the high priest. Each man had pledge a vow to forsake his race, ruler, family, and beliefs in order to serve justice. The council muttered amongst them for what seemed to be an eternity. Tavir peered to his right. Solon stood rigid and silent as if none of this mattered to him. Perhaps, it was just his elven half? Elves rarely showed any emotion in public. He peered over his shoulder to see

Vashti sitting at attention, carefully listening with her sensitive hearing to every word being said.

"Enough," the high priest silenced the council. All eyes diverted to Aejeon. The high priest rose from his seat and glanced down at the witness box below his tier. King Tritan sat glaring at Solon with a deadly look. "Solon," the high priest called to his son. Solon lifted his gaze to his father, bowed and stood up with reverence.

"The Atlantium?"

"Sir?" Solon asked.

"Be honest with me, son. Speak to me as my son and not as a criminal speaking to the high priest. These charges that stand against you are serious."

Solon nodded, "Yes, father."

"We have heard King Tritan's side of the argument. I cannot dismiss the fact your misdeeds have coincided with Prince Kilean Dragonson's Soul Sickness or the fact that General Roan has died from Milk of the Dragon. It looks like you knew what Tayla had planned and tried to save the prince. If that be so, we should be grateful for your deed but still it is disturbing to know you are involved in this tracery," the high priest asked, pointing to the human spirit.

"No, sir, you have it all wrong."

"Then tell me, Solon. What is the truth?"

"None of these three instances are related. I had sex with the princess. It was consensual. She gave the Atlantium to me so that I would be able to visit her in areas of the ocean where my body cannot go. I didn't know that I would have to use it on Prince Kilean."

"You're an immortal, son."

"Oh, I know, father. But there are still areas of this planet that even an immortal elven form cannot linger. After we had sex, I grew so cold that I had to leave her, even though she wanted more from me."

"King Tritan," the high priest asked never keeping his green eyes off of his son.

"My daughter admits she loves your son but she did not tell me that it was consensual nor that she gave the Atlantium to him."

Solon protested, "Of course, not. She's your youngest. Call her forth and let her tell her story. She will tell you that we have been together many times."

"Do you have a relationship with this woman, Solon?" a merman councilman asked.

"Yes."

111

"But it is forbidden," a stout human councilmember said. "The Dragon Lord Guardian can only mate with the Dragon Lady Guardian. No one else."

"And where am I supposed to find her? Hmm, tell me. We have no contact with the Dragon Lady, her temple, her army, her Dragon Master, dragon or her guardian ever since the veil was lifted between hers and King Tavir's kingdoms! I have needs. My mother was a sex slave. The high priest and high priestess have twins plus one child each from a sex slave. The genetics are more dominate from the sex slave in the child from that union. I can't always control my urges even though I'm an elf! You want me to be of sound mind then let me fuck whoever I want to until we find Princess Iona's guardian!"

Aejeon grunted, shaking his head. "Tritan?" he asked the merman king below him.

"I will drop the charges. He may continue the relationship he has established with my daughter until his mate had been procured. I will ensure she takes certain precautions when she is with him so she doesn't spawn," he sighed then disappeared.

"Release my son," Aejeon ordered the guards beside Solon and sat down as the cuffs came off Solon's wrist. Solon nodded to his brother, Drayson, standing on the platform below the witness tier. Solon rubbed his wrists, lifting his eyes to his father.

The high priests eyes fell upon Sina and Roan. "General Roan Tharg," the elf's voice boomed with authority. Roan stepped forward, bowed regally then stood upright. "Which sister did you drink from?"

Roan grinned, "Why should I tell you?"

Aejeon slammed his hands on podium, rose and snarled at him. "You have no right to speak to me in that manner, General!"

"Ah, but you're not...." Roan began to speak then disappeared.

The councilmen, soldiers, Solon, Sina, Vashti and Tavir all spoke to each other with shock and dismay. Chaos reigned in the chamber. "Find him!" Aejeon bellowed to Drayson.

"Yes sir," Drayson replied. He ran across the room, shouting orders to all his soldiers. Group by group they all disappeared. Aejeon glared down at Sina with a deadly look.

"It wasn't me. I...."

Suddenly a portal opened in the middle of the hall. Tavir and Sina parted to allow the portal to open wider. All eyes glared at Thalos entered into the chamber carrying an unconscious Iona. The council rose at the sight of the new Dragon Lady while K'Lara and Lethos followed behind them. Tavir couldn't keep his eyes off of K'Lara. His eyes glanced up and down her tight fitting black catsuit framing her perfectly athletic body. He never heard a sound nor took notice of anything going on around him. She was his world.

"Tavir," Aejeon's voice telepathically entered his mind. The king shook his head then looked back at the elf. "Kiss her and get it over with."

"Gladly," Tavir walked to K'Lara, gently placed his hand on her cheek and kissed her. K'Lara wrapped her arms around him and returned his kiss with more passion. "Oh, I missed you," Tavir whispered, with his forehead on hers.

"And I you. I'm so...I'm so sorry, Tavir. I...."
He placed his finger on her lips, "Shh, all is forgiven. Thank you for the priestess you chose for me. She was a good wife and mother to my son."

"Was?"

"Elarya went mad about a year ago. I had sought help from the council. High Priest Aejeon explained there is a relatively rare disease that affects the Elven brain. He called Maelgrum. He said it can affect elves as young as 200 years old. My wife had just celebrated her 200th the month before she began to have headaches and nightmares. I should have known something was wrong when she started to have them but I didn't think anything of it and to be honest, she told me the headaches weren't that bad. A month later, her appetite decreased and she was sleeping more. She began wandering the hallways, talking to herself. Kilean and I would try to interact with her but she would have fits of confusion where she didn't know who we were or where she was. It only grew worse when she couldn't control her magical abilities."

"Shit."

"Yes, that's when I brought her here." He exhaled a deep breath. "She's dying," he muttered.

"Does Kilean know?"

Tavir nodded slowly. "He refuses to visit her."

"Where is she?"

"With her parents. The council had enough mercy to allow her to die with her family. I'm glad they did. Her disease will only grow worse. She'll lose her magic, go blind and then forget everything and everyone she knows. It's a horrible way to die. She pleaded with me before we came here to end her life. I think in that brief rational state she was in she realized what was happening to her."

"Her father is an elder healer."

"Yes, and he was very grateful that we returned her to him so she could live the last of her days under their house."

"Does the council know what caused it?"

"They told me sometimes when an elven's memories are removed and then restored the magic they used to do so can cause the disease to lay dormant until the elf's mind matures."

"Shit," K'Lara muttered.

"I haven't told Kilean how his mother had contracted the disease. He's not handling his mother's situation well. At least becoming a Dragon Lord has helped him to focus on something other than his mother."

"Does Kilean have siblings? Most elves only have about four children?"

"Kilean is our eldest. He's nineteen. He has two sisters, Sharia is sixteen and Phoebe is twelve. His brother, Ryo, is ten."

"How are they doing?"

"Ryo and Phoebe are in a state of denial. Sharia is being strong for all her siblings. She knows Kilean has a duty to serve as the new Dragon Lord so she does everything she can to make sure he stays on task. She took Ryo and Phoebe to visit my wife's family in the borderlands while I helping Kilean with the Rite of Dragon Souls. They do not know what has befallen upon their brother."

"I am so sorry to her of your family's situation."

"Thank you, K'Lara. I care about her but I don't love her. I know she could always see that in my eyes."

"Did she use the spell I taught her?"

"She did and it soothed me some nights when I couldn't stand to be without you."

"I knew she would take care of you. I'm only sorry that I..."

"...I told you, K'Lara. I have forgiven you. You will and always have been the joy to my heart."

K'Lara smiled, kissed him deeply and stepped away. She held his hand as she approached the high priest. "My daughter has been poisoned by the Gleaning Chair. Thalos and Lethos have been treating her. She grows stronger for a bit but then it declines. The dragon soul is healing her womb but the poison is in the bloodstream."

The council returned to their seats. Aejeon turned to Solon. "Solon, take Princess Iona to the healers. Lay her beside Kilean. Join their hands together. Perhaps being together might help both of them. I'll send Sina when I am done with her."

"Yes, father," Solon bowed and took Iona from Thalos arms. He walked to the back of the chamber and disappeared.

Thalos glanced at Sina, "Good to finally see you. Where is your sister?"

Sina waved her hand, "Long story, Thalos."

"Lethos, I can sense something is bothering you," the high priest said.

The human dragon twin nodded. "May I ask something of the council before I speak?"

"Ask," a draconoid councilman nodded.

"Queen K'Lara was punished for her crime of being dissuaded into accepting King Nomiki as her husband. I understand Draco and Razil are giving her a second chance so that she might be able to accept her position as Dragon Lady Ambassador. She would be reunited with King Tavir, which by the looks of it wouldn't be that bad."

All eyes turned to Tavir and K'Lara. Tavir held K'Lara close to his body with his arms around her waist, gently kissing the side of her neck. She nudged him with her elbow. He lifted his eyes to see everyone was staring at them. Tavir cleared his throat and stood upright. "Sorry. It's just..."

The high priest huffed with a grin. "She may not be an ambassador yet but you two obviously are still attracted to each other. So much so you have forgotten how ill both of your children have become?"

"Oh, I haven't forgotten," they said together.

The high priest nodded. "Go. I'll transport both of you to your room. Make love to her as long as you two need to clear your heads."

"Yes sir," Tavir said, picking K'Lara up in his arms. They kissed deeply then disappeared.

12

Soft light filled the large bedroom. Tavir sat on the edge of the bed with K'Lara on his lap. He couldn't believe she was actually here. Oh, thank the gods, she was here. They hadn't stopped kissing and groping each other since they had arrived into his elaborate bedroom only a few moments ago. He pulled away with a large grin, staring at the zipper of her cat suit. "You know a Dragon Master isn't supposed to sleep with the Ambassador," he said then gripped the zipper with his teeth and pulled it down exposing her large breasts.

"Fuck the rules," she snarled, pushing Tavir onto his back. She removed the top of her cat suit. Tavir pulled on her tit chain making her purr like a kitten.

"Gods, you must be soaking wet between your legs."

"Care to find out?"

Tavir grinned as she pulled down his pants, threw them to the side then removed her catsuit. Her gorgeous body hadn't aged a day since he saw her. He grabbed her by the waist as she threw her catsuit to the floor and pulled her underneath him. Tavir couldn't stand it any longer. He removed his shirt, threw it, lifted her legs and inserted his penis. She arched her back with a low moan of delight. She was so wet! He could feel the chains between her legs gently pull the lips even wider to give him more access. The more he thrust, the more she reacted with sensual moans and groans.

"Gods, I've missed this," Tavir exclaimed kissing her nipples.

With arms and legs embraced they kissed and rolled all over the bed, never completely satisfying their intense hunger for each other. Sweat lubricated their bodies. Heavy breathing, intense moans and groans filled the air. They just couldn't control themselves. Why should they? It had been over thirty years since they had last been together. Thirty years was a long time to wait when the love of your life couldn't be near you, especially when you had never physically been intimate, only your souls.

"Oh, K'Lara," he hissed as she rocked back and forth on his hips. He held his hands on her waist, never taking his eyes off his beloved. Gods, she was so magnificent. He loved to watch the tit chain on her breasts move back and forth as she madly pushed her ass against his hips. His hands slid to her thighs. Fingers found her clit. She screamed his name, rocking even faster and harder. She was a masterpiece.

"Oh, dear gods," she repeated in between her sensual groans. She breathed harder. "Yes, oh gods, yes!"

Tavir grinned, "You missed me?"

"You're so big!" Tavir chuckled. He wasn't about to let her have all the fun. He pushed her underneath him and slammed his penis deep inside her. "Oh, shit! Tavir, oh gods!" Tavir peered between her legs. Her silver cord had expanded towards her ass. "Ass plug," he questioned kissing her earlobe.

"Fuck yes. It's growing into a fucking full penis. I'm...oh...yes...hmm...feeling you and the dildo in my ass. Oh gods!"

"Hmm, I could have fun knowing your sex girdle still works."

K'Lara glared at him with a grin. "Do your worst, Tavir." She kissed him deeply. Arms and legs embraced they changed sexual positions several times only heightening their sexual encounter. Tavir moaned deeply with her on top. He was about to cum hard inside her. He just couldn't stand it any longer. The pressure was too great. He burst his seed inside at the same time she orgasmed. K'Lara silently grinned, pushing one last time to make certain all of him was inside her.

"Damn," Tavir muttered, staring at his ceiling as K'Lara lay beside him. She laid her head over his heart, rubbing her hand on his chest. Tavir wrapped his arm around her. He turned to her with a serious face. "Our children," he whispered.

K'Lara closed her eyes with a drawn out sigh. "Iona told me Tayla was in the temple with her and Kilean," she explained, opening her eyes. "I had no idea but I'm scared that the council will blame me for it."

"K'Lara, I will protect you."

"How? It wasn't me who helped her. I didn't even have access to my daughter when she went to the temple. I only reunited with her after she had received the dragon soul."

Tavir nodded. "I was with Kilean when it happened. The transfer occurred but he never received it. When he told me Tayla had the soul, I was confused. I asked Solon about it but he is as confused as I am. The council suspects me of treason."

"No," she gasped, rising up on her elbow. "Tavir...."

Tavir raised his hand to her cheek. "I doubt they do any longer. Why would the high priest release me if he thought I committed treason? Besides I believe Roan may be the one who is guilty of that and his disappearance might prove it."

"Disappearance?"

"His soul disappeared from the chamber while the high priest was interrogating him."

"But how?"

"I don't know."

"Where did he go?"

"I don't know that, either."

K'Lara exhaled a deep breath and rolled onto her back. "Lethos and Thalos told me that my sister disappeared from her punishment and is being held captive by Prince Zurggash."

Tavir rose on his elbow and leaned over her. "When was this?"

"She was taken while she was in custody of the God of the Dead."

"K'Lara, I'm so sorry. I didn't know."

She nodded. "It's all my fault that our world is falling apart. If I hadn't been so naïve then none of this would have happened."

"You can't take all the blame," he said turning her face towards him with his hand on her cheek. "I know everything about you, my love. You were hurt and extremely emotional due to your family circumstances at the time. It was your emotions that had blinded you to the truth. Now you are atoning for them, aren't you?"

"But our children are suffering because of me."

"Well, not entirely because of you. General Roan and Asa had a hand in what happened between us, did they not?"

"I suppose so but...Tavir...I'm scared for Iona. She's...well....she's not me."

"Good. I hate to think Kilean was sleeping with you. I might get a bit jealous."

K'Lara slapped her hand on his chest. "I mean Iona...her father didn't allow her to prepare for this. I did the best I could while I was alive but after my death, all hell broke loose in my kingdom. You just don't understand the terror Prince Zurrgash brought to my people. I'm worried about them."

"K'Lara, there has to be a way to help your daughter and save your kingdom."

"I have been trying to figure that out for some...." A knock on the door interrupted them.

"Mother," Iona's voice called gently from behind the wooden door.

Tavir rose to his feet, grabbed his robe and placed it on. He exchanged a look with K'Lara as she began to rise. He shook his head. K'Lara pulled the covers over her body. Tavir's robe covered his naked body leaving a portion of his body visible. A young, blonde woman dressed in white royal robes stared up at him with a look of astonishment. "K'Lara, what's with all the cloth on her body?" he asked, scanning the dress up and down.

"Nomiki raised her after I died. And not very well, might I add."

"Hmmphf," he nodded. Iona stared at his visible penis.

"Who are you?" Iona asked lifting her eyes to his.

Tavir smiled. "My name is King Tavir. My son is Kilean."

"Oh," Iona replied lightly, trying to avoid gazing at the slit of his robe. "I...ugh...I"

"Child, don't stutter. I know the relationship you have with my son. It is the same I have with your mother. Come inside."

Tavir glanced at K'Lara with a look of disapproval as Iona walked into the bedroom. He closed the door while K'Lara tapped the bed beside her. "I thought you were sick, sweetie?" K'Lara asked, holding Iona.

"I was but when I woke I was completely healed. I asked for you. The elves attending me said you were in here with your lover?"

K'Lara smiled. "Tavir is the former Dragon Lord."

"Oh," Iona gasped looking at Tavir then back to her mother. "So he's the one...uhm...you did...uhm."

"The one I had sex with in the Plains of the Dreams?" Iona nodded. "Yes. He's my soul mate. My true love. We didn't think the physical bond between us had remained but obviously it did."

"Very obvious," Tavir grinned.

"Why would the bond break? Can it?" Iona asked.

"It can," Tavir explained walking to the foot of the bed. "The bonding of the dragon souls unites our souls with the dragons. But it leaves an unquenchable thirst to have sex in the physical realm with each other. That is relieved during the Rite of Dragons. But should the Dragon Lord and Dragon Lady not bond during that ceremony the sexual energy withheld drives them insane until one dies, leaving the other depressed."

"That's what happened to you?" Iona asked her mother.

"Yes. I thought my illness and death would have been sooner. I'm grateful it wasn't so I could have had some time with you."

Iona swallowed hard. "If Kilean and I don't...how is it then that you two needed to have...uhmm...?"

"Sex," Tavir offered.

"Yeah," she whispered.

Tavir shook his head. "I don't know, Iona. Nothing makes sense. The bonds between us should have been severed and our illnesses should have occurred much earlier but it's almost as if we are being protected somehow."

K'Lara grinned. "Whoever it is, I would love to thank them for letting THAT happened between us. Damn, Tavir. It was better then we had in the Plains of the Dreams."

Tavir smiled. "Too bad we can't do it again."

"Why not?" Iona asked, looking between the two of them.

"She's not my mate, yet," Tavir explained. "Shit, you're General Roan Tharg's mate."

K'Lara sighed, "I wouldn't want him to fuck me for anything. I would only do so out of duty. That traitor ruined our lives and what does that council do but make me Iona's Dragon Master matching me with him!"

Tavir shook his head, turned away from her and cussed to himself. "You will have to bond with him when Iona and Kilean complete the ceremony."

"Ugh, Tavir, don't remind me."

"How fortunate for you he doesn't have a body."

"Tavir, we can't ignore that Roan has disappeared."

"No, and when the council finds him he may find himself in more trouble than he's already in."

"Mother," Iona called to her mother. K'Lara turned to her daughter. "How do you become King Tavir's mate?"

"I have to prove to the council I am worthy enough to become your ambassador. Which isn't going to be easy to do."

"Where are we? My dragon twins have disappeared. I saw Kilean beside me. He's very ill."

"Deathly," Tavir answered, pouring wine with his back to them.

"How can we save him?"

"I don't know, Iona. The only way to do so is to retrieve his dragon soul. We know Tayla has it. We suspect General Roan Tharg is involved but to what extent, we can't determine. He and Asa have disappeared. Wine?" he explained then asked, holding a glass out to her.

Iona shook her head. "I don't drink."

Tavir laughed, placing the glass down. K'Lara threw a throw pillow at him with a serious look. He sighed, picking the pillow up and threw it on his side of the bed. "Nomiki," she warned him.

"Ah, I'm sorry Iona. You must know I didn't choose him for her. General Roan killed the man I chose to be your mother's mate then presented Nomiki to your mother. She couldn't recognize him for who he was. It separated us and our kingdoms."

"Are you alive?" Iona asked as Tavir sat in a chair next to the bed.

Tavir nodded. "I am. I never died but I was seriously ill, mentally and physically. The headaches were severe. My mind felt as if it would burst from my skull. It stopped ten years ago."

"Mother died," she whispered.

"Yes. I do hope that you and Kilean can survive long enough to save each other."

K'Lara wiped her hands down her face with a drawn out breath. "Tavir, if my daughter is awake. The council will know of it soon. They'll want to interrogate her. And..."

"Stop it," he demanded, rising from his chair and lowering the glass of wine to the table. "I will not let us be separated or our children's lives be placed in jeopardy."

"I'm already being punished!"

"It's a second chance, K'Lara. They aren't going to separate us. We were created to be together just as our children are. They know that!"

"What if they decide to start all over?"

"Oh, please. You're overthinking the situation. Our world is falling apart. The dragon population has seriously declined since we were separated. Think of the hope that lies in which we are together helping the new Dragon Lord and Lady. You want to redeem yourself so we can live together then you know what you have to do. You have to help our daughter and son unite."

"What does he mean live together? Aren't you two together now," Iona asked?

"No, sweetie," K'Lara explained. "When the previous Dragon Lord and Lady become Ambassadors they are given the honor of dwelling together as husband and wife. The council allowed Tavir and I to mate because the urges inside us were too hard to ignore. But there will come a time when I will have to leave his bedroom and never be with him again until I prove that I am worthy enough to assume my rightful place at his side."

"So in order to save your relationship, Kilean and I have to set things right?"

"No," Tavir answered. "You do."

"Me?" Iona questioned. "But how can I do that? I don't even know anything about this world and the laws that govern it."

"Listen to your mother, Iona. She can guide you. You have to help the council retrieve Kilean's Dragon Soul then complete the Rite of Dragons with him. It's the only way to save our world."

"But I don't even know where to start."

"We have to go back, Tavir. The council was holding the dragon twins. Perhaps, they have the answers from them that we seek."

"Hmm," Tavir nodded. "I want to visit upon my son first." He turned to Iona. "The council had your hands clasped together. Did you feel anything from Kilean?"

"No, should I?" Iona asked.

"Damn," K'Lara and Tavir cussed together. K'Lara rose from the bed, grabbed her catsuit and hastly placed it on.

"How long do you think they have?" K'Lara asked.

"Solon said five days but that shouldn't have happened so soon."

"Maybe it's my daughter?"

"K'Lara that's nonsense, they have already been in communication telepathically. Why stop now?"

"Maybe..."

"What did I miss?" Iona asked firmly, stepping between the couple.

K'Lara sighed, placing her hand on her daughter's shoulder. "Kilean's soul is attached to your own, that's how you were able to telepathically communicate with him. The telepathy is a gift from his soul. When you are given a dragon soul it merges with your own but it doesn't completely change whom you are. It just enhances it. In the beginning there was one Dragon Rider soul but it split into male and female. Every generation that dragon soul reproduces into male and female form. The Dragon Lord and Dragon Lady can sense each other because they are technically of one soul. If you can't feel Kilean then his part of the soul is lost."

"But he's...what?"

"I don't have time to explain, daughter. Go back to Kilean. Hold

him. Kiss him. Do whatever it takes. Just get his attention!" She looked to Tavir. "We have to approach the council."

"Indeed," Tavir replied with a serious tone. "The sooner the better. Go, Iona. Now!"

Iona nodded, turned and ran out of the room. Tavir picked up his clothes, dressed then walked swiftly out of the bedroom with his beloved. Hoping to the gods, they weren't too late to save his son.

13

Drokap Castle – Kingdom of Saloron

Darkness consumed the small cell in the back of the catacombs with a slight green light spilling gently through the slit below his cell door. For the first time in his life, Kilean wished he didn't have the soul of a Dragon Lord. Unlike, any other creature in the known world, the soul of the Dragon Lady or Dragon Lord was an extension of the host's body. He could see, feel, touch and do anything else as if he was in his body. Kilean shivered, sitting naked on the floor with his arms wrapped around his legs. He thought he could hear the screams of other captives crying for help in between their blood curdling yells for mercy. The rich stench of blood, vomit, and his excretions filled the air. He knew his body was suffering from Soul Sickness but wondered what would happen if he was united with the Silver Dragon Soul while his own soul was badly beaten. Would his body suffer?

Kilean peered up at the walls surrounding him. No light. No window. It was hard to tell how much time had passed since his soul made the journey from his body to this dreadful place. He lowered his head with a drawn out sigh. He couldn't give into the despair. His eyes lifted to the torture table in the middle of his cell. Dark stains of his own blood upon the marble table reminded him of the intense session he had with his unknown interrogator. Deep bruises and cuts littered his almost broken body. Every muscle ached in protest to the harsh treatments he had endured from an invisible force. He had tried to identify his interrogator numerous times but the only clue he had was an invisible entity subjecting him to unspeakable methods of torture and a deep male voice. Somehow he had to get a message to Iona. Perhaps, if she knew where he was, she could think of a way to save him. Whoever was holding his soul captive didn't want to kill him but make him so weak he couldn't escape back to his body.

A sharp clanging sound of a door opening caught his attention. He quickly stood, aggravating his many wounds.

"What do you want?" Kilean screamed, running towards the door only to be jerked backwards by the green energy chain connecting his right ankle with the wall. It vibrated as it gleaned more energy from his soul. Kilean fell to his hands and knees, struggling to breathe. He lowered his head and shook it. "No more. Oh please, dear Gods, no more." He collapsed on the ground, barely able to stand, the chain increasing the ferocity of his energy pull. He pressed his forehead on the hard, firm ground. Kilean closed his eyes praying desperately for it all to end. Just how long were his captors going to keep him here? What would happen to his soul once his body died?

Kilean stared at the green glow of candlelight illuminating from the sconce next to the door. He couldn't recall how many times he had studied the cavern, trying to come up with an escape plan. But it was always useless. The more he fought his restraints the more energy they took from him. He lowered his head with a drawn out sigh. He couldn't give up. His people depended upon him. He needed Iona. He couldn't feel his legs. He thought he felt his breathing, maybe even his soul's heart?

The wooden door clanked. He thought he was just imaging the sound. He lifted his weary eyes to see a man and a woman stand before him. The humanoid woman with large purple dragon wings extending out of her lean back walked behind the man. Tayla closed the door behind Prince Zurggash and locked them in.

"Prince Kilean Dragonmoon. I am honored to meet your acquaintance," Prince Zurggash gloated holding a large wooden box in his hand.

"Who are you?" Kilean asked staring up at the muscular man.

"Oh well, Tayla, did you hear that? He doesn't know who I am."

Tayla grinned, crouching before Kilean. She lifted the young prince's chin with her hand. "What do they teach Dragon Lord's these days? Tsk tsk, such a shame that you don't know your own history, boy. This mighty ruler is Prince Zurggash and I am Ta…."

"Tayla the Damned," Kilean finished then spit on her face.

"Well, well. How is that you know me but not my husband?"

"Fuck you!"

"I believe we already did that. You are a wonderful lover but nothing like my nephew."

Kilean growled moving away from her but she wouldn't release her tight grip on his chin. She raised him in the air one handed looking up and down his body then threw him backwards with a mighty roar. His back thumped hard against the wall. He slid down, dazed and confused.

"Bring him to the table. I wouldn't want our pet to attack his master," Prince Zurggash ordered.

Kilean shook his head and came to his senses just as his body appeared on the marble table.

"No," He protested as the chain wrapped around the length of his arms and up his legs to his waist, pinning him down. He arched his back, trying to free himself but the chains only made him weaker.

Tayla stood behind him with her talon fingers lightly stroking the side of his head. He heaved knowing what would come next. He had felt those talons before. So these were his interrogators. There hadn't been just one but two. He lifted his eyes to the humanoid dragon twin then screamed out in pain as she dug her talon deep within his mind.

"Find the information I seek, Tayla. I'm growing quite bored with his answers," Prince Zurggash ordered.

"Gladly," she replied then pushed deeper into Kilean's mind. Oh Gods, the pain! The piercing pain! His couldn't breath. He couldn't think. He couldn't see. Was he screaming? Images flashed through his mind as she shifted through his brain. He had to protect the Draconian secrets. The more he fought her advances the deeper she pushed. He was screaming. That had to be his voice he was hearing. Oh Gods, when was this all going to end?

"Enough. Don't kill him," Prince Zurggash ordered, waving his hand.

Tayla ripped her talons out of her victim's mind. Kilean heaved, wanting to vomit from the entire experience. He stared up at the tall curved ceiling not able to think. At least he didn't need to think in order to breath or for his heart to work. He could hear his captors talking but .....

"Kilean," Iona's voice broke through his gaze. Could it be? Had Tayla done something to make it easier for him to communicate with Iona?

"Iona," he thought, ignoring his captors' conversation.

"Where are you?"

"I don't know. Help! Oh Gods, help me. I'm badly hurt."

"Your body seized."

"How are you near my body?"

"I'm at the temple. I met your father. I can sense you but I can't see you."

"Tayla. I'm being held captive by Tayla and Prince Zurggash. Tell my father. I'm in an ancient cave. Green lighting… as big as if a dragon can fit in here. There are others here. I can hear them being tortured but can't see them. Iona. Help me. Please, help me. I'm being tortured."

"I need more …." The connection between them suddenly broke. He pounded the back of his head out of frustration. Tayla and Prince Zurggash were still talking without taking notice of him. Thankfully, they didn't know he had been talking to Iona. At least there was hope.

"Prince Kilean Dragonsun," Prince Zurggash greeted approaching the table with the box in his hand. "You are quite stronger than I had expected. Tayla tells me that she can't glean the information I seek from tapping into your mind. One would wonder if you're part elf."

"My mother is elven."

"Ah, that's explains it," Tayla said, walking next to her lover. "I would have never suspected Queen K'Lara to have chosen an elven priestess for his father. But it does make sense. There are rumors that K'Lara was learning to become an enchantress before her sister died."

"Why doesn't he show the markings of an elf, then?"

"Human and Elven DNA mixed together are quite strange it can create a halfling, human or elf. In this case, it had to be human because no matter what race a Dragon Lord or Dragon Lady is mixed with they will always be human."

"Interesting. You will give me what I seek, Dragon Lord."

"I will never serve you!" Kilean yelled then spit in the prince's face.

"He's still a bit feisty for everything I did to him," Tayla said, rubbing her hands on Prince Zurggash's chest from behind with a close eye on Kilean.

"Do what you want with me. I will never…," Kilean paused as Prince Zurggash opened the box he held. A silvery glowing orb spilled soft silver light towards Kilean. Kilean stared at the magical orb, fully relaxing under its soothing embrace. It glowed, warming his soul with energy, wanting to merge with his own soul yet unable to do so from its own captivity. Kilean stood straighter, taking in what little the dragon soul could offer him. He breathed in the scent as if it was life it itself.

"That's enough," Prince Zurggash claimed, closing the box and locking it with magic. Kilean's spirit returned to its weakened state. He sagged with his head lowered. "If you want more of that then you will give me what I seek."

"Never," Kilean pushed out.

"Dear boy, don't be stupid. It's so beneath you." The prince nodded to Tayla. He watched her as she roared loudly, fully expanding her wings then muttered in an ancient language so soft Kilean couldn't hear her words. The chains tightened. Tayla grasped him hard from the shoulders and ripped her talons down his body. He screamed as her claws shredded his torso stopping at his waist. She pushed him down and bit him hard on the stomach, clenching her teeth deep in his gut. His eyes bulged at the sheer pain. She couldn't kill his soul. Not as long as his body was alive, but damn! His lungs burned. It was hard to breath. Her teeth had cut into his stomach and gut. His body shook uncontrollably with shock and pain. Tayla rose over him, licking the blood from her lips and hands.

"I bet he wishes he was dead," she sung thoroughly enjoying her masterpiece.

"Let's try this again, shall we," Prince Zurggash said, holding Kilean's chin with his hand. "Now," Prince Zurggash said, handing the box to Tayla. "You're going to say the spell that will transfer the dragon soul's desire to merge with your soul to mine."

"I don't know what you're talking about."

"I told you not to be stupid," the prince yelled, tightening his grasp on Kilean's chin. "There will come a time when your body dies and I will kill you if you continue to play games with me!"

"I'm look forward to my death, asshole!"

"Tayla," Prince Zurggash grinned, releasing Kilean's face.

Tayla spread her wings and transformed into a large dragon. She flew above him and slammed her foot on his torso, breaking every bone. Kilean gasped. His blood had splattered all over the table. The pain! It was almost too much to bear. She landed with a thump as he stared dazed and confused into nothing. He could vaguely hear his interrogators.

"A bit too much, my love," Prince Zurggash commented, examining Kilean's body.

"Oh, too hard? Hmm, maybe I should try again," she spoke.

"No, no. He's coming around."

"Such a pity, I so wanted to play," she said, transforming back into her human self.

Kilean gazed between them, fearful what they would do to him next but determined not to give into them.

"It would be in your best interest not to keep lying to me, Prince

Kilean Dragonsun. My aunt wants to play. I wouldn't wish that on my worst enemy," Prince Zurggash whispered the last part. "Now, let's try this again, shall we? The Silver Dragon Soul. I possess it but I can't use it as long as it wants to merge with your own soul. I have tried numerous spells. Nothing works. My only choice is for the transfer spell to be casted but I can't do that without you," the prince quietly said. "Be a good boy and help me."

"I can't."

"You can't or won't?"

"I don't know it."

"Tsk, tsk. Wrong answer. Tayla, burn him," the prince commanded.

"No," Kilean protested loudly as he and Tayla changed places. She opened her mouth and breathed fire on his legs, methodically moving up his body. She made certain to only give him light burns but still it was enough to almost drive him mad.

"Are you done being difficult?" Prince Zurggash asked as Tayla backed away.

"I can't give you what I don't have! The Dragon Lord's soul merges with the Silver Dragon Soul until the time comes for a new Dragon Lord. It leaves the old Dragon Lord and merges with the new."

"Common knowledge, Dragon Lord. What I want is the knowledge of the soul you possess that you would never tell another person."

"I...I...I don't know what you're talking about. That's all I know about the dragon souls."

"Tsk, tsk, you are going to make this harder than it has to be, aren't you?"

"I swear on all the Holy Draconian Orders I know nothing more than what I'm telling you."

"You're more of an idiot than I thought you to be, then. Do you know why your body has Soul Sickness?"

"Tayla stole the soul from me."

"True but there's more to it than that. Soul Sickness isn't a punishment. It's a side effect of the intense need both you and the Dragon Soul have to merge. Sometimes, it has rarely happened but I know it has at least ten different times in history, either the Dragon Lord or Dragon Lady is physically or mentally too weak to go through the Bonding of Dragon Souls ceremony. In that case, they develop Soul Sickness. While they suffer, their Dragon Master and Guardian chose someone from the warrior caste to replace him. In fact, it was your great-grandfather who was chosen to replace his former Dragon Lord when the Dragon Lord's son was ill with a very deadly strain of Meloxian Syndrome. You wouldn't be the new Dragon Lord had that man lived through that disease."

"I know the story but I don't know what he did to make the transfer. Honest."

"This is pointless," Tayla sighed, placing the box on her hip. Prince Zurggash looked up at her then back to Kilean.

"The spell, Kilean. I won't ask so nicely next time."

"I...don't...know...it," he emphasized every word.

The prince growled loudly, rising to his feet. He swiped his hand sending a large brick across Kilean's face, breaking his nose. The brick disappeared. Kilean gasped. The prince kicked him in the head, sending Kilean backwards screaming. He moved his large foot down to Kilean's neck and pressed his foot on it, causing Kilean to scramble for a breath.

"St...uh...op," Kilean pushed out, pounding the prince's foot.

"Tell me the spell then I'll think about it."

"Guardian...my guardian keeps it hidden...hmm...no Dragon Master is allowed...to...hmm...know the spell.... we...might...misuse it. It...changes...from one...Dragon Lord...to another. So...even if I ...did...know...of one...it might...not...work...for me."

Prince Zurggash removed his foot with a snarl. "Torture him as much as you want, my love. He's all yours," he said, taking the box from her. "Just remember you can't kill him. His soul will remain until the body dies. Have fun," he grinned and kissed her. Kilean heaved at the monstrous sight of Tayla as Prince Zurggash disappeared from the cavern.

"This is going to be fun, Dragon Lord," Talon grinned.

For the first time, Kilean felt his heart beat.

14   Temple of the Sun

Iona ran as fast as she could down the elaborate hallway with no idea where she was going. Twisting, turning, it seemed wherever she went the hallways took her someplace she didn't want to go. Her mind raced with overwhelming concern for Kilean. His voice had sounded weaker than usual and filled with great fear. What kind of things were Tayla and Prince Zurggash doing to him? Horrible images filled her mind. Tears strolled down her cheeks. She hadn't known Kilean for long but she knew she loved him. She couldn't imagine life without her Dragon Lord.

"Oof," she reacted bumping into someone, stepping back and looking up to see who was in her way.

"Iona," her mother's voice startled her.

"Mother," she cried, fully embracing her, sobbing profusely.

K'Lara looked at Tavir then back to her daughter. "We've been looking all over for you. The council needs to speak to you. Drayson went to the healing chamber but you weren't there. He returned claiming such, which only frustrated the council. They sent Lethos, Thalos, Tavir and I to find you along with half a dozen guards."

Iona lifted her head, heaving. "I'm sorry. I was trying to find the council chamber."

Tavir stated, "You can't. It's hidden by magic. The only way to enter is to possess the magic it takes to open the portal. Why aren't you with my son?"

"I was. He said to find you."

"He's awake?"

Iona shook her head, "No, I reconnected with him."

"That's great news, sweetie," K'Lara smiled.

"No, you don't understand. I could speak to him telepathically but I couldn't see his body. I really wish I could. I feel useless. He told me things but I can't figure out where he is."

"Where he is?" Tavir asked.

"Tayla and Prince Zurggash, they're torturing his soul. His body seized several times. The healers say he is only becoming weaker."

"Tavir, that would explain why his condition is accelerating," K'Lara explained to her lover with urgency.

"Where?" Tavir demanded to Iona.

"I don't know. He…he…he said he's in an ancient cavern with green lights. The cavern's big enough to hold a dragon. He also said he can hear others but can't see them," Iona explained.

"You don't think…." K'Lara started.

"…he wouldn't…"

"…he might. We never could find him and that place is protected by the dragon magic that only a dragon twin possesses. Tayla could have opened the portal for him."

Tavir pivoted and ran back down the hall yelling, "Drayson! Drayson!"   Iona stared down the hallway until the panic stricken king disappeared around a corner. She turned back to her mother. "You know where he is?"

"We might but we have to return to the council first." K'Lara wiped the tears from Iona face. "You felt his emotions in there?"

Iona nodded. "He's terrified. They're doing something to his mind, mother. I don't know what but it's affecting our ability to communicate with each other. I don't want to lose him. I love him."

K'Lara placed her hands around her daughter's face. "The council will do everything they can to help him. You have to trust in them."

"But you don't, do you?"

K'Lara swallowed hard. "I have no choice. Iona, I made decisions in my life when I was in your stage that caused so many problems. I have to atone for them or risk losing my life. The council holds my fate in their hands."

"It's not fair."

"Be careful of your words, daughter. The council doesn't trust you, yet. You are my daughter and in their eyes the problems we face now are only an extension of what I started."

"But I want to be the Dragon Lady. I want to help set things right."

"Tavir and I believe you but it's going to take time to convince the council that you are able to lead. They are confused as we all are as to why Tavir and I still are attracted to each other and why you are able to be Dragon Lady. There are many things that have happened that don't make sense to them and they are flustered because they don't have all the answers. Yet, it is their responsibility to ensure the next Dragon Lady and Dragon Lord are prepared for their duties. Just do whatever they ask from you."

"Princess Iona," Drayson's voice echoed down the hallway.

K'Lara lowered her hands and stepped to the side. The elegant, elven commanding officer bowed before her as Tavir stepped beside K'Lara. "King Tavir has informed me of the situation," Drayson said rising to full statue. "Can you tell me anything else?"

Iona shook her head, "I didn't see anything. I only felt his feelings. He's terrified and confused. We tried to speak further but the connection between us was severed abruptly."

"Did you feel anything before that happened?"

"Only his emotions."

"Drayson?" Tavir asked.

The elven commander turned to face the couple. "I don't know. It sounds like they are torturing his mind not his soul but that should be protected by the Dragon Lord soul and if it is his mind they are focusing on then Iona's mind should be affected as well."

"Because we are of one soul?" Iona asked.

"Yes," he answered her then turned back to the couple. "It could be that the Soul Sickness is protecting her from feeling the same fate. I'm sorry. I don't have any more answers than that."

"Saloron," K'Lara muttered.

"Sounds like a hold in Drokap Castle," Tavir stated.

"What is that?" Iona questioned the trio.

"An ancient castle the dragons once held where they tortured humans and the other races during the War of the Dragons in order to gather vital information from their enemies. The magical properties of that place are so dangerous that Draco and Razil hid it from all the races after the war was over," Drayson explained.

Tavir closed his eyes taking a deep breath. "That place," he started. Drayson placed his hand on the king's forearm. Tavir opened his eyes.

"We will find him."

"That place. The magic it holds. My son's soul is as corporal as his body. He...he may never be right in the..."

"Tavir, we won't let that happen. I promise you."

"But how are you going to find it? It moves from time and place so no one can ever access it. I don't understand how Tayla even found it to begin with."

"I'm not concerned with that at the moment. What I am more concerned with is finding your son and healing his mind and soul. We cannot lose the Dragon Lord."

Tavir nodded.

"Holy mother of the gods," K'Lara exclaimed with an abrupt thought. The men turned their attention to her.

"Queen K'Lara?" Drayson asked.

K'Lara grabbed Iona by the arms and looked squarely at her. "Think real hard, Iona. You possess the Golden Dragon Soul. It would have connected with the Silver Dragon Soul. We know Tayla has it. Did you feel it when you were there?"

"Mother?" she asked.

"Answer her. I think I know where she is going with her thoughts," Drayson persuaded.

"I was only focusing on him. I didn't...I mean it felt normal as it always has except he was terrified...I...I...I'm sorry...I don't know how to tell between my own soul connecting with Kilean than my dragon soul doing so."

K'Lara released her hands and turned to Drayson. "Is there a way she can call for the Golden Dragon?"

"I don't know. I've never heard of a Dragon Lady doing so before she has physically bonded with the Dragon Lord."

"But," Tavir interrupted. "The Golden and Silver Dragon Souls are always united. They should be able to connect telepathically, shouldn't they?"

"The Silver Dragon Soul isn't in a body," K'Lara said.

"How do you know that?" Tavir asked.

"Because Tayla and Prince Zurggash are torturing your son and I would bet they are only doing so because they need the Dragon Soul Transfer Spell."

Tavir grinned, "I had forgotten about that."

"What is that?" Iona asked.

"He wouldn't have that information," Drayson said. "Only my ... shit. You don't think Kilean would have told them where to find it do you?"

"Kilean doesn't have a weak disposition due to his mother's elven blood but push my son too hard and he might. He's more human than a halfling."

"Humans are the weaker of all the races. Shit! Solon wasn't in the healing chamber and I have no idea where he went."

"Could he be meditating," K'Lara asked.

"Perhaps so, but if he is he won't be anywhere he's so easily found."

"What?" Iona asked confused as Drayson turned, said a spell in ancient elven so low they could barely hear him. Iona glanced between the couple and Drayson. "I don't understand."

"It doesn't matter right now, Princess Iona. Get in the chamber. Your mother will explain in there," Drayson said in front of the opened portal.

K'Lara took Iona's hand. "Come," she said guiding them inward. Iona turned back as they crossed the barrier.

"You will find Solon," Tavir asked.

"I will. Go and tell the council what you've learned. I may know where my brother is. We will find and heal your son, Tavir. You have my word."

Tavir clasped Drayson's forearm. "Thank you," he said then walked into the portal.

15

Iona paced inside the large council chamber, anxiously awaiting the arrival of Solon and his half-brother, Drayson, ignoring the constant chattering between the council members. It seemed like hours since she had told her mother, King Tavir and Drayson of Kilean's location. They had all rushed into the magical chamber, informed the council of what she knew and then after much debate she was asked to call forth the Golden Dragon Soul. She had tried everything she could think of, even accepting help from all the races to do so. But in the end, nothing had worked.

Iona lifted her eyes to Vashti. The large female dragon sat proudly watching Iona carefully. Iona swallowed hard at the sight of Vashti's yellow eyes. At first Vashti had scared her. She had never seen a real dragon before, well except for when the Silver Dragon Soul had approached her. Her father had told her plenty of stories of dragons devouring humans and causing mass carnage. She could still remember the terrible nightmares she had had of dragons killing her entire family and massacring her people. It was hard to trust Vashti because of them. But she had to. Amidst those memories were delightful ones filled with Kilean telling her wonderful things about his dragon. Vashti and Kilean shared a deep connection that only a dragon rider and his dragon could ever have. She respected Vashti only because of that relationship.

"How did you contact Kalesh the first time?" Sina asked beside Thalos and Lethos.

Iona shook her head. "She came to me."

"Think, Iona, what were you doing when she did so?" K'Lara asked on the other side of the chamber standing next to Tavir.

"I...I...I was...mother..." she huffed.

"Great gods," Tavir exclaimed. "Did it have something to do with sex?"

Iona opened her mouth then closed it. "Don't be so embarrassed. You're the Dragon Lady, for gods' sake. Everyone knows you're a very seductive woman that needs constant sex!"

Iona swallowed hard. "Speak up, child," the high priest encouraged.

Iona stepped turned in circles, peering at everyone. She exhaled a deep breath, staring up at High Priest Aejeon Trajeon. "I had emerged from the Draconia Temple of the Gods from a very satisfying encounter with Kilean and Tayla. My body was craving more from Kilean. I was desperate for his touch. A dragon dildo appeared beside me. I used it and was thinking of Kilean while doing so. I was pleading for him to join me. The experience was intense. I ended up on the floor, doggy style and double stuffed. I came really hard. Afterwards, Kalesh appeared and told me who she was. She had apologized for the intense desire to mate because I am untrained. She said I have to be careful with my desires until I can be fully trained."

Thalos stepped forward and asked, "When you were with us she didn't appear?"

"No. The only time I have heard her voice or seen her was with that encounter." Silence filled the chamber as everyone exchanged glances. "What?" she asked breaking the silence.

"Could it be possible?" King Tavir asked the high priest.

"What?" Iona asked.

Aejeon Trajeon shook his head. "I have never heard of it but the souls are sensitive to each other."

"But," Sina interrupted. "Why would Kalesh apologize for the urges she is facing unless...?"

"...she can't control them herself." Thalos finished.

"I don't understand. Aren't the dragons supposed to be superior to humans in all matter?" Iona said, approaching the council.

"Normally, they are, but that is in a world where female and male energies are in balance. The Dragon Lord and Dragon Lady have not been so since your mother was unable to complete the transition." Aejeon answered.

"But, I'm here now," Iona protested. "Shouldn't that mean the worlds are balanced?"

"No, your highness. While it is true that you and Prince Kilean's souls have been united, you still have not balanced the male and female sexual energies. That cannot happen unless both the Silver and Gold Dragon Souls take their place within their respective hosts and the hosts have endured all the rituals that are demanded upon them before they assume their place. Kalesh is unbalanced because her mate does not dwell inside Kilean. We have never had this happen before, Princess Iona. Your mother and Kilean's father had completed the Bonding of Dragon Souls."

"So...Kalesh is fixated on mating with her half?"

"Seems so."

"There may be a way of contacting Kalesh," Lethos said approaching the small group. Everyone turned towards him. "Iona said her body was reacting to the effects of the orgy she had in the temple and the only way she could eliminate it was for Kalesh to provide a vibrator while she was thinking of Kilean. What if we lured Kalesh out by recreating that event?"

"We don't have Kilean," Thalos countered.

"No, no. I don't think we need Kilean," King Tavir interjected.

"Tavir?" K'Lara asked.

"All your daughter has to do is believe she had that encounter. The power of the mind is a strong thing. Just merely watching sex can cause one to experience an orgasm."

"True, but mainly so in humans. They are the weaker of all creatures," Aejeon agreed.

"I propose we use the Dragon Twins to recreate the circumstances with Iona. When she cums hard and is left wanting more, we abandon her to her mind. Then she can be seduced by her own desires, Kalesh will have no choice but to soothe her in order to keep Iona from losing her mind."

"A female dragon twin is forbidden from having sex with the Dragon Lady."

King Tavir slowly approached the podium. "Aejeon, these are not normal times. The Dragon Twins were created to help the Dragon Riders heal in all manners; physically, sexually, emotionally and mentally. We cannot find my son without Kalesh's help and we can't draw upon her help without the Dragon Twins. We have Sina, Thalos and Lethos. Let this occur, please. I beg you not only as father to father but as the Dragon Lord's ambassador. If the gods of the races should object I will soothe them. Please, Aejeon."

The grey haired, noble elf peered at Iona with longing eyes. "It will only work if you consent to it and you must not see the Dragon Twins in your mind but that of Kilean and Tayla."

Iona swallowed hard. "To have sex in front of...."

"Iona," the tall, stern elf leaned on his forearms. "You will always have sex in front of people. It is part of being a Dragon Lady. And you won't always have sex with Kilean, either. There are certain responsibilities that you must abide by as Dragon Lady. What we are asking of you is not something that is out of pure voyeurism. It is your duty. Your mother once disregarded her duties as Dragon Lady. Will you follow in her footsteps?"

K'Lara walked swiftly in front of her daughter and pushed Iona behind her. "That isn't fair!"

"Queen K'Lara this conversation has nothing to do with you."

"But it does. Her father never taught her our ways. You can't punish her for my mistakes."

"It will not be your mistake if she chooses not to abide by her duties. But it will prove that the Dragon Lady's bloodline is tainted."

K'Lara heaved, shaking her head. She turned quickly towards her daughter, placed her hands on Iona's upper arms and looked sternly in her daughter's eyes. "You have to do this. Don't worry about what I think of you. Just do whatever they are asking from you."

"Mother," Iona whimpered. "It's not .... I mean....to have sex in front of my mother."

"Iona," K'Lara sneered, tightening her grip. "You don't understand. If our bloodline is deemed tainted then the council will kill both of us and find another to replace us. It won't be a clean, painless death, either. Trust me. It is rare for the council to ever take such action against a noble lineage but it has been done before. I think only once and it was a very, very, very long time ago. I have heard stories. Now, do what they want. Don't protest. I love you," K'Lara sternly instructed, kissed Iona on the forehead, then walked back to Tavir.

Iona swallowed hard. She stared around the room taking in everyone's gaze at her. All she wanted was Kilean but to do so this way seemed so unnatural. Then again, much of what she had been through since she appeared in these lands had seemed unnatural to her. Every time she had spoken to Kilean about her concerns he just reassured her it was alright. She wondered what Kilean would tell her now. He'd probably just reassure her and tell her to have fun with it. Fun. Well she couldn't deny she had absolutely enjoyed all the experiences she had had so far.

"Your highness," Aejeon called to her. Iona lifted her eyes to the elevated platform where the high priest and council sat. "Your decision?"

"I will do so."

"Good," Aejeon rose from his place. "The sexual energies emitted from the Dragon Lady are too intense to ignore. The council members have taken a vow of purity and my wife is not here to join me. We will leave the chamber. Vashti," he called to the dragon.

"High priest," the dragon's head nodded with respect.

"You will remain my eyes and ears throughout the entire procedure. Should Kalesh appear and open the portal. All will enter except you. Contact me telepathically once they have stepped through the portal and it has closed."

"I will."

"Good." He looked down to Iona, K'Lara, Thalos, Lethos, King Tavir and Sina. "Be safe in your journey."

"Thank you," they answered.

"We will need a bed," Thalos said to the high priest.

"And bondage," Iona provided. All stared at her. "We used the straps. And there were sex toys. We used them, too."

Aejeon smiled briefly at her. "There is hope for you yet, Princess Iona." He waved his hand. An elegant king sized bed appeared in the middle of the chamber with leather straps on the tops and bottom of the bed. A long table with a variety of sex toys appeared beside it. Two more beds and tables with sex toys laid on either side of the room. "Have fun. Your bed and toys will disappear when you are finished. You will have to have ten orgasms before it does so, just as it was in the ceremony, each harder than before."

"Agreed."

"High Priest," Sina called to Aejeon. The elegant elf nodded in her direction. "What of the Dragon Twin she doesn't choose. He will need to be satisfied. We have a former Dragon Lady and Dragon Lord. Could they, since we are having an orgasm, satisfy him?"

"It is most highly irregular to do so, Sina."

"I understand but this isn't normal, either. Surely, the gods wouldn't want a Dragon Twin to be corrupted."

"Your sister has already been so."

"And shall we lose another by depriving him of what he needs in order to maintain the balance he has with his brother?"

High Priest Aejeon looked at the small company then back to Sina.

"He only participates with King Tavir and Queen K'Lara during the reenactment. Afterwards you take care of them while she masturbates."

"Agreed. Thank you."

"You're welcome."

Iona watched as the council members and elves disappeared.

"Well then, shall we get started?" Sina asked as the group gathered around her. "Which Dragon Twin do you want, Iona?"

"She was very appreciative of the efforts I made upon her body while my brother was away," Thalos grinned.

"Only after she wasn't scared of your dracnoid body," Lethos argued slapping his brother's chest.

"I, ugh, I," Iona grinned. "I really like both of you but Thalos excited me more because he's not human but then again, Kilean is human so maybe..."

Sina stepped closer. "Iona, it doesn't matter who is more human. The more you like him the easier it will be for you to associate him with Kilean. Kilean is an amazing lover."

"I forgot you have had sex with him," Iona sighed.

Sina placed her hand on Iona's arm. "Don't let that hinder you from doing what needs to be done. Kilean loves you. My sexual relationship with him is only out of duty. I am his servant just as Lethos and Thalos are yours. We were created to serve in all capacities in order to heal the Dragon Lord and Dragon Lady." Sina removed her clothes and dropped them to the floor. Iona stared at the humanoid's large breasts. They were enormous! Sina placed her hands underneath her breasts and pushed them upwards. "Kilean drinks from these just as you feed from your Dragon Twins penis. There is nothing wrong with what we are, Iona, nor is there anything wrong with the relationship we have with our rider. It is the way of things. Now," she said lowering her hands. Iona stared at Sina's tit rings, the chain between them, peered at the hip chain then lifted her eyes to Sina.

"I have all of that, too."

"Yes, to enhance your sensual experience. Iona, choose the Dragon Twin you are most attracted to so we can begin."

"Thalos."

Thalos removed his clothes and placed them in the pile with Sina's clothes. Lethos, K'Lara and Tavir walked to the bed on the right. Iona watched her mother, Lethos and Tavir undress then turned back to the Dragon Twins.

"Undress," Thalos instructed then checked the bondages on the beds.

Iona slowly dropped her clothes. She stared down at her slender body then back to the Sina. "I started with Kilean. We talked about many things. We were both nervous. I laid on the altar. He kissed and fondled me."

"And you had sex?" Sina asked.

"No. It was a new experience for me. I was shocked at the sensations I was feeling. He got off, took his pants off and had me touch his penis. I was so new at everything he wanted to make certain I was comfortable. He said we could go as slow as we needed to."

"What happened after you talked?" Thalos asked.

"I sat on his lap and played with a vibrator. It made him want me."

Thalos grabbed a dragon vibrator. "Then let's start there," he said, sitting on the edge of the bed. "Sit on me," he said. "I'll help you."

Iona complied. She spread her legs wide, leaned back on Thalos' strong chest. Thalos' slender fingers found her clit. She moaned and rocked as he gently stroked her with his other arm around her waist. "Think of Kilean," he whispered in her ear between her sensual moans. Iona nodded taking the vibrator from him and inserting it inside her. Thalos' placed his hand on her large breasts, fondling her tit bars.

"Oh, yes," Iona moaned, imaging the experience she had with Kilean. She could feel his breath upon her neck. His warm kisses. "Kilean," she moaned wave upon wave in her lower stomach heightened as he played with her nipples. Up and down, back and forth. Oh, she needed him. She needed him so badly. She could feel his penis grow hard between her legs. His sensual moans. She wanted to continue but... "Uhm, he told me to get off because I was making him want to be inside me," she pushed out of her lips. "That's when Tayla appeared."

"Good, get off him," Sina instructed.

Iona removed the vibrator and got to her feet. She stumbled a bit then turned to Thalos. Thalos dragon penis was fully erect and hard. "Damn, I can see why he needed to be inside her," he muttered, standing upright. "She's fucking hotter than her mother when she was that young."

"What happened after Tayla came?" Sina asked.

"Kilean and I had problems having sex in front of her so she disappeared. I laid on the table, was bound and he played with the sex toys on me. He left the clit vibrator on me and we had the most amazing sex. Then Tayla reappeared. I changed places with Kilean and sat on his face. He ate from me while Tayla gave him a blowjob. Tayla and I kissed. It made him even more excited than before. Tayla sat on him while he continued to give me oral sex. I got jealous. I changed places with Tayla and suckled him. We then gave him a double blowjob. I then straddled Kilean backwards while Tayla played with my clit and Kilean's balls. We did that for a time then I dismounted. Tayla took over. I changed places with Kilean. Tayla was on top of me as Kilean fucked her from behind. I didn't like that part. We ended up on our sides. Kilean fucked me from behind while Tayla had a dragon vibrator and ass plug inside her. Tayla massaged me. We all came hard and it was over."

Sina looked at Thalos then back to Iona. "I don't think I have to do everything exactly as she did to get you to believe we are Tayla and Kilean."

"Why not?" Thalos asked.

"Because what she is describing is how Asa and I would mate with Kilean. There are some differences but not so much that if I change what I do it would make her think any less of what was happening. Iona was forced into a servant role, not as a participant."

"But I enjoyed it," Iona argued.

"When you were jealous, did she ever focus on your needs?"

"No."

"That's because you weren't important. The needs of a Dragon Twin or Sex Slave are never important. It is the needs of Dragon Rider who come before our own. She wanted Kilean to be appeased. I can do the same thing to Thalos and make you believe he's Kilean."

"If I wasn't important then why did she want me there?"

"Because she needed a Dragon Twin to help her and she didn't have one. Her twin is dead."

Thalos stepped closer to the women. "What's the plan, then?"

"We'll start with what always excites a man and work our way to the actual intercourse."

"Which is?" Iona asked, with an arched eyebrow.

Sina grabbed Iona's breasts. "They love to watch women have sex. It excites them," she explained then licked Iona's nipple. The two women embraced, licking each other, stepping backwards until Iona fell onto the bed. Sina flipped Iona onto her stomach, pulled her ass upward and kissed her bottom. Oh, she felt so good. How could a woman make her feel so good? Sina pushed Iona onto her bottom and moved her to the edge of the bed, separated legs as she licked and fondled her breasts. Iona sat on the edge of bed, fully taking in Sina's delicious, seductive kisses all over her body. They kissed passionately then turned their faces to Thalos. Thalos grinned, holding his erect penis in his hand. They rose from the bed, each taking an arm and guiding him onto the bed. Sina and Iona strapped Thalos to the bed.

Iona quickly climbed onto the bed, took his penis into her mouth and suckled with her eyes closed thinking of Kilean. Oh, he tasted so good! She could hear Thalos' sensual moans and groans in between kissing Sina. She was so hot for Kilean! Iona couldn't control it any longer. She straddled Thalos and pushed his penis deep within her. "Oh, Kilean," she moaned, leaning back on Thalos legs. "Oh, you feel so good!" Iona rocked her hips. Sina turned to face her with her ass on Thalos face. Thalos thoroughly giving her oral sex while Sina played with Iona's clit and breasts. Up and down, Iona rocked. The immense sensations driving her crazy. "Kilean, oh, yes, more! My love, fuck me harder! More!" She screamed, clearly seeing Kilean satisifing her. She screamed leaning back as an orgasm overcame her. Iona huffed between her teeth with immense pleasure. She rotated backward then rocked again. Iona felt her ass widened. Sina licked her finger, placed it inside Iona's ass, removed it then placed an ass plug inside. "Oh, gods," Iona cried, pushing even harder. Wave after wave rolled through her lower stomach. She leaned back and screamed with delight at the touch of Sina's hand on her clit. "Oh, ugh, ugh, Kilean!" Faster and faster she rocked as Sina said, "Fuck you. It feels so good." Sina slapped and sucked on Iona's tits, "Oh, yes!" Sina leaned over and licked her tit as she continued to massage Iona's clit until Iona could no longer stand it. "Kilean!" she cried out then dismounted.

Sina and Iona smiled at each other then leaned over Thalos' penis. The two women stared at each other for a brief moment, kissed passionately then shared Lethos' penis between them. Back and forth, they each licked the draconoid penis bringing the same experience she had had with Kilean to her mind. The more she suckled, the more she wanted Kilean. She just couldn't stand not having him inside her. Something overcame her. She could feel the sensual power inside her growling for more. She pushed Sina away with a snarl. "He's mine. Kilean's mine, bitch!"

Sina grinned. She unstrapped Thalos, nodded to him and changed places. Iona's sexual thirst grew even stronger. "You can have both of us, Iona. Kilean, fuck her from behind while she gives me oral sex," Sina instructed lying on the bed holding her legs open. Iona crawled on the bed and suckled Sina's clit. She gasped as she felt Thalos' penis enter her from behind. Iona closed her eyes, fully taking in her lovers' deep assault. She loved the feel of his hand on her breasts and his finger playing with her clit. She lowered her mouth back to Sina's clit and licked it several times. Deep moans and groans filled the air. Sina's cries crew even louder. Sina pushed Iona backwards. Thalos caught her. "Get on the bed, Kilean and Iona. Lay on top of him with your back on his chest. I think you will both enjoy this," Sina ordered.

Thalos and Iona complied. She spread her legs wide. Sina licked Thalos' penis then inserted it back into Iona as she sat upright. Iona moaned loudly. Iona straddled her lover's waist leaning back on her arms. Her breasts bounced up and down as she rocked in unison with him. "Fuck, fuck me harder, Kilean!" she cried out, arching her head back. Sina pushed her over and placed an ass ring into Iona's asshole. Harder, faster, Iona rocked as the ass plug became another penis and vibrated in unison with her lovers'. "Oh, oh, oh!" she screamed reaching another orgasm. She descended. Sina climbed on top of Thalos', faced him and rocked as Iona straddled Thalos' face facing Sina. She closed her eyes as Thalos suckled her juices. "Shit, Kilean. Oh…," she whispered then was interrupted as Sina passionately kissed her. The ladies embraced, moaning sensually in between Thalos' moans. Sweat filled their bodies. The dildo in Iona's ass pushed even harder. She rocked back and forth, "My love. Kilean. Oh, my love! Yes, yes," she growled fiercely taking hold of Sina's shoulder. She emitted loud roar. Sina pushed her off Thalos. Enraged that the woman would deny her satisfaction, she lunged towards Sina but was interrupted by Thalos charging at her.He rolled on top of her and kissed her.

The couple kissed a long time, slowly denying what she wanted the most but she didn't care. Kilean's kisses were amazing. He lifted her legs, fondled her clit and pushed his penis inside her. Iona grinned with delight in between her sensual moans. Sina came from beside her, played with Iona's breasts and clit. The seductive human dragon twin climbed over Iona's face and rubbed her own clit. She descended upon Iona's mouth. Iona grabbed a dildo from the table and pushed it hard inside Sina. Thalos leaned over and kissed Iona. She bit Thalos' lip as she orgasmed hard several times. He arched his back, closed his eyes and moaned loudly spilling his seed inside her. "Oh, shit, Iona," he muttered with one more thrust then rose off the bed with Sina.

Iona smiled with utter bliss, closing her eyes. "Kilean," she said.

"Did we accidently satisfy the dragon," Sina whispered to Thalos, removing the dildo and ass plug.

"I don't know. Did you hear the dragon inside her," Thalos asked. Sina nodded.

The couple patiently watched Iona peacefully lay still. Iona's slowly opened her legs. "Hmm, more Kilean," she moaned, massaging her clit. "Oh, gods, Kilean I need more."

"There it is," Sina said, motioning for Lethos to join them as the couple moved to their own bed. Lethos ran towards the bed on the left, leaving K'Lara and Tavir as they embraced.

"Kilean, oh, gods, Kilean I need you," Iona cried, rising from the bed. The sex toys and bed disappeared. She wandered aimlessly around the room dazed between the sexual encounter and her needs. Where was she? Where was Kilean? "Kilean!" she screamed, mindlessly searching for her lover. Her body craving for his touch. She thought she had felt something behind her. She turned to see a large dragon shaped dildo laying on a cloth on the floor. She knelt with her legs spread across the cloth and inserted the dildo. Instantly, it went to work. She rocked her ass, playing with her aching tits. "Oh, yes," she moaned, leaning back. Harder and harder it pounded inside her. She leaned onto her hands and knees. Tentacles erupted from the dildo, touching her clit, activating the dildo in her ass and surrounding her tits. Every sensual place on her body erupted with sheer delightful sensations. Iona breathed hard as the large dildo did its job. Sweat poured down her down her body. She almost couldn't stand its strong intensity. She roared loudly at the strongest orgasm ran through her entire body then collapsed from exhaustion.

Kalesh emerged from her body in her full glory. The Golden Dragon peered around the chamber at the other people. "What is the meaning of this?" the ancient dragon demanded of Iona. "Why am I in the council chamber?"

"I'm sorry, Kalesh," Iona said, rolling onto her back. She wiped her face, removed the dildo and ass plug then peered up at the large dragon. "I need your help. You're the only one who can help me."

"I am not to be used by you. You can't control what you don't understand and you can't understand when you don't have your mate."

"Kalesh, you're the only one who can save our mates. I know you hunger for him. I feel it."

"Hmm, so you tricked me into appearing beside you?"

"I had no choice," she argued sitting up. She grimaced at the slight pleasantly painful sensation in her lower stomach and rubbed it. "The

Silver Dragon Soul is being held by Prince Zurrgash at Drokap Castle."

"Drokap Castle? The location of that place changes in time and realm frequently. How am I supposed to help you?"

"You are connected to the other soul, which means you can open a portal to wherever the soul is."

"I can, but that is only when the Dragon Lord or Dragon Lady desire to visit the other's mating chamber."

"But surely it is the same?" a naked, sweaty, breathless Queen K'Lara asked rising from her bed.

Kalesh turned to face her former host. "K'Lara, it has been too long."

"Yes, it has. What of my question? Surely it has to be same process. You're tied to the soul not the person because you and your mate used to be one soul. One would believe the only reason you crave to be with the other dragon soul is to remedy the separation between you that was caused by the separation of your soul."

"It is true."

"Then surely you can open a portal to take yourself to it."

"I have to have a host in order to do so."

"You have one," K'Lara said, pointing to her daughter.

"But my mate does not."

"Why should that matter?" Sina asked, rising from her bed.

Kalesh turned to the dragon twins. She shrugged her shoulders. "I supposed it does not. The energies are tied together. I can feel his urges as much as he can feel mine. But Sina, the portals are to be used so I can mate with him while the Dragon Riders mate."

"My son is with the soul," Tavir argued. "He just doesn't possess it. We can remedy that if we can rescue both my son and the soul."

Kalesh turned back to Iona. Iona slowly rose to her feet with her mother's help. "Please, I love him and our world is lost if we don't rescue them."

"I cannot help you fight whomever you encounter."

"I have my friends to help me do so."

"The portal is only for the Dragon Lady and Dragon Lord, not their friends."

Iona stepped towards the dragon soul. "Why are you fighting me?"

"I am not. I am only guiding you."

"Kalesh, we can save Kilean and your mate but I need help in doing so. I understand what the portals are for just as I understand what I did here today to call you forth isn't normal."

"There are rules and regulations for a reason, Iona."

"Sometimes the rules are meant to be broken for the betterment of everyone."

"Those are very dangerous words, you speak."

"I'm not asking for the destruction of our world. I'm trying to save it. Please, open the portal so my friends and I can save what has been taken from us."

Kalesh looked around the room then nodded. "I'll open it as soon as everyone is dressed and ready to go."

"Thank you."

"You're welcome."

16

Drokap Castle – Kingdom of Saloron

Drip. Drop. Drip. Drop.

The constant sound of water dripping somewhere in his cell was going to drive him insane. He really hadn't noticed the obnoxious constant dripping until his screams had ended and his tormentor had left him. He wondered if she had done it on purpose. Bound to an enchanted rock slab, laying in his own vomit, urine and sweat. His bones, tendons and muscles had been methodically broken and torn until he couldn't stand the pain any longer. She should have just let him die. But no, Tayla had enchanted the slab with enough healing power to slowly heal his wounds so she could tear him apart limb by limb as much as she wanted to. Torture. Heal. Torture. Heal. Torture. Heal. The cycle just never ended. He could feel his mind slowly begin to crack under her methods. As hard as he tried he just didn't know how much he could keep going on like this. A part of him couldn't wait for the Soul Sickness to kill his body. Perhaps his soul would be released from his torment. But he knew there were certain rituals that had to be followed after his death in order to secure his soul within the Draco's Hall. He would find peace and paradise as long as his soul wasn't with his body. This. Was. Never. Going. To. End.

Kilean lifted his head off the table he was bound too and peered at his broken body. He lowered his head with disappointment. Every muscle, bone and tendon hurt beyond his wildest imagination. He wasn't certain just how long Tayla had tortured him for this time around. He could barely remember anything other than the sounds of his screams echoing off the cavern walls. The wicked dragon twin had done everything she could think of to make his life a living hell. But there was one thing she could never have – his hope in Iona. He knew he had spoken to his love. He believed he had. Was it just faith or had they truly communicated with each other? What was taking her so long?

Kilean closed his eyes, taking in the brief respite he found in his empty cell. He just wasn't certain how long Tayla was going to leave him alone to recover mentally and physically. It wouldn't be long. That was for certain. She had enchanted the table to keep him alive not comfortable.

The Dragon Lord braced himself at the sound of a portal opening and footsteps. He had to be mentally prepared for whatever else she had planned for him. It was just too simple to let him die. No, he was her toy. Her battered, ugly toy she was going to chew up, spit out and damage until she could no longer do so. However long that took her.

"Kilean, oh gods, Kilean," Iona's voice resonated in his ears but he couldn't believe she was actually here. Tayla had used all kinds of mental tricks to get inside his thoughts. Some of which, had made him question if his holding back on information from the one seeking it was wise. But then he would come to his senses, realize where he was and what was going on then deny Tayla the information she was seeking.

He cringed at Iona's gentle touch on his cheek. "Get away from me," he sneered, turning his head to face the other direction.

"Kilean, it's me, Iona."

"Tayla, you tried this before. I'm not telling you anything that you don't already know."

He felt someone else's presence next to his bed and winced out of view at the sound of his father's voice. Tavir took Iona's hand in his own. "He's been tortured, Iona. He's not himself. You said so."

Iona nodded her head with tears falling down her eyes. Kilean jerked his limbs at the sensation of someone messing with his metal bonds. "Get away from me," he screamed, severely fidgeting as he turned his head to face the image of K'Lara at his feet.

K'Lara lifted her hands with a serious look towards him. "We're here to help."

"Liar," he bellowed at the top of his lungs.

"Kilean, you can't make any noise. Please. We don't want the guards, Tayla or Prince Zurggash to know we are here."

"They already know. You're working for them! Leave me alone," he demanded, shifting his body back and forth to avoid her touch. He spit in her direction.

K'Lara grabbed his shins, bore down her weight and stared deeply into his eyes as he panicked. "Prince Kilean Dragonsun! Listen to me very closely. You may not recognize me but you sure as hell should recognize them," she yelled, pointing to Tavir and her daughter.

Kilean sniffed his nose and swallowed hard. He heaved turning his face towards Iona and his father. Tears ran down his cheeks. "A trick. They aren't here. Tayla," he turned back to K'Lara. "Why? That form is seductive enough. I like the large breasts I can see from the opening of your catsuit but...,"

"He's your son, alright," K'Lara sneered towards Tavir.

Tavir chuckled. Kilean peered at the unfamiliar woman, back to his father then to K'Lara once again. Could her words hold meaning? Oh, what was he thinking? It was just another trick to get him to lower his defenses.

"Fuck you," he bellowed in her direction.

"Oh, I'm sure you would like to but I'm off limits to you, Prince Kilean. I'm Iona's guardian and her mother," she emphasized the last part.

Kilean grinned. He had her. Now he knew the truth. "Queen K'Lara's dead, TAYLA!"

He heard a deep sigh from his side. Someone placed a gentle hand on the side of his cheek. He fidgeted then surrendered to Iona's mouth gently touching his own. He slightly opened his mouth taking in her delicious kiss. There was no doubt about it. It had to be Iona. NOBODY ever kissed him like her. He kissed her with more passion, fully taking in her tongue. His heart skipped a beat. Oh, gods she was here! His message had worked. "Iona," he whispered pulling his mouth away, staring deep into her blue eyes. "A dream?"

Iona smiled. She lowered her hand to his waist and caressed his cock. "Oh, by the gods," he declared, arching his head back.

She grinned releasing her grip. "Well?" she questioned.

"Not a dream. Definitely not a dream. I don't feel that way with any other woman."

Kilean moaned, fully relaxing as much as he could on the slab. He was barely holding it all together as it was. "May I?" K'Lara asked with her hands on his ankle cuffs.

"Their enchanted so I couldn't break them. I have tried, before, numerous times."

"Do you know the spell?"

Kilean shook his head. "Only that a dragon twin can break it."

"Well fortunate for us we have three."

"Three?"

Klara moved to the side. He saw Sina, Thalos and Lethos magically working on breaking the spell that locked the door. Kilean heaved with gratitude. "Oh, by the gods," he gasped, lowering the back of his head as K'Lara approached the twins. He couldn't believe his luck. Iona had not only come with their parents to save him but had brought dragon twins with her. He was so grateful! He relaxed as she gently stroked his battered cheek.

"How bad is it?" Tavir asked him.

Kilean shook his head, crying.

"It's going to be alright, Kilean. We're here, now," Iona coaxed.

"Why did you come?" he asked with his eyes closed.

"Why wouldn't we? We all love you."

"I hurt all over, Iona. My mind is confused. I can't think. I can't…"

Tavir interrupted him. "Just relax, Kilean. It will all be over soon."

Kilean opened his eyes and turned to face his father. "I tried so hard, father, to be brave and strong. My mind is fragile. I screamed so hard, so many times I don't know how I even have a voice left. She did things to me. So many terrible things."

"She won't any longer. We're going to take you home. Just rest, my son."

Sina approached him between his father and Iona. "How you holding up, lover?"

Kilean huffed then grimaced as he felt something on his ankles. He screamed, arching his back while Thalos and Lethos cast a spell on the cuffs. Sina held him down by his shoulders as the men worked their spell. "Stay strong, Kilean. The ward is more powerful than we first thought but we can break it. You have to remain calm so it thinks you are not trying to escape."

"Oh, by the GODS!" he bellowed even more, heaving and fidgeting.

"You can do this, Kilean. Just keep your mind on Iona. Think of how much you love her and the life you want to have with her. Slow your heart and breath. You know how to do that."

Kilean whimpered, keeping his eyes on Iona. Tears cascaded down his bruised cheeks as he calmed down. He couldn't believe she was here. His beloved, naïve young lover had blossomed into the companion he always wanted. He loved the way the light shined on her blonde hair. Her large breasts just barely covered by the slits in her white tunic. His eyes scanned up and down her body. Had her dress become more revealing than before?

He heard his metal ankle cuffs clank open. He moved his feet. He could freely move his feet. Kilean sat up on his elbows, moving his sore legs. "Lie back down. We need to remove the cuffs," Sina ordered him as Thalos and Lethos walked around the slab. Kilean complied. "Iona stand over him so he sees you. Kilean keep your eyes on her," Sina ordered. Everyone moved into place.

He screamed and tensed his body as they worked on the cuffs. "Focus on me, not the pain," Iona directed him, placing her hands on the side of his head. He heaved peering up at his beloved. Oh, by the gods, she was absolutely gorgeous!

"I'm sorry," he cried to her.

"For what?"

"I should have known better. I should have known that it was a trap but I was so caught up in the moment. I wanted to believe it was all real."

"Kilean, you didn't know that Tayla wasn't who she told us she was."

"I should have. I knew the story of who she was. I know all the races never use that name anymore because of who she is. But….oh, gods," he sneered, lifting his face to the twins.

"Lay back down and don't fight us. The spell's complicated," Thalos said.

"Kilean, do what they say," Sina instructed.

He glanced at the dragon twin, laid back down and focused on Iona. Iona rubbed the sides of his head with her thumbs on his temples. "Hmm, feels good."

"I'm glad. I don't blame you for any of it."

"You should. I knew better."

"I doubt that. By your own words, the world you come from is out of balance because of what happened between my mother and your father. Your people had lost any hope that we would ever be mated. It would make sense for you not to receive full instruction and faith that what happened has."

Kilean inhaled deeply hearing the clank of the metal cuffs. "Get me off. Get me off," he bellowed, trying to descend from the table. Tavir caught his son in his arms and lowered him to the ground just as metal blades descended from the ceiling into the slab and two metal pieces with spikes rose from the sides, converged together and slammed into the bed.

"Holy shit," Iona cussed backing away from the bed just in time to miss the blades.

"A little insurance that if I ever escaped from the cuffs I wouldn't leave that thing in one piece," Kilean explained, lying on the ground in his father's arms. He cringed, placing his hand to his forehead. "She knows I'm not there. She'll come for me," he declared to his father.

"That isn't going to happen," K'Lara declared, lifting her two swords from her back. "I have the counterspell. Tavir, stay with our children. Sina, you're with me. Thalos, Lethos, find the prisoners and release them. Let's go," she demanded. The spell on the door lifted. Everyone left.

Kilean clutched his father's tunic with a loud moan just as Iona joined them. Tavir cradled his son's broken body, safely in his strong arms. "What," Tavir asked, pulling Kilean closer to him.

"My body?"

Iona knelt beside him. "It's as handsome as you left it."

"Be serious, Iona," he sneered, his naked body shivering. Tavir removed his coat, placed it around his son and caressed him trying to keep him warm without hurting him.

"You seized many times. The healers say you don't have much time left before the Soul Sickness kills you. But I am certain it won't kill you. All we have to do is find the soul, have sex, it'll join your soul and all will be well."

Kilean chuckled, then gasped several times in pain, clutching his father's shirt. "Slow deep breaths, son," Tavir instructed.

Kilean nodded, complying with his father's instructions. He turned to Iona. "If this doesn't work...," he started.

"You can't think that way!" she yelled at him.

"Iona, you're being idealistic. You already told me the healers do not have faith that I will survive this."

"What do they know? They're elves?"

Kilean smiled, "Elves know so much more than humans do."

Iona grabbed his chin and lifted his eyes so they met his. "You get this through your thick skull! I am not giving up on you and you aren't going to give up on me. You liberated me. I will not live a life without my dragon mate."

"There can be another mate."

"I don't want another. I want you," she declared then kissed him passionately. Something powerful stirred inside him. Something he shouldn't feel but did. He wrapped his arms around her, pushed her to the ground and climbed on top of her. He didn't know where he had the energy to mount her but it was intense! He leaned back, feeling the calling. It was so strong. His hands caressed her body. Stronger, deeper. He could sense it. But he didn't know what to do. He knew what he wanted to do. Oh, gods, how much he wanted to do it with her.

"Dad," he muttered, his hands undressing Iona without his thought. "What's wrong," Tavir said.

"I can feel it."

"Feel what?"

Iona grinned with a reply, "The Silver Dragon Soul. It wants to mate with my Golden Dragon Soul. I can feel Kalesh inside me. She's roaring with passion."

Kilean peered down Iona's naked body. He grinned at the sight of her tit bars, the chain between them and the hip chain descending between her legs. "Oh, gods, I want you so bad!"

"I can tell," she nodded to his large, firm, erect penis.

He extended his arms and leaned his head back taking in the silvery smoke descending throughout the room. "It's healing me so I can mate. The last time I saw the chest, Prince Zurggash had it. He's obsessed with it. He must have opened the chest to stare upon the Silver Dragon Soul. The Dragon Souls felt each other and it's come to mate."

"Iona," King Tavir looked at the blonde beauty. Her fierce face filled with intense sexual desire only had eyes for his son. Her hands groped Kilean's strong body. "Mate, both of you, now. Don't let the souls be disappointed," he ordered, stepping to the back of the cavern.

His father didn't have to tell him twice. Kilean and Iona wrapped their arms around each other, kissing and groping. Heat rose between their sweaty bodies. He thrust his penis deep within Iona. Her deep moan of delight, enticed him even more. Oh, gods, all he wanted was her! They rolled with their arms and legs embraced. She sat on top of him, rocking fast back and forth. "Oh, yes! Oh, by the gods, yes," he bellowed, arching his back, fully taking the immense sexual pleasure in. He pushed her underneath, lifted her legs and took her harder than he had ever before. She was so fucking wet and horny! Their hands couldn't stop touching each other. He leaned over her, placing his fingers in her mouth. The slick movement of her tongue recalling to his mind the amazing blow job she had once given him. She heaved and moaned sensually as he bit her nipple in between his deep thrusts. Oh, she was so perfectly addicting! He couldn't get enough of her. He laid

his complete body on top of her, allowing the sweat of their bodies to lubricate each of his movements as he nibbled on her earlobe.

He didn't even see it coming but felt the fierce silvery smoke envelope them as they rose in the air. The mixture of gold and silver smoke encasing them in a cocoon. They roared loudly in response to the overwhelming deep orgasms they experienced repeatedly. They bit and clawed each other in response to intense, dragon like sexual appeasement. Loud moans filled with sensual screams of delight filled the area around them. He didn't even know he could make sounds like that. Suddenly, he arched his head back, opened his mouth wide and inhaled the strong, silver smoke. Kilean roared fiercely with the strength of the Silver Dragon Soul in unison with Iona as she roared with the Gold Dragon Soul at the strongest orgasm either of them had ever felt in their lives. The couple disappeared.

17 Temple of the Sun

Kilean inhaled a deep breath, opened his eyes. He stared up at the large crystal quartz descending from the ceiling over his bed. It lightly glowed, pouring healing rays of light upon his body. It took him awhile to figure out just where he was. The warmth of the glowing light brought healing peace upon his body and soul but he just couldn't get over the strange sexual sensations he was feeling. It was almost as if the dragon spirit inside him wasn't appeased with the bonding he had with its mate. Images of Iona came to the forefront of his mind. An unquenchable desire to touch her. Kiss her. Be with her.

He could lay here all day long, thoroughly enjoying the respite thinking only of her. Kilean slowly closed his eyes briefly enjoying the feel of his soul in his body. A part of him wanting to stay here forever but he knew he couldn't do that. His father, K'Lara and the dragon twins were trapped in Prince Zurggash's fortress.

Kilean opened his eyes, bolted upright and held his hand to his forehead as a sharp wave of dizziness overcame his senses. Every muscle in his body ached. He was so weak all he wanted to do was lie back down. Hadn't Iona said his body had seized several times. No wonder he was weak and sore. But he couldn't just lie there. No, there was work to be done. A duty to his people and his mate. He lowered his hand, sat upright and blinked several time to still his mind.

He exhaled, ever so grateful to feel his heart beating inside his chest. He peered down at the simple white tunic and loose pants covering his body. The multicolored healing crystals of all shapes and sizes lining his bed delivered the strength he needed to heal. Oh, how great it felt to be back in his own body. He grinned rubbing his hands down his face then examined his entire body. Nothing was broken, bruised or cut. He didn't feel ill anymore. Iona had been right. The Silver Dragon Soul had entered into him just in time to save him from certain death. But now he had another problem. He was so horny he needed relief or the dragon inside him would make him go mad with desire. He had to find Iona.

Kilean rose to feet, grabbed the robe beside his bed, placed it on and walked out of the small chamber healing pod. Nurses walked back and forth through the transparent clusters of healing pods, treating patients with all kinds of injuries and illnesses. He tied the robe around his middle to the bulge in his pants then walked down the long hallways.

"Your highness," an elven healer greeted him from the nurses station. The tall, elegant elven man walked around the station with a large grin. "I had feared the worse for you. I am glad you're awake. If you please, let me examine you?"

"I don't have time. Where's Solon?"

"I don't know, my lord. He remained with you for a time then left to meditate. I know his brother is looking for him."

"And where is he?"

"That I cannot tell you, either."

Kilean huffed with frustration, trying to walk past the elven healer with no luck. "Sir, I must insist that you allow me to examine you. Soul Sickness is a very serious, deadly ailment to have. Sometimes when patients have a terminal illness they will recover just before they die."

"I am not ill. I have the Silver Dragon Soul. Now, please. I appreciate your utmost concern for my well-being but I need to find my mate. I know she was with my father, her mother and the dragon twins. I can only assume she was in the council chamber. I can't get into that chamber without the spell. Solon knows it. I need him."

The elven healer stared at Kilean with disappointment. A moment of tension spread between them. "You could be insane with illness," the elven healer said without emotion.

"He's not insane," Solon bellowed from the long hallway leading the central healing pod.

Kilean smiled over the elven healer's shoulder at the sight of his guardian walking quickly towards them with Iona by his side. The elven healer stepped to the side. Kilean ran to Iona, embraced her then pulled away with his hands on the side of her face. "Are you alright?" he asked.

"Yes. No. I mean I'm..."

"...fighting the urge to rip off my clothes and take me?" Iona grinned with a nod. "Me too. All I can think about is you."

"I was like that after the first time we were with the dragons. Kalesh gave me a dragon dildo to ease the sensation."

Solon explained, "It's a side effect of the bonding. The dragons are nesting and preparing your bodies for the bonding ceremony. Normally, the Dragon Lord would be appeased by the High Priestess and the Dragon Lady by the High Priest in order for them to know what kind of lover suits you best. They use the information they glean to help them decide which priest and priestess they should chose to present before the Dragon Lord or Dragon Lady as potential mates for the other. It is a ceremonial bedding for each of you to bond with each other's spiritual leaders but as we do not know where the High Priestess is, it cannot be done. I would highly recommend that we continue with traditional rites of passage as much as possible."

"I don't want to be with anyone other than Kilean," Iona protested

"I understand that, Iona, but it is not that simple. Kilean will not be your husband, only your lover. He will choose your husband from his priests."

"And who will be his wife if I don't have a High Priestess or priestesses?" Solon silently looked at the couple. "You don't know, do you?"

"It isn't a simple matter. No one expected any of this to happen. We thought the days of the Dragon Lord and Lady were over the day your mother turned her back on her duties."

"My mother was tricked into believing my father was her lifemate. She didn't turn her back on her duties because she wanted to!"

Solon raised his hand. "Iona, I didn't mean any offense. The matter still lies before us. The council doesn't trust you because of what your mother did. If you are going to win their trust then you have to strictly prescribe to all our customs, traditions and laws. You must allow my father to ceremonially bed you."

"He's right," Kilean admitted.

"What?" Iona gasped loudly in Kilean's direction. "But..."

He placed his finger on her lips. "Your mother did it and so can you."

Iona opened her mouth and licked his finger sensual. "Oh, don't do that," Kilean hissed pulling his finger out of her mouth and held his engorged crotch.

"You want me," she teased.

"Of course I do! But I can't physic..." he paused, exchanging glances between Iona and Solon.

"Kilean?" Solon asked.

"The bedding ceremony. It only appeases the dragons, right?"

"Technically, yes, but it's a way...."

"I understand what it is for, Solon. Iona's right about one thing. The world is so unbalanced that I can't go through all of the rites of passage in the Draconian Codex. Iona would have no choice but to choose a sex slave as my wife. There's no one to guide her. But I have to be appeased. Perhaps, we can give her duty and desire?"

"How so?"

"Oral sex. She gives me a blowjob then you can escort her to your father for the bedding ceremony. The Dragon Lord and Dragon Lady go their separate ways then rejoin again to ride each other's dragons. Am I correct in that assumption?"

"You are."

"That doesn't mean she can't give me oral sex," Kilean said, raising his eyebrow with a devilish grin.

"Kilean, this is most highly irregular."

"So has everything else we have done so far. Iona didn't have a priest when she first felt the urge after the incident between us and Tayla. She was appeased with a dildo. I need a fuck and I don't have the High Priestess to do it for me. You know our bodies can't return to their normal state after we return from that ritual without a good fuck. So Solon, please let her do what I need. I'll even let you watch. I know how much you'd enjoy that."

"Hmpf," Solon huffed.

"Sounds like fun," Iona said, slipping her hand down his pants.

"Oh," he hummed, almost falling backwards as she rubbed his cock. "Oh, gods," he moaned, placing his hand on the nurses station. He closed his eyes taking a deep breath, breathing in rhythm with each of her strokes.

"Very well, Kilean," Solon huffed, crossing his arms.

Kilean kicked off his pants, grabbed a chair, sat in it and spread his legs, holding his erect cock upwards. Iona knelt on the ground before him, placing her hands on his strong upper legs then kissed his inner thighs. She smiled with delight, licking her plump lips as she removed the top of her dress so Kilean had a fill view of her tits. Softly, she took hold of his penis and brushed the tip of it against her nipples. Kilean grinned. He always did like her big breasts. The fingers on her other hand tickled his balls. He inhaled a deep breath, through his clenched teeth. The strong sensation of sensual desire became even more enhanced. She lowered his penis and brushed her long hair across his balls. "Oh, shit," he exclaimed, widening his legs.

Iona slowly licked the tip of his penis with her tongue. "Fuck, Iona," he swore, moving his hips. She peered her eyes upward, catching his gaze as she descended her mouth upon his erect cock.

Kilean breathed deeply with each slow stroke. Back and forth, she moved in perfect rhythm and speed, licking and sucking while playing with his balls in her hand. He moaned sensually with each perfect stroke. "Oh, baby, yes," he muttered, holding tight to the chair's arms and arching his head back. She alternated her strokes with the flick of her tongue licking the tip. Each flick making him react even stronger. He couldn't speak anything other than her name. Up and down she bobbed, perfectly flicking her tongue in all the right places. Iona moved her mouth away, looked him straight in the eyes and rubbed his cock. He heaved through his teeth.

"Like it?" she asked.

"You're fucking amazing!"

She grinned devilishly, then licked the length of his penis. "Fuck," he moaned. He leaned his head back, letting the sensual pleasure overwhelm him. Stroke. Lick. Suck. Play with his balls. Her mouth alternating between his balls and penis. He breathed faster and moved his hips in unison to her perfection. "Oh, yes, Iona!" he screamed as she moved his balls all around the insides of her mouth. She was going to make him cum hard!

Iona moved back to his penis. He lifted his head and stared at her bare breasts. Just the sight of those gorgeous mounds! He leaned back. "Oh, I'm going to cum hard! Ugh, gods," he moaned loudly, placing his hand on top of her head. "Oh, yes, Iona. Oh, by the gods, Yes!" Faster she moved, sliding back and forth. He moaned loudly, grasping the side of the chair. Kilean arched his head back, breathing hard. He could barely keep his legs straight. He gripped the sides of the chair with all his strength. She was fucking amazing! "Oh, fuck me harder, Iona. Oh, Iona, yes!" The more he cried out, the faster she suckled. His face became red. His heart beat hard in his chest. He was almost there. Just a few more….. "Oh, shit, oooohhhhh" he bellowed, cuming hard in her mouth.

Iona grinned, rising with his sperm fully in her mouth. She placed her hand on his chest and swallowed it in front of him. "Tasty," she smiled. Kilean heaved with delight, almost falling to the floor.

"Damn. You're not the sweet, innocent girl I knew," he grinned with delight.

"You don't like me, anymore?" Iona asked.

"No, no. I love it." He gently kissed her. "Thank you."

"You're welcome."

Kilean pulled up his pants, took a deep breath, gathering his senses then walked with Iona back to Solon. Solon and Iona stared at him. "What?"

"Your clothes," Iona said.

"My clothes?" he asked, slowly accenting the syllables.

"You didn't notice the change when you put your pants back on?" Solon asked.

Kilean glared down at his body. Thick, leather black pants clung to his legs, tight enough to highlight his bulging crotch. A long leather, sleeveless duster hung off his shoulders illuminating his strong chest and arms. He lifted his eyes to Solon and Iona. "My official uniform?"

Solon answered, "I'm surprised they gave it to you. I didn't think Draco and Razil would have approved of the manner in which you chose to appease your urges."

Iona asked, "Does this mean they will approve if he does the same to me?"

"Probably not," Kilean answered. Iona lifted an eyebrow towards him. "You have your High Priest. I don't have my High Priestess. In all manner of speaking, you are the highest-ranking woman in this temple. That is probably why they approved of it. You will, after all, make the decision in the end as to whom you chose to be my wife."

Iona sighed, "I have only had sex with the Dragon Twins and you. I..."

"...Iona, you will have sex with more men than them. I know it has to be hard for you hear that. But it's true. We are not only the enforcers of the Draconian Codex but we regulate everything that has to do with sex from the priesthood to the mere peasant. Don't feel ashamed of what you do. At the end of the day, I know where your true loyalty lies. With me. And mine will always be with you." He kissed her gently on the lips. "I love you. I would never ask or allow anything to come between us."

"Alright, I'll do it without hesitation but only because you asked

me to."

"You won't regret it, Iona. He's very experienced and knows much about what gives a woman the greatest of pleasures. Even more so than I." He turned to Solon, "Take her to your father's chamber, inform him she is ready for the ceremony then tell Vashti to meet me in her chamber."

18

The enormous Dragon Chamber towered above the sacred grounds atop the Temple of the Sun. Kilean sat on the windowsill with his back against the wall staring out at the rolling highlands bordered by the dense forest of the Elven homeland. He had visited upon the Elven lands many times as a child, whenever Elven customs dictated ceremonies and festivities. He had often times loved spending time with his mother's family. Kilean stared at the borderlands, thinking about his mother and her family. Tears cascaded down his face. A part of him wanted to seek his sage grandparents' advice. They were over 450 years old. Certainly, they would know a solution to his messed up mind? But then again, he couldn't bear the thought of them knowing of what Tayla had done to his body, let alone his mind.

He lowered his head between his bent up knees and released his tears. His heart ached with the regret that his father, Iona's mother and the dragon twins were still locked away in that horrible place with Tayla and Prince Zurggash. He could feel phantom pains of the evil dragon twin's marks upon his body from where she had ripped him to shreds with his talons. Every now and then he heard the screams of those left behind as if they were still with him. Those horrible screams. He had thought when he had returned to his body that all his mental pain would have disappeared. At first, it had. The healing light of the crystals hadn't eased his sufferings only masked it. He had felt the first singe of pain, anger and resentment when he had encountered the elven physician. No wonder the healer thought he was still unwell. He could sense the dis-ease inside Kilean. Kilean had tried to keep his temper down so neither Solon nor Iona knew something was wrong.

Iona's blowjob on him had done him wonders. He had felt relaxed afterwards but it didn't take long for the memories and feelings to creep back into his mind.

Kilean exhaled a deep breath. A soft breeze blew through the dragon sized rectangular glass-less windows large enough for a dragon to fly in. The journey through the temple to the Dragon Chamber was small enough for a human to climb but not so much for a dragon. He knew Vashti would have to fly to her chamber.

He peered up at the sky with thoughts about those he had left behind in that evil place. Every now and then he could hear his own screams and thought he had smelled the mixture of blood, urine and sweat. Kilean looked up at the sky wondering where his dragon could be. It wasn't like Vashti to ignore him. Kilean sighed with disappointment. He didn't know just how long he had been sitting on the windowsill but it sure felt like an eternity. Maybe, it was because he couldn't keep his mind off of what Iona must be doing with the high priest. A part of him, even though he had enjoyed his experience with Iona, had desperately wanted the elven high priestess to bring him the greatest amount of pleasure a mere human could handle.

"Ugh," he moaned, wiping his hands down his face. He turned his face towards the large chamber. He saw his torture chamber! The screams of others mixed with his own. Those horrible smells. The pain. Oh, gods the pain! He clenched his hair, lowered his head between his legs and sobbed uncontrollably. He clenched his fist screaming in between his sobs for a long moment. He couldn't go back there. No, never again. He just couldn't do it.

Kilean caught his breath, feeling the familiar gusts of wind from a dragon landing nearby. But he didn't move. Frozen between the past and his present, he just didn't know what to do or how to control what he felt. "Kilean," Solon's voice mixed with Tayla's.

He pushed Solon away from him. "Don't touch me!"

Kilean heaved staring at the room before him. There was nothing there but his dragon and guardian. But how could that be? He had seen in it. It was right there. Wasn't it?

Solon and Vashti peered at him with a look of immense concern. He wiped his face, blinked several times then reopened his eyes. It was all the same. No smells, noises or the sight of that dreadful place. He was safe at the temple.

"I...I...I'm sorry. I ...," he waved his hand then walked towards the wooden door to the circular stairs. Vashti quickly turned around and barred him with her tail from leaving. "Vashti, please," he begged.

"No, your mind isn't right. I can feel it."

Kilean shrugged his shoulders, never taking his eyes off the door. "I'm bonded with the Silver Dragon Soul."

"That wouldn't do to your mind what I feel inside you."

"Get out of my head, Vashti," he bellowed turning to her.

"I can't. You're my rider. Our minds are one. Why won't you let me see what is tormenting you?"

"Because I don't want to see it."

Solon peered at Vashti then back to Kilean. "Kilean," he guided, taking a step towards his younger charge. "Vashti told me she can feel dark thoughts inside you. I am concerned, as is the council."

Kilean shook his head. "I...I...I thought since I was back in my body it would all end. I thought the Silver Dragon Soul would heal me, but I keep seeing my torment under Tayla's hand. I don't want to."

"That is good news."

"No, it's not! You don't know what I went through," he screamed, then turned to crying.

"We can't locate Drokap Castle," Vashti informed.

"I can't help you."

"Kilean, that's not true. You can. These memories you're reliving. If you remember the right details, then perhaps I can figure out where the fortress is and I can rescue them. It's dragon magic that binds Saloron to its time and place."

Kilean breathed deeply, staring up at the domed ceiling above them. "Vashti, please," he begged.

"Don't you want to rescue your father, Iona's mother and the dragon twins?" Solon asked.

"Of course I do," he bellowed, turning to them. He pointed to his head. "It hurts, Solon. You have no idea how much it hurts. More than I can even bear. I...I don't want to remember any of it but the Silver Dragon Soul won't let me forget."

"And have you considered perhaps the soul is trying to tell you something important?"

Kilean huffed, "By reliving my torment?"

"Kilean, I won't even begin to imagine what Prince Zurggash and Tayla put you through. Iona has told us of what she knows of it. But you have to think. Vashti says she can take a rescue party to rescue everyone but she needs an idea of where to go. The only people who know the spell to open that portal are dragon twins and we seem to be fresh out of stock with them."

"Vashti can't control time and space. I don't know how you plan to do that."

"There has to be a spell. The dragons have given you your official clothes. That means you are one step closer to assuming your position. I may be able to open the portal as soon as Iona is blessed by the power of the dragons."

Kilean swallowed hard. He sniffed his nose and swiped his hand under his nose. "How is she?"

"She was bit nervous when I took her my father's chamber. I left her with two of his servants so they could prepare her for the ceremony. My father was on his way to the chamber when Vashti and I left her. The council desires you and Iona maintain your preparations for the bonding ceremony while we plan a rescue mission to save your father, Queen K'Lara and the dragon twins. My brother is gathering his best men."

"And what is the plan if Iona and I aren't to participate?"

"Drayson and I will ride Vashti to Drokap Castle. Once we breech its wall, Drayson will open a portal for his soldiers to invade the castle, capture the prince and Tayla and rescue our missing."

Kilean nodded. He exhaled a deep breath, peering at his dragon. "You're in deep pain, Kilean. I feel it. But you are never going to release it without telling us what we need to know." Vashti instructed.

"When I was in there....was your mind affected?" he asked his dragon.

"No, the spell that was cast over your thoughts can't touch the mind of a dragon. It is too weak. Merging your memories into mine will not do if that is what you are thinking."

"It would be better than carry them around myself without sharing the pain."

"Kilean, I am suffering from Dragonlust. My capabilities are not fully functioning. I want to share your pain. I truly do but I am not strong enough until after I have my first mating season."

Kilean sighed, "I really need to find that dragon."

Vashti chuckled. "I couldn't agree with you more but this matter is more important than that. The elves have been able to sustain me for a time."

"How?"

"Kilean, don't be a stupid human. You think your kind are the only ones that have implements of satisfaction to ease a certain craving when one cannot be appeased by their own kind?"

"Oh," he gasped with understanding.

"Drokap Castle," Solon redirected the conversation

Kilean shook his head. "Solon, it was horrible. I really don't want to think about it."

Solon stepped closer to his charge. He placed his hand on the young man's arm.

Kilean nodded with a sniff of his nose. He pushed back his fears and dug deeper into his mind. Harder and harder he tried to recall every detail but…"Two moons. One blue and the other orange. I remember because I used them to keep track of time outside my window. They rose at different times and came together at the height of the night only to split again towards dawn. It was cold, so very cold. I was naked the entire time and I could never stay warm, despite the fevers. I think time moved faster wherever I was because I thought it had been decades since she told me, but I never aged as such and when Iona came to me she didn't look any older than when I had been with her."

"Good. That's a start. What else do you remember?"

Kilean stared down at the floor, trying hard to access the hidden memories he knew he had. Vashti comforted him, "It's alright, Kilean. You're safe. I know the memories have to hurt you."

Kilean sobbed, nodding. "It was so hard, Vashti. She tore my body so many different ways. She burned me alive. She…." his bit his lip, shook his head, and walked away. Kilean took a few steps and turned to Solon. "I don't want to remember!"

"Kilean, you must. Just a few more details and I'll have everything I need to tell the council so we can work on the spell to rescue them."

"She…" he paused remembering something. "There was…uhm…I don't know…a bright light. It wasn't always there. It came into my room as if…uhm…it was hard to describe. I had never seen anything like it before. I could feel it's sorrow. It peered down at me with such sadness as if …. As if it was a trapped spirit. Oh, that doesn't make sense. Who can trap a spirit?"

"The sun, was it brilliant yellow, almost white?"

"Yes, it was. I remember now. The spirit would bath in it. It had a chain that lead from its ankle to the ground. It wasn't always there. Strange thing was, that thing felt somehow familiar to me."

"You should, you're half elf," he said. Kilean looked at him with a look of confusion. "There have been rumors among the elves that

Prince Zurggash has infiltrated the world of elven spirits."

"How is that possible?"

"I do not know. I didn't think it was possible for anyone to travel to the Elven land of the dead because it is another realm and the gods haven't spoken of it."

"Then how do you know?"

"The gods may not be speaking but a few of our ancestral spirits have visited upon the seers proclaiming their torments. Kilean, it is of the utmost importance that I speak to the council concerning these revelations. In the meantime, perhaps you cannot heal because you are looking at this from a human perspective?"

"Pain is pain, is it not?"

"Yes, but each of the races have their own way of handling painful memories. Kilean, your pain is affecting your personality and behavior as if a spell has been cast over you. Go to your family in the borderlands. Let them heal you."

"I haven't set foot upon those lands since mother went mad."

"Your mother is honored among all elves for being chosen to give you life. They cherish you. I'm quite certain they will help you overcome this ailment."

Kilean swallowed hard, walking over to the bay window and stared upon his mother's homeland. He had missed his grandparents, aunts, uncles and cousins. "What of Iona?" he asked with his back turned to them.

"The Draconian Codex says the future Dragon Lord and Dragon Lady are to share a ride on their dragons together. It never mentions where that ride is to originate. I will send word to Vashti when Iona has emerged from her bedding ceremony. She can join you in the borderlands."

Kilean slowly nodded. He wiped away his tears and sniffed his nose. "My father?"

"I will have him and Queen K'Lara escorted to you once we have rescued them. Kilean, do not delay. You need to heal."

"I'm a weak human."

"You are not! The blood of the elves runs through your veins. Go to your mother's people, Kilean! They are the only ones who can help you heal. Don't you trust me?"

"I do."

"Then trust that I know what I am talking about. I am half elf just like you."

"Except your mother was a dwarf. She gave you those large, funny looking feet of yours."

"Eh," Solon muttered then grew serious. "Kilean?"

The Dragon Lord exhaled a heavy sigh, pushing his hand down as he walked to Vashti and climbed onto her back. He laid his head down between her shoulders. "Take me home to my mother's people," he said.

Vashti elegantly nodded to Solon, rose to full stature and took off out the window. Kilean hung onto her scales for dear life as they ascended into the air.

19

The sweet fragrance of roses and hibiscus lingered in the air of High Priest Aejeon's round, elegant bedchamber. Rose petals littered the marble floor and king sized poster bed with passionate red curtains. Iona stood naked in the middle of the room with only a silken robe around her body, openly displaying the front of her body. Her skin shined from the residue of the sacred mating waters the high priests' servants had bathed her in. The warm waters had felt so sensually pleasing she could still feel it's presence upon her senses. She turned hearing the pod door open. Her eyes stared upon the high priest. Clothed only in a robe that didn't close in the front, she could see his very long, large penis halfway erect already.

Iona swallowed hard. His body was amazing! Long, tall, perfectly formed. She couldn't help but bite her lower lip in embarrassment.

"Ah, you like elves," he said, stepping to a wooden table on the side of the room with a pitcher of red wine and goblets.

"I'm sorry. I didn't mean to be rude," she apologized staring at his long grey hair the hung loosely down his back.

"There's nothing to apologize for child. Your body will react to what it desire. It helps me to choose the right mate for you."

"I don't want another mate. I want Kilean."

The high priest sighed, lowering the pitcher and glass down. He turned towards her. "Iona, you are not the first Dragon Lady to tell me you want to be your Dragon Lord's mate. In every way, you are. But it is of the utmost importance that the line of successions for Dragon Lord and Dragon Lady are not corrupted by a child from that union. That is why you will never give him a child."

"Never? But we have sex."

"Your womb will never produce a child for him. Draco and Razil have cursed the womb of the Dragon Lady so she will only bare her husband a child and not the Dragon Lord. Kilean can spill his seed in you all he wants to but it will never produce."

Iona's face fell. "Why!"

"As I said, it is to preserve the genetic makeup for each line of succession." He picked up a glass of wine and handed it to her. "Drink."

"What is it?" she asked taking the glass from him.

"Something to give you strength, immense passion and the greatest of pleasures." She stared into the cup then back to him. "Iona, I have done this with your mother, grandmother, great grandmother and so on back with your female ancestors and never have I ever poisoned them."

Iona shrugged, "Seems to me you should know what I like by now if you've been with them."

"Each woman is different. Drink please. Then give me your goblet and remove your clothes so I can examine you."

Iona sipped on the delicious wine. She swallowed, deciding it was quite rather good, she took a larger chug. "It's nice. Has a flowery taste to it," she said between sips.

"It tastes different for everyone who drinks from it. It's quite interesting that you are tasting the flowers, though."

"Why's that?" she asked then drank again.

"The only woman in your line of ancestors to taste the flowers was your great, great, great, great, great, great grandmother, Alareeah."

"Queen Alareeah. My mother told me about her when I was little. She was the first Dragon Lady of my line. She had been a servant to the previous Dragon Lady and had been chosen to replace her the day the Lady had died."

"Yes, Alareeah's parents were elves."

"But...I'm human."

"Alareeah and the Dragon Lady had been travelling by themselves through the Kinarder Wilderness. The wilderness has always been a very dangerous place filled with nomads and rebels. Alareeah's dragon had offered to take her through the wilderness to her destination at the Sacred Fount of Jalvern. But she had rejected the offer claiming she needed to take the pilgrimage only with her servant."

"Does the Dragon Lady always take such pilgrimages?"

"No, no one knows why Lady Celeste decided to take such a

journey. She was large with child at the time. There are nymphs who live in the waters in the pool of Jalvern where the sacred fount is located. If captured they must bestow the seeker with any wish they desire, except raise the dead or force someone to love you. Some say Lady Celeste was unhappy with her life and sought to end it."

"Why, she was with child?"

"I cannot say. Her guardian pleaded with her that if she wasn't going to take her dragon then at least she should allow her to go with them. Lady Celeste consented. The ten-day journey only lasted five days when the rebels attacked. The rebels were brutal. They left everyone for dead. There was no hope for Lady Celeste nor her child so the guardian had no choice but to cast the spell to transfer the Golden Dragon Soul into Alareeah. She told Alareeah to run back to the castle then she died a few moments after Lady Celeste did."

"It seems odd that the rebels wouldn't have wounded Alareeah as much as they did Lady Celeste and her guardian."

"There were many who thought the rebels had attacked to ensure Alareeah was given the soul. Some do not agree that only the humans can be a Dragon Lady or Dragon Lord. They feel the dragons favor humans because humans are less likely to revolt against the dragons."

"And what do you believe about my ancestor?"

"I was not even born, Iona. I cannot cast a judgement unless I have solid evidence to prove my case."

"But if you had too? You're elven. Do you agree with what the dragons do?"

"I am the high priest. It is my duty to do so and not question."

"You said my ancestor was an elf. How am I human?"

"Alareeah's daughter was just like Kilean. She had to mate with a human because all Dragon Lady and Dragon Lords have to be human."

"But there was an exception made in her case?"

"Draco and Razil made her human once she had accepted the passing of the soul."

"They can do that? Make one species into another?"

"The gods can do anything they please, Iona," he instructed holding out his hand for the empty goblet. She handed it to him. "The examination is to ensure that no matter what mixture of species you are, you are majority of human."

"One would think you would do that before the soul came into me."

Aejeon chuckled, placing the cup on the table as she dropped her robe to the ground. He turned to face her. "You will always be human, Iona. It is the way of things. I do find it intriguing though, that you desire to be with an elf. You are so far removed from your ancestor that you shouldn't have elven DNA in you. Spread your legs."

Iona complied. He cupped his hand between her legs, placed his hand on her back and pushed his fingers inside her. She gasped with delight, leaning against his strong hand as he pumped his fingers. "Human indeed," he said pulling out his fingers. He paced his hands on her breasts and fondled her tits, periodically kissing her nipples and suckling. Iona moaned with delight.

Aejeon bit her nipple and pulled back. She moaned, smiling, He did the same with the other one then stepped backwards, taking a clear view of her body. "Not every species is going to excite you like that. The test is simple. I have gathered priests from each of the five alliance races – merman, draconian, human, dwarf and halfling."

"I thought there were six?"

"I will represent the elves."

"Ah."

"They will greet you with the traditional way one greets a Dragon Lady."

"Which is?"

Aejeon stepped close to her, kissed her nipples, bowed between her legs and stuck his tongue inside her. "Holy shit," she exclaimed, stepping backwards and taking hold of the footboard. He rose to his feet and swallowed. "That...uhm...is that...?"

"A formal way to greet the Dragon Lady. Of course, you would have more restraint as to not show pleasure and displeasure when it is being conducted."

"And how does one greet the Dragon Lord?"

"Kiss the end of his penis then give him one stroke of a blowjob while rubbing his balls."

"Lucky person whomever we cum to."

"Indeed. That person is considered very blessed to receive that while they are greeting either you or Kilean because it doesn't happen very often."

"How could it not?"

"You and Kilean won't always have so many people greeting you at once and you would have greater self-control. Normally, you two would make love before a greeting like that ever happened so both of you would have discharged. The cum and seed of the Dragon Rulers is very powerful and has been known to give a blessing to it's bestowed for twenty-four hours."

Iona peered at the door then back to the high priest. "Ah, don't worry about the priests. Your body will choose the given races then we will all have sex with you. That way I can gauge how well you react to each of them. Which one you are stronger with and which one you like the least."

"How can you when you will have sex with me?"

"Not me, Iona."

"But you said you represent the elves."

"I do. Solon will conduct the evaluation."

"Solon!"

"Don't be so shocked. He used to help me in all spiritual matters before he was assigned to Kilean's household," he explained, walking to the door. Iona watched him carefully as he disappeared out into the hallway. She took her robe, placed them onto a chair next to wall then turned as the door opened again.

"Iona," Solon nodded, dressed in his best clothes. He grabbed a pair of low raised pedestals from under the bed and placed it on the ground before the foot board. "Step on it," he ordered.

She stepped the strange boxes, showing her exactly where to stand with her legs apart.

"Are they too far apart," he asked.

"No, just right," she answered, not able to lift her eyes.

"Good," he answered then tied her waist to the footboard of the bed with a thick, silken cloth. "Normally, I wouldn't have to do this but you are untrained. The cloth will help you from falling over. Place your arms along the edge of the bed. There are metal cuffs there I need to use around your wrists. I'm going to cuff your ankles to the bed as well so you can't close your legs."

"Alright," she whispered.

Iona got into perfect position. She breathed deeply lifting her head while Solon worked. She almost didn't feel the restraints being closed. She wondered what the high priestess would have done to Kilean, had the temple been available. Her mind wondered to Kilean. She knew his mind wasn't right. His behavior had changed somewhat but she knew that had to do with what Tayla had done to him. She only hoped he could find healing.

"Iona," Solon called to her. She lifted her eyes to him. "Are you ready?"

Iona nodded. "Each man will enter one by one. If I take his robe then it means you like that race and he will then exit the room, naked, to show everyone your decision. If I do not, then they leave in disgrace for their race. The men chosen to represent their race have the perfect bodily proportions for the race they come from. Any questions before we begin?"

"So the best of the best have been chosen for me?"

"Yes, physically, mentally, sexually and emotionally."

"I like that," she grinned.

Solon ceremoniously walked down the aisle to the door, opened it and...

"Drayson," Iona gasped as the elven commander walked into to the room. The door closed behind her.

"Your grace, may I introduce to you the Ambassador of the Elves," Solon declared as Drayson lowered his robe, revealing an even finer body than his father. She glanced at the brothers with shock. Solon answered her silent questions. "The ambassadors are chosen from the best of stock out of all the races. They are especially prepared for this event. Everyone from all corners of Draconia are outside. The people have been waiting for this moment for a very long time. Portals were created just so all the races could attend this event. The men are usually bred for such an event but seeing as we didn't know the line would continue the breeding programs had stopped after your mother hadn't completed her bonding rituals. When the races learned of you, Iona. Word has spread quickly across the lands to find the right men for this event. Drayson is the best the elves have and the elves only thought it suitable that the son of the priest and priestess be chosen among them."

"But I haven't been in your lands long."

"The news had spread to the temple when you were brought to your dragon twins. Now please, your grace, if you will."

"Oh, of course." Iona closed her eyes, cleared her thoughts and opened to find Drayson before her. She smiled at his fine body. He bowed elegantly. "Your majesty. Pleasure and blessings be bestowed upon you for eternity," he softly blessed her then kissed her gently on her left nipple. Iona gasped as he pulled on her tit then suckled. She could barely keep her breath as he did the same to her other breast. Drayson lowered himself between her legs, places his long elegant hands on her thighs, licked her clit and inserted his tongue. "Oh," she moaned, barely able to keep from quivering as he removed his tongue and swallowed.

"Seems father was right. She loves a good elf. She was reacting to my body long before I touched her," Drayson said to his brother.

"I saw it, too," Solon grinned picking up his brother's robe from the floor.

Iona heaved several times, staring at Drayson. "You need to control yourself. There's plenty more races to choose from, Iona."

"If I can catch my breath long enough to do so. Shit," she swore, lowering her head. Drayson chuckled then walked out of the room. Loud cheers erupted outside the chamber. "Whose next?"

"What do you want?"

She lifted her eyes to Solon. "Sex with that elf," she nodded to the door.

"Not yet, Iona. We still have to find the others."

"I could make this simple for you. I like elves, humans and draconians. I'm not sure about halflings, dwarfs, fairies or mermen. How does a merman have sex with a human?"

"You'd be surprised with what a merperson can do."

Iona smiled, biting her lower lip. "Merman," she declared towards the door.

"Excellent choice."

20 Lundy Hollow – The Borderlands

Tanyl closed his eyes with his hand laying gently upon the ancient Maple tree next to the small pond. He smiled, feeling its positive energy restored. The great healer had spent months tending to the trees in the forest close to his cottage after a vicious infection had infected the trees. He hadn't been shocked that the negative energy had invaded the borderlands. The world had been out balance ever since Queen K'Lara had been tricked into believing King Nomiki had been sent to her by King Tavir to be her husband. The Temple of the Moon had disappeared along with the High Priestess, the Dragon Maidens, the Dragon Lady's Dragon and the priestesses. In his six hundred and fifteen years of existence, he had never experienced the world so out of balance. Oh, there had been times when the male and female energies were slightly out of balance. But nothing like this. And it worried him. There had to be balance between male, female, negative and positive energies in the world or one would overtake the other. He opened his eyes hearing his younger lifemate approach.

"How is she?" Amara asked, placing a wooden bucket next to the pond.

"Better," he turned to greet his wife with elegance and grace. Amana Trejilon had been the love of his life for four hundred years. He had never given marriage a thought, dedicating his life solely to the healing arts. One day, Amana had appeared in his woods with several deep wounds from a Salendar Cat. She had been foraging in the forest when the cat had brutally attacked her, leaving her for dead. Her brother, a member of the King's Guard, had found her and brought her to Tanyl for healing. He had been able to extract the deadly poison from the cat's fangs and heal her wounds. It had taken him months to save her and in those months they both could feel something between them. But he was a hundred years older than her! Tanyl had dismissed her advances then released her from his care when she was well enough to return to her family. After she had left, not a day went by when he couldn't stop thinking about her. Frustrated, he had sought her brother out at the palace who in turn had told him his sister was feeling the same way. There was only one reason they would be so drawn to each other. Elves mate for life and the urge to be so passionate with someone was a sign that they were each other's lifemates. They went through all the Elven rituals and married.

He turned hearing the sound of his grandchildren's laughter in the woods. A slight smile came upon his face at the sight of his youngest daughter, Eletha, and his granddaughter, Sharia, walking slowly towards a wooden bench close to the small clearing where his wife had planted flowers. "It's good to see her out of bed today," he nodded to the mother and daughter.

Amara turned her gaze to the sight. "She was waking up when I left for the village this morning."

"Did she remember her children?"

"Just Sharia. Have you noticed her sleeping habits?"

"There hasn't been a day since she arrived that I haven't been closely watching her. I had thought the arrival of the children would have helped her."

"She's more alert."

"I had hoped she wouldn't be."

"How can you say that? She's our daughter. There is hope."

"There's no hope for her, Amara. We have to face the fact that our daughter is dying."

"You're one of the greatest healers known throughout the elven realm. You of all people should be able to save her."

"I can't!"

"Tanyl, Maelgrum is only supposed to affect the familiar line of the High Priest and High Priestess, should they decide to join the priesthood and they undergo The Cleansing. I'm not from that line and neither are you, so how could it be that she has Maelgrum? Perhaps you and the council have the wrong diagnosis."

"They don't," he muttered under his breath.

Amara stepped closer to her husband, placed her hand on his chest and stared deeply into his brilliant hazel eyes. "Tell me," she whispered.

He placed his hand on top of her own. "No. This is my fault and I take responsibility for it. She is ill because of me. I should have stopped her."

"You came to this forest a little before I was born. No one knows your family nor where in the borderlands you are from."

"Amara," he warned.

"You live a life of a recluse yet want for nothing."

"Don't."

"Some people are scared of you because they don't know your family. There are so many stories about you that it's hard to decide which are true and which are not."

"Please, I beg you, wife, don't proceed further with this conversation."

"You're my husband, Tanyl. Don't I, of all people deserve to know the truth?"

"That truth causes problems."

"You just alluded to me that you are member of the High Priesthood."

"Amara, no more questions. Please," he sneered, pushing her hand down, he turned and walked away. He paused in between two ancient oaks, wiped his hands down his face and exhaled a deep breath. He had kept his true identity a secret for a little over 400 years and now all his secrets were threatening to be revealed because he had allowed his daughter to join the priesthood. How could he have been so stupid! He knew every initiate had to provide proof of their lineage so the family of the high priesthood wouldn't scan those they were related to. He should have told his daughter the truth instead of falsifying her lineage papers. But he had never expected for her memories to be restored. Tanyl took a deep breath, gathered his senses and turned to face his confused wife. "The length of how long one suffers from Maelgrum until their death varies from elf to elf. I was hoping she wouldn't have to suffer for a long time. The illness is debilitating. It will eventually consume her to the point that she will be as helpless and useless as a newborn but unable to think on her own. She'll suffer from hallucinations so severe she won't be able to tell reality from fiction. I should have never allowed her to go to the temple," he muttered, clenching his fist.

"Tanyl, she wanted to serve the gods. You could have told us that you were descended from the highest ranking of elven society."

"It is not something I want, Amara. I chose this lifestyle for a reason."

"What did you do? The highest caste of Elven society never dwell among our people. Your minds and capabilities are completely different than even the royal family."

"That is because the family members of the high priesthood are only interested in separating themselves from Elven society. I do not. I never have agreed with the lifestyle my family had demanded upon me. I didn't do anything to cause me to dwell in seclusion. I chose it for myself. I was afforded more freedom to do so than anyone else in my family because of who I am."

"That being," she asked.

Tanyl shook his head, "No." He wiped his hand down his face and walked away from her, paced then turned back to her. "I should have stopped Eletha when she told us what her intentions were. She was only a hundred and fifty when she left us for the temple. Not a child but not fully mature, either."

"She wanted to serve the gods. You should understand that, being who you are."

"Oh, I do, Amana but there were other ways for her to do so. I have faithfully served our gods as a master healer for a little more than three hundred and seventy five years. Our eldest son serves in our king's army as commander. One of our daughters is a knowledge keeper in the Great Library and the other one teaches in town. Soldier, sage, teacher – these are all notable professions for my children. But her decision? She had no control of where her fate could lie. Once she had entered into the Temple of the Moon and declared her intentions, her life laid at the mercy of the Dragon Lord and High Priest!"

"Eletha did well. She passed the Shifting and when King Tavir's great grandfather had examined her in the Forbidden she was chosen to serve as a priestess. She honored the gods with the sexual services she had provided to the Dragon Lord's army. She was proven many times, Tanyl. Her own children from the time she spent as a priestess are some of the most desirable of sex slaves, even though she doesn't know she has two other daughters and a son. It was an honor that she was able to catch Queen K'Lara's attention. Once she married King Tavir, the high priestess restored her memories. We have a relationship with our daughter and her children."

"But to lose her to a disease that was caused by the restoration of her memories?"

A loud scream from the plain behind them mixed with the sound of a dragon wings caught their attention. The grey haired Elven couple glanced at each other then quickly ran to the edge of the forest.

"Stay with your mother and siblings," Amara yelled at Sharia, seeing her granddaughter sprint towards them. Sharia turned back to her family.

Faster and faster, the tall Elven couple sprinted through the woods, the screams growing even louder as if something was falling out of the sky. Tanyl's heart skipped at beat at the sight of his grandson falling faster towards the earth. "Kilean," he screamed, sprinting faster. Kilean's body landed with a loud thud mixed with the sound of cracking bones.

"Oh, gods," Amara cussed.

Kilean screamed even louder, grasping his head, rolling around in a mad fit, crying in between his screams.

Vashti landed hard. "What happened," Tanyl demanded to the dragon then turned to his wife. "Get my bag and don't tell his mother or siblings he's here."

Amara nodded with understanding then ran back into the woods. Kilean wouldn't stop screaming. "It wasn't like this at the temple. He became more agitated the further we traveled," Vashti explained.

"How did he fall? He's ridden you plenty of times," he asked trying to calm Kilean with no effect.

"He didn't. He jumped. His mind isn't right, Tanyl."

"What did they do to him?"

"It wasn't the council. Kilean had Soul Sickness."

"How can that be? Sharia told me he was completing the Rite of Dragon Souls the day they left for here. He should have received the soul and then be in preparation for the Bonding of Dragons."

"Tayla."

Tanyl clenched his jaw, rose to his feet and glared deeply at the dragon with a stern look on his face. "What happened?" he emphasized both words.

Vashti told the middle aged elf everything from how Tayla had stolen the soul from Kilean, of Roan and Asa's disappearance and betrayal, and of the council's investigation. Vashti told of K'Lara's return, the unification of K'Lara and Tavir and of Iona. She told of how Kilean's soul had been captured, imprisoned and tortured at Drokap Castle. She didn't go into great detail of how Kilean had been rescued, saying she didn't know the detail because she hadn't travelled to the castle with Iona, but she did tell of Iona's efforts to save Kilean. "Solon said when he had approached Kilean in the healing bay, Kilean was highly agitated. He was calmer around Iona."

"Where is Iona?" he asked.

"Completing her bedding ceremony."

Tanyl nodded slowly then carefully studied Kilean's highly agitated state. "Are you certain he was tortured at Drokap Castle?"

"I am. King Tavir, Queen K'Lara, Sina, Lethos and Thalos are trapped inside the keep. We had all thought Kilean and Iona would be able to escape with them but when Kilean received the Silver Dragon Soul the souls had transported them back to the temple. Solon is a working on a spell to open a portal to the keep using my dragon magic."

The wise Elven healer turned towards the woods then peered back at his grandson with a heavy heart. "His mother came here to die, Vashti."

"I am sorry, Tanyl. But if anyone can heal him, you can."

The compassionate healer shook his head. "If he has what I think he does, then there is no cure. He will be in extreme agony until he has a heart attack and dies. Which by the looks of him, won't be that long."

"There must be something you can do for him."

"It's Dragonflame, Vashti. Look at him. His face is flushed, he's highly agitated and paranoid. He's cowering like a scared child. I can sense his mind is shifting back and forth between the memories of his torture and his hallucinations, both of which are only feeding his extreme paranoia. His heart won't be able to keep up the stress he is placing it under. Perhaps, if he was calmer I could extend his life a few more days?"

"What is Dragonflame?"

"A deadly poison, only found at Saloran. I've read of accounts from during the Dragon Wars about it. It is the only reason I know it exists and what the symptoms are. It was forbidden by the Draconian Codex because of what it does. Every prisoner at Drokap Castle who was being tortured, and there were not many who weren't, was forced to inhaled the deadly toxin. The toxin works its way along the person's nervous system and settles in their mind, leaving tiny traces on every single nerve. Whenever the prisoner is tortured, the noxious pores excrete more pressure upon the nerves, enhancing the pain to an almost unbearable rate. When the victim isn't being tortured their infected mind believes they are. They recall every sensation and experience so vividly they loose their mind. The length of time between insanity and the heart attack that causes the body to become so weak it can barely operate depends upon the species of the victim."

"Kilean's a Halfling. Shouldn't his elven half heal him faster or at least prolong his life?"

"No, Vashti. He's not like his siblings because he is the Dragon Lord. He is as human as his father."

"And the soul? Why isn't it healing him?"

"The soul has merged with his soul and mind. Kilean's mind has been poisoned thus so has the dragon soul's mind. I don't know how to save him, Vashti. I don't even know if there is a cure."

Vashti peered at Kilean. "He has several injuries from the fall."

"He won't let me heal him. Vashti," he called to the dragon. Vashti looked at him. "You have to bring Iona to me. Their minds are merged because of the spirit dragons. She might suffer the same fate as Kilean. I just don't know. The people don't need to know the Dragon Lord and Lady have been corrupted."

"Agreed. Will Iona die as well?"

"I don't know. I don't believe Dragonflame has ever been used on a Dragon Lord and Lady. At least, I haven't found any record of it. My daughter is a keeper at the Great Library. I would like to ask for her help but I don't want to alarm anyone in the capital of what has happened."

"Solon wants discretion. He has more resources at his disposal than the elves do."

"I understand. You said Iona was able to calm him?"

"Yes."

"Then hurry, Vashti. Bring her to me."

"I will. Take good care of him, Tanyl," Vashti said, ran down the plain and took to the skies.

Tanyl watched Vashti disappear then gently stared upon his grandson. Kiliean laid on his stomach, a hand clawing in to grass, his other hand clutching his chest, heaving and sobbing as he tried fidgeting. He gently walked towards him then paused hearing Sharia yell Kilean's name.

"No," Tanyl ordered raising his hand and stepping between them. "Leave him, alone."

"Grandma said you needed the basket," she cried, holding the basket out with tears in her eyes.

"Just set it down, turn around and go back to your mother."

"But...is he...is he dead? He's not moving anymore and where's father?"

"No and it doesn't matter right now. Please, Sharia. Leave us. No one is to know your brother is here nor are they to come to him. Do you understand?"

"Yes, grandfather," she sniffed with her eyes on Kilean. She never moved.

"Sharia," he calmly called to her after the sound of Kilean's deep moan. She lifted her blue eyes to him. "Go to your mother."

She nodded, sniffed her nose then ran back into the forest.

He felt a hand on his boot and turned his hazel eyes downward to see Kilean's hand on his shoe and his eyes looking up at him. "Help me," Kilean breathed then fell unconscious.

Tanyl crouched next to his grandson and felt for a pulse. "Heart attack," he sighed recognizing the signs. "Hurry up, Vashti," he muttered with his eyes to the sky, knowing with dread his grandson wouldn't live to see the rest of the week, if he even had that long.

Drokap Castle – Kingdom of Saloron

21

"What the hell were you thinking?" Solon bellowed as he burst into Tayla's empty bedroom in the lower level of the castle. He peered around her small private quarters. Her queen-sized bed was neatly made. Soft light descended from the light globe at the top of the cavern. Solon huffed, crossing his arms across his chest. Of course, his lifemate wouldn't be around when he needed her. He walked around the dimly lit room, surveying every piece of furniture and belongings he was already familiar with.

Solon picked up a small round, ruby encased trinket box he had given Tayla fifty years ago thinking about their relationship. He had always been a devoted follower of the Draconian Codex since his birth two hundred years ago. He had thoroughly enjoyed his station in life, as the son of the high priest, a priest and then as a tutor to King Tavir and as a guardian to Prince Kilean. He never thought he would fall in love with Tayla, quite the contrary. But most of the stories told about her were just made up to make her look like a horrible, despicable creature.

"And make certain they don't find the prisoners," Tayla's voice bellowed from behind him. He lowered the trinket, turned and glared at Tayla as she closed the door behind her. "What are you doing here?" she asked.

"You told me you weren't going to kill Kilean!"

Tayla rolled her eyes, lowering her shirt to the ground. Solon gulped hard at the sight of his beloved's naked, bronze torso. She walked towards him, rubbing her nipples with a grin.

"You were saying?" she asked, lightly caressing the side of his face as he stared upon her large breasts. Solon pushed her to the bed and tackled her underneath him. He grabbed her throat and snarled. "I missed you, too, husband," she forced out.

"Shut up. Sex isn't going to make this any better."

"Aww, sex with you makes everything better for me."

"Tayla," he yelled, pushing her head back, released her and walked away.

She coughed several times, trying to catch her breath, holding her hand to her neck. "You know that temper of yours is going to kill you. You best let me relax you."

"You told me you weren't going to kill him," Solon bellowed in her direction.

"Who? I do have many prisoners in this place. Prince Zurrgash wants...."

"Oh, shut up. I know he's just your puppet." Solon paced the room for a long moment then pivoted to her. "Kilean is special to me."

"You should have told me you knew the spell to make the soul go to someone new then I would have never had to force him to have Soul Sickness."

Solon huffed between his clenched teeth then charged at his wife. He smacked her hard on the cheek. "Soul Sickness is one thing. I could explain that by blaming you. But Dragonflame. You fucking poisoned him with Dragonflame!"

Tayla roared, shoved him to the ground and sat on top of him. "Hit me again, husband, and I swear it will be your last," she threatened, pinning him down.

"Fuck you," he spat at her.

Tayla rubbed the spit from her face with a grin, "I really would love it if you would."

"Kilean."

The draconiod dragon twin sighed, leaning back on his waist. "I had no choice. My nephew greatly desires the soul and told me to have fun torturing the boy. I knew from your reports that Iona might try to rescue him. She seemed by your accounts to be a formidable woman."

"She's stronger than she knows. The Elven in her is stronger than the human even though it shouldn't be."

"How is that possible?" she asked, caressing Solon's chest.

"I don't know. She is so far removed from her elven ancestor that it shouldn't be. Are you certain Nomiki is human?"

"Yes."

Solon pulled her lower and licked her tits with his tongue.

187

"Hmm," Tayla moaned with great delight. He suckled, paying close attention to both her tits then whispered, as his fingered her body. "Kilean?" he asked.

"Oh, hmm, don't you want to fuck first."

"No, but I wouldn't mind torturing you sexually until you give me what I seek, wife," he informed, turning so she was on the floor underneath him. Solon removed his clothes, the rest of her clothes and threw them to the side. He held her hands over her head as he groped her breasts and neck with his mouth while pushing his erect penis just so it was barely touching her.

"Oh," she hummed, closing her eyes and arching her head. "Not fair. So not fair. If you're going to put it in me then do so, don't just let it wait at the opening."

Solon chuckled, nibbled on her ear then whispered, "Why Dragonflame? You said you thought Iona was coming. Kilean was already affected by how you tortured him."

"I only learned you knew the spell after I first interrogated him. Prince Zurggash has put an order for your capture. He believes if I torture you then you will give us the spell."

"Oh, how kind of him. And would you?"

"I can't penetrate the temple."

"Tayla, would you is not the same as can you?"

"No, alright. I didn't want to hurt you. I love you. But you can't expect me to deny him what he wants for very long, Solon. We need my nephew if this plan of ours is going to work."

Solon slowly entered his penis into her vagina. "Oh, yes," she moaned with a giant smile. Her smile fell as he quickly removed his penis.

"Like that," he whispered.

"Always have with yours. It's so much longer and thicker than my nephew's."

"Good. I'll give you more if you're honest with me. Agreed?"

"Uhmm hmm."

"Why didn't you contact me when you knew I had the spell?"

"Why didn't you tell me you had it so I could avoid torturing him?"

"Tayla, I'm asking the questions, not you." She sighed deeply. "If you knew the truth the prince would have required you to capture me. Then you'd have to kill both Kilean and I. The spell only works if the Dragon Lord is dying. I wasn't and I still am not willing to kill him for that soul."

"You said it yourself, he has to die for the transfer to occur."

"There are other ways."

"If Kilean dies then the soul is free."

"Don't be stupid, wife. It's beneath your intelligence. Those souls bond to the Dragon Lord and Dragon Lady's mind and soul. Thus, when you poisoned Kilean's mind with the Dragonflame you corrupted the Silver Dragon Soul as well."

"He didn't possess it. Prince Zurggash has it."

"Not anymore. It merged with Kilean after Iona and his father rescued him and because it did so, it too is ill. So even if Kilean dies, the soul is useless to you. It's dying too! And since Iona and the Golden Dragon Soul are merged with Kilean and the Silver Dragon Soul they will die too."

"Shit."

"Shit is right. You should have contacted me. Because, my love, you damned the entire plan with that little scheme of yours."

"What else could I have done?"

"You could have made him mad. If he was found to be mad, then the council would have demanded of me to remove it from him. He would have died from Soul Sickness but at least that's not as horrible as the death you've decided to give him with Dragonflame."

"I thought you didn't want him to die?"

"I don't but I know you can survive Soul Sickness. His father did."

"Only because Queen K'Lara died fir...," she grinned with understanding. "You would kill, Iona."

"Without hesitation," he claimed pushing his penis several times deep within her.

"Oh, baby," she inhaled through her teeth. "Oh gods, yes."

Solon kissed her nipples then her mouth. "If you had given me the time I would have been able to help you trap Iona so you could steal her soul too. The souls were hungry for each other. We could have tricked Kalesh into thinking her new host was unsuitable. All you had to do was hold Kilean, not torture him nor poison him. Iona is the interloper, not Kilean."

"There's an antidote."

"Oh," Solon said.

"It was developed by the dragons in case a prisoner become of such high value that they needed to create a cycle of healing, torment, healing, torment, etc."

"Interesting. A cycle of mental strain upon a body and mind already suffering."

"They were methodical, if not efficient in their torturing methods. Which by all accounts, I can clearly say you are as well. Fuck me!"

"The antidote, where is it?"

"In the chest by the door. It will only take one vial but you will need a vial for Iona and Kilean. Will you please fuck me already!"

Solon kissed her passionately, got on his knees as she leaned upright on her hands and opened her legs. He pushed hard in her as he played with her nipples. "Oh, yes," she moaned, arching her head back. Faster, harder he pushed, making certain to hit the right spots. She bit her lower lip making sexual noises of delight. Solon grabbed her hips. He slowly moved his fingers down her firm stomach to her clit. "Solon!" she screamed his name as he played. He loved hearing her plead his name. Solon pushed her legs over her chest and fucked her even harder. She giggled, playing with her tits.

"Oh, yeah," Solon heaved. "Fucking bitch. Oh!"

Tayla grinned leaning back on her elbows, thoroughly enjoying the sensual pleasure as her husband pushed her legs out. "Ah, I missed you."

"Hmm, me too." Solon removed his penis. "Get on all fours, bitch. Ass in the air."

"Gladly," she enthusiastically complied. Solon pushed her lower to the ground, held his hand on her ass and tickled the tip of his cock on her ass driving her crazy. He grinned positioning his penis close to her vagina, tempting her. "Oh, fuck. Oh," she moaned.

"I missed your beautiful, fucking pussy," he said then pushed his penis deep inside her.

"Oh, you feel so good," she moaned.

She lowered closer to the ground as he pounded, never stopping her exclamations of delight. "Oh gods! Oh gods, baby. Yes! Oh!" Solon pulled her ass closer to him, going deeper and faster with each thrust. She leaned up on her arms, never stopping her sensual adorations of what a fine job he was doing. He pushed her back down, leaned his full strength on her lower back with his hands and drove into her even harder.

"Scream, baby. Yeah, like that," he coaxed her. He breathed hard, making certain every thrust hit her harder than before. Just as she was beginning to get used to it, he pulled back and slowed his thrust. Slowly, he pulled his penis out and then back inside again, several times, nearly driving her insane as he held her ass. He turned her onto her back, held her leg up and pushed on her breast as he continued his assault. Sweat poured down her body. Solon moved his hand from her breasts to her neck, squeezing just enough so she could barely breathe. He leaned over her body as he pushed with a sexual grimace as her elations rose. Her tits were growing hard. Her face was flush. She was going to orgasm any moment. "Don't you fucking cum, bitch. I'm not ready for that," he yelled, rolling her onto her back. He grabbed her hands behind her back, pushed her flat, spread her legs and took her again while holding her hands with both of his.

"Oh, gods. Oh, gods. Oh, gods," she cried out.

Solon bit his lower lip, breathing hard as she called his name. He could feel the pressure in his body. He pushed even hard, periodically slapping her ass. "Oh, yes! Fucking yes," he yelled then released his seed at the same time as she orgasmed. Solon grinned, exhaling a deep breath. His wife never moved. "Gods, I love it when I leave you exhausted," he muttered, removing his penis then bit her ass.

"Mhhm," she relaxed. "Me too." Solon rose, never taking his eyes off her gorgeous naked body. "I have intruders," she muttered with her eyes closed, completely sprawled out on the floor.

"I know. The council said Iona had travelled with Queen K'Lara, King Tavir and the Dragon Twins. What are your plans for them?"

"I'm not certain yet." She rolled over onto her back with a confused look. "You said the soul is inside Kilean? How do you know what's happened in his cell?"

"He and Iona are in the temple."

Tayla leaned up on her elbows. "Since when?"

Solon sighed, placing his clothes back on. "Have you not been paying attention to anything I've said, Tayla? The Dragon Souls were hungry for each other. The Golden Dragon Soul provided a portal for Iona, her mother, King Tavir, Sina, Lethos and Thalos to come here and rescue Kilean. Their plan had been to ask Kalesh to transport them back but the dragon souls were so hungry for each other Iona and Kilean bonded spiritually then were transported back to the temple. All that remains is a physical bonding to solidify that union. Once they do that, I can't remove the souls."

"They were alone?"

"No, King Tavir is trapped in Kilean's cell."

Tayla rose to her feet and stumbled, almost not able to walk. Solon chuckled as she stabilized herself with a hand on the footboard. "Shut up," she snarled.

"I like it when you're weak. You're usually the dominant one. I thought Dragon Twins were supposed to be the strong ones."

"We are but we don't compare to a member of the High Priesthood." Solon grinned with a bow of gratitude for the compliment. "The Dragonflame."

"What about it?"

"I couldn't deliver it to Kilean personally so it's in the air in his chamber. It doesn't leave that chamber. Everyone who has been in there has been exposed. It doesn't affect anyone who has been in there for a short amount of time but it does...."

"Shit, Tayla," he threw down his cloak. "What the fuck were you thinking!"

"I was thinking it would only be Kilean in there. He would be dead by the time Iona would find him but obviously not."

"Obviously," he huffed. He rubbed his face and paced the floor. "Gods damn it!" He paused turning around to her. "The posion only works if the prisoner is being tortured?"

"As far as I know, why?"

"What do you mean as far as you know? You're usually more thorough than that."

"Prince Zurggash didn't give me enough time to fully research its effects upon different races and what is happening to them physically while they are exposed. He's too rash in his thinking. I couldn't stop him. He wanted me to place it in the air when I told him I couldn't get close enough to Kilean. He told me it would only remain in that chamber."

"Do you know what will happen if you kill all the dragon twins, Queen K'Lara and King Tavir? Kilean and Iona need them if they are to continue their iniatations."

"I thought you didn't want that to happen."

"Well we obviously can't stop it now that you have poisioned the gods' damn fucking souls!"

Tayla sat on the side of the bed, clenching her teeth. "We have to work together, Solon, if we are going to restore Draconia to the old ways."

"Oh, I completely agree," he snarled grabbing his cloak, putting it on then walked to their chest. "You cannot allow your nephew to interfere with our plans, Tayla. He has to think he's in charge. All the blame needs to be on him, not us."

"You have a plan, husband?"

"Not yet. What of Roan and Asa?"

"Asa's pregnancy is going well. Prince Zurggash is working on a way to save her life. He's making great progress on the solution. He's taking the knowledge we have already learned from when I used my body to store the Silver Dragon Soul inside me."

"Good. And Roan?"

"I stole his body from the mating lands, healed his soul and restored him to his body. He's been given the position as General of the Black Dragon Army."

"He must like that."

"Very much, so. He's also enjoying being able to spend time with Asa instead of hiding their relationship. I know they truly believe that my nephew is in charge and not us. The prince still hasn't figured out that you're my lifemate. He thinks I'm completely enjoying the incestal relationship we have."

"And are you?"

"Hell, no! You're a better fuck than he is."

Solon laughed, "Is that all I am to you, Tayla? After all these years of marriage? A good fuck?"

"Solon," she sighed. "I love you. I shouldn't because of who both are. It's forbidden, but I don't care."

Solon grinned a devilsh grin towards her, taking ten vials of the antidote from their chest. He closed the lid, placed them in his leather satchel then kissed her. "I love you."

"Hmm, love you, too."

"Don't do anything to your intruders but do make them believe and the prince believe you are trying to kill them. We'll find another way to glean the power we need to face the dragons."

"How many more options are there?"

"I don't know, Tayla, but there has to be a way. I have to go. I told Drayson I was in my private study researching an antidote for Kilean's condition. He's busy fucking Iona at the moment."

"Oh, really? She has a thing for elves does she?"

"Halflings, humans, dracnoids and elves. Especially, elves. Gods, Tayla, you should have seen her when Drayson presented the elven race to her. It would have made you horny."

"I doubt that. Go," she said then cupped her hand around his face with a grimace. "I was wondering."

"What?"

"Can you check on something for me?"

"What's wrong?"

"I don't know. This time. It felt different. I felt something pop inside me."

Solon's face fell. "Shit," he swore. "I was trying not to go that deep in you."

Tayla shook her head. "It might be nothing."

"But it could be something," he lowered his eyes to her lower stomach.

"If I am and the prince has figured out how to save the life and child of a dragon twin then all the better, right?"

"Yeah, I guess so."

"You guess so?"

"If you felt the pop then how are you going to explain to the prince that you're carrying my child?"

"I might not be."

"You said you felt the pop inside you."

"Solon, it was rough sex. You could have burst one of my sensual nodes. I am having a hard time walking. It's known to happen when the sex is rough. I've popped nodes before."

"Hmm," he nodded then kissed her. "Be careful, my love."

"I will. Go. I'm going to rest a bit then go torture my new friends," she said laying on the bed, pulling back the blankets and snuggling in.

Solon sighed, opened a portal then disappeared.

22   Temple of the Sun

Warmth filled her deliciously aching body as Iona sat naked submerged up to her shoulders in the pool sized, rectangular, hot tub. She closed her eyes with the back of her head leaning on the wall. Surreal happiness filled her entire being. Her thoughts strolled to her last sexual encounter. Drayson has been fucking amazing! The mere recollections of their encounter was enough to make her horny. Too bad she was alone. She could use another sexual encounter. She smiled to herself, leaning back, allowing her sexual girdle to appease her. The sex chains pulled apart the lips between her legs, allowing the warm water to wash upon her clit, bringing her periodic bolts of sensual pleasure "Hmm," she moaned lightly, as the dildo pushed deep inside her. She braced her hands on the side of the hot tub, leaned back and let the dildo do its thing as her mind wandered to thoughts of Kilean. She imagined his hand touching her. His lips upon her breasts. Everything seemed so real.

"Your grace," Solon's voice startled her. Iona opened her eyes and gasped at the sight of Kilean's guardian standing in her room.

Solon raised his hand to her. "Don't be startled. I'm sorry if I was intruding on your personal pleasure."

Iona opened her mouth to say something then closed it remembering what her mother had taught her. There would be moments in her life when she could allow others to see she was being sexually satisfied. She cleared her throat, pushed the thought of Kilean to the side and became the noble women she was destined to become while the dildo continued its assault. Iona leaned against the wall. "How is Kilean? Any news on finding the spell to free my mother, King Tavir and the Dragon Twins?" she asked with authority.

Solon smiled, "You learn quickly. I haven't known many Dragon Ladies who were able to separate their minds from their phsycial pleasures so soon after their bedding ceremony. Usually, the entire experience leaves them wanting more so, much that they crave the Bonding of Dragons to be expidated."

"Oh, it's not a thought that hasn't crossed my mind," she sung, rocking her hips.

Solon smiled. He lowered his light tan satchel on the round end table by the pool. "I sent Kilean to the borderlands to be healed by his grandfather."

"Grandfather? I didn't think he had any family other than his father."

"King Tavir doesn't have any relations that are still alive. Kilean's mother, Eletha, is an elf. Elves have a lifespan between 800 to 900 years. His mother turned 200 last year. Her parents and other members of her family still live in the borderlands. Her father is the most famous healer in Draconia."

"He seemed more agitated then usual the last time I was with him. Did his behavior grow worse?"

"Yes. Vashti said he jumped off her back before she had landed."

"He did what? Is he ok?"

"He broke his arm, leg and possbilty a few ribs. But it is hard to tell to what extent his injuries are. He won't allow anyone to examine him. Tanyl believes his grandson suffers from Dragonflame. There is no known cure but I may have found one."

"Oh!" Solon peered at her with a curious look. "I mean, oh?" She held up her finger, closed her eyes, leaned back and allowed the sensual waves overtake her until she couldn't stand it any longer. "Shit," she exclaimed, reaching orgasm then exhaled a deep breath, relaxing as the dildo disappeared and her sex cords returned to their normal position. Iona wiped her face with the warm water then swam to side of the hot tub. She learned her arms on the edge, pressing her breasts close to the wall.

"I would be careful in that position," Solon advised her.

"Why?"

"The walls are enchanted to give whomever you desire to join you in that pool or yourself the greatest amount of pleasure, possible. You can have sex parties or use the hot tub for healing. I'm surprised you didn't figure out how to turn the sensual sensors off."

"There's a switch?" she asked, turning around. "I hurt all over, a good hurt mind you, from my bedding ceremony. Your father brought me in here once Drayson finished fucking me. Gods, that brother of yours is amazing."

"He's a member of the High Priesthood, such as I am. We are born into it and we possess the most sensual skills known on the planet. No other caste or race can compare to the wisdom, talent and skills we have."

"Damn, so you," she said pointing to him.

"Yes. The switch is on the upper right hand corner of the pool. It's not visible. Put your hand on the tile and it will turn to a healing pool for you."

Iona nodded, turned back to where she had been and searched. She found the tile above the corner of the pool and placed her hand upon it. The tile suddenly glowed from a deep red to cool blue. She heard a clanking sound coming from the pool. Iona turned to find the shelfs and dildos from all races retreat back into the pool wall only to be replaced with large crystals of various colors illuminating.

"Release your hand. The crystals have four settings for how intense the healing should be. Low, Moderate, High and Severe. You should only need low to massage your muscles," Solon guided. "How long have you been in there?"

"I don't know. Not very long, I supposed. It felt good when I got in. My body kept wanting more and the water felt so nice. That's not the first time my sex girdle was activated."

"I suppose not. The water is enchanted by either the healing crystals or a main sensual orb lodged in the middle of the pool on the pool floor."

Iona peered down the floor where a large circle laid, obviously hiding the orb under water. "Hmm," she moaned walking deeper in the water with her hand on her lower stomach. "I haven't been feeling well even though I did like the experiences. I keep remembering what my father and brothers did to me and then for some reason my body reacts to it as if it has been happening to me all over again. The sex has been helping me to keep my mind off of it but I can't have sex every moment of the day, can I?"

"Depends upon the circumstances." Iona's face fell serious. "I am being serious."

"Well fuck."

"Fuck indeed. Stay in there and relax. Let the waters heal your body."

Iona closed her eyes taking in the warm and blissful healing waters. Her head pounded fiercely. She placed her hands on her forehead, leaned over and felt the urge to hurl. Iona could hear Solon speaking but just couldn't make out the words. Why did he sound like he was underwater? She lifted her face, heaving. Everything seemed to be blurry. Her heart felt like it would burst our ofher chest. She couldn't feel her arms. Her stomach turned. Was there something sticky and wet on her face? Mindlessly she walked around the hot tub, ignoring the strange noises all around her. Her foot slipped. She fell backwards, falling downward in the depths of the more than six foot deep end of the pool. Iona gasped for breath but her body was useless. Farther and farther her body descended to the body of the pool. She fidgeted, struggling to breathe or at least make her way back to the top. Oh, gods. She couldn't die like this!

"Iona," Solon's muffled voice filled her ears. She thought she heard a splash but it was too late. She closed her eyes, crying internally, panic stricken. This was it. Oh, gods, she didn't.....

Someone strong had placed their arms around her. Faster and faster her body was being lifted to the top. She wanted to reply. She wanted to scream. Her body rolled onto the hard marble floor of the chamber but she couldn't breathe.

"Shit, what happened to her?" she heared Drayson's voice calling to Solon from the entrance to the aquatic chamber.

"She drowned but not completely. There's still time for us to use our magic to heal her," Solon ordered as he emerged from the pool.

"Are you sure? If the heart has stopped we can't bring her back. It's forbidden to raise the dead."

"Just fucking do it!"

Drayson ran to Iona's side, tapped her on the cheek and called her name but she couldn't reply. He felt for a pulse. "The heart is weak but manageable." He placed his hand right hand flat over Iona's heart, opened her mouth and leaned over her. Drayson muttered the ancient Elven spell in Coptic Elven. Moment later a sliver wisp of wind emerged from his mouth, slithered through the air and poured deep in Iona's mouth. He made it way down her throat and into her lungs. His hand illuminated a warm glow over her heart. A peaceful bliss radiated all over her torso. She suddenly gasped, opening her eyes wide, turned to the side and vomited water. Drayson rubbed her back as she projectile vomited the mixture of water and vomit. "Co...co...cold," she muttered, shivering uncontrollably.

She felt Drayson pick her up. Iona placed her arms around his neck and cuddled close to his chest. "Solon, why is she feverish?" he asked as his younger brother dressed.

"Dragonflame. Kilean was poisoned by it when he was being tortured. I believe since the Silver Dragon Soul inhibited him after the soul was poisoned, it has poisoned the Golden Dragon Soul as well. Iona's ill because her dragon soul is reacting to it's mate," Solon explained as Drayson carried Iona to the king size bed at the far end of the chamber. Solon pulled back the covers as his brother laid Iona in the bed. She clung to the covers that Solon pulled over her. It was so hard to breathe. She gasped and heaved; her body not able to move.

"Kilean must be close to death if your assumption is right," Drayson observed.

"Mo...uh...mothe...," she pushed out.

"I've organized a rescued party. Vashti is ready to go. All I need is the spell from my brother in order to get in there. I hope he has found a way."

She took a painful deep breath, closed her eyes and reopened them. She didn't know how long she had been unconscious but it must have been awhile for when she had reopened them Solon and Drayson were discussing matters admist the supplies he had brought.

"Solon, Drayson," High Priest Aejeon's voice echoed in the chamber. She turned to find the high priest walking quickly towards them. "Has she healed?" he nodded to Iona.

"Not exactly. Why did you leave the sensual sensors on," Solon asked. "I didn't."

"Father, she didn't know it was on that setting nor did she know how to change it to a healing pond."

Aejeon cocked his head at his sons. "I left it on healing, Solon. I knew she didn't have the right training. How long was she in there for?"

"I don't know but that's not what has her bedbound," he said, taking a vial of aqua blue liquid from his satchel. "She's dying."

"Is Kilean that close to death that her dragon soul has sensed it?"

"Her drowning helped her current condition," Drayson added.

"Drowning?" Aejeon asked.

Drayson nodded. "Solon and I saved her but her body is so weak that's she's barely able to speak."

Aejeon glanced at Iona then back to his sons. "Vashti told me you have assembled your men."

"Yes sir," Drayson said.

"Solon, what have you discovered in your library?"

"I may have a cure for the Dragonflame. I found a brief mention of how the dragons used to cure victims they had poisoned just so they give them enough respite so they could repoision them. The cycle continued until the body had grown so accustomed to the routine of healing and torture that they had no option but to kill the person being interrogated."

"I knew the dragons were methodical but I had never heard of that before."

"It wasn't something they wanted to be known. I had to search deep within the ancient texts just to find the cure. There is only one problem, father."

"That being?"

"The poision has never been given to a Dragon Lord nor a Dragon Lady. We know the biological compostion of their lineage is quite unique. They hold genetic markers of all the races. I don't know what this cure will do to them. I can assume Iona and Kilean are linked in their ailment from the spiritual connections they have through the souls they possess. I can cure their bodies but I am hoping it will do the same to the dragon souls. I just don't know if I can cure the dragon souls."

"We must try."

"It would be useless to give the antidote to Iona while Kilean is still suffering from the effects of the poision in his bloodstream. I need them to be together while it is administered. Vashti can carry us there."

"No, I know a faster way."

"Is there anything faster than a dragon?" Drayson asked, arching his eyebrow.

"Yes, a portal."

"But you don't know where to lock the portal anchor to," Solon countered. "I only told you that I sent Kilean to his grandfather in the borderlands. You never knew where his mother was from, only the general area. You don't like to know the exact location where the priests and priestesses come from."

"Trust me, Solon. Drayson, pick up Iona and bring her to us."

"What of Vashti?"

"I will send for her once we know Kilean and Iona are safe. Solon, did you find the spell to Saloran?"

"I did," Solon answered.

"Good. We will use it after we know the future of the Dragon Mates is secure."

Drayson walked to the bed, picked Iona up in his arms with a blanket wrapped around her and walked back to his family. She gripped the end of his black leather armour, trying to breath. "I gave her Elven breath but it's not working well in her lungs," he explained as his father felt her burning forehead.

"She's burning with fever. It could be the cause of it."

"Will she make it without the antidote in her?" Solon asked.

"I believe so but I am not certain. Grab your belongings," Aejeon ordered then turned his back on his sons. Iona's teeth chattered. Her eyes rolled and she convulsed in Drayson arms.

"Shit," Drayson exclaimed, lowering her to the floor. Harder and harder she thrashed for what seemed to be an eternity. Aejeon turned to see what was causing the commotion. He knelt beside Iona. "Give it to me, Solon. I can feel the dragon soul struggling to maintain its connection with her body," he demanded, holding out his hand.

Solon laid his bundle down and rummaged through his sack. He pulled out the tube of blue liquid and handed it to his father. Iona's seizure stopped. She moaned, turning her head to the side. Aejeon gently placed his hand underneath her head. She looked up at the wise elf. "Sip. Do not drink too much," he guided. Iona complied. She closed her eyes as Aejeon pulled the tube away from her and handed it back to his youngest son. "We have to hurry. Pick her up. We leave at once," he ordered, rising to his feet and began the portal enchantment.

23

Lundy Hollow – The Borderlands

Amana sat on the wooden bench against the wall in her medium sized guest bedroom, carefully watching her husband tend to Kilean in the simple, wooden framed, king sized bed. Her heart ached with the thought that her daughter and grandson were dying. She exhaled a deep breath, wiping her slender hands down her beautiful face.

She had always been proud of her youngest daughter, Eletha, for proving herself at the temple worthy enough to be the Dragon Lord's mother. What an honor! Amana had enjoyed a wonderful relationship with her youngest daughter until the day Eletha had showed advancing signs of Maelgrum. There were moments her daughter was completely lucid but most of the time she lived a life of dreadful hullicinations, memory loss and paranoia. Tanyl had told her time and time again there was nothing he could do to save their daughter. It would only be a matter of time before she became so debilitated, she wouldn't be able to eat nor drink. She would die a death of starvation or her heart would simply give out from all the strain put upon her body. She knew it would happen but the mother inside her couldn't help but beg and plead to the Elven gods for a cure. Then to learn today that her husband could have prevented all of it! The only reason she had sent Sharia to give Tanyl his basket is because she was so irate at what he had done she couldn't bear to look at him. This was their daughter! His secret had cost the life of their daughter!

She clenched her jaw with tears strolling down her face, rubbing her temple. This couldn't be happening, but it was. "Amara," Tanyl's soft voice entered her ears. She wiped her tears, sniffed her nose and peered up at her husband. How could he not be tormented by the sheer fact he had doomed their daughter to death and now their grandson was dying from Dragonflame? Damn the man and his ability to keep his emotions from everyone.

"His fever has fallen."

"Good. Why isn't he awake, then?" she asked in harsh tone.

"The fever has fallen too low. He's cold to the touch and will only grow colder. It won't be long before he passes into the next realm. You should speak to him. I'll tell his siblings of his condition. They should speak to him as well."

"What of our daughter?"

Tanyl shook his head. "She doesn't remember him, my love."

"Hmpf," she huffed rising from the bench. He grabbed her by arm and looked sternly at her.

"Say it," he urged her.

She huffed, pulling her arm away from him. "You doomed our daughter to her fate and now she can't even say farewell to her son! What were you thinking?"

"The life I had at the temple is not one I desired for my children."

"Then you should have stopped her!"

"And do you honestly believe that she would have listened to me? Amara, she's stubborn. Eletha, would have done whatever she wanted to do. She's always been that way."

"At least," she cried, heaved then began again, "at least she would have known what to expect from there and your family wouldn't have wiped her memories."

"And we wouldn't have Kilean, if I had."

Amara shook her head with a sniff of her nose. "I don't understand."

"It is against the Draconian Codex for any member of the High Priesthood family to become the mother or father of the Dragon Mates."

"Why?"

"Because we are considered sacred." He exhaled a deep breath, looked at Kilean then back to his wife. "I'm sorry. How many times do I have to say it?"

"Do you mean it?"

"Of course, I do! Don't think for one moment I haven't been torturing myself over it. I couldn't celebrate with you and Eletha when our daughter rejoined our family after she was chosen to marry the

Dragon Lord because I knew the dangers of what could happen to her mind and body. I earnestly prayed to the gods it would never happen but it did. There's no cure for Eletha. It's my pain. I caused it by my own foolishness in thinking that I could hide my true heritage from my family. I hate to admit it. I really do. I love all our grandchildren. But I know we would have had a better life if I had told Eletha the truth and had presented her with the sacred lineage papers. Then none of this would have ever happened. She would have been trained as one of the highest ranking priestesses, she is owed, due to her caste through my lineage."

"Why didn't you?"

"Amara, I feared, and still do to this day, if you had known the truth of who I am among the high priesthood you would deem me too sacred to be your husband."

"That's absurb. I love you."

He kissed her gently on the top of her forehead. Amana chuckled. "What?" he asked pulling away from her.

She looked up into his eyes. "The sex. I should have known something was up with you when we had sex. By the gods, you are amazing in bed!"

Tanyl chuckled, "Well, thank you."

She placed her hand over his heart. "I'm sorry, too. This is just...hard. Very, very hard. We don't even know where Kilean's father is and I know if Tavir knew his son was this ill, he'd be here. He should be able to say farewell to his son too, should he not?"

"Of course." He placed his hand on his wife's hand. I'll sit down with the children, tell them what is going on then let them come to say their farewells. Stay with Kilean. He won't wake."

"I will," she said, removing her hand from his chest. She silently watched him exit the room and close the door behind him. Amara quietly picked up the quilt she had made from the foot of the bed and raised it over Kilean. She knew he already had several blankets over his shivering body but what would one more do?

Amara stroked the side of Kilean's pale face with her long finger thinking about when he was younger. He had been such a sweet, rambunctious child. Always playing outside, listening to the tales she and Tanyl had told him. Sweet memories flooded her mind. "You're so young to die like this," she whispered. "My little sweet, Halfling. I hate that you have to depart from this world. You should...."

"This way. Put her inside next to Kilean," she heard what

sounded like Tanyl's voice order someone. Amana rose from the bed just as the wooden door burst open. She peered at the tall, blonde younger Elven men enter into the room in front of a man who looked like her husband but had different clothes on. Drayson laid Iona beside Kilean, tucked her and clasped her hand with Kilean's.

"Tanyl, what's going on?" she asked him.

The mysterious man glanced at her then ignored the inquiry. He walked over to Solon. "You have the antidote ready?" he asked.

"Solon, Kilean's closer to death than Iona," Drayson observed. "We have to act quickly."

"But you said there isn't a cure and who is this, Iona?" Amara pestered the mysterious man.

He pushed her away and turned back to Solon. "Can you inject them with it or does it have to be swallowed?"

"I'm not certain."

"Be certain, Solon. We can't lose him. He's close enough to death for you to transfer the soul to a new Dragon Lord but his brother is not old enough to assume his position and we don't have a replacement for Iona. If your cure doesn't work we lose everything," Drayson bellowed.

Solon pulled out two needles and the potions. "I packed them just in case but I must...."

"Tanyl, who are these men?" Amara demanded upon the mysterious man ignoring the sounds of someone walking into the room.

"Get out of my house!" Tanyl bellowed from the door, pointing towards the entryway.

Aejeon turned to face his twin brother. The fraternal twin brothers almost looked identical.

Amara gasped, speechless she couldn't stop looking at the two.

Solon and Drayson stared at the view of their father and uncle side by side. "Holy Shit," Drayson cursed.

Tanyl slammed his fist in Aejeon's face, sending the high priest stumbling backwards and falling on his bottom.

"Well, is that any way to treat family?" Aejeon asked, rubbing is sore jaw.

"You lying piece of shit. How could you?" Tanyl demanded, kicking his brother on the side.

"Oh, is this about your daughter?"

"You should have been able to sense who she was when you slept with her at the initiation. You had every right to investigate. That's why we slept with the intiates to feel their spirits and read their genes."

"Well maybe," Aejeon yelled, rising to his feet, "if you hadn't cast such an impressive misidentification shield on her mind and body I would have!"

Tanyl huffed, shaking his head. "You could have broken through that shield."

"You've always been better at spellcasting than I, Tanyl. I have never been able to break your spells."

"We have the ability to break through all magical contractions and essences."

"I'm your twin! Twin magic is more powerful than any other magic known to all the races. If you cast a spell, I can't break it and it's the same, vice versa." Tanyl exhaled a deep breath through his clenched teeth. "You can't blame me for something you knew I could never penetrate."

"Oh, you penetrated her alright," Tanyl hissed.

Aejeon pointed to the bed. "Can we discuss this later? I have to save them."

"There's no cure."

"My youngest son has found one."

"Sons?"

"Two sons and a daughter."

"From our sister?"

"No, I couldn't go through the rite without you taking our other sister."

"Oh, shit. The prophecy," Solon cussed. "It all makes sense." All eyes peered at him as he stood over Iona.

"What prophecy?" Amara asked, still stunned.

Tanyl answered, "Double moons and double suns come together to join as one. The salvation of the Draconian Ways shall merge together from within the flames. Solonified to destroy the word from within. Only the four high kings and queens shall live to create the world anew."

"You left because of that?" Amara asked her husband.

"I left because I didn't agree with our parent's interpretation of the prophecy. They believed the only way to save our world was for Aejeon and I to marry our twin sisters."

"Double moons and double suns," Aejoen interjected. "You damned this world with your actions, Tanyl. There's nothing we can do to save it."

"Then prepare the people for the worst, Aejeon! Our caste has no right to keep the prophecy that was given to us over 1,000 years ago from the people. Even the kings and queens of each of the allied races have no idea that there is an end to this way of life. Why do you insist on following the strict codex when you know there is no hope for the future?"

"You want me to panic the world?"

"No, I want you to trust that the rulers of the seven races are smart enough to understand what is happening and is yet to come to their people. You are only going to allow more chaos and rebellion in this world by not informing the people of the reality of this situation!" He turned back to his wife. Amara glanced at her brother-in-law.

Aejeon glared at his twin. "You've always been idealistic, Tanyl."

"And you've always been too rigid in your thinking!" Tanyl yelled towards his elder brother.

"Being rigid in our beliefs is the only way to prevent catastrophe. Something you have never appreciated," Aejeon hissed.

Tanyl clenched his jaw, clutching his fist. "So that's what you want, is it? For me to leave my wife, children and grandchildren in order to appease what our parents believe to be a reality?"

"I would if you could but you can't. No one can," Aejeon muttered.

"Why not?"

"You've been gone too long, Tanyl. Prince Zurggash killed our sisters fifty years ago in one of his uprisings in order to stop the propehcy."

Tanyl gasped in shock. He stared at his wife then fell into a chair, utterly defeated. He lowered his face into his hands as Amara approached him. Aejeon continued. "Their deaths devasted our mother. She killed herself in the Lagos Drago."

"Why didn't...," Tanyl started to ask as Amara rubbed his back.

"Father," Drayson yelled from Kilean's side. All eyes lifted to the younger elf. "He's not breathing."

"What," Aejeon yelled, quickly walking over the bed as Tanyl rose suddenly. "Solon, the antidote," he barked to his other son.

"I had to prepare it with the spell before I placed it in the needle," Solon explained, pushing the needle into the top of the tube next to Iona.

"How long has he been dead?" Tanyl barked, walking next to his brother.

"I don't know. A minute, maybe two? He was fine, barely breathing but he just breathed his last," Drayson stampered.

"It hasn't been five minutes," Tanyl said to his brother.

"Move," Aejeon ordered, pushing Drayson out of the way. Drayson stumbled backwards as his father opened Kilean's mouth. He peered up at his confused younger son. "You only a have a very brief time in which we can hold his body and soul together. You have to deliver the antidote as soon as you hear him gasp. We can accelerate the healing process so his heart will remain beating."

"It's against the law to return a soul to its deceased body," Solon objected.

"Not for twin magic. Just do it." Aejeon turned to his other son. "Drayson, you must return immediately to the temple. Find your grandfather. Tell him to come quickly and bring the reunification stones."

"The reunification stones? What are those," Drayson questioned.

"I don't have time to explain. Just do it, then take your army and rescue the others from Tayla. Bring King Tavir and Queen K'Lara here! Go! Now!"

"Yes, sir," Drayson nodded, cast a portal spell then disappeared into the portal. The portal closed.

Aejeon and Tanyl exchanged a knowing glance. The high priest lifted his left palm in the air. Tanyl joined his right palm to his brother's palm. They closed their eyes and began to chant an eerie sounding Coptic Elven spell. The cryptic sounds resonated in the air all around them, engulfing the mysterious life force floating unseen in the room. A long silver stream of magic erupted from the twin's mouths, intertwining with each other in a beautiful, whimsical pattern to Kilean's mouth. Its magic drove deeply down Kilean's throat. The silver threads gently emerged tetancles from the stream, fully engulfing Kilean's body. Kilean laid silent for a long time. Tears flowed down Amara's cheeks. Oh, gods, how she hoped whatever her husband and his brother were doing would work. She didn't know much about magic, let alone twin magic. She fidgeted with her skirt. Suddeny Kilean's body arched. He gasped widely opening his eyes. Solon leaned across Iona's body and pushed the hypodermic needle on the side of Kilean's neck. Kilean closed his eyes and fell silent just as the last of the magic left Tanyl and Aejeon. The twins collapsed.

24
Drokap Castle – Kingdom of Saloron

K'Lara paused in the middle of the damp, dark corridor with her curved swords lowered. She paced up and down, looking in all directions.

"What's wrong?" Sina asked, standing against the marble wall.

K'Lara shook her head. "I don't know. How long do you think we've been in here?"

"It can't be that long, can it?"

K'Lara sighed, returning to the humanoid dragon twin. "Sina, time runs differently in Drokap Castle. I feel as if I've been walking up and down the same corridor. The sounds of the prisoners aren't getting any closer, yet I know I have to be close to them or at least making my way towards something."

"I've been feeling the same," Sina sighed, moving closer to the guardian. "I just thought I was disoriented because Asa and I are separated." The raven haired beauty walked past K'Lara and examined the same hallways. Darkness and dread consumed the inner sanctum but Sina pushed through all of it, seeking the Male Dragon Twins with her mind. She turned back to K'Lara.

"Can you feel Thalos and Lethos?"

"No. I'm sorry K'Lara. It was difficult before without having access to the Temple of the Sun but now it's even harder without Asa. I've been feeling stranger than usual."

"Because of Asa."

"I would know if she is dead but I can't feel it yet, I know she is with Roan's child. She'll be dead once she gives birth unless Roan knows something I don't."

"Hmm," K'Lara nodded. K'Lara rubbed her eyes then peered towards Sina. Her eyes sight became blurry. She blinked her eyes again yet the world around her never cleared. A wave of dizziness overcame her. K'Lara stumbled back, dropping her swords and ran into the wall.

"K'Lara," Sina called to her, grabbing her by the arm to stabilize the warrior queen. Iona's mother pressed her hand against the wall and lowered herself to the floor. Blood tricked down her nose. She gasped for air, just barely breathing. Sina tapped her on the cheek. "K'Lara, stay with me," she said as K'Lara closed and opened her eyes.

"Air...it's in the air..."

Suddenly a dragon roar erupted from the down the hall followed by a billow of flame streaming quickly towards them. Sina turned to see Tayla in dragon form charge towards them. She instictivly transformed into a dragon, roared loudly and breathed flame. Sina's flame blocked Tayla's flame from reaching her human friend.

"Bitch," Tayla cursed disappating the flame and charging even faster towards Sina.

Sina charged towards Tayla. The dragons roared loudly, the echoes of their battle cries echoing off the ceiling and walls as they crashed into each other.   K'Lara closed her eyes amidst the intense battle between the dragons. She desperately wanted to remain conscious but her weakened body just wouldn't allow it. She fell to the ground then slowly opened her eyes against her body's desires. The blurry vision of the loud dragons fighting caught her attention. Suddenly, Sina transformed back into her human state, slid across the floor and tried to rise but stumbled.

"Let's end this once and for all, Sina," Tayla roared, charging towards the women with thick, rich, red blood trickling down her sides and wings. Sina tried to change back into a dragon but couldn't. Tayla laughed. "Stupid girl. Looks like the poision I placed on my talons is working."

Sina gasped to K'Lara then tried to morph yet again but couldn't. Closer and closer Tayla drew upon them.

"Do something. I can't move or think," K'Lara pushed out of her mouth, trying to remain awake.

"Having trouble connecting with Thalos and Lethos," Tayla laughed. Sina grabbed K'Lara's sword and glared at the incoming dragon. "Thought it was because Asa joined Prince Zurggash, did you?"

"What have you done with my sister," Sina demanded, standing like a warrior in front of K'Lara.

"You have the wrong questions, Sina. You should be asking what have I done to Thalos and Lethos," she bellowed swiping her front paw towards Sina. Sina beautifully moved to the side, ducked and turned to avoid Tayla's paw.

K'Lara's breath slowed. She lowered her eyes. She could hear the brave battle happening all around her but just didn't have the strength to open her eyes. Bones breaking. The clash of metal hitting against bone. Screams. Roars. The smell of fresh blood. Oh, gods she hoped Tayla wasn't besting Sina. She wanted to move. She wanted to help Sina. K'Lara tried to call forth the will but her entire body was paralyzed. What in the name of the gods had Tayla used against her? It had to be something that would only affect humans. Humans. Shit! Tavir. Oh, gods, was Tavir like this and what had she done to him? Panic filled her mind. Anger filled her heart. She had to move! She had to help Tavir!

"Queen K'Lara," Drayson's voice filled her ears. How could she hear him? It had only been her and Sina. She felt his hands on her face, one lightly tapping her cheek yet she was too weak to respond. "K'Lara, listen closely if you can hear me. Kilean and Iona are safe in the borderlands." That perked her attention yet she couldn't express it. Thank the gods the children were away from here. Drayson continued, "My father ordered me to bring you and King Tavir to them but I am bringing everyone because the only way to cure all of you can be found there. My uncle should know of the spell you and King Tavir are under and be able to heal both of you so you can rejoin your children."

K'Lara pushed through the spell with everything she had and opened her eyes. She stared at the sight of blood all aroud the corridor. Sina's unconscious, broken body laid on the floor in a pool of blood with an Elven soldier tending to her. Drayson peered behind him. "She's alive. Tayla wasn't here when we arrived. I assume she left both of you for dead, which," he turned back to her. "Tells me the poison inside you will kill you. I need to transport both of you immediately. My men have already secured King Tavir, Thalos and Lethos. Tayla did the same to King Tavir, Thalos and Lethos as she did with Sina. We know all of you have been poisioned by Dragonflame but what is making you paralyzed isn't that poison. It will only become worse with time. King Tavir has been exposed to the Dragonflame longer than you, Sina, Thalos and Lethos. We had to sedate him because he is losing his mind from the Dragonflame. Solon has a cure for Dragonflame."

K'Lara closed her eyes with sheer relief. Thank the gods her

daughter, Kilean and Tavir were safe. She could finally rest. She just hoped her willingness to rest didn't mean an eternal rest. She felt Drayson pick her up. She could hear him say the portal spell then order his men inside the portal with Sina's body.

"Stay strong, Queen K'Lara. Don't die," Drayson encouraged her then stepped through the portal.

Lundy Hollow – The Borderlands

25

Onas stood silently watching as the reunification stones emitted their mystical healing properties upon his twin sons. He walked around the large bed, thoroughly surveying Tanyl and Aejeon's progress. He had felt their souls rejoin their bodies but they still weren't awake. It didn't surprise him, though. The Reunification Stones had been created by Draco and Razil only for the use to heal twins and restore their magic. It was always necessary to use them whenever one twin was ill or injured, the other twin would feel it too. Death, illness, injury, magic; all shared by the other. Perhaps, he had been too late?

Tanyl moaned, wincing his eyes then slowly opened them. He groaned at the sight of his grey haired, elegant, seven hundred year old father, removed the stone from his forehead and sat upright.

"Thank you," Tanyl said.

"You're welcome. How do you feel?"

"Weak. I have a headache and I'm sick to my stomach. Aejeon have stomach issues?"

"No, but your body hasn't completely realigned to your soul yet, either. You need to rest." Tanyl nodded, closing and opening his eyes. "What is it?"

"I know that look," he said, moving his eyes towards his father.

"We need to speak but it can wait until you are completely healed."

"I can't rest knowing you are upset with me."

"Hmpf. I am more than upset with you. I'm livid." Tanyl nodded, peered at his twin then back to his father. "Let your brother rest. Are you strong enough to walk?"

"I believe so."

"Then come with me, Tanyl."

The healer removed the stones from his body, rose from the bed and stumbled. His father grabbed his arm to stabilize him. Tanyl placed his hand on Onas' chest, took several deep breaths then rose to full stature. "Alright?" the older elf asked.

"I think so."

"Good, put this on," Onas said, taking his son's pants and robe from the back of a chair and handing it to him. He watched as his son dressed. "Why?"

"Why?"

"That robe and pants are fitting for an upperclass elf but you were born into the highest caste. Why reject that?"

Tanyl huffed, tying the ends together. "You still don't understand, do you, father. I do not reject who I am."

"If you believe as such then you would have never left the temple to...to...to live like a hermit."

"Our world never started to fall apart until Queen K'Lara and King Tavir didn't complete the Bonding of Dragons."

"Tanyl, it could have all been avoided if you and your brother had joined with your twin sisters. The two houses your unions would have created would have been powerful enough to protect and preserve the Draconian Ways."

"You can't possibly belive a decision I made three hundred years ago has damned our entire world?" Onas lifted an eyebrow with a stern look. Tanyl sighed. "Rebel activity has only increased since you left us. The fact that Prince Zurggash and Tayla were able to infiltrate the Dragon Mates inner circle only supports the fact that the days of our end is growing closer. And despite your so called efforts to prevent disaster, you have participated in the corruption of the Dragon Mates lineage."

Tanyl sighed, "Eletha "

"Eletha. What the hell were you thinking?"

"I didn't think she would make it as far as she did within the temple. I thought if I gave her such a low caste lineage she would never be chosen for the Dragon Lord Mother contest."

"It doesn't matter what caste or race a priestess comes from, Tanyl. The high priestess would chose three of her best priestesses to present to the Dragon Lady as mate for the Dragon Lord. You should have expected a daughter of a high priest would possess the sensual skills and talents to appease any race."

"I had hoped if she wasn't trained from an early age and because she is only half high priestess she would never be able to tap into that part of her."

"This naïve way of thinking is why you shouldn't have left the temple in the first place!"

Aejeon moaned, turning his face towards them then fell silent.

"Come, we must let your brother wake on his own," Onas said, pulling the blanket higher on Aejeon's body.

"Where are we going?" Tanyl asked.

"Not very far. This is a very large cottage but not as large as one I would have built for you," he said, walking to the door. Tanyl rolled his eyes. He always hated his father's way of making everything a mystery. Why couldn't his father just tell him what he obviously wanted to. "Tanyl."

"I'm coming," Tanyl said following his father out of the room.

"It is a very impressive place for something so...so...so quaint," Onas said, nodding to the arched ceiling then back to the marble floor in the long hallway.

"It's bigger on the inside than it appears on the outside for a reason."

"That being?"

"I didn't want people to visit me because they felt they had to. Honestly, I didn't really want to be a healer, either. I wanted to live a life in seclusion but I healed one elf from a disease that commoners believe is fatal and then word spread that I was a master healer."

"And how did you keep from going mad from the sexual urges before you married Amara?"

"I visit the local temple in disguise. I have over fifty pseudomyns I used so the temple doesn't start to suspect anything. Their priestesses service my needs."

"Still use them?" Onas asked after a long moment of silence.

"Amara and I have a rich sexual life. She pleases me three, mostly four times a day. She doesn't know I must have the encounters in order to maintain my health. She thinks I do it because I love her."

"And do you?"

"Yes, very much so. Most of the times we are together is out of love. I can't imagine being with any other woman. There are times, though, when she is not available that I have to use those spells and the priestesses but she doesn't know of it. But now that she knows who I am, she might figure that out."

"What caste is she from?"

"Military."

"A caste one step lower from the high caste. You could have done better, Tanyl."

"She has the stamina to maintain the intensity of our encounters."

"She's not of noble blood."

"Why does that matter? I'm not even supposed to marry outside our own caste."

"For a reason, Tanyl," he said turning around the corner and opening the door to Kilean's bedroom.

Tanyl gasped seeing his daughter full of life, talking and laughing with Kilean, Iona and Amara dressed in a beautiful, simple tunic with a sharp crescent at the top exposing her breasts but hiding her nipples. Black leggings hid her skin from view. The hem of her tunic reached the top of her thighs. Eletha rose from the bed, turned and greeted him, "Father."

He turned to his father, wide mouth, unable to speak.

"I healed her. She is as if she had never been sick before."

"How? There is no cure."

"There is but it is so costly that it is best if no one knows of it." Onas pulled out seven bright pink and two dull blackened crystals. He placed the blackened crystals in his son's hands. "You know what these are?" the Grand Priest asked.

"Draco's Life. When a High Priest turns six hundred he retires and his eldest son becomes the new high priest. He is secluded at Lago Draco in order to receive eight crystals that will heal his body and extend his life for two hundred years. The first must be used upon the elf's eight hundreath birthday. Your birthday is today, father."

"It is. I was at Lago Drago when Drayson found me this morning. I was contemplating giving the crystals back to Draco so I could die today and be with your mother. Drayson said Aejeon told you what had happened to your mother?"

"He did. Why?"

"You broke your mother's heart when you left the temple two hundred years ago. She missed you terribly but she was not reminded of it on a daily basis because she served as Grand Priestess. When your sisters were murdered fifty years ago, the saddess was too much for her. She couldn't bear the loss of her children. Aejeon's wife had tried to help her through it but it was too much. No one knew she had crossed the barrier to the Pools of Askarlar until it was too late. I found her floating face down in the Lago Drago the following morning."

"Father, I am so sorry," he said, placing his hand on his father's forearm.

Onas cleared his throat, wiped away his tears and continued, "This morning, I extended my life with that crystal. When I arrived to your cottage, I saw Eletha in the gardens and wondered why the Dragon Lord Mother was here. I knew she was ill but word had not come to me of what she had been suffering from. Solon told me everything. I was shocked. I couldn't allow another member of our family to die and I certainly couldn't allow you to feel the pain of a child's death so I did what I had to do to save her. I traded a life for a life. I persuaded her to join me by the pond and used the crystal to heal her. She knows everything, Tanyl."

Tanyl stared at his daughter then back to his father with tears running down his cheeks. "Thank you."

"You're welcome. You just remember what a great sacrifice I made for you today, Tanyl, and when I die in 800 years you better not forget why I didn't make it to 1800 years. Because, son, this entire situation is your fault. I leave you to your family and we will speak later. Send for me should you find you need to return to your bed," he said, pushing his son's fingers over the two crystals. Father and son exchanged a glance. Tanyl wiped his tears and sniffed his nose. He walked into the bedroom, closing the door behind him.

"Father," Eletha called to him, walking up to him.

Tanyl placed the crystals into the inner pocket of his robe then held her face with his long hands. He smiled seeing life again in his daughter's green eyes. "Eletha," he whispered, thoroughly examing her with all the love he could give. "I am so sorry. So, so, so, sorry," he cried, lowering his head to her shoulder.

"Grandfather told me everything," she said. "Mother explained to me why you kept the secret from us. Father, I understand...."

"You shouldn't have to," he said, lifting his face. "No, I was wrong. Your sickness and everything that has happened since...my father's right...it's all my fault. Forgive me."

"I wouldn't have Kilean or the other children if I hadn't done what I did. Mother told me about my two daugthers and son born from my priestess duties. I remembered them even before she spoke to me about them."

"You remember them?"

"I remember giving birth seven times and not four but I don't remember raising them."

"You didn't. They are sex slaves. They were raised by the Mistress of Priestesses and Lord of Priests. I only hope my father will rescue them from the life they lead because of you."

"Kilean," Iona said from her side of the bed. Tanyl and Eletha walked quickly to Kilean's bed. Kilean moaned, tossing and turning then fell silent.

Amara informed, pulling aside Kilean's blanket so Tanyl could examine his grandson, "I bandaged his head. He has a small cut on the back side of his head. His elbow is badly bruised and he broke his arm close to the elbow. He has three broken ribs. His right knee is bruised, the leg is broken and the ankle is sprained."

"Concussion?"

"He is showing signs of such. He's nauseated, can't remember anything you tell him, sleeps a lot, can't speak very well and has headaches."

"What about his attitude?"

"I'm not sure, Tanyl. He and Iona woke up yesterday evening. Iona's fine but I told her she needed to rest to regain her complete strength. Kilean...well...he comes and goes. When he is awake, he's very confused and has the other symptoms I told you about."

Tanyl sighed, sitting on the side of the bed. "He's fortunate that's all that's wrong with him after that fall he took yesterday," he explained, examining his grandson.

"Did he fall or jump?" Eletha asked sitting in the chair next to the bed.

"Eletha, it wasn't him who fell from the sky. He was mad from the Dragonflame inside him."

"Which he got when Tayla tortured him," Iona completed the thought, sitting upright.

Eletha clenched her teeth, "His father?" Iona bit her lower lip. "Iona, where is his father?"

"He thought you were dying. We all did."

"I was. Where is Tavir, Iona? If he knew his son was deathly ill he would do anything to save him. Yet, my husband isn't here."

All eyes peered at Iona. "He was reunited with my mother."

"And?"

"You're not upset? He's your husband."

Eletha sighed, "Iona, Tavir doesn't love me nor I of him. We married out of obligation to provide him with an heir. I always knew he loved your mother. That's why I used the spell she had taught him to make my body look like hers whenever Tavir wanted to have sex with me. If they are together, then I am happy for them."

"Oh."

"Where are they?"

"Kalesh came forth, opened the portal and we all went Drokap Castle. King Tavir and I remained with Kilean while my mother and dragon twins left his chamber to rescue the others Kilean told us had been imprisoned there. After mother and the others left, we released Kilean but he felt the urge to mate with me. The Silver Dragon Soul was calling to mine. We had sex, he gained the Silver Dragon Soul and then our souls portered us back to the temple. I awoke in the chamber. Solon brought me to Kilean. When we arrived in the healing pod we found Kilean highly agitated and needing sex. Solon had suggested we find a sex slave for him but he wouldn't have it. He demanded Solon allow me to fulfill his needs. We knew we couldn't penetrate each other so I gave him a blow job and swallowed his cum."

"Shit," Eletha cussed, turning to her father. "He knew better. I know Tavir raised him better than that."

"What?" Iona asked.

Tanyl raised his hand to his daughter never taking his eyes off Iona's body. He glanced between the very thin two strips of fabric descending over her shoulders to form a v meeting at the hem of her skirt. "It might just be your son knew what he was doing, Eletha."

"How? He knew he needed to complete the Bonding of Dragons with Iona before he could ever touch her and the only way to start that ceremony is for the female to submit to the male with oral sex and then the male to the female."

"But he wasn't in his right mind. He may not have known he was poisioned but he knew his body was weak from his soul being tortured. Dragonflame affects the mind and body no matter how it is administrated. Look at their skin. You can barely see it. I think he started it for a reason but couldn't articulate what he was doing. Your son is a very intelligent young man, Eletha."

"What are we looking at?" Amara asked, stepping next to her daughter.

"Watch Iona's skin. You can barely see it but if you concentrate hard enough you will. Her uniform makes it easy enough to see it in the breasts. The straps are only large enough to hide her nipples." He nodded up at Iona. "Stay still."

"Alright," she replied.

All eyes studied her body. Suddenly a light glow of gold traversed from her heart throughout her torso and down her limbs. "Holy shit. That's not supposed to happen, yet." Eletha gasped, turning to her father.

"What is that?" Amara asked.

"Her dragon soul is preparing her body to mate. The only way it does that is if the Dragon Lord activat...," Eletha paused, glanced at her father. "He..." she pushed her father aside and lifted Kilean's blanket. A silver glow traveled throughout Kilean's body. She lifted her eyes to Iona. "The cum. You swallowed all of it?"

"Yes, why," she asked.

Eletha turned back to her father. "We can still unite them."

Tanyl nodded. "I was afraid with his injuries all hope of their bonding would be lost but Eletha, Kilean did right by demanding what he did of Iona. He knew he had to preserve the union. I don't think he jumped off his dragon out of madness."

"Then why?" Amara asked.

"He must have had a rational thought that he couldn't allow the Dragonflame to overtake his mind before someone figured out what he had done to Iona. He jumped to clear his mind with pain but didn't realize that the Dragonflame would only intensify the pain."

"So now what?" Amara asked.

"We wake him up and have him finish what he started," Eletha said, changing places with her father.

"Finish?" Iona asked.

Tanyl lifted his gaze to her. "I assume my brother had you go through the ceremonial bedding."

"Yes, it appeased me for a time. Drayson, by the gods he was the best lover I had out of all of them, but even he couldn't completely appease my sensual desires. I needed more. Your twin took me to a pool where I could have sex and healing."

Tanyl nodded, "I know the pool you speak of. Did you choose sensual or healing?"

"I didn't know it has a healing setting until Solon found me. I couldn't stop wanting to have sex. I thought it was from the pool when Solon told me what the waters did."

"It was not. You need to let Kilean give you oral sex and there must be witnesses. I believe the dragon souls are trying to mate and if they are it will allow the Bonding of Dragons to occur within the timespan it should. If not, then the two of you will go through what your parents did. I know Kilean doesn't want that for either of you."

Iona nodded. Kilean moaned as he opened his eyes, "Hmm, Mom."

"What of his injuries?" Amara asked.

"I don't believe the souls will aggravate them. They may temporarily heal him so he can do what must be done. Once they are finished he will return to this state until he is well enough to assume his role but they will help in the healing process," Tanyl explained.

All eyes turned to Kilean. Kilean grimaced looking around the room. His eyes fell on Iona. He smiled. "Iona," he called.

Iona crawled onto the bed. "Hi," she whispered, placing her hand on his bare chest just above the bandanges around his torso.

"Hmm," he moaned, arching his back then falling silent.

"Kilean," she called to him. He turned his face towards her. "You started the bonding in the healing pod?"

Kilean nodded then grimaced. "I was in so much pain, Iona. I didn't think...ugh...I didn't think I would survive. You needed to be the one to live not me."

Iona gently caressed the side of his face. "Finish it."

"So much pain."

"You have to finish it, son," Eletha said.

Kilean turned to his mother. "How? I can barely breathe without pain. My head...can't think...can't."

Tanyl interrupted. "Take your mind off the pain and finish what you started. The Dragon Souls will give you enough relief to appease them. Just do it, Kilean. You don't have much time. Today is the sixth day."

"Shit," Kilean swore. "I don't want either of us to be like our parents. I'm weak enough. It will take me first. I've already had Soul Sickness."

"Kilean," Eletha called him.

He turned to face his mother. "I saw what the sickness did to your father. So did you. You know death will not come right away nor does it matter what state you are in it. It could be Iona who dies not you. You have no way to control that. Mate with her, son. I don't want my son to become like his father. And I really don't believe you wanted that either or you wouldn't have begun the Bonding of Dragons with Iona. I know you are in pain and I know you want to make love to her."

"I do."

"Then do it. Start by giving her oral sex and if the dragon tempts you to penetrate her then do so. My parents and I will bear witness to it."

"What of the others? I haven't chosen a husband for her and she hasn't chosen a wife for me."

"I'm not concerned about the others who are supposed to participate. That has nothing to do with your union with Iona. It is only a formality to appease the people."

Kilean motioned for Iona to approach him as his mother removed his left arm from it's sling. She crawled closer to him. "Sit on my face but please be careful."

"I will." She lifted her skirt, spread her legs and sat over his mouth. Kilean placed his hands on her hips and kissed the inside of her thighs. She moaned with a smile. He breathed between her legs then gently kissed her clit. "Oh," she bit her lower lip. Kilean chuckled then worked on her other thigh, repeating the process, causing her to purr like a kitten. Her clothes disappeared. He slowly moved his tongue, licking every sensual spot. Kilean laid his tongue flat, letting her rub against it. Iona closed her eyes, braced the headboard and rocked. He licked her clit, nibbled on it and suckled sending spasms of delight throughout her body. She leaned over as he continued to his rhythm assults of licking, nibbling and sucking. Kilean pulled her ass apart, allowing her sex girdle to insert an ass plug as he played with her.

"Oh, gods," she screamed, arching her back. She panted even harder as Kilean thrust his tongue inside her and started a new rhythm. "Shit, oh Kilean, yes!"

His hand reached up to her breasts and fondled her tits as his other was between her legs, playing with her clit. "Oh, oh, oh, gods," she cried out between his thrusts. He moved his fingers to her mouth. Iona suckled in perfect rhythm of his licks. She closed her eyes, allowing the waves to overtake her. Faster and harder he licked her until she couldn't stand it any longer. She climaxed. He swallowed her cum, pushed her to the other side of the bed then climbed over her. The couple kissed passionately, rolling around in the bed with arms and legs entangled. The fierce roar of dragons erupted throughout the room. Tanyl smiled as he looked around the chamber. Silver and Gold shadows danced on the walls, floor and ceiling. Everything was perfect. He looked back at the bed. Kilean sat on his knees, pushing his penis deep within Iona as he played with her tits. "Oh, yes, hmm, oh, Kilean, yes,

Kilean!" she moaned, wrapping her legs around his waist then sat upright, pushing his penis even deeper. They wrapped their arms around each other's back and kissed passionately. Kilean lowered her back to the bed and laid on top of her and pushed even harder. They rolled all over the bed, experimenting with different sexual positions, each more intense than the previous. Sensual moans and groans filled the air. Their hands clawing each other's bodies. Their mouths kissing each other's skin so hard they were sure to leave teeth marks. Hitting, kicking, kissing, fondling, groping, clawing, around and around their bodies moved on the bed like some natural dragon mating dance.

Amara took her husband's hand. He smiled at her. "It's beautiful," she whispered.

"It is."

"Oh, gods," Kilean yelled, sitting upright over Iona. Iona pushed him backwards and sat on top of him.

"Yes, oh fucking yes!" she proclaimed, rocking harder and faster with Kilean's finger on her clit and her hands on his chest. She inhaled deeply just as Kilean pushed her underneath him with her torso over the side of the bed. He held her legs and fucked her so hard her body bounced up and down. She placed her hands on the floor. "Kilean, fuck, oh fuck!" He pulled her upright, held her in his arms and guided her hips. Tanyl was quite certain his grandson had given Iona at least six or seven orgasms.

"Kilean, it has to be ten. Don't cum until the tenth. The dragons won't like it. You have to control the encounter not the female," Tanyl guided. Kilean nodded with understanding. "I've counted at least six, maybe seven. You should be able to feel every time she has one. They will come faster the more you give them to her. How many?"

"Eight," Kilean said just as Iona screamed. "That's the eighth."

"Keep it up. Give her one more then cum with the second. You have to cum at the same time as her so make certain you time it right."

Kilean pushed Iona onto her back then kissed her from head to toe. "Oh, shit," Iona whispered as he reached her clit. She arched her back with a long sensual moan. Kilean placed his fingers inside her and pumped with his thumb on her clit. She fidgeted.

"You're so fucking wet," he said then pushed his penis back inside her.

"Oh," she proclaimed loudly, taking him in her arms. They rolled around in the bed, groping, biting, kissing and kicking.

Eletha asked her father, "You think he'll be able to control it?

She's been coming so hard, I'm shocked it hasn't made him cum already."

"He can do it, Eletha. He's a quarter high elf and he's the Dragon Lord. Sina and Asa have been training him well for this."

"Kilean, shit," Iona screamed with her legs on his shoulders and back arched.

A wave of dizziness overcame Tanyl. He blinked several times blocking out the sounds of his grandson's ceremonial bedding. Tanyl tried to contact his father telepathically but his mind just was too weak to send the message. His stomach turned. He grasped his wife's arm with his eyes closed.

Amara stepped closer to him. "What's wrong?" she asked, placing her hand around his waist.

He shook his head. "Hmm, I need to...return to our bed...finish healing." He opened his eyes at the sound of Kilean and Iona loudly declaring they had reached the last orgasm together. Tanyl's eyes rolled back and he fell unconscious.

26

Iona slowly opened her eyes and turned towards Kilean. Her heart broke at the sight of her slumbering husband. He slept peacefully with his head bandaged, bandages over his torso and his arm in a sling. His broken leg was in a splint propped up with several pillows all the way down to his sprained ankle.

"Good morning," Eletha said, lowering a bowl of half eaten stew on the side table.

"Mm, morning," Iona yawned, carefully rising as to not wake Kilean. She peered down at her body with a curious look. The simple white tunic had completely disappeared only to be replaced with gold and silver lines running seductively across her skin, twirling in circles around her breasts, across her stomach, back, buttocks and down her legs. A long breetcloth of gorgeous white material lined with gold and silver with the emblem of the gold and silver dragons ran from her waist down to the floor. She peered up at her mother-in-law.

"The dragons changed your uniform as soon as you fell asleep. Kilean has the same markings and breethcloth you do. Your tattoo is still on your body. You'll use that to harness the power of the dragons whenever you need their sensual strength."

Iona looked back down, took note of the tattoo then looked back to her mother in law. "I don't have a top to wear?"

"You don't need one. You're the Dragon Lady now. Your royal cloaks are on the chair over there. They appeared along with your crowns this morning."

Iona walked over to the simple wooden chair and paused at the sound of Kilean's long groan. She turned around to see Eletha had moved to the side of the bed with her back to her. "Shh, Kilean. It's alright. Rest, my son. You did good. Your plan worked. You are the Dragon Lord and Iona is the Dragon Lady." Kilean fell silent. Eletha rose from the bed and walked over to Iona.

Iona nodded to Kilean. "Is he going to be okay?"

"In time, yes. His broken ribs were dangerously close to his lungs but the dragons have repositioned the broken bones so they won't puncture the lungs. He awoke before you did and was starving. He ate some stew then went back to sleep."

"I'm hungry, too."

"I'll get you something to eat," Eletha said, rubbing her hand on Iona's bare arm.

"What happened to your father? I saw him fall after Kilean and I finished the Bonding of Dragons yesterday."

"He hasn't fully recovered from when he and his twin secured Kilean's soul. He's resting with Uncle Aejeon in bed. My mother has been with him ever since. She told me he is recovering peacefully."

"That's....."

The door opened quickly. Solon said a spell and waved his hands towards the wall. The room expanded and three more beds appeared. The elf turned to Iona, peered at her outfit then said. "How? Nevermind the how," he said then ran out of the room. "Drayson, bring them over here," he yelled out in the hallway.

"What's going on," Iona asked Kilean's mom.

"I don't know. We better get out of his way," she said, moitioning for Iona to move backwards.

A few moments later, Drayson arrived with an unconscious K'Lara in his arms and placed her on the bed. "Mom," Iona yelled, starting to take off but was held back by Eletha. She fought to get past the taller elf.

"Let them do what they must for her," Eletha said as Drayson ran out the door just as Solon carried in the unconscious, badly beaten Tavir and laid him next to K'Lara.

"Tavir," Eletha gasped, loosening her grip. The women watched as one by one the brothers brought in badly beaten and unconcious Sina, Thalos and Lethos. They placed Sina in her own bed then placed Thalos and Lethos in their own.

"Where's father?" Drayson asked.

"Still recovering. Our grandfather is still here. I can take you to him," Eletha said.

"I can't keep Tavir unconscious for long. Solon, can you deliver the cure to them while I get our grandfather. He'll know what was used on K'Lara."

"Are you certain?" Solon countered.

"It's only effects humans and if we don't do something then we'll lose her."

"I can find the spell."

"We don't have time to look in your stupid books! Her heart is trying to fail and her lungs are almost there! The spell is working too fast. Grandfather should know all the spells ever created. Just give them the Dragonflame antidote!"

Solon nodded. Drayson turned to Eletha catching his eye on Iona's body. "Wha...huh...your majesty," he graciously bowed onto one knee then rose quickly. "Forgive me for...."

"Drayson, go," Iona interrupted with the order. She turned to Eletha "Take him to your grandfather and hurry. I don't want my mother to die."

"Of course," Eletha said then let Drayson out of the chamber while Solon delivered a hypodermic shot to King Tavir.

Iona quickly walked to her mother's bed, sat down beside her and held K'Lara's hand. Solon loaded another hyperdermic needle, leaned over Tavir and pressed the needle into the side of K'Lara's neck. "It won't heal her but it should slow down the progression of the poision," he said then turned back to his table and loaded another needle.

"What happened after we left? Who did this," she asked never taking her eyes off her mother's still, beautiful face.

"I don't know much, Iona. I was procuring the sex slaves for Eletha when Drayson and his army arrived. All he told me was to help him. None of them were conscious."

"You're a healer like your uncle."

"I am a scholar and a guardian, not a healer. If you want answers then it would be best if you asked my brother."

Iona watched Solon administer the antidote to Sina. She gasped, moaned then rolled onto her stomach. "Sina," Solon called to her. Iona rose with authority and walked towards Sina's bed. The draconian humanoid, pushed Solon away, sobbing.

"Sina," Solon comforted, kneeling before her so he could see her face.

"I am nothing but a human."

Iona asked beside Solon, "What do you mean you are nothing but a human?"

The raven haired beauty slowly lifted her eyes in Iona's direction then gasped. "How," she mumbled.

Iona sighed, exchanging a glance with Solon then back to Sina. "Kilean started the Bonding of Dragons in the healing pod."

"Aw, hell," Solon swore standing upright. "I should have known he was up to something when he had demanded that you give him a blowjob," Solon snarled towards Kilean.

Sina heaved, reaching out to Iona with a bloody hand. "It worked. I'm glad."

Solon turned to the twin, "Did you know about it?"

"How could I," Sina cried then grimaced with pain.

Iona knelt beside her and took her hand. "Sina, what happened?"

"Your mom and I....trapped in a long corridor....we were following screams but never could reach them." She took a deep breath then painfully continued. "K'Lara stopped...she was confused then fell ill...couldn't move...Tayla attacked us...I transformed into a dragon and fought her...I was winning...hurt Tayla bad."

"How bad?" Solon asked curiously.

"Not bad enough to stop her...I was so focused on the fight...She sliced through my side with her talon...hurt a lot...kept fighting...became human and couldn't transform back to dragon...She..."

"Roll over," Solon ordered.

Sina looked up at him. "If she sliced your side then made you become human I may be able to draw out some of the poison and be able to use that to determine the type of poison used," He explained rummaging through his medical bag on end table between her bed and the male dragon twins' bed. "I can assume it's the same for Thalos and Lethos?"

"I don't know," she cried, rolling on her back.

"Did they see any healers at the temple?" Iona asked, helping Sina remove her shirt.

"I assume so. They're wounds have been cleaned, bandaged and they are wearing new clothes," Solon answered, stepping to the side of the bed with a knife and clear glass tube. Iona tossed Sina's shirt to the floor and stared at the blood-stained bandages over Sina's torso. "Which side?" Solon asked.

"Right," she answered, peering her at the long curved mark of blood from just under the armpit to the top of her stomach.

Solon moved to step around the bed. "Give it to me. I'll do it. You just tell me what to do," Iona ordered, taking the knife and glass tube.

"Sit up," Solon guided, helping a very weakened Sina upright. Her head fell downward as she struggled to breathe. Sina turned her eyes to Kilean as Solon carefully unwrapped her bandages.

"I wish I was well enough to heal him. How bad are his injuries?" Sina whispered to Iona.

Iona peered over her shoulder. "Three broken ribs, broken arm, broken legs, sprained elbow, knee, ankle and a bad concussion."

"Damn," Sina swore lowering her eyes.

"You trained him well."

"Hmm, thanks."

Solon guided, "I haven't removed all her bandanges. Can you get to the wound?"

Iona lifted the thin layer of cloth bandages wound around Sina's chest. "I can."

"Good. Make a small incision into the cut and gather some of her blood into the vial. She's a humanoid dragon twin so her blood is red. Anything that doesn't look like blood will be a remnant of the poision that was used on her."

Iona carefully lifted the cotton bandage over the long incision. She peered at the nicely bound work the healers had done to Sina's skin without stiches, looking for the right place. A small line over her ribs showed promise.

"I'm sorry," she whispered to Sina.

"Just do it," the humanoid answered.

Iona nodded then went to work. She pressed the tip of the blade onto of the magical incision and cut into it. Sina roared loudly, arching her head back as Solon held her still. Iona ignored her cries. The dragon twin's red blood flowed downward for a few second with no sight of any different coloration. She had begun to worry that perhaps Sina was losing too much blood, too fast. But then she saw it. Small trickles of lime green blops in the blood quickly grew so Sina bleed green instead of red. "It's thick," Iona claimed, placing the vial next to the wound so it could drain.

"Get as much as you can," Solon advised. "I'll have to close that wound soon or she'll bleed to death. She had lost a lot of blood when Drayson had found her."

"I thought you didn't know what had happened over there."

"I only know what Drayson told me. Hurry up, Iona. She's losing consciousness."

Iona lifted the glass vial up to show it filled with the lime green substance. Solon leaned over, placed his hand on the wound, said a quick spell and lifted it away, showing the incision has completely disappeared except for a long scar. He immediately wrapped the bandages around Sina's torso, tied it up and laid her back on the bed. Her head flopped to the side as she slept.

"Thank you," Solon said, taking the vial and knife from Iona.

"You're welcome. Is she going to...?"

"I don't know, Iona. I must analyze the poison first. Stay with them. I'll be back with an antidote as soon as possible," Solon said. He walked to the center of the room, opened a portal then disappeared.

Drokap Castle – Kingdom of Saloron

27

Solon ran through the portal, threw the vial against the wall sending it crashing in pieces to the floor and kept running down the dark hallway as the portal closed. His heart beat heavy with deep concern for his wife. Sina had said Tayla had been greatly wounded but not enough to stop her. A loud roar emitted from the hallway on his right. His heart skipped a beat. He turned to his right, ran down the hall, took another left then another right. Louder and louder, Tayla's roars lifted in the air until he came to a T in the hallways. He took a step to the right then backed up again seeing Roan step into Tayla's dragon nest. Two guards guarded the entrance.

"Shit," Solon swore to himself, leaning his back against the wall. He listened carefully to the conversation between Roan, Prince Zurggash and Tayla.

"Can you morph back into your human form?" the prince asked.

"My wing's broken." Tayla complained.

"What happens if you morph with a broken wing?" Roan asked.

"I don't know. I've never had one before!"

"My love," the prince tried to coax her. "Roan is only trying to help you. You have several large lacerations, you've lost a couple of talons and your wing is broken. I don't know what your injuries would do to you human form but you must have some. You're part dragon and part human. Your injuries will affect both. We're only trying to heal the human part, too."

Tayla let out a deep sigh. "I don't have the strength to morph back into a human, Zurggash. Let me rest, husband. Please."

"I will. You did good, Tayla. Kilean and Iona will be defenseless without their dragon twins."

"Thank you. I'm tired."

"Go to sleep, Tayla. Roan and I will take care of the rest of the plan. We'll check on you later?"

"Hmm."

"Roan, we need to check on Asa in your chamber then we will plan the invasion."

"Yes, sir," Roan said. "What of my guards?"

"We won't need them. I strengthened the shield and moved the temple after Commander Drayson rescued his people. The only way into the temple is to know the exact portal spell to always be able to find the temple."

"They found it before."

"Yes, that bothered me. I know Iona found this place because of the spirit dragons. I am assuming, but I may be incorrect, that once Iona and Kilean disappeared, they were able to tell Drayson where to find the others. I didn't want to take any chances of the temple guards finding us again so I reconfigureated our location and the spell. We have to go, Roan. Our plan is working."

"Understood."

Solon peered around the corner. He watched Prince Zurggash and Roan step out of Tayla's chamber. Roan dismissed the guards. The four of them disappeared down the hallway then turned to the right. Solon quickly turned, ran down the hallway and entered Tayla's large circular chamber. He closed the wooden door behind him and stared at the large brown dragon. The smell of blood and vomit lingered in the air.

Deep incisions badly mutilated her body. Her left wing had been set and bound close to her body. He silently walked towards her with tears. "My love," he whispered with his hand out.

Tayla opened her eyes and turned her face towards him. He swallowed hard seeing her right eye cloudy from where she had been struck in the eye. "Solon," she whispered with dark purple tears.

He gently stroked her nose. "How did this happen? You're the strongest dragon I know of. You should have been able to kill them and not sustain these many injuries."

"I'm with your child. That's the only explanation. A dragon twin loses her ability to fully combat another dragon when she is carrying a child."

"Does the prince suspect anything?"

Tayla shook her head. "No, but it won't take him long to figure it out."

"But you have fucked him? Haven't you?"

"Of course I have."

"Then Tayla, just tell him the child is his."

Tayla blew steam out of her nose. "That would take a miracle and I'm all out of those at the moment," she snarled.

Solon stepped backwards with his hands raised. "Tayla, you have every right to be in a foul mood. But listen to me carefully. We can't lose the deception we have created with your nephew. He has to be blamed for everything."

She huffed, lowering her head to the ground. "Did the posion work?" she asked after a long moment of silence.

"Yes, the dragon twins are helpless. But we have another problem." She lifted her good eye to him. "Kilean and Iona have completed the Bonding of Dragons."

"How the hell?" she growled.

Solon anxiously moved his hands. "Shhh, Tayla. I don't know how far Roan and the prince are in the hallways and your voice car...."

The door handle suddenly moved. Tayla nodded for Solon to move behind her. He ran behind his love and hid in the back with Tayla's tail curved around him.

"Tayla?" Roan asked opening the door as she lowered her head. Prince Zurggash entered behind him.

"I'm...umm...," she lifted her eyes to her nephew.

The evil prince entered the room with a curious look. "What is it?" he demanded, pushing Roan aside. Tayla blinked her eyes several times then groaned. "Tayla," he called to her sharply. "What's wrong?"

"I was thinking..."

"...and..."

"...well it occurred to me I may know why my strength was weakened during the attack. If I'm correct, then I will need your help."

"Anything. Just name it."

Tayla swallowed hard. "I'm with child," she whispered.

Prince Zurggash's face fell. He stared, speechless at Tayla's big eye. "Your...uhm," he looked to Roan. Roan shrugged his shoulders. He looked back at Tayla. "You're certain?"

"Do you have any other explanation for my weakened condition?"

"No. But Tayla if you..."

"...it worked on Asa. It will work on me as well. We already know I have carried the dragon orb in my womb and I delivered it to you."

"That was a spirit not a child!"

"Well if you didn't fuck me so well then maybe I wouldn't be like this!"

"I appreciate the compliment but shit, Tayla, this disrupts everything! You won't be able to do anything for at least nine...uhm....how long?"

Tayla sighed, "I don't know. My human body wasn't showing yet so maybe I'm about two or three months along."

The prince rolled his eyes. "That is still six to seven months where you're incapicated. I can't do this without you."

"I'm not dying. I'm with child! Your child! Get out. Just get out."

"I'm not saying I don't want the child. Our invasion plans are more important then raising a family. We agreed not to have a family until the dragons were overthrown."

"I didn't exactly fucking plan to have a kid yet!"

The prince huffed, crossing his arms. "Get rid of it."

"What!"

"You heard me. Abort the kid."

"Oh, hell no! You're an idiot if you think I'm going to do that. You need an heir and who knows what the child of a dragon twin and the spawn of a dragon twin will create."

"She's right," Roan interrupted. The prince turned to face Roan. "Asa and I's child will be the spawn of a resurrected human and dragon twin. I have no idea what that will create. It is forbidden in the Draconian Codex as is the union you have with your aunt, but what if the dragons created those restrictions to control the population and species that inhabit Draconia."

Prince Zurggash nodded. "Interesting point." He turned back to his aunt. Tayla lifted an eyebrow at him. "Fine, but you will aid me in every way you can."

"Of course, I will," she agreed. "And you the same?"

"How...?" he turned to Roan with a thought. Roan grinned. He turned back to his wife. "Of course. How could I have forgotten. A pregnant dragon twin is more sensual as if she is molting or menstruating. I will appease those desires when you have them, Tayla."

"Thank you."

"You're welcome. Just don't forget your duty to me."

"Never, my love. Please, let me rest."

The prince kissed her gently on the tip of her nose then exited from the chamber.

"Congratualtions, Tayla," Roan said before he left the room and closed the door behind him.

Tayla blew smoke out her nose and released her grip on Solon. He slowly moved aroud her body, carefully examing every battle mark. "You're healing nicely for the battle to have been only a few hours ago," he said, moving towards her.

"Thank the gods I'm part dragon," she huffed.

"Tayla, I'm sorry. I never meant..."

"...I know." She cleared her throat then continued. "K'Lara?"

"My grandfather will figure out the counterspell. It should be a simple remedy if you used the spell you told me about."

"I did. What happens now that we couldn't stop Kilean and Iona?"

"We manipulate them into believing the dragons are wrong."

Don't miss out on the next installment of
THE DRACONIAN RAPTURE series

DOUBLE MOON, DOUBLE SUN

Read on for a preview...

Lundy Hollow – The Borderlands

Soft moonlight filled the quiet rectangular room. Queen K'Lara Dragonmoon slowly opened her eyes. She moaned feeling her complete body ache. At least she was feeling something. She pulled aside the blankets and sat on the side of the bed with her head hung low. K'Lara stared down at her body. Her jet black leather catsuit was open from the top to her waist in a V like shape showing her entire torso. Her tit chains bounced lightly as she moved. She peered down at the dragon claws tattoos holding her breasts. For some reason, she could feel power illuminating from the dragon tattoo that began across her back with its arms around her sides. The claws holding her tits and meeting between her legs. But how could it be that her dragon tattoo was caressing her with power? It was just a tattoo now. The soul resided in her daughter, not her.

K'Lara wiped her hands down her face, trying to ignore the strange sensation. Iona was the Dragon Lady, not her. None of what she felt was real. It couldn't be.

"Sorry about the catsuit. You're heart stopped and we had to massage it to get it started again while my grandfather delivered the antidote," a woman's voice said.

K'Lara slowly lifted her eyes and swallowed hard at the sight of Eletha offering a glass of water. "Eletha," she whispered, taking the glass. She drank then placed the cup on a table. "I...uhm...Tavir told me you were dying."

"Grandfather cured me."

"Grandfather?"

Eletha grabbed a stool from beside the bed and sat down before K'Lara. "My grandfather is the Grand Priest."

"Holy shit! So Kilean....is...oh my gods...it's completely illegal...did Tavir know?"

"I didn't even know, K'Lara. My father is High Priest Aejeon's twin brother."

"Your marriage is illegal. Oh, by the gods, do you know that Tavir and I...."

Eletha nodded. "I know. Iona told me," she sighed. "I told your daughter I don't have feelings for Tavir."

K'Lara huffed. "The Dragon Lord's Mother always has feelings for her Dragon Lord and the Dragon Lord Father has for the Dragon Lady. It's to ensure unity so the children grow up in a secure home." K'Lara moaned, feeling the surge of her tattoo grow even stronger. She rose and placed a hand on the nightstand, stabilizing herself.

"What the...?" Eletha cried, rising from the stool. She stared over K'Lara's shoulder.

K'Lara turned around to see Tavir's naked, unconscious body levitating in the air with silver strands cocooning his entire body. She could see between the cracks of silver strands of energy his tattoo glowing brightly.

"Shit," Eletha said glancing at K'Lara body. K'Lara peered down to see her own tattoo glowing.

"What's happening? I feel as if I have to mate. I shouldn't feel like that. I'm not the Dragon Lady," K'Lara pushed through her mouth as her clothes disappeared. She glanced upward and stared at Kilean's elevated body cocooned in golden strands of energy.

Eletha turned to see her son fully encased and Iona sexually aroused just like her mother. "Get on the bed with my husband," she said to K'Lara never taking her eyes off Kilean and Iona.

"Eletha," K'Lara asked.

"Just do it. I don't know why I'm telling you to do so but I think you must."

"Tavir's your husband, now. I have..." she paused thinking about their reunification. "We couldn't keep our hands off each other. It was as if we were meant to be together. Our tattoo's and my sex girdle had activated when Tavir and I had sex. It wasn't supposed to be like that. Not since Iona and Kilean joined together."

Eletha turned to face K'Lara. "Tavir's not my husband. He has never been. He's always been yours. Even when we made love he was fucking me, K'Lara. I used the spell you taught me to appease him. I loved him but he never loved me."

"I'm sorry. The sensual and emotional pull between the Dragon Lord and Dragon Lady is intense."

"And by all accounts from you and your daughter, you and Tavir still feel that pull even though you are no longer the Dragon Lord and Dragon Lady but what if everyone has it all wrong."

"What do you mean?"

"There has never been two dragon lords and ladies. Normally, the former dragon lord and lady become the current dragon lord and lady's ambassadors to the gods. But everything was changed the day you missed your Bonding of Dragons with Tavir."

"Double moons, double suns," K'Lara gasped with understanding then crawled into the bed allowing her intense sensual desires to prepare her.

K'Lara closed her eyes, feeling silver energy strands descend from around Tavir's body to between her legs and on her breasts. She inhaled deeply through her teeth, opening her legs and arching her back as a strand entered her. The intense sensual experience nearly took her breath away. She rocked her hips as the energy aroused her. Her tattoo glowed even brighter. She didn't know what was going on but she sure as hell liked it.

About the Author

Bestselling author Allison Bruning originally hails from Marion, Ohio but full time RV's with her husband and their Australian cattle dog, Lakota Sioux. Allison is the bestselling author of several novels, short stories, children's books and a poetry book. Allison's educational background includes a B.A. in theatre arts with a minor in anthropology from Sul Ross State University in Alpine, Texas. Allison received National Honor Society memberships in both Theatre Arts and Communication. She was also honored her sophomore year with admission into the All American Scholars register. She holds graduate hours in cultural anthropology and education. In 2007, Allison was named to Who's Who Among America's Educators. She is also the recipient of the Girl Scout Silver and Gold Awards. Allison received her Masters of Fine Arts in creative writing at Full Sail University on June 28, 2013. She is an educator, writer, speaker, screenwriter, film director, choreographer and business owner. Allison's interests include Ohio Valley history, anthropology, travel, culture, history, camping, hiking, backpacking, spending time with her family, and genealogy.

www.ingramcontent.com/pod-product-compliance
Lightning Source LLC
Chambersburg PA
CBHW050341030726
47503CB00008B/2549